Want to Know a Secret?

Want to Know a Secret?

Sue Moorcroft

First published in hardback as *Family Matters* by Robert Hale in 2008

Published 2010 by Choc Lit Limited
Penrose House, Crawley Drive, Camberley, Surrey GU15 2AB
www.choclitpublishing.co.uk

The right of Sue Moorcroft to be identified as the Author of this Work
has been asserted by her in accordance with the Copyright, Designs and
Patents Act 1988

A CIP catalogue record for this book is available
from the British Library

ISBN-978-1-906931-26-1

Mixed Sources
Product group from well-managed
forests and other controlled sources
www.fsc.org Cert no.TT-COC-002063
© 1996 Forest Stewardship Council

Printed in the UK by CPI Cox & Wyman, Reading, RG1 8EX

In memory of my father
Walter Moorcroft
1932–84

He would have been pleased

Acknowledgements

With grateful thanks to Sloane Helicopters, Sywell,
for allowing me to visit; to Alan for telling me exactly
how my helicopter prang should happen and Sheila for
taking me to see one that had landed hard. To Roger
for making the introduction, answering flying queries,
reading the manuscript and pointing out the ugly sentences
(even when they weren't).

Thanks to Jean Fullerton, supernurse and author,
for pointing out where details of hospital routine
and drugs needed work.

Special thoughts for 'Natasha' from Northampton
and thanks to Nigel Spratt and Linda for sharing
their experiences.

As ever, thanks to the Choc Lit team for their
unending support, and all my friends at the wonderful
Romantic Novelists' Association, ditto.

Chapter One

Two towering policemen filled Diane's kitchen, incongruous amongst the splatter and clutter of dinner preparation and her hand sewing litter draping the chair backs. She touched the fabric, as if the blue satin intended for a prom dress would keep her knees from buckling. 'How badly is he hurt?'

The older, taller of the two officers hovered closer. 'Our information is that Mr Jenner's in no immediate danger but has been injured. He was helped at the scene and taken to Peterborough District Hospital.'

Diane imagined the busy A47 on Gareth's route home and an ambulance nosing its way through traffic chaos to their silver Peugeot bent and twisted. And Gareth trapped inside. She swallowed. 'Where? Did it happen, I mean?'

'The helicopter in which Mr Jenner was a passenger unfortunately crashed on take-off from Medes Airfield, this afternoon.'

'*Helicopter*?' Relief whooshed through Diane, slackening the sinews that panic had tightened. For an instant she thought that her head might actually snap backwards like a puppet with a string cut. 'Helicopter? He's as likely to be in a flying saucer.' She laughed, flopping into a kitchen chair and flipping her waist-long plait over her shoulder. As if Gareth would somehow magic himself into one of those clattering monsters when he should be fitting ventilation units to industrial buildings!

The policemen exchanged glances. 'Is your husband here, Mrs Jenner?'

'Well, no he's late – but Gareth works all the hours that God sends, he's probably been held up in the wastes of some

1

industrial estate. One of the last people in the civilised world not to have a mobile phone, is Gareth.'

The older policeman smiled kindly. 'If you're convinced of a mistake, we can radio a colleague at the hospital to double check.' He even shut his notebook, as if that was that.

'I think you'd better. He has a fuzzy old tattoo at the top of his right arm, a capital G. If the man in hospital hasn't got that, it's not Gareth.'

'That ought to settle it.' The older man nodded his young colleague out of the back door to make the necessary call while he chatted easily to Diane about how she liked living in a village way out here, isolated by the splendour of the Fens.

In less than two minutes the young officer returned. 'G-golf, top of right arm,' he reported. 'I'm afraid it sounds like your husband, Mrs Jenner.'

'Oh.' Cold with shock, Diane fumbled her way into a jacket against the June evening and her new burgundy shoes from the hall cupboard. The shoes felt cold and stiff without tights. A sale bargain, they clashed with just about everything, including the turquoise skirt and top she was wearing, but now wasn't the time to be particular. She must see what had happened to Gareth.

She'd never ridden in a police car before. Perched on the back seat feeling sweatily sick, she watched swaying nettles tangle with froths of cow parsley as the car swished up the straight Fen lanes between fields divided into rectangles, brown soil embroidered with green crops. The land was flat for as far as the eye could see and deep dykes drained water to the sea that had once made a marsh of the people-made landscape, but was now miles away. The older constable kept up his amiable conversation. 'Flat up here, isn't it? We don't normally get up so far towards Holbeach and Spalding. Not many windbreaks.'

'People from outside the area do tend to feel the wind.' Although she responded automatically, Diane's mind was churning. What the hell had Gareth been doing in a helicopter?

'And it was a special dinner you were cooking, was it?'

'Silver wedding anniversary.'

He glanced back over his shoulder. 'Never! You don't look old enough.'

She flushed. 'I married young.' Her heart was drumming with apprehension. Gareth might not be a husband sent by angels to make her life heaven on earth but he was her husband. This morning, he'd given her a card, *To My Wife on our Silver Wedding Anniversary*. He'd known that she was cooking a celebration dinner: lamb steaks with herb butter; new potatoes, broccoli and baby carrots from the garden. He'd smiled and dropped a rare kiss on her cheek. 'I'll be home on time.'

Instead, he'd been in a helicopter crash. How badly did you have to be hurt for the hospital to send the police to inform the next of kin?

In the thirty minutes of the journey to Peterborough the dread grew that the answer was, 'Very badly'. The car turned off Thorpe Road and parked between A & E and Outpatients by an ambulance with *East Anglian NHS Trust* on the side in dark green.

'Here we are, Mrs Jenner.'

Floating through the automatic doors on a cloud of unreality, she found herself the baton passed efficiently from the policemen in the car to a PC Stone, who was exactly what the public expected of a copper – a big, stolid man with buzz-cut hair and a mission to keep her calm. Positively oozing positivity, he must have been top of his police class in reassuring silently freaked women in their best clothes and the wrong shoes. 'I'm assured that your husband isn't in any danger, Mrs Jenner. And he's in good hands. I'll tell you what I know so far.' A & E was busy but he found her a blue vinyl chair in the waiting area. Her legs wobbled and she dropped down onto it, wiping a prickle of sweat from her top lip.

He fetched a cup of water and she sipped while he repeated everything the first two policemen had said in his deeply reassuring policeman's voice and she made herself listen and nod. It was real. It was happening.

Presently, he rose. 'I have to go back behind the scenes to see what I can find out. Will you be all right here?'

'Yes. Thanks.'

'Should I contact someone? You might like to have a relative with you?'

Bryony. But her daughter was far away in Brazil, working in an orphanage full of beautiful, black-eyed waifs who had almost nothing, but considered themselves lucky not to have to scavenge on the street, according to her letters. Bryony would have to be told. But not yet. So far away from home, it would be cruel to frighten her until Diane had concrete information. Bryony's childhood of illness and narrow squeaks made Diane shield her automatically. Also, Bryony and Gareth's relationship had been what Bryony declared 'shitty' before she had left, so Diane wanted to know exactly what shape Gareth was in before she prodded that sleeping tiger.

'The Norths are over there, if you don't want to wait alone.' Constable Stone gestured over his shoulder.

Diane didn't understand what he meant by 'Norths', but knew that to wait alone was exactly what she did want. The hospital procedure was familiar from all the times they'd brought Bryony here in the throes of an asthma attack, clutching her inhaler, white-faced, eyes frightened. The staff

4

worked their way down to you and you just had to wait.

'I can call my brother if I find I need anyone.' She tried to imagine Freddy abandoning his big, comfortable house in leafy Orton Longueville to sit beside her on these crowded seats. He would in a heartbeat, of course, if she asked him. But it had probably been a long time since he entered an NHS hospital. Much more likely companions were Ivan and Melvyn, who would willingly charge in to keep vigil for their big brother. They'd take over. They'd tell her not to worry, sit either side of her and be grim and demand to see every doctor in the place.

No, she'd wait alone, listening to the vending machine's satisfied gurgles as a steady procession of people fed its coin slot. A group of teenage lads laughed and swore. Kiddies, pale and whiney, red and sleepy, crying, noisy kids that should've been in bed instead of arguing in the children's playroom, waited while their siblings had their broken limbs and split heads seen to.

'Diane?'

She jumped. A man loomed over her, his black leather jacket shining dully and his thick dark hair looking freshly cut.

'Yes?' she answered, cautiously.

He took the seat the policeman had vacated and smiled. 'I'm James North, Valerie's husband.'

Sorting rapidly through her memory, Diane failed to locate a James or a Valerie North.

'Valerie was in the crash, too,' he added, as she hesitated. Then, patiently, 'You know who Valerie is, don't you? Valerie North?'

She blinked. She hadn't had time to wonder if there were others in the crash. 'If you're her husband, I'll take a stab that she's your wife.' And, realising she'd been unnecessarily curt, 'Does she work with Gareth?'

His brows went up. 'Of course not.'

'I'm afraid I don't know, then.'

His eyes narrowed intently. 'You don't know who Valerie is?' He leaned nearer, as if he could hypnotise her into divulging all she knew. The leather jacket brushed her hand; cool, sinuous.

She resisted the urge to check out its stitching to see if it was as well-made as the rest of him. 'Should I?'

Frowning, he murmured, almost to himself, 'I don't know.'

His grey-eyed scrutiny made her feel like a specimen under his microscope. She put on the crisp voice she used with the bank to cover up a dread of uncovering unpalatable facts – this time that Gareth had been with this man's spouse. A chill rippled through her guts. 'You're talking in riddles. How about simply telling me what's going on between my husband and your wife?'

'For God's sake! What could be "going on"?' For an instant something blazed in his eyes and she realised with a little shock that behind his show of patience, James North was smouldering with anger.

Before Diane could bark back that that was exactly what she wanted to know, a pale and untidy young woman rushed up, big-eyed as a fawn. 'Dad – look at *Pops*,' she hissed, a hand fluttering towards an older man who, drained of colour and sunk in a chair, was foraging vaguely in the folds of his jacket.

'Hell,' muttered James. In four strides he was at the older man's side. 'I'll get it, Harold.' His big, deft hand extracted a bottle from the old man's jacket pocket. In seconds a tablet was beneath Harold's tongue and his collar and tie had been loosened. James had even found time to reassure the young woman twitching beside him. 'He'll be fine in a minute, Tamz, when he gets his breath.'

Relief, then uncertainty, flitted across her face. 'I forgot about his medication, didn't I?'

'You did fine, you fetched me, you did the right thing.' James smiled and his daughter smiled tremulously back.

James North turned the beam of his attention back to Diane. 'Could you sit with Harold and Tamzin while I see if I can organise somewhere a bit quieter?'

Not waiting for an answer, he launched a charm offensive at the woman behind reception desk, his low voice warm and his smile persuasive. 'My father-in-law's not well, he has angina –'

Diane dropped into the empty chair beside Harold. 'Any better?'

His large, old man's nose was threaded with red veins, white hair lay neatly to one side and his eyes were kind. Already, the blue tinge was leaving his lips. 'Getting that way.' Hands slack and palms up in his lap, he nevertheless managed a trace of grim humour. 'Shocks can do old codgers in. I shall have to point it out to my children.'

Diane was reminded of her father. Peter Wibberley hadn't possessed much of the friendly dignity in this man but he, too, had spoken 'nicely' and automatically dressed in a jacket, shirt and tie whenever he left the house.

'Pops will be much better soon.' Tamzin's bony hands moved restlessly. 'The pills are well good.'

'Good.' Diane smiled. She'd first taken Tamzin for about sixteen, with her waiflike figure and James North as her sheepdog, but now she saw that Tamzin's eyes were much older. Sadder. Reflecting the world in the grey of her eyes. She spoke like a princess who'd learnt the vernacular from the servants, inserting 'well good' clumsily. She would've been pretty if not such a scarecrow. 'His colour's improving already.'

'Reassuring,' Harold murmured.

Then James was back. 'There's a room we can use. They'll let us through a security door.'

When Harold had gathered his energy, they herded along the corridor, James stationing himself at Harold's elbow as well as resting a hand on the thin shoulders of his daughter as if to ensure that she didn't get lost. He settled the older man in a room that was cramped but better than the busy, noisy area they'd just left. 'Tamz, will you stay with Pops for a few minutes?' His eyes settled purposefully on Diane. 'We'll organise hot drinks, shall we? We could all do with something.'

Fifteen paces outside the door he took her arm and shunted her firmly to the side of the corridor, letting two wheelchairs whisper past on fat, rubber tyres, stooping to bring his head closer to hers. 'You coping OK?'

Diane breathed in the faint smell of new leather from his jacket. 'Don't worry about me. Although it would be helpful if you'd explain who everybody is and why I'm supposed to know them.' She lifted her brows.

'I was beginning to suspect that you hadn't a clue.' James rubbed his hand over his hair. When he spoke again he had rediscovered the patient tone that Diane was beginning to find seriously annoying. 'It's quite straightforward. Tamzin is my daughter. Valerie, who's had the accident, is my wife; you've got that bit. And Harold is Valerie's father. Of course, Harold is Gareth's father, too, so Valerie is Gareth's half-sister.'

Diane stared. She went cold. She went hot. She felt as if she'd been caught up in some freaky dream but the smell of the hospital and the pinching of her new shoes were quite undreamlike. 'Gareth's father?'

'Yes.'

'And sister.'

He puffed out a sigh. 'Half-sister. Obviously.'

Diane groped for sense and reason. 'But – '

As if to make up for the sigh, James returned to being overly patient. 'I think Gareth's told you about Valerie and me and our three daughters? Natalia, Alice – and Tamzin.' He nodded at the room they'd just left.

'But you can't be talking about Gareth *Jenner*,' she interrupted. 'He hasn't got a father.' She knew this as certainly as she knew where the sun rose – unless someone had been messing with the celestial mechanics. Perhaps that was it! A shift in the universe might explain Gareth's presence in a helicopter and how, when she knew so well that his family consisted only of a mother (deceased) and two brothers living in Peterborough, he'd somehow acquired a father and a sister. She shook her head, trying to clear it.

There had to be an explanation. Her suspicions had hovered earlier around the idea that Gareth was having an affair with this Valerie North but now that seemed comparatively tame.

Was she drunk? Was James drunk? Had somebody slipped him something? His slate grey eyes with their huge black pupils were fixed on hers with unnervingly hypnotic effect. 'Do you think there could have been two Gareth Jenners admitted tonight?'

A corner of James's mouth curled. 'I understand from my brother-in-law, Gareth Jenner, that his wife's called Diane Jenner. And, somehow, I can't see there being two of you, too.'

'No,' she agreed, baffled. Someone *must've* been messing with the celestial mechanics, then. It was the only explanation.

Back in the little room furnished with squashy turquoise chairs, James removed the lid from a polystyrene cup of tea for his father-in-law. 'How are you, now?'

Harold, pale but no longer chalky, grinned, unconvincingly.

'Right as ninepence.'

James touched Diane's arm, the heat of his fingers making her jump. 'The introductions are a bit late but this is Harold Myers, Gareth's father. And my daughter, Tamzin.'

Diane offered her hand and found it enfolded between both of Harold's. In contrast to James's, his fingers were chill and clammy.

'I'm so pleased to meet you – at long last!'

She returned his smile, searching his face for some echo of Gareth to support the preposterous idea that he could, indeed, be Gareth's father. To her, Gareth had always resembled his mother, the same hard mouth and rock-set jaw. But now she could see that Harold was smiling at her with familiar eyes; warmer, on Harold, but exactly the same combination of hazel and green. 'Gareth's father,' she marvelled softly. *But Gareth doesn't have a father. Gareth carries his illegitimacy like a chip on his shoulder as big as a boat.* Growing up in an era when illegitimacy was a positive scandal, he'd suffered for his mother's haphazard fortunes with a defiance matched only by his determination not to blame her.

Harold squeezed Diane's hand. 'Thank God that Gareth isn't in any danger. Broken bones heal. We'll get him and Valerie moved to the new Ackerman Hospital as soon as possible.' He took out a clean handkerchief, ironed neatly into a square, to dab at the corner of his eye.

Ackerman was a private hospital. Gareth didn't have a private hospital income. He barely had a new-pyjamas-for-hospital income. Diane opened her mouth, flicked her gaze around the surrounding faces then closed her mouth without speaking. Tamzin, hair hanging like straw, looked as if she'd already been in bed when news of the accident came. Harold was obviously bone tired, and James had the air that this was just one more day when the cares of the world had descended upon his shoulders. They had enough to worry about without Diane blurting out, 'But we can't afford a private hospital!' No doubt there would come a point when she could explain to the staff, discreetly, why Gareth would remain in the arms of the NHS.

'The helicopter must have come down with a bang,' Harold observed. 'Valerie was always telling me how safe it was. How do you think it could have happened, James?'

James shrugged. 'Mechanical failure? Cross wind? That's the Civil Aviation Authority's province. There will be an enquiry, I expect.' His voice was even but, again, Diane caught the glitter of anger in his eyes.

'Do you really think Mum's going to be all right?' Tamzin sniffed. 'I mean, she's not going to ...?'

James threw an arm around her. 'Tamz, she'll heal. We'll just have to be patient for a few months.'

'What on earth were they doing in a helicopter, anyway?' asked Diane, idly. The police hadn't been able to provide any information beyond the preposterous fact that Gareth had been the passenger in a two-seater Robinson R22 helicopter that had crashed on take-off at Medes Flying Club. If they drove the country route to visit Gareth's brother, Melvyn, she and Gareth passed the flying club, on the edge of Peterborough, without ever entertaining the notion of turning in under the matt black iron archway, past security. That was for other people, people in a salary bracket that Jenners only dreamed of.

Her enquiry seemed to rouse James's annoyingly patient tone again. 'Valerie got her private pilot's licence for helicopters last year. She often takes Gareth up on his days off.'

'On his *what*?' Diane spluttered her coffee all down her chin.

Silence. Wariness crept into James's dark eyes. 'Is there

anyone you want me to phone? To be with you?'

Diane was an old hand at not allowing subject changes as a question-avoidance tactic. Even blessed with what her mother used to term a 'silvery' voice, she wasn't easily talked down. 'What do you mean by "Gareth's days off"?'

James shrugged. 'Since Gareth took semi-retirement, he only works Tuesday to Thursday, right?'

Diane stared. 'Tuesday to Thursday,' she repeated, faintly, wondering how this could be when Gareth's working week apparently also encompassed Monday, Friday and most Saturdays. Even the occasional Sunday. 'So, Gareth's taken semi-retirement, discovered his long-lost family and spends his spare time whizzing around in helicopters?'

A grin flashed across James's face, filling his eyes with suppressed laughter. 'It doesn't normally sound quite so ludicrous – but, yes.'

She refrained from retorting that ludicrous was exactly what it was, because she so desperately needed to understand what the hell was going on. 'And you know who I am, yet you've never met me?'

Smile fading, James acknowledged, 'No. Owing to health issues.'

'Whose?'

'Yours!'

She made her eyes big and puzzled, a trick that could make even the bank manager responsive. 'Oh dear, am I ill? What on earth can be the matter with me?'

James exchanged a look with Harold.

She pounced. 'You don't know!'

'Of course I know! Gareth explained – that you have a nervous complaint, compounded by agoraphobia.'

'Why didn't he bring you to our house to meet me?'

Harold smiled a weary and gently perplexed smile. 'But you don't like meeting new people, Diane, do you?'

Diane studied first Harold's helpful smile, then James's puzzled frown. They meant it. They genuinely believed what they said. Her heart began to beat hard. She fought to keep her voice steady, the voice of a sane, rational person that everyone would believe in. 'Have I behaved tonight like an agoraphobic with a fear of meeting people?'

James watched her. Eventually, he admitted, 'I suppose not.'

Breathlessly, almost as if she didn't know if her input were welcome, Tamzin added, 'We all *wanted* to meet you. We wished we could.'

'Meeting would have made everything clearer,' Diane agreed, before picking up her now cold coffee and withdrawing into meditative silence.

PC Stone left the hospital, having gathered information for his report and satisfied himself that no one was about to die.

The corridors began to quieten.

James tried to relax, but the chair wasn't made to loll in. He felt stiff and bristly. As first Harold and then Tamzin fell silent, he was able to watch Diane Jenner out of the corner of his eye. Her expressions, flitting across her face like a slide show, told him that her thoughts weren't sweet. It had been an education, meeting her. Mindful of everything he'd been told about her precarious health, he'd made a huge effort to cater to her fragility – although the last thing he needed was an extra person to treat like china – and she'd reacted with the kind of outraged disbelief that she might reserve for an amiable drunk with a turd in each hand.

She made him want to laugh. And she made him want to throttle her when she gave him that politely scornful stare and demolished every statement he made.

A reassuring doctor brought news, first that Gareth had

gone down to theatre to have pins in his wrist and fingers, a plate in his leg and an external fixation device – whatever that was – screwed into his pelvis, then of Valerie's multiple leg injuries, a similar pelvic device and a collapsed lung. James received the news stoically. 'On the whole, it's slightly better than I expected. Gareth and Valerie have been lucky. Helicopters aren't designed to bounce.'

'Neither Gareth nor Valerie will be on a ward for some time,' the white-coated doctor added. 'You might be better going home for some sleep.'

'I'll stay,' Diane returned, instantly, as if preprogrammed to rebut any idea she didn't originate.

James looked at Harold, who looked as if he could sleep for a year. 'I'll take you home.'

Harold shifted. 'I'm not sure … Valerie's my daughter. And Gareth, I've only known him a couple of years –'

'A couple of *years*?' murmured Diane. James looked at her sharply. Harold was obviously shattered by the shock of having his child – his children – badly injured and he didn't need Diane interrogating him, not now.

James tried Tamzin. 'And I think you've had enough.'

Tamzin clutched her chair, her pleading eyes melting his heart. 'I want to see Mum when she comes round.'

James patted her arm, avoiding words like, *careful*, *medication* and *rest*. 'I could drop you off at your sister's. Nat won't mind you crashing in her spare bed. She'll fix you up with night things and something to read.'

Shaking her head mutinously, straw hair quivering, Tamzin's voice tightened, a great tear trembled on her lashes. 'I want to see *Mum*.'

James had to relent. 'All right, we'll take Pops home and pick up Mum's stuff.'

He noticed Diane watching them gather their things. 'Rather than staying here alone, you could come with us,' he offered.

'No, thanks,' returned Diane, cordially. 'I'll be OK.'

'Fine.' It might be a struggle to look after his exhausted father-in-law, his waif-like daughter, *and* this agoraphobic nervous wreck half-sister-in-law of his wife's who never left home. But, unaccountably ... here she was out.

Still, she was a woman alone in the middle of the night, far from home, and she'd just sustained a series of bruising shocks ... He sat down again, ready to cajole her into co-operation. 'It might be better if –'

'– you stop knowing what's best for me. Because I'll probably slap you if you use that patiently patronising voice on me again.'

He frowned horribly to disguise the almost overwhelming urge to laugh at her awful politeness. 'I'm not patronising.'

'You bloody well are, you know.' She patted his hand. 'I'm not a child, I'm not an imbecile and, as we now all know, I'm not ill. So I'm the one who makes up my mind. OK?'

Chapter Two

'Oh-kay,' he conceded.

Diane watched them leave, the big man and his lame ducks, leaving behind them only silence and space.

She fetched herself another drink and settled down in contemplation of her world gone mad. Two years, Harold said he'd known Gareth. *Two years.* Had Gareth's behaviour changed in that period, had he been more than usually secretive? Done anything that should have alerted her to the fact that for two days of each week he was not at work, but ...

... where? Almost any other man who was leading a double life would have a mistress tucked away. But Gareth's secret, it seemed, was a nice family.

She was word perfect on the story of Gareth's childhood and how Wendy had brought him up any way she could. In the sixties, the benefit system hadn't been what it was now. Unmarried mothers had found it hard to scrape by and, like many others, Wendy had drifted into a relationship, trading sex and housekeeping for a man to put his roof over her family's head. Or surviving on jobs that paid peanuts.

So why hadn't she made Harold cough up for Gareth's keep?

Diane's eyes grew gritty as the wee hours stilled the antiseptic corridors. James returned with weary tread, a wraith-like Tamzin drifting beside him, just in time to be allowed in to see Valerie.

And Diane's vigil was rewarded when she was shown in to see her *poorly, battered, but stable* husband. 'Just ten minutes tonight, please.' The nurse consulted Gareth's chart, pen in hand. 'He's just about conscious but we'd like him to rest.'

'I understand,' breathed Diane, staring down at the bed

Gareth's face was grotesquely swollen. Diane had difficulty recognising this purpling balloon-head as her husband. Every feature was puffed, distorted and discoloured beneath his incongruously normal thatch of iron-grey hair. His jaw was swollen shut, there was an enormous egg at the left side of his forehead and that, and the eye socket beneath, were flooded a dark angry red. He looked as if an elephant had pirouetted on his head.

But he was evidently sensible enough to recognise her and, un-Gareth-like, groggily search out her hand with his chilly fingers. His other hand, the right, was encased in plaster and plastic troughs.

The distortion of his features seemed appropriate, somehow, as everything Diane thought she'd known about this elusive, self-contained man had warped, too. He was inclined to guard what was his and she'd always known he wasn't good at sharing. But finding his natural father two years ago and keeping it a secret ...

She glanced at her reflection in the huge window. Her hair hung long in its neat plait, her clothes were, admittedly, self-made, but then that was her *job*. What was he so ashamed of?

It might've relieved her feelings to round on him with ferocious questions but she kept her anger to herself. Habit. Long habit. She never roused Gareth's temper unnecessarily. She liked to have her challenge all worked out in her mind before she incurred his house-shaking rage or punishing silence. And she had been punished plenty, in recent years.

'So,' she observed. 'You survived.'

'Uh.'

She took the grunt for assent. 'The doctors say you'll recover.'

'Uh.'

'I expect you're woozy.'

'Uh.' He closed his eyes. His breathing deepened.

Sliding her hand from his, she turned to the scarred locker beside the bed and opened the drawer. Beside a handful of change lay his wallet, black and soft with use. She'd bought it several years ago at John Lewis's one drizzly, dank December morning, £24.99, as a Christmas gift. He'd said one from the market would've done just as well, £4.99 or even less, but she'd argued that this would last longer.

She'd never had it in her hands since the day she gave it to him; they respected one another's private space so far as things like wallets were concerned. Gareth was particular that way. But now, defiantly, she flipped open the snap. Her purse was housing mainly moths and she'd need money to get home.

Cards in the card sleeves, including one Bryony had sent with her contact details in Brazil. Lonely in the note slots, a twenty-pound note and a five.

She fingered the leather thoughtfully. Its substance suggested further paperwork in there somewhere. Her fingertips found the smooth oval tag of the zip to the inner compartment and she ran it gently along the top edge, *ZZZzzz*.

The inner compartment was full of twenties.

She almost dropped the wallet in shock. Heart picking up, fingers stiff and trembling, she counted. Twenty. *Twenty twenties*! She stared at the lightly mauve notes, unable to remember the last time she'd held twenty twenties. A fortune. She'd almost exhausted the housekeeping for the week and there might be all kinds of incidental expenses for her to meet while Gareth was in hospital. And why should

Gareth squirrel away dosh, when things were squeaky tight at home?

Slowly, she slipped out two notes and dropped the wallet back in the drawer.

Twenty twenties. Eighteen twenties, now.

After a moment, she picked up the wallet again and extracted another three twenties. Then five more. That was fair. Halvies.

She jumped to see that Gareth's eyes had opened. 'I'll be back tomorrow.' Her voice emerged matter-of-factly, as if she were the type of wife who routinely rooted through her husband's personal possessions.

Gareth said, 'Uh,' again, moving his head and then sucking in his breath in pain. She could almost hear the protests he was too ill to make.

She licked her lips. 'You'd better sleep.' The unfamiliar substance of two hundred pounds clutched in her hand, she crossed the room slowly, waiting for objections and reprimands to bound after her like maddened cats. But Gareth said nothing. Two hundred pounds. The notes felt soft and thick, coated with the prints of all the fingers they'd passed through, fingers perhaps more used to holding a wedge of notes than hers were. Two. Hundred. Pounds. She'd never suspected robbing her husband would be so empowering. Fun, in fact.

The door shushed as she opened it and clunked softly closed behind her. She let out her breath.

In the corridor, James was pacing, glancing at his watch. Lines of fatigued grooved his face. 'I thought you must still be here. I waited to run you home.'

She rubbed her temples, her mind still on the blast of Gareth's outrage that had never come. 'But I live way out in the country.' Her eyes went to Tamzin, who was propped against the wall, eyes huge with weariness.

'Purtenon St. Paul. I know it.' He pressed a flat chrome button and the lift doors opened.

She didn't want him to take her home, didn't want to have to be grateful, to satisfy his obviously over-developed protective streak by needing his help. Proudly, she flourished the stack of twenties. 'Don't worry, I just raided Gareth's wallet for taxi fare.'

James stepped back to allow her into the lift, Tamzin drifting in beside her. The doors breezed shut and they stood in the small space for a few silent seconds until the doors opened again in the foyer where a cleaning crew were buffing the floor. Through the main doors, the night they stepped into was cool and fresh. And damn! The taxi rank was empty. Diane tutted. She'd been looking forward to putting some of her ill-gotten gains to frivolous use.

Gareth so disliked frivolity.

She turned back. 'I'll ask at reception for the number of a cab company.'

James groaned, rubbing a square hand over his hair. 'Please, Diane. It's nearly morning and you've had a shock and I can relax if I know you've made it home. Let's not bicker about it. Just get in the fu – in the car.'

Diane glared up at James. His gaze met hers. She hesitated. He looked really tired yet – judging by the obstinate set of his mouth – was apparently unwilling to abandon her, a woman he'd never met until tonight – a fairly awkward and ungrateful woman he'd never met until tonight. She found herself looking at his mouth, as she examined the thought and wondered what she had to prove by refusing his kind offer.

'Give in,' Tamzin advised. 'It's easier in the long run.'

Tamzin didn't like riding in the back of the car but insisting that Diane sit in the front beside her father was the sort of courtesy her parents had drummed into their kids.

The sky was just thinking about turning silver and pearly. She could sit in the middle of the back seat and watch it, occasionally letting her gaze slide over to the still figure of Diane Jenner.

Uncle Gareth's wife! How strange was that? For two years they'd referred to her as 'Mrs Rochester', the unbalanced wife that Uncle Gareth hid away and cared for so heroically.

Diane was well unusual, with a gaze to read your soul and an impressive ability to resist doing anything she didn't wish to do. She certainly wasn't suffering from any nervous, emotional or phobic difficulty so far as Tamzin could see. And Tamzin would know, because of Her Condition.

So, either Diane had made a *mega* recovery ... or Uncle Gareth had been telling porkies.

Mega recoveries were rare. So. Uncle Gareth hadn't wanted them to meet his wife. That was totally pants.

Natalia and Alice would be as mad as hell to have missed this skeleton rattling out of its closet tonight, and their father taking ages to catch on that the facts about Diane Jenner weren't facts at all. But James had asked Tamzin's sisters to stay at home. Valerie wasn't in danger, Nat was working shifts and Ally was in the middle of accountancy exams. Tamzin, as usual, hadn't been given an option; James had just said, 'Come on, Tamz.' Because of Her Condition he wouldn't leave her home alone when anything bad happened – not that she'd wanted to be left at home. She'd wanted to see her mum. And now she had, so broken and bruised. Her dad would be watching her like a hawk for days, if not weeks.

Nat and Ally were lucky; strong and confident and well-adjusted, with healthy lives full of healthy problems like annoying boyfriends, impossible bosses and killer hangovers. She loved Nat and Ally. She wished she *was* Nat or Ally.

Depression was a bastard.

She yawned. She hadn't got up till lunchtime but she longed to retreat to her cool sheets. On bad nights she would only lie and stare at the ceiling, but still she loved the cocoon comfort of her bed. Bed. Her heart lurched to remember Valerie strung up like a fly in a web in that hospital bed. It was so crap that Valerie had been hurt. Really hurt. Tamzin felt a familiar hollowness in her chest. It would be ages before Mum was home. Could Tamzin hack undiluted James for so long? Her father got so stressed about her getting better it made her feel guilty that she couldn't.

Valerie placed less importance than James on things like washing and dressing. Possibly, she didn't always notice whether Tamzin had. That was cool. Less pressure.

Yet, the baby of the family, Tamzin's childhood memories included perching proudly on her mother's lap at parties in her Laura Ashley dresses and white knee socks while Nat and Ally, less malleable and less pretty, careered around with sashes untied and lace ripped. Valerie loved parties, having always been beautiful and vivacious so that men made idiots of themselves over her, which made her dead snappy with Dad, sometimes, because he refused to be made angry by them.

Tamzin had a special connection to her mother – they closed their eyes to each other's problems. She wiped her eyes with the back of her hand as the car purred through the dawn and wondered how her mother would take to Diane Jenner. Uncle Gareth had been a lovely new audience for Valerie's toys, the big stone house, the Alloy Blue TVR Tuscan 2 Targa, the 4-wheel-drive Lexus, the flying.

But Diane didn't look the type to be easily impressed.

'Where's your place?' James asked Diane, politely.

Diane stirred and stretched in the dark grey light. 'A couple of miles. Drop me by the village green, if you like. I can walk down the lane.'

James glanced across at her. 'At night?'

'It's getting light.'

He made a performance of peering out. There was no colour yet in the fields or hedges and the streetlights were still alight as they neared the village. Tamzin could have told Diane that she was wasting her breath. James wouldn't drop Diane anywhere but safely at her front door. 'Just tell me where to find your house,' he said.

Shrugging, Diane sent him down a main road between brick houses topped with tile, turning left just before a huddle of new properties advertised as 'executive residences'. Nowhere near as big as our house, Tamzin thought. Over a small bridge, they crossed a dyke where the water looked like weak tea without milk in the first of the sun's rays and ran down a lane between a string of redbrick houses with hedges. The flatness of the surrounding fields was typical of the wide expanses of the Fens where most of the scenery was sky and the pylons marched like robots.

The Mercedes rolled along quietly. James glanced at Diane. 'Bit bloody lonely down here. Do you often walk it alone?'

One of Diane's shoulders lifted. 'I have to get from A to B.'

Tamzin couldn't decide whether Diane was hostile or amused at James's concern. Concern was kind of a habit, with him.

They pulled up outside one of the redbrick semi-detached houses and Diane opened the car door. 'Sorry to have put you to so much trouble at the end of a long night.'

Tamzin climbed out, too, intending to move into the front seat. The first streak of pink had appeared overhead and she hunched her shoulders against a chill morning breeze.

'I'll see you in,' said James.

Diane halted, her long plait settling over one shoulder. 'See me in?' She examined the thirty yards between the car and her house. The corners of her mouth twitched. 'Oh. OK. Um, thanks.'

Tamzin grinned as her father, scowling at being humoured so obviously, trailed Diane up the concrete path to what probably used to be a council house. The front garden was long and the shrubs they brushed past were silvery with dew and spider webs. Something squelched under Tamzin's shoe. 'Gross,' she muttered.

Diane led them to a side door that opened into the kitchen. In the light of a bulb shaded by taut white cotton, they all blinked. 'As you can see,' observed Diane, gravely, 'quite safe. It's very good of you to worry, of course.'

'Right.' James turned for the door.

But Tamzin couldn't stop gazing at her surroundings. This kitchen was out of a museum! White Formica worktop, chipped and scarred, white tiles, greying grout, a freestanding electric cooker crouched on quarry tiles, more Formica on the units on the wall. It would have been straight out of the 1970s, except for the fresh pink emulsion with a stencilled grapevine arcing above the washing machine.

Well old! And *tiny* compared to their house, with the gables of six bedrooms studding the red-tiled roof and four cars parked in the garage at the end of the drive.

Her mouth was quicker to react than her sluggish brain. 'Whoa! Does Uncle Gareth live *here*?'

Diane halted, that disconcerting gaze homing in on Tamzin in a way that made Tamzin want to suck the words back out of the air. Seconds passed in silence. Without removing her gaze, Diane reached down thick, yellow mugs from behind a glass sliding door of a wall cupboard. Her voice had taken on a note of steel. 'I can't let you go without something to keep you awake on the drive home.' She filled the kettle, plugged it in, and scraped out two kitchen chairs. 'Please – sit.'

'We ought to get going.' James turned for the door.

'A cup of tea first,' Diane contradicted firmly. 'And a chat. That would be ... helpful. Please.'

Tamzin watched her father hesitate, pinned by blue eyes. There was something about Diane, something good and valiant. And difficult to resist. Tamzin suspected that if Diane didn't get what she wanted now, she'd lie in wait for them at the hospital. She sighed aloud and dropped into a chair. Slowly, her father joined her, frowning like a goblin.

Diane made tea in a pot, with tea leaves and a strainer.

Then she folded her arms on the kitchen table, pushing aside a bundle of blue fabric, a tattered blue pincushion and a pot of sequins. 'Why are you so astonished that we live in this house, Tamzin?' She glanced around the kitchen. 'It's modest but it's a perfectly respectable house, bought and paid for.'

Picking up the yellow mug, although the tea was hot, Tamzin protested, feebly. 'I'm not astonished.'

Diane's voice softened as she poured her own tea, brewed Guinness-dark. 'Tamzin, I've had a bad day.'

'Tamzin's very tired,' James cut in, in his *in charge* voice.

Diane twinkled at Tamzin. 'Are you too tired to answer, Tamz?'

Tamzin sighed and dropped her gaze to Diane's top. It reminded her of a clear sea on a summer day, the glitter of the sun on embroidered waves suggested by a spangling of golden beads and – now she looked more closely – fleets of tiny silver buckles. Cool.

She ventured. 'I suppose I thought Uncle Gareth would live somewhere different.'

'Different? Bigger, smaller, prettier, uglier, upmarket, downmarket?'

'Upmarket,' Tamzin selected miserably, unwillingly, aware that she was toiling deeper into hideous poo and wishing James had been content to drop Diane at her gate.

'Upmarket.' Diane mused. Her hair caught the light as she nodded. Tamzin fixed her gaze on it. Such a strange colour; properly pale blonde. Moonlight. Star shine. Pearl. Unexpectedly beautiful. 'Why would you expect Gareth to own a house that was "upmarket"?'

James tried again with the authoritative voice. 'This isn't our business.'

'That's a get out.' Diane stretched absently, putting her hands behind her head and making her shoulder bones crack, the fabric of the loose satiny top tightening against her body.

Tamzin was horrified to catch James all too obviously blinking his gaze back up to Diane's face.

Diane dropping her arms. Suddenly.

And James blushing as hot and red as a chilli.

Oh gross! Tamzin felt the sting of mortified tears. Her father had *looked* with that lips-parted expression men reserve for breasts – and let Diane catch him. And they were looking at each other and then not looking, glances flitting around the room like birds with no perches, before their gazes tangled once more.

'Because of the money,' Tamzin blurted, to deflect attention from James's cringeworthy behaviour.

Diane's gaze flicked back to Tamzin. 'Money?'

'Pops gave him money.' Tamzin's voice shook.

Diane's body flexed and quivered as if silently absorbing a blow. Her eyes grew enormous. 'Gareth would never accept charity. He wouldn't claim low-income benefit, even, when our daughter was younger.'

Decisively, James jumped to his feet. 'Then obviously we're mistaken.'

Diane continued speaking to Tamzin, as if they were old friends, her eyes intent, yet vulnerable. 'Do you know how much?'

Tamzin hesitated. 'I don't know a figure.'

'Roughly? Please?'

Anxious tears were building and building. And if she cried, Diane would feel sorry for her, might slide her arms around her and stroke her hair. She might like Diane to stroke her hair. But she wouldn't like Diane to feel sorry for her. She swallowed hard. 'Quite a bit, I think. Plus the cottage.'

Diane flinched. Dawn was bursting through the kitchen window now, lighting up Diane's hair pink-apricot. Her skin was soft and clear, the lines fine at the corners of her eyes. Valerie's grooves were deeper, but then Valerie wasn't exactly a health freak and the puckers around her lips told of all the cigarettes she'd smoked, no matter how much stuff she had injected. Diane's face was young but her hands were old; rough and red and work-worn where Valerie's were soft and manicured –

'What cottage?' Diane's voice was a whisper.

James answered this time, his voice deep and gentle. 'On the outskirts of Whittlesey.' He hesitated. 'Harold's owned it for years. Apparently he once bought it for Gareth's mother.'

Diane's eyes emptied. There was a long silence. Slowly, she touched Tamzin's hand. 'Thanks. I won't keep you if you want to get off to bed now.' A tear welled and skittered down her cheek. She batted it away with the back of her hand, lurching to her feet and turning blindly.

Tamzin scraped back her chair, seeing a danger with sudden appalling clarity. 'Careful!'

But James was already there, snatching at Diane before her hand made contact with the chrome kettle. As if it was one shock too many, Diane piped out a sound between a laugh and a sob. And, without either of them seeming to do more than sway, James's comforting arms were around Diane and Diane's head was on his shoulder, and James was pushing her plait out of the way so that he could pat her back, murmuring that he was sorry that she'd had so many bolts from the blue and Diane hiccupping that it was hardly his fault.

Tamzin returned slowly to her chair. Her father was well weird, the way he seemed to be able to care for just about everybody in the world.

Chapter Three

Diane dialled carefully, preparing for that little pain at hearing Bryony's voice, so real, clear, dear and familiar, when she was actually so heartbreakingly far away.

But Bryony had to be told about Gareth before she disappeared off to work at the orphanage.

She gripped the handset. A succession of clicks. The ringing tone. It rang for a long time but it was six in the morning in Brasilia, although ten a.m. in Purtenon St. Paul. One of the girls Bryony shared with answered eventually with a cross, 'Yeah?' Six girls lived in the same house, although so far as the landlord knew there were only four.

'Can you get Bryony for me, please? This is her mum.'

'Jussa minute.'

Usually, Diane would wait out such delays tense with frustration that her frugal five minutes was ticking away.

But today she was unconcerned at racking up the phone bill. Gareth could afford it.

Bryony's arrival on the other end of the line was surprisingly quick, her voice high with alarm. 'Mum? It's so early! Are you all right?' Her young, over-emphatic voice rushed from the phone.

'Hello, darling.' For a second, Diane couldn't find any further words. Her instinct was always to protect Bryony, not to be the one to cause her pain. She hugged herself, longing to hold her daughter. 'I'm fine – I'm afraid it's Dad. He's not in any danger but he was in a crash –'

A gasp. 'Oh my *God*! How bad –?'

'He's very bashed up but the important thing is that he'll heal. But he's broken his right arm and fingers, both legs and his pelvis.'

She dealt patiently with three minutes of, 'Oh, my *God*,' and, '*So* can't believe it!' before Bryony's common sense began to function, 'Should I come home?'

Diane was ready with a firm reply. 'No, don't come haring back, he's quite out of it at the moment and you'd just be wasting your opportunity in Brazil.'

Bryony sounded relieved. 'Because I will, of course ... but it would take ages to get the dosh together to come back.'

'That's why I don't think you should do anything hasty.' *Dad could pay.*

'Keep me in touch, then. I wish you had a computer, Mum. I could get you fixed up with Skype and we could talk for, like, nearly nothing. Tell Dad ...' She paused. 'Tell him I'm thinking of him.'

'Of course I will.' It wasn't until she put the phone down that she realised Bryony hadn't said, 'Give Dad my love.' She sighed, standing alone in the tiny, white-painted hallway, the cold striking up from the chipped tiles and chilling her feet. Bryony and Gareth not getting on well in the months before Bryony went away had troubled Diane, but Gareth and Bryony had each shrugged off her anxious enquiries.

She wiped her eyes. She hadn't broken the news about Gareth's secret family – Bryony's family, too. She was still wrestling with that.

James North returned in the early afternoon driving Gareth's silver Peugeot with Tamzin following in a dark grey Lexus. Pausing in her task of gazing glumly at her white, crumpled, sleep-deprived reflection in the tiny mirror on the wall, through the kitchen window Diane watched them arrive. 'Damn.' An abortive attempt at daytime napping had left her head thick and throbbing with the horrible realisation that her life was emptying fast, her marriage even faster and her husband was a phoney.

And now she had to face the man she'd wept all over last night and his waif-like daughter.

She watched James stride up the garden path, Tamzin dawdling behind. She opened the door and James dangled the keys that normally lived in Gareth's pocket. 'I've brought your car back – thought you'd need it for hospital visiting.'

'Thank you, I'd begun to wonder where it was. Where had he left it?'

'At the flying club. The keys were retrieved from the 'copter wreckage, so the police gave them to me.'

'Right.' Diane smiled at Tamzin to avoid the sympathy in James's eyes. Tamzin was so slender that her head seemed too heavy for her neck. Even her freckles looked too big. Somewhere in her chest, Diane felt compassion stir. 'How's your grandfather today?'

A small smile. 'Better after some sleep. How about Uncle Gareth?'

It seemed strange for this fluttery girl that Diane had met only yesterday to refer to Gareth as 'uncle'. 'He'll mend. And your mum?'

'The same.' Tamzin didn't move from just inside the door. 'The collapsed lung's scary because she smokes way too much. But the doctors say there's nothing to stop her recovering.' She was quiet but not timid. Both smile and eyes were reminiscent of her father, except for her personal elements of trouble and need.

In the new reality that Diane had been tossed into last night, Tamzin was her niece by marriage. Gareth's other niece and nephews were a part of Diane's life, normal, boisterous, sometimes sullen, sometimes marvellous, teenagers or children. The offspring of his brothers. The cousins of her child. She was a part of their family and they were a part of hers, she knew their birthdays and whether they were taking exams this year. Tamzin was related to her in exactly the same degree as they were, as Ivan's son, George – Gorgeous George as Bryony called him – who'd arrived at the house last week to show off that he was allowed to drive his mother's car. A visit he'd cut short abruptly as he rediscovered how much he missed Bryony.

James was quiet – probably frozen with horror, seeing her in the daylight with her piggy cried-out eyes and a robe that had been a cheap buy ten years ago from a market stall. She'd never got around to making a replacement for the thin, shiny garment that had once been a pretty forest green but was muddy now with years of washing.

Pulling the dressing gown tightly closed as she belatedly remembered the nightdress beneath, once white but now ivory with age, she felt a flush of indignation. It was no sin not to have money! Gareth's wages didn't go far when he so often felt the need to help his brothers, family being family and blood being thicker than water. As their 1930s' house had run into the major maintenance issues of a new roof and damp proofing over the years they'd had to extend and increase the mortgage periodically to cope. Money was always spoken for. Always.

Bryony had been a delicate child, plagued by asthma, bronchitis and tonsillitis. Her sickliness had been the reason they'd never had another baby and the reason that Diane had never quite got around to formal employment, even as Bryony grew up and, to an extent, out of her childhood maladies. Diane had made what money she could from her sewing, tailoring blouses and embroidering skirts for other people, wondering whether she ought to embark upon a midlife reinvention, perhaps to emerge at the end as a post-office counter-clerk with a salary, sick pay and a pension. But it was so difficult without a second vehicle. Lack of transport was a serious omission in Purtenon St. Paul, threaded as it was like a bead on the long string of Fenland lanes. To get a job she needed a car. To get a car she needed a job. 'It's time I dressed,' she said, suddenly.

Tamzin moved immediately towards the door.

James put a reassuring arm across his daughter's shoulders. 'We only came to bring the car. No doubt we'll come across each other at the hospital. They're being moved to the Ackerman about three this afternoon.'

She nodded. 'Yes. I had a phone call.' Some admin person with a practised coo *just* to confirm for Mrs Jenner that the Ackerman Hospital *were* expecting Mr Jenner, and his room *was* ready and the ambulance arranged.

'Call me if you need anything,' said James, as he turned for the door.

'Interesting, isn't she?' asked Tamzin, as they drove away in the Lexus.

James flicked her a glance. He had never quite got used to the ghost that his daughter had become over the past couple of years, often silent, always sad. Words like 'interesting' from her were as rare as a heap of food on her plate. 'If you like a woman with a tongue like a hedge cutter.'

Tamzin giggled. 'She has not! You're just peed because she doesn't follow your orders.'

James let that one go. 'So why's she interesting?'

'Because she's been kept secret, I suppose.' Tamzin screwed up her face. 'Why would Uncle Gareth do that? Why would he live in such a teeny, ordinary house? Why didn't Diane know about the cottage? Or the money? Why didn't she know about any of us? Maybe it's us that Uncle Gareth kept secret, not her?' As if the prospect was too much for her she leaned her temple against the door and closed her eyes, signalling that she no longer wanted to talk.

'Both,' James answered, anyway. 'And the underlying

reasons behind that will probably prove interesting, too.'

He lapsed into silence as the big vehicle eased along the lanes. Diane certainly was 'interesting'. So resilient. Yet vulnerable, the way that she'd curved into his arms, her hair brushing his hand, her body quivering as she'd fought back her tears.

The way that they'd spoken to one another, for ten seconds, as if they'd known each other forever.

And although she'd cried, although she'd accepted his shoulder just for a few moments, he'd had the feeling that here, for once, was a woman who didn't need his strength.

She could be strong. Sensible. Competent. Motivated. He thought that Diane Jenner could be anything she wanted to be.

'She was embarrassed!' Tamzin's eyes flew open to examine the idea. 'We caught her in her nightie and she didn't like it. That's why she sounded stressy and obviously wanted us to go. It was probably you, Dad, because you're a man.'

James let his mind conjure up Diane's robe doing less to cover her scantily clad breasts and more to gather them up nicely. That had been interesting, too. 'Probably,' he agreed mildly, quite happy to take the blame for Diane's poor welcome.

He didn't distress his fragile daughter by airing his opinion that any awareness of James's masculinity that Diane might have experienced had been minor – compared to her vulnerability. Because, last night, she'd been caught without her armour.

After the Norths left, Diane showered and, to make up for being caught in ancient night clothes, changed into one of her favourite outfits, a white blouse criss-crossed irregularly by salmon-pink ribbon, and black jeans with a helix of the same salmon-pink chain stitch winding evenly up the left leg; clothes that made her feel less the ragged relation.

She picked up the car keys and felt a chink in her gloom. She was going to drive the car.

Although she'd passed her test at seventeen and, in fact, it had been through her snazzy British Racing Green Mini Cooper that she'd met Gareth just over twenty-five years ago, when he had stopped his scooter to help her change a flat, she now scarcely ever got into the driving seat. In fact, she'd driven this car precisely once.

If Diane wanted to leave the village when Gareth was at work she strode up the lane and across the bridge to catch one of the buses that trundled three times a week a torturous route between the hedges and into Peterborough or, in almost exactly the other direction, Holbeach. If she went out in the evening it was always to deliver a garment in the village or to accompany Gareth to visit his family, when, traditional man that he was, Gareth would drive.

Isolation was a feature of living in Purtenon St. Paul but Gareth had been intent on this rural idyll for them, as if living even on the edges of a town or city would automatically condemn his family to the grotty streets of his childhood. He wasn't swayed by his brothers' families surviving happily in modern housing on perfectly pleasant estates with schools, shops, cinemas and McDonalds within walking distance.

But, like any idyll, the rural existence had its drawbacks – Diane was driven bonkers by the seclusion. Bryony used to escape by going home after school with friends in Holbeach, Gareth fetching her at the end of the evening. Diane had no such convenient friends. In fact, living Gareth's idyll, working from home, not being mobile ... it was difficult to make friends at all.

It wasn't even cheap to live in Purtenon St. Paul. The nearest supermarket was half-an-hour away by car and the village shop had everything from Christmas trees to carbolic – everything except bargains.

But now, hospital visiting was expected of her. And the car was all hers.

Carefully, she adjusted the seat, the headrest and all the mirrors – Gareth would grumble when he was able to drive again but that wasn't going to be just yet. Her internal butterflies danced a little jig – it was amazing how tense she felt behind the wheel – and she turned the ignition key. The engine responded instantly, *vrummm*!

'Driving's not difficult,' she blustered aloud, as she eased the silver Peugeot up to the turning point further up the lane. But, as she moseyed along cautiously between the verges and the fields she was glad there was no one around to see her jerky progress.

Suppressing the adrenaline rushing around her system she flicked left to join the next lane, which took her to the main road, although there were only sheep to see. She flinched as she changed down to second to squeeze the car over the narrow bridge. Whoo-oops ...! But she made it without touching the sides, laughed in nervous delight and successfully negotiated the right at Main Road towards Crowland and Peterborough.

Once on the open road she felt her spine relax as the car co-operated beautifully, moving left or right according to her direction, slowing when she pressed on the brake. After five miles of being overtaken in irritated little rushes by other vehicles she let her foot weigh down the accelerator and began to enjoy the liquid sensation of speed and the little bob the car gave over bumps.

'This is OK,' she told herself, slackening her death-like grip on the steering wheel. 'Dead easy.'

It all seemed so on the long lanes, the steering so light but positive that she even began to sing along to the radio in breathy little bursts as she made her way over the lengthy straights, faster and faster.

But she overcooked it when she arrived too quickly at a corner and the car wallowed unpleasantly, as if in imminent danger of plunging sideways into the unwelcoming depths of the roadside dyke. 'Shi-hit!' she cried softly, stamping on the brake and spinning the wheel frantically between suddenly sweaty hands.

The car halted. She opened her eyes. She was still on the tarmac. Or three wheels were, which was acceptable. She wiped her forehead and, shakily, restarted the engine that had stalled because, all her limbs being taken up with steering and braking, changing gear had been a task too many. She drove on more cautiously.

Set about with groomed lawns and coifed conifers the new Ackerman Hospital looked like a red-brick lantern, the upper storey smaller than the lower and crowned by a cupola of glassed-in offices. Diane stepped into the hushed building as if entering a church, surveying the navy, tan and deep raspberry pink carpet, the smiling staff, the plants twisted artfully up trellises. It didn't look like a National Health hospital but it smelled no different.

A groomed, dark-haired nurse showed her into Gareth's hotel-like room, although she felt sure she would've been successful at locating it by its room number. He lay quietly in the white bed. 'He's slow, after his concussion,' the nurse explained, kindly. 'Just let him sleep when he wants to.'

Diane found herself clutching the nurse's arm. 'But he's lost all his teeth!'

The nurse patted her hand. 'They're still there. Under all that swelling – aren't they, Gareth? They'll reappear, in time. Should I get somebody to bring you coffee, or tea?'

For some time, Diane sat beside Gareth's bed, drinking coffee, gazing at him as he dozed, waiting for him to rouse for more than a few seconds at a stretch. She'd expected that he'd be more alert. That there would be conversation.

With nothing to occupy her she began to worry about the journey home. Whizzing through the lanes had been OK once she got used to it but the journey had become a bit fraught once she met the A47, sucked around roundabout after ever-busier roundabout and squirted out onto the hectic dual carriageway that was Paston Parkway. The hospital's position between Paston Parkway and open Fenland meant that at least she didn't have to brave thundering Soke Parkway into the bowels of the city, as she would have if Gareth had remained in the district hospital.

But still, she glanced at her watch. Often.

She sipped her coffee and studied Gareth's bloated head and plastered arm, all that could be seen protruding from the sheet. His fingers, in their troughs, were purple sausages. They made her wince just to look at them.

But his injuries didn't give her amnesia about his unforgivable lies.

She sighed. She wished she'd brought a magazine.

She brooded on the hateful thing he'd done.

She fidgeted.

Rush hour was approaching. The thought was like cold custard in the pit of her stomach. Gareth was hardly aware that she was there ...

She slipped from the room, anxious to put the city behind her before the dreaded five o'clock brought traffic like a rush of demons from the mouth of hell.

After leaving Purtenon St Paul, James drove home to Webber's Cross, Tamzin almost silent beside him.

'I ought to go into the office,' he said, experimentally. 'I'm supposed to be in a Health and Safety meeting, this afternoon.'

After a moment, she nodded. 'OK.'

He turned onto the A47. 'But I could video conference it if you'd feel better with me at home.'

'I'll be OK. What about Mum?'

'I won't stay late. I'll be home in time to take you to see her in the early evening.'

'OK.'

He wished he knew exactly what she was thinking; Tamzin, so fey next to Natalia and Alice. How could Valerie dismiss Tamzin's problems?

'Sure?'

'Sure.'

Still, he hovered in the hall, as she trod silently up the dogleg stairs and across the gallery landing, until he heard the sound of the television coming from her room. 'Ring me if you need me,' he shouted. He gathered up his briefcase and his keys. Either he had to spend some of his time in the office or give up his job. He couldn't stay at home with Tamzin for the whole period that Valerie languished in hospital. It would be months.

But he'd talk to his CEO, Charlie Hobbs, about working from home a couple of half days a week. Till now, he'd relied on Valerie being at home with Tamzin at least part of the time. When she wasn't flying, lunching or shopping.

His desk, when he reached it, was half-buried in paper. He frowned. Furness Durwent was meant to be a high–tech, paperless environment, but you just couldn't cure some staff of the stickies habit. Several coloured envelopes scattered across the wooden veneer proved to be Get Well Soon cards for Valerie. 'Pretty bloody quick,' he muttered, flipping them into a pile and sliding them efficiently into his briefcase to take to the hospital, later. He raised his voice. 'Lawrence!'

Lawrence, who looked about fifteen but had a first in politics and business studies and was up for the next manager's job that became available, was already halfway through the door. 'Here,' he said, with an air of mild reproach that James should think he'd need to be called.

James grinned. 'What do I need to know?'

'Nothing urgent. You've got a shitload of email but everyone knows about the accident so I've been able to fend some people off. The Health and Safety meeting's been put back until Tuesday.'

James halted. 'I told you I'd be here.'

'But Charlie went to some working lunch and has stayed behind, schmoozing a potential new big client with a toy factory. They're looking for a new supplier of printed circuit boards.'

James grunted and sat down in his big leather chair. Damn. He could have worked from home. He dropped his BlackBerry on the desk – now that he looked, he could see a text from Lawrence in his inbox, probably telling him the meeting had been postponed – and joggled his mouse to bring his computer screen to life. 'For their production systems or their toys?'

'Automated toys. They do educational stuff.'

'OK, thanks.' He watched Lawrence return to his desk and become instantly immersed. His type of man. Saw what needed to be done and did it.

James could divert his calls to Lawrence, now that the meeting was off. Should he go home? He checked out of his window. His corner office looked straight up the Frank Perkins Parkway and he could see that the traffic was slooooooow … Might as well be here working as sitting in a queue fulminating.

The 'street view', as the offices at the front were designated, was meant not to carry the prestige of the rear 'field view', where fields could definitely be seen, over the roofs of some smaller units and a yard full of containers.

Charlie had a field-view office but James preferred to see the traffic. It gave him a feeling of being connected to the real world. If he were due in a meeting with visitors, he could keep an eye out for their arrival. His life was made up of meetings. Production was the core of the company and if there was a meeting in the building, it seemed as if James, as production director, needed to be in it. Health and Safety. Training. Equipment maintenance, equipment purchase, budget, IT, HR, sales, planning and control of production, quality, timescale, costs ...

Did he ever do any real work, these days? He'd become a communication hub, meeting after meeting, email after email, assigning the managers to write his reports for him to edit into his own words.

He knew he was good in meetings. He enjoyed keeping everything in his head, listening silently, absorbing the reports of others, computing their decisions. Rectifying them. Nobody minded James's input because it was never political – there were no blades between shoulders. And he rarely offended, because he took care to make his methods non-interfering. A note on someone's pad, a text or email to their BlackBerry ... the colleague would glance at it and move smoothly on to cover the point.

If Charlie was chairing the meeting he'd say, 'Let's just wait until James has made sure our web's neatly constructed. James? Can we move on?' Charlie referred to James as Spiderman. If the meeting was going well he might even joke, 'Did I get everything, Spidey?'

At his last appraisal, Charlie had said, 'For whatever reason, James, you were born with the ability to make things work. If I can get you to sign off on a project without frowning, I know we're OK.'

James loved his job. Loved the feeling of being in control. In charge. And, if he were honest with himself, important.

Processes. Systems. Overviews. Anticipation and foresight –

His BlackBerry buzzed. He glanced at the screen, then took the call. 'Tamzin? OK?'

'Should I ring the hospital to find out how Mum is, do you think?'

He checked his watch. 'We'll be seeing her in a couple of hours.'

'I just want to know if she's OK. Didn't they say we could ring the nurses' station to ask? I know they don't want us ringing her room until she's begun to improve.'

He considered. 'If you really can't wait a couple of hours, I suppose you can ring.'

A pause. 'Can you ring?' Her voice was small. Then she brightened. 'No, I'll ask Ally to do it. She's off work on study leave this afternoon because of her exam this evening. I'll ring her.' Before he could express an opinion, she'd ended the call.

He sighed as he dropped the BlackBerry back on the desk, turning to his desktop pc and frowning at his crowded inbox. There were a lot of messages with *Valerie* in the subject line. Opening the first, from Amaguchi San, his opposite number in the Japanese office, he tapped out a rapid reply, *Thanks for your kind concern. It's early days but Valerie will recover from her broken bones etc. It'll mean quite a time in hospital, though. James.* Before sending the message he copied the text and zipped through the rest of the enquiries about Val by clicking *reply* and then pasting in the same message and clicking *send*.

He paused to text Tamzin. If yr ringing about Mum, u better ask about Uncle Gareth, 2.

It seemed to him that Diane Jenner was so independent/ bloody-minded that if Gareth took a turn for the worse, she'd set out to cope on her own, no matter how much help she needed. It might be better if he had reports on Gareth, too, in case he had to divert any of his attention to the Jenners.

Gareth had been an unexpected branch to grow on the family tree but Val was much fonder of him than James would have expected, considering his blunt manners and his uncomfortable upbringing. Valerie was amused and entertained by Gareth. It wasn't in her to feel compassion – leave that to Harold – but she genuinely enjoyed Gareth's company. Once or twice she'd undiplomatically banged on about her privileged childhood but Gareth seemed more fascinated than resentful and eager to spend time in the North household. In the helicopter. In Val's car.

James had wondered. What about his poor, mentally sick wife? He had occasionally pictured a sad-faced woman with her nose pressed up against the window, waiting for her husband, her only link with the outside world.

But all the time, that wife at home had been quite normal.

He grinned as he opened an attachment to an email, a report from Cherry in HR about training requirements in the coming quarter. Diane Jenner seemed to be coping admirably with the fact that Valerie had nearly killed herself and Gareth with her stupid antics.

The lines of Cherry's report blurred suddenly.

Valerie had nearly died.

The thought revolved slowly as his eyes focused again and his heart resumed its normal rhythm. He tried to imagine what would have happened – the grief of his daughters. Tamzin, especially. Tamzin would have been in bits. He tried, and failed, to imagine Tamzin coping.

He shuddered. Once Valerie was well enough he was going to give her such a bollocking. Fucking Valerie.

He returned to the report's introduction, trying to concentrate, trying to deny to himself that he had just suffered something unpleasantly like shock.

That's what had changed his whole adult life, fucking Valerie. Made him a married man and a father way ahead of schedule, tied to a woman who had picked him as her life partner for all the wrong reasons.

Or maybe for pragmatic reasons. Maybe she'd recognised a man who would never let anything bad happen to her.

But she had overlooked a fundamental fact: it could be hard for two people who loved and respected each other, and had stuff in common, to live together without bloodshed.

Let alone those who would have been happier apart.

As a kid, he'd assumed, naively, that he would someday meet a woman he'd fall in love with and with whom he would want to be. Simple.

Things hadn't worked out like that and, in principle, he could leave Valerie right now. But he wouldn't, for all the reasons that he had never left Val – he had no cause to go. No hatred between him and his wife. No love between him and someone else.

And then there was Tamzin. Poor, fragile Tamzin, needing support even though, perhaps taking her cue from her mother, she sometimes treated James as if he were the enemy.

Instead of her only friend.

Chapter Four

Over the following weeks, Diane developed a routine of working at her sewing machine in the mornings and visiting Gareth in the afternoons, when the roads were relatively quiet, leaving the evenings free for Ivan and Melvyn if they wished to keep their brother company. 'You can have some evenings, if you want,' offered Ivan, handsomely.

'Gareth wouldn't like me driving in the dark,' she responded, truthfully, because Gareth generally had some objection to make to any idea she put forward. Which left her free to do her hand sewing in the evenings while the best television programmes were on, enjoying having custody of the TV remote.

She even became accustomed to 'going private'. The hotel-like hospital had a pleasant serenity. It was the task of the nurses and doctors to keep a close eye on Gareth's head trauma and the things that pinned him together; Diane's was to interact with him. As he wasn't exactly up to games of cards or even keeping up his end of a conversation, she sat beside his bed and updated him on life as it went on without him.

'Only bills in today's post – I'm opening all your letters now. The lady in your wages office says that you're entitled to three months' on full pay before the company reviews the situation. That's generous, isn't it? After it stops, we'll have to claim statutory sick pay, I suppose, because you won't be fit to return to work in three months. You've always refused to claim benefit, but the bills must be paid, and the mortgage.' She flicked a glance his way in the hopes of reaction but was disappointed.

With Gareth unable to prevent her investigations she was beginning to get to grips with the tricks he'd exerted to maintain control in their marriage. 'I'm enjoying the novelty of being in charge of the bank account. Money's a little less tight than before. You're spending nothing, of course, and shopping for one is cheaper than for two. And Ivan and Melvyn aren't likely to approach me for a sub with you in hospital, are they? Also, somehow, your salary is quite a bit higher than I understood.'

Gareth regarded her through the slit eyes in his lurid head. His expression, on that bloated face, was impossible to read.

She could have added: *'Isn't that funny, Gareth? Especially as you've only been working a three-day week. Your hourly rate must be nearly double what you told me.'* But he needed quiet and calm; the doctors and nurses said so. So she just smiled sweetly at him to let him know: *I'm on to you, mate.*

At the end of the hour she patted his chest, an area that was free of plaster. 'I'll leave you to rest.' And breezed from the room that he was stuck in, knowing that she'd irritated him with her cheery reports of ferreting into areas that he'd hitherto guarded from her eyes. Out in the corridor, phones rang, nurses raised reassuring voices, cheerful porters piloted gurneys and she strolled through them feeling pleasantly revenged by her liberty.

Sometimes she came across Harold and his veined face would brighten. 'I'll duck in and see Gareth after Valerie, my dear!' There was no sign of the pinched pallor of the night of the accident; he was hearty and energetic.

Occasionally she'd catch sight of James's dark figure striding in to see his wife and he'd grin at her as if enjoying a private joke, but he visited mainly in the evenings. No doubt he had a job to do on weekdays. Once she saw Tamzin with two young women so like her – except rounded and robust – she knew even before Tamzin introduced them that they must be James's other daughters, Alice and Natalia.

'Poor Uncle Gareth!' they chorused, corn-coloured hair swept up with bright ornaments behind their heads. 'Bless him! His poor face!'

'Yes, *bless* him,' agreed Diane, wondering if she'd look as insouciant if she wore her hair so carelessly whisked.

Her visits became more interesting as Gareth improved. His facial swelling began to deflate, sinking his eyes into violet rings. Teeth began to twinkle through his gums and he began to form recognisable words. He was just like a giant baby.

Diane measured his progress as carefully as any nurse.

On the day when she judged him to be adequately responsive, able to carry on a conversation and suck up liquidised food, she sat back in the visitor's chair, cupped her knee in her linked hands and stared straight into his blackened eyes. 'Why didn't you tell me that you'd found your father?'

Gareth stilled.

She allowed the silence to stretch.

His head sank back onto the pillow. 'Can we leave this for a bit, Diane?' Suddenly his voice was weak and fatigued and the clarity of his diction took a giant stride backwards: 'Han ee eave iss ver a bi, Dia?' And a peevish note, as if Diane should have been more considerate than to bother him with trivialities.

She rocked a little in her chair. 'It's been left long enough, Gareth.'

He closed his thick eyelids, slowly, as if in pain.

'Why didn't you tell me that you'd found your father?'

The eyes remained closed. But it seemed as if he'd accepted that the inevitable moment of confession had come when he asked, 'Do you know how Valerie is?' his diction clear again.

'I don't even know *who* Valerie is.' Diane paused at the

quiet knock that heralded the appearance of refreshments. She supposed such service was one of the things that Harold was paying for. Or it might be Gareth footing the bill, of course, with his newfound wealth. She hadn't bothered to enquire.

Her coffee was fragrant and freshly poured into a white china cup from a filter jug. Gareth's was provided in a blue plastic cup with a 'chimney', reminiscent of Bryony's toddler days. Diane stirred in sugar with a clinking spoon. The door hushed shut behind the auxiliary.

'Why didn't you tell me?' she repeated, lodging the spoon in the saucer.

Gareth sipped in silence.

She fixed her gaze on his eyes. 'Why didn't you tell me?' The same quiet, reasonable tone.

His eyes closed, firmly, blocking her out.

'Why didn't you tell me?'

The eyelids flipped open to display blazing eyes. 'Because he's *my* father. OK?' His voice dripped sarcasm.

Diane felt the blood boil into her cheeks at the echo of her own words. *They were* my *parents!* Remembering herself shaking with determination as she confronted Gareth about the will.

She moistened her lips. 'It's because of the money.'

Irritably, he closed his eyes again. 'What?'

'The reason you didn't tell me. It's not because Harold's your father, it's because he gave you money and you didn't want me to share it. You didn't want my life made easier, for me to have a car, or a new TV, or clothes that I hadn't made myself. Not even a new pair of winter boots! You gave yourself an extra two days off a week to enjoy with Valerie and Harold and told them I was mentally ill.'

She waited. Then began again. 'The reason you didn't –'

'Yes!' Gareth turned his head sharply, making himself

wince. 'The money. Obviously the money. Because we don't share decisions about money that comes to us from our parents – *do we?*'

The palms of her hands prickled with fury.

His eyes burned balefully as he massaged his fattened jaw with his fingertips. Probably it was aching now with this unaccustomed talking. Or through gritting his loosened teeth in his swollen gums.

'Gareth, I had my pride.' The familiar cry that epitomised all her confused and hurt feelings towards the parents who'd tried so hard to control her, even from the grave.

He rolled his head on the pillow. 'We couldn't afford pride.' Again, the hand, to soothe the jaw he was meant to be using only gently.

'And before Bryony went to Brasilia, when I wanted to see if we were eligible for various low-income benefits and you went ballistic, it was nothing to do with *not taking handouts* or *not being a charity case* or *not wanting anyone to think you couldn't look after your family*. It was because you knew your horde, your stash, the treasure that your long-lost father had given you, would come to light?'

Silence.

Outside the window the blue sky was ragged with piebald clouds racing before a stiff breeze. The double-glazing hushed the thunder of traffic to a whisper. Amongst the trees, birds could be seen but not heard. Diane leaned her elbows on the bed. Her heart was beating not fast, but hard, as though running in seven-league boots. 'We could've afforded another car.'

'We could have had another car ages ago – if you'd challenged Freddy.'

And Diane looked at him and saw that he was ugly. Not because of the swelling or the bruises, but because of what he'd let his grudge make him do – hide his wealth and his family away like kinky perversions. 'Do you remember when we were happy?' she murmured. 'When it didn't matter that we had no money, it was us against the rest. My parents tried everything they could to come between us when they were alive and you let them achieve their aim once they were dead.'

He shook his head. 'You let them achieve it.'

'It was only money.'

He grimaced. 'And we only didn't have any.'

Diane left the room, shaking. The traffic would be gathering impetus as the dreaded rush hour approached but she couldn't command her disobedient legs to carry her to the car. She felt as if she were made of drumsticks, stiff and clunky, held together with brittle old thread.

In an embrasure beside a tall window facing the hospital gardens she discovered a water dispenser that turned the sunrays into a rainbow, and a comfy little chair in plum leather with a cushion in the same fabric as the curtains. She sank down, weedy in the wake of battle. She so rarely confronted Gareth; long experience had taught her it wasn't the best way to manage him. And the scene had been ugly with old sores and unsettled scores.

No, she wasn't really surprised that he hadn't told her about Harold because of the money. It had always been about money, about the days when she had money and he didn't.

Not much more than twenty-five years ago, when they began to get serious, Gareth had been prepared for resistance from her parents. He wasn't stupid. He knew how the world worked and that *fitter from a council estate* wouldn't be on Peter and Karen Wibberley's list of prospective sons-in-law. He'd expected a chilly reception when Diane took him to meet her parents.

But they had both been shaken by the depths of Peter and Karen Wibberley's repugnance.

Sitting back in his imposing house with a fragile teacup in his hand Peter Wibberley hadn't pulled any punches. 'And what do you do?'

'I'm a fitter at Greatorex Packaging.'

'And where do you live?'

'The Brightside Estate.'

Peter Wibberley's silver hair was combed straight back, his moustache darker grey. He nodded sadly, as if his worst suspicions had been confirmed. 'I am not the sort of father,' he pronounced, 'to expect to vet my daughter's friends. Normally, I trust her judgement.' He sipped his tea.

Diane felt her palm sweating, where it lay in Gareth's hand as they sat side-by-side on the sofa.

'However,' Peter continued, 'I think we might as well be straight from the outset. We had envisaged something – someone – very different for our daughter. I can't imagine your relationship with Diane lasting and my wife and myself will not be acknowledging it.'

Karen Wibberley turned to stare at Gareth, her hair permed into a fuzz of mousy curls. 'She's only eighteen. Eighteen! We have to protect her from … people like you. From herself,' she added, as if Diane wasn't even there.

A crackling silence. Then Gareth rattled his cup and saucer onto the coffee table and strode from the room.

Diane flew after him in tears of fury, hair sticking to her cheeks. 'Gareth, I didn't know –'

'Well, now you do,' he said, without breaking stride. 'Now you fucking-well know.'

Gareth had sulked for a fortnight, a fortnight during which Diane's parents had been kind but unyielding. Gareth Jenner was out of her life. Good. If she accepted that then they would forget the whole unfortunate episode and things would go on just as before, with Diane bathed by her parents' approval.

But then Gareth rang Diane at work, from a callbox. 'Let's talk,' he suggested. That night she lied to her parents about her movements and met him at a restaurant. 'It was a bit of a sodding shock,' he said, grimly, 'that shit your parents handed out. I thought that if I kept my nose clean and worked hard it would be enough in this so-called classless society. I didn't think it mattered where me mum brought me up. I thought what mattered was what I made of myself.'

Diane was forlorn. 'I thought they'd be OK when they met you.'

Gareth sliced through his steak with suppressed violence. 'Some bloody hope! I suppose that there's no point in asking you to marry me, now.'

Her mouth dropped open.

'No, I shouldn't have asked.' He took a slug of his beer. Diane drank wine in restaurants but Gareth hadn't taken to it. 'Blood's thicker than water. You have to please your parents.'

Anger set her face on fire. 'I'm not twelve, you know.'

He went back to his steak, shrugging her off, dismissing her point of view, just like her parents had. 'But you're a bit of a hothouse flower. Not exactly hardy. No, you'd do better to wait for the right bank manager to come along. Or doctor, or accountant. Do right by your mum and dad.'

And, somehow, she'd found herself flinging his bitter resignation back in his face. 'Rubbish! And don't tell me I'm a hothouse flower; I'm perfectly resilient. I'm not like my parents, valuing people for superficial reasons.'

He let his eyes lock with hers, took her hand and raised it to his lips. 'So you'll marry me, then?'

'Yes!' The word had spurted from her in triumph. How

victorious she'd been as she stalked in to demonstrate to her parents and, perhaps, to Gareth, that she wasn't to be dictated to. 'We've something to tell you. Gareth proposed tonight and I accepted.'

She'd felt the first stirrings of uncertainty as her father's face went puce and the newspaper slipped from his lap.

Gareth even went forward to offer his hand. 'I know I'm not what you want for your daughter, you've made it quite clear. But we'll stick together and have a bunch of kids and give them a grand life. Not like me, who never knew his father.'

'Oh, my God,' breathed Karen, through fingers spread across a horrified mouth.

And there were no congratulations or sherry or questions about the future. There was just that horrified, disappointed hush. And a squirming in Diane's belly that wasn't completely joy at her betrothal.

That very night, they planned a wedding for six months ahead, at the register office, of course, because Gareth had never been christened and never went to church. It all felt quite unreal but, fuelled by her parents' anger – 'We're waiting for you to come to your senses!' – Diane took to the marriage a determination to make it work, a savings account just big enough for the deposit on an ex-council house in Purtenon St. Paul, and a green Mini.

From time to time she'd actually been impressed at the unremitting, freezing bitterness with which her parents treated her husband and, to a large extent, herself.

'I've been brought up to take a few knocks. I can cope,' Gareth said, often. 'Don't fall out with your parents over me.' He'd been good about years of stilted Christmases with his parents-in-law, the only time they ever shared with Diane and Gareth, and later Bryony, their cushioned existence in their big house with cleaners and gardeners, new cars and all the status symbols. He'd been there for Diane when her mother had died, the rift between them unhealed.

When the time came, at her father's graveside Gareth had stood beside her, although he'd later told her that it was just to be certain that he saw the mardy bugger safe underground.

Anticipation had been shining from his eyes when she arrived home a few days later after talking to Freddy about the estate. 'Straightforward, is it, the will?'

Diane hung up her camel-coloured coat. 'Very.' She turned, slowly, slowly, reluctant to face him. 'I'm not in it.'

His face turned to stone. 'You're joking.'

Her hair was up behind her head, tightly, making her head ache. She began to drag out the clips, her scalp prickling as the strands unwound. 'It's all there in black-and-white. The whole lot goes to Freddy. Freddy's embarrassed.' She reached over to her coat and extracted paperwork from one of the large front pockets, tossing it on the table between them. 'He's even provided me with literature about how to contest a will under the Inheritance Act.'

Gareth snatched at the papers, relief sweeping his face. 'That's very fair of him. Your dad was always investing in things, wasn't he? He must have been worth a few bob.'

'Oh yes. The estate is valued at about two million, including the house.' She dropped down into a chair. Nausea had held her throat in its hands for most of the day as she'd tried to come to terms with what her parents had done. She was weak with disbelief. Grief. And such bitter disappointment, not over the money that had been withheld, but the love.

Gareth's face flushed. 'My God, we're millionaires, bar the formalities. Fucking millionaires! We'd better get a solicitor. How long do you think it'll all take?'

'I'm not contesting the will. Freddy has offered to cut me in for half. All he has to do is sign a thing called a deed of post-death variation.'

Gareth sank into his chair. 'You gave me a few nasty moments. But there you are, it'll be sorted in a few weeks. Freddy's all right, we might've known he wouldn't try and snaffle the lot.'

Diane stared. Blinded by pound signs, Gareth wasn't getting the point. Fury burned in her gullet and she spoke the words that changed her world and had made their marriage, for the past ten years, an empty thing. 'I refused. My parents have disinherited me. I don't want their stinking money.'

It was fully ten seconds before he spoke, his eyes horrified. 'Don't be stupid,' he managed eventually, hoarse in disbelief. 'Don't be bloody stupid! Money, even some money, even if you only accept forty per cent, or twenty, it'll make all the difference to our lives. We're still talking hundreds of thousands, Diane. It's your right, it's your inheritance. It's yours! Don't you see? Taking the money is the very thing to do *because* they don't want you to have it. We'll be getting back at them.'

Her guts melted with misery as his voice climbed, but she didn't waver. 'I have my pride, Gareth.'

And then he was lunging across the table, roaring into her face. '*We can't afford fucking pride*! You're entitled to that money. Pride's all very well for you but it's me who's working my balls off, scrounging for every hour of overtime.'

Tears flooded from her eyes but she hadn't wavered. 'They're my parents and it's my decision.'

Chapter Five

Trembling, Diane filled a waxed paper cone with the cold, crystal water as the dispenser gulped and glugged. Tiny sips moistened her mouth but didn't ease the thudding in her chest. Her fingers shook as she drained the cone and refilled it. Money. So much trouble in her life had been over money.

Like the ugly little scene over her mother's jewellery when she and Freddy had pitched in to help their father after their mother's death, she processing the debris of the funeral and Freddy going upstairs with his father to help sort out Karen's things.

But when she'd carried cups of tea up to the others she'd heard Freddy sputter, 'Of course I can't accept it!'

And her father, clutching her mother's leather jewellery case. 'Look, Freddy, you know as well as I do that your sister will let that bloody man get his hands on it. I just couldn't stand it if your mother's and grandmother's jewellery turned up in second-hand shops all over Peterborough.'

Placing the cups on the nearby chest of drawers Diane wiped sweaty palms on the back of her jeans. 'Stick it up your arse, then,' she suggested, pleasantly.

Freddy had followed her down, taking her hot hands in both of his. He wore contact lenses, in those days, and his eyes were always pink. 'You're the daughter, you should have her jewellery. Dad's not himself.'

Diane had to find a tissue and blow her nose. 'He is himself, Freddy. I thwarted him ten years ago and he's been an unforgiving bastard ever since. Just think of the Christmas when he gave me a mixing bowl and you a gold watch. When he said he'd bought a hundred premium bonds for

Bryony – and then "kept them for her". He very obviously doesn't want me to have Mum's stuff so let's just give it to Sîan. Mum treated your wife more like a daughter than she did me.'

'You can pass it on to Bryony. I haven't even got daughters.'

That's when Diane had hesitated. There was more to be thought of here than her own bloody-mindedness. 'It can go straight to Bryony,' she decided, shakily. 'Will you keep it for Bryony, please, Freddy? Put it in your loft or something until she's grown up?'

Freddy had sighed, opened the box, worn at the edges, and gazed at the dull glint of gold set out amongst the compartments. 'I suppose so, if you're certain.' And that's where it had been put and, she presumed, where it still was.

The corridor at the Ackerman wasn't busy but against the background squeak from a trolley, the hiss of the lift doors and the rustling of occasional feet across thick carpet, a shrill, rapid, grief-stricken voice split the afternoon. 'You're making an excuse. Inconvenience! I bet you wouldn't – ' The voice was female, young and uncontrolled.

Then a man's voice came in reasonable, measured counterpoint, his words indistinguishable.

A door burst open and the young woman's voice hurried closer. 'It's just an excuse. Mum will be fine by the time she comes home.'

Diane turned her head.

The man: soothing, calming. 'It's nothing to get upset about, I promise. Let's not worry about it, now. It'll be a while before she'll be well enough to come home, anyway.' The couple came into view. The young woman racing ahead was Tamzin North.

And, prowling behind, James, focused on his daughter.

Tamzin, eyes wild and chest heaving, plunged like a pony to avoid his comforting arm. 'You should tell me what's going on. I'm not a baby!'

'I just told you.' James was all reason, not displaying anger, not raising his voice. His eyes flicked to Diane then returned to his daughter. 'It's just what your mother and I think is best, for now.'

Tamzin's eyes darted about his face. The pitch of her voice veered a degree nearer to reasonable. 'It's just for now?'

James gave a sudden smile. Diane noticed his lips again, too full for a man really, but she liked to watch them as he spoke. 'We haven't put a time limit on it. Your mother's been injured and we have to accept one or two practicalities. That's all.'

Tamzin's expression began to clear. The tension that had puckered her face receded and her fists unclenched. For the first time, she acknowledged that they weren't alone. 'Oh, Diane, hello.' She sniffed like a child with a cold.

Diane managed a small smile. 'Hi.'

'How's Uncle Gareth?' Another sniff.

'How's your mother?' Diane didn't even want to think about Gareth, let alone transmit progress reports. She fished a clean tissue from her bag and offered it.

Tamzin seemed to wake up to her woeful appearance and grabbed the tissue to wipe her face and blow her nose. 'Much the same. Won't be coming home for ages yet.' She stuffed the tissue into the pocket of aged and shapeless jeans and turned to her father. 'There's a little coffee shop on this corridor, perhaps Diane has time for a latte?' She looked disproportionately pleased at the prospect.

As James murmured easily, 'Perhaps she has?' Diane blinked at Tamzin's transformation from stressy mess to hospitable young woman, recognising the poise from the sort of childhood she'd had herself – private school and lots of socialising at her parents' house, the scene of almost weekly parties: bridge, dancing, after golf, pre-ball.

She ignored an unexpected twist of nostalgia. She'd long since left her parents' lifestyle behind and the pleasure of coffee shops was one of the many economies she'd made in her bull-headed determination to make her life with Gareth Jenner.

James's gaze was fixed on her, as if Diane's acceptance of the simple invitation was of peculiar importance. She was glad of an excuse not to fight the manic traffic all the way to the green Fen lanes and an empty house, so smiled at Tamzin. 'Sounds great. Lead the way.'

The coffee shop was small, just ten bentwood tables staffed by a lady in a white top and a red gingham tabard trimmed with rick-rack braid. Once only seen in school needlework lessons rick-rack was currently hot in Diane's sewing supplies catalogues. There was no accounting for fashion.

Tamzin appointed herself hostess. 'Would you like something to eat, Diane? No? Just a latte?'

Diane, as suggested, ordered latte, having only ever heard of it and curious as to what all the fuss was about. When the pale, creamy liquid was set before her in a thick pan of a cup she was satisfied. Until she saw James's cappuccino with cream and chocolate sprinkles.

Cream and chocolate sprinkles would've been great.

'Do I call you Aunt Diane?' Tamzin glanced at the coffee placed before James and Diane – plus biscuits for James – as she accepted mineral water herself.

Diane wrinkled her nose. 'I think we could leave off the "aunt". None of my other nieces and nephews uses it.'

Tamzin seemed in the mood for conversation, her eyes over-bright. 'I love your jeans and top, you wear such wicked stuff. It's well strange.'

The top was a fine linen shirt with shiny chrome eyelets zig-zagging down one side, threaded with scarlet leather laces and tied with fat tassels. The jeans had dinky little zips in odd places, topstitched in emerald green.

Automatically, Diane sat back to display the outfit. 'This is what I do, I make one-offs, and sell a lot of it to a shop in Peterborough. I wear my own stuff as a kind of walking advertisement. It's all very highly decorated. I was making boho before boho was invented.'

'It's so cool. Really random but pretty. Do you, like, take orders?'

'Customer commissions? Of course. Mainly evening wear, for ladies who want something you won't get at John Lewis or Debenhams.' She stirred her latte.

'What could you make for me?'

Beside her, Diane felt James start slightly, and wondered wryly whether he'd just seen himself as the guy footing the bill. Oh well, he looked as if he could afford it, with a leather jacket that she kept wanting to trail her fingers across and midnight blue polo shirt that fitted just so. 'Anything you want, so long as the fabrics are suitable. I don't do rubber or vinyl or anything.' She winked.

Tamzin giggled. 'No, nothing weird. I was thinking, like, freaky tops. And decorated jeans.'

Tamzin turned to link her father's arm, beaming up at him with a smile, their spat, apparently, forgotten. 'I haven't had any new clothes for ages, have I?'

His eyes crinkled. 'You're positively overdue for some.'

'You're not such a sad Dad.' She planted a sudden kiss on his cheek before swinging back to Diane. 'Can I talk to you about it? One morning? I know you visit Uncle Gareth most afternoons. I come to your house, right?'

'Tomorrow, if you like,' Diane agreed, unable to read James's expression but wanting, as much as the welcome commission, because Rowan at the shop was really stingy with what he paid her, to see more of this bright Tamzin who'd suddenly burst on stage like an actress. All the clothes Diane had seen her in so far had been atrocious; it would be fun to do her justice.

'My mother likes to see me in autumn colours but my favourites are turquoise or hot pink.'

'Turquoise would look really good on you,' Diane agreed.

And Tamzin went on and on, talking with her hands and giggling. Presently, she fluttered off to the Ladies, still calling back over her shoulder about beads and fabric, like a child who doesn't want to waste time peeing but can't put it off any longer.

James turned to Diane the instant his daughter stepped out of sight. 'You're *amazing*.'

Diane was caught off guard. 'Why?'

'That's the nearest to normal she's been for two years. If you knew how much I wanted her to take an interest in her appearance but it's all I can do to get her to brush her teeth. And you just wander in and – She has problems, I suppose you realise? Adolescent depression. She seems mainly to dress in gardening clothes – when I can coax her out of her dressing gown, that is.' And suddenly his warm hand was closing about Diane's. She could even feel the pulse in his thumb. 'Thank you!'

Diane flushed, her fingers tingling. 'I don't think I did anything; it's just a coincidence that what I do interests her.' Then, cautiously, 'She certainly swings from one mood to another. I suppose she's been knocked off balance by what's happened to her mother?' She glanced down at their fingers curled together, his so big and capable. She hoped hers didn't feel incredibly workworn and rough.

He released her suddenly and used the hand to rub tiredly over his face. 'She has a special relationship with her mother and occasionally comes out batting wildly on her behalf, completely unasked. That row you overheard – I just suggested that Valerie had a bed of her own when she eventually comes out of hospital. It's practical. She might still be in plaster.' He hesitated, as if debating how much to say. 'Tamzin viewed it in the worst possible light. That I was trying to avoid intimacy with her mother. She has a thing – a fear – about us splitting up. She has fears about lots of things.'

Then, in a rush, taking her hand again as if he couldn't get his feelings across without touching her, he fixed her with his dark grey stare. 'If Tamzin doesn't turn up tomorrow, I hope you'll understand. Persist. Make her another appointment. She sometimes just ... runs out of steam. Stays in bed. She describes her depression as living in a labyrinth of caves. Every time she makes it out of one cave she finds she's walking into another, just as grey and festooned with cobwebs as the last one. She only ever sees the sun in the distance but some things make it seem closer – I think that her interest in your work might be one of those things.'

'I'll be patient,' she promised. Her heart rate had picked up, as if his enthusiasm was transmitting itself to her through the touch of his hand.

'I wish more people would just show patience instead of treating her as if she's feeble.' His hand fell away, leaving her feeling suddenly cold.

'Did it just come on? The depression, I mean.'

He grimaced. 'During her first year at university she began to be overwhelmed in certain situations, unable to organise herself. She attracted the attention of some bullying bastards and began not to eat.'

'Is she anorexic?'

'That isn't the diagnosis. The doctor calls it unhealthily thin.'

'If she'd been to university she must be older than I thought.'

'Twenty. She was the baby of the family, of course. Valerie says I've babied her too long.' He sent her one of his fleeting smiles. 'Tamzin's so fragile, she brings out the guard dog in me.'

'I'd thought sheepdog,' she joked, gently, to disguise the compassion she felt for him as he tried his damndest for his child. 'It must be horrible for her, to feel like that. And your wife must be out of her mind with worry about her, too.'

James's eyes shifted to the wall behind Diane's head. 'Most mothers would be.'

His silence made Diane feel awkward. She wished Tamzin would come back. It seemed time for a change of conversational direction but none of the subjects they held in common were particularly cheerful – the accident, Gareth's deceit and now Tamzin's difficulties. She opted for the accident as the best of a bad bunch.

'Have the authorities given you any indication of what the problem was with the helicopter? Why it came down, I mean?'

His eyes flicked sharply back to her face. He checked over his shoulder and saw that Tamzin was walking towards them. Words rat-a-tatted out of him like bullets. 'Oh, I have a good idea what the problem was. Valerie forgot that alcohol and flying don't mix.'

Chapter Six

'That took ages. There are only two and they were both busy.' Tamzin was slipping back into her chair before Diane could react to James's shocking statement. 'Diane, we're going to see Pops. Why don't you come?'

Diane tore her gaze away from the anger in James's eyes. 'Yes,' she agreed, slowly, trying to process information and invitation simultaneously. 'Yes, I think I'd like to. It's not as if there's anything spoiling at home.'

From the car park, the dreaded rush hour looked every bit as ferocious as Diane had feared, but she tucked her car in bravely behind James's Mercedes. She was getting less nervous about busy roads and her hands only sweated a little bit. And James was either considerate of her modest progress or he always drove like an old woman on a sunny Sunday.

Harold lived in Castor, a village to the west of Peterborough shown on maps as Castor and Ailsworth, it being so difficult to see where Castor ended and Ailsworth began. Castor was beautifully kept, from the neat green umbrellas outside the pub to the village hall ornamented with Village of the Year awards. Harold's home stood back from the road, an impressive thatched-roof house with fish-eye dormers over several sparkling bow windows, and a porch supported by massive oak posts twisted and split with the seasons. The garden was a small park of exemplary grass and architectural trees. James pulled up on the turning circle of gravel outside the front door and Diane crunched to a halt beside him.

Harold, dressed casually – still a shirt and tie but an olive buttoned-up cardigan instead of a jacket, and leather carpet slippers – seemed delighted with his extra visitor. 'Diane! Come in, come in.' His white hair was thin and looked incredibly soft, like a baby's. He ushered them into a sitting room with tapestry upholstery, a carved sideboard and oil paintings in gilded and decorated frames.

As she sank into a vast high-backed sofa, Diane breathed in the scent of furniture wax with the slightest accents of age and dust, complemented by warm grass and rose petals from the windows open to the spacious front windows. The fragrance of childhood.

Either the unbelievably comfortable sofa or the day's confrontation made her feel almost as if she could go to sleep. The others discussed Valerie's condition and treatment, but she just let the words drift past: plaster, pins, pelvis ... external fixation device.

Presently, Harold disturbed her reverie. 'James and Tamzin already have plans but would you stay and dine with me? Just a casserole – Mrs Munns usually makes twice what I eat and it will save you cooking.'

Diane beamed, nestling still deeper into the cushions. 'That would be *lovely*.'

James offered Diane a business card, having added his private numbers to it in pen. *Furness Durwent, Printed Circuits. Production Director – James North*. Stiff white card with a discreet logo. 'It makes sense if we swap contact details.'

Digging out an old shopping list from her jacket pocket Diane wrote her home phone number on the back. 'I haven't a card.'

'Mobile?' he suggested.

She flushed. 'I haven't got one of those, either.'

He paused. 'I think there's a pay-and-talk one at home somewhere if you'd like to use it. It might be useful, whilst

Gareth's in hospital.'

She smiled gratefully but – as usual – didn't feel the need for his help. 'Thanks, but I'll be fine.'

After James and Tamzin had gone, Harold made a fresh jug of coffee and Diane kicked off her shoes and curled her legs up on the sofa. 'This house reminds me of my parents' home. They liked the same type of furniture.'

Harold added a spoonful of brown sugar crystals to her cup, fine porcelain with a tiny handle and the gilding worn off the rim with use. 'I understand from Gareth that your parents were not cordial towards him.'

She threw him a glance. She didn't – couldn't – discuss her parents with many people. With Gareth his antipathy always got in the way and with Freddy it was the money. 'My parents gave me a lovely childhood full of holidays and activities and love. They sent Freddy and me to decent schools. The house was always full of people; there was a boat on the River Nene, summers in France, winter skiing in Switzerland. And always love. Lots and lots of love.'

'Sounds idyllic.' His emphasis on the first word made his comment a question.

She nodded, stroking the delicacy of the old cup in her hands. 'So long as I was a good daughter, it was. Mum was accommodating about friends staying or cheering me at hockey matches and swimming galas and running me to music lessons. She was content to be the person who made things possible for everybody else, while Dad ruled the roost.'

The fragrant coffee took her attention and she paused to sip. She did like coffee. Much more expensive than the loose-leaf tea that she generally drank at home. She was so used to economy that she rarely yearned after luxuries she didn't have but she had always envied people who could afford rich, dark coffee.

She fixed her eyes dreamily on the brick-and-stone hearth, the fire basket cloaked for the summer with a brass peacock-tail screen. 'I had a strong-willed father.' She smiled. 'But I grew up strong-willed, too, and I began to fight him.'

'One needs a bit of backbone.'

She sighed. 'It could all have been different. If Dad hadn't taken one look at Gareth and ordered me to dump him. If he'd discussed his worries and explained where he saw trouble for us instead of wagging his finger in my face and roaring, "He isn't our kind."'

'Indelicate,' Harold agreed.

'He should have given me a bit of time to discover the differences between me and Gareth –' She ground to a halt, realising that she was all but confessing to her newly discovered father-in-law that her marriage had been a mistake. She cleared her throat. 'I became incredibly stubborn. The more he raged against Gareth, the more I flouted him. It seemed right to follow my heart rather than do as I was told.'

Harold's lips twitched as he poured more coffee. 'Yes, it's a pity that my son's not of sufficiently good family.'

Diane let her head fall back as she laughed. It felt almost unfamiliar; she hadn't seemed to have done much laughing since Bryony got on the plane to Brasilia. 'Isn't it ironic? I wish I could tell my father about you.'

'I wish you could, too,' sighed Harold. 'It would be comfortable to be able to change the past.'

The grandfather clock in the hall bonged, six resonant chimes. Diane waited for the last to fade before suggesting, diffidently, 'Would you mind telling me where you've been for most of Gareth's life? I have a lot of blanks to fill.'

Harold's face sank into deeper folds. He put down his empty cup and steepled his fingers. His voice was bleak. 'I'm afraid it was all too common a story in those days. I was young and I got a girl in trouble. I'm not proud of it. Father owned a big shop with several departments and our family, we thought ourselves grand. We had cars and we even went abroad on holiday.'

Abroad. Diane remembered going abroad, feisty France and dreaming Italy, the excitement of visiting a country with a different climate, foods, smells, sounds, language, culture and people. Since her marriage she hadn't managed even a cheap break in Spain because Gareth liked a sturdy British holiday in July at a seaside holiday camp with his brothers and their families, so that if the weather wasn't great there was always good company. The three brothers never seemed to tire of each other.

Diane hadn't ever suggested linking up with her own brother. Just imagine Freddy's face if she'd suggested a fortnight in a static caravan site with a clubhouse and a crowded outdoor swimming pool! Freddy took his holidays in La Manga in a big villa with a spacious private pool surrounded by high walls.

He had the money – as Gareth never ceased to remind her.

Harold cleared his throat and applied his neat handkerchief to his watering eye. 'Wendy worked in Father's department store. Tight skirts were all the thing and she was so tall and willowy the fashion could've been designed for her.'

'You're *kidding*,' Diane breathed. Even over a quarter of a century ago, when Diane had first known her, Wendy hadn't been within four stone of 'willowy'. Tall, granted, but with a body that was a series of pears and tyres, topped by a set of turned-down, worn-down features.

Harold tipped his head against the back of the chair. 'Stupidly, I got Wendy pregnant. I thought a great deal of her but still I took advantage, didn't take proper responsibility. Perhaps I thought that kind of dreary obligation was for other people. I was the boss's son! I had an Alvis and a flat of my own, very nice. Going about with a girl like Wendy was not uncommon for a young man used to a bit of class privilege. Oh, yes, it survived the sixties, you know!'

'Certainly do,' Diane murmured, thinking of her father.

'My friends referred to her as my bit of fluff and were perfectly pleasant to her, as long as I didn't take her to the wrong places. I wasn't expected ... didn't have to ...' Angrily, he shook his head. 'I didn't have to treat her as I would a daughter of a family friend – with respect. And I didn't introduce her at home.'

Diane grappled silently with the image of gruff, forceful Wendy being Harold's *bit of fluff.*

'Anyway. When she told me she was having my baby I'm afraid I failed to offer to marry her. I arranged to buy a little place for her instead, where I could visit her and the child. Gareth.' He laughed bitterly, a suggestion of colour coming to his face. 'I didn't even attempt to explain *why.* I simply thought of my parents' shame if I were to "marry beneath me".'

'I suppose that's how things were, then.'

'But I was arrogant. I didn't think of Wendy's feelings at all. And she, of course, was too smart to fool.' He managed a small, painful smile. 'She came along to see the cottage. I explained how I'd be responsible for her finances and she wouldn't have to worry. "I'll keep you," I said. The next day, she didn't turn up for work, nor the next, nor the next. When the personnel lady tried to trace her she found no forwarding address. I never saw Wendy again. Gareth has been very blunt –' he coughed, 'about the hard life she lived, subsequently.'

For the first time in her life, Diane felt a flutter of sympathy for the abrasive, pugnacious woman who had been her mother-in-law; too late now, because Wendy's cider-drinking, cigarette-smoking, lard-eating lifestyle had brought an end to her several years ago. She sighed. 'Whatever pride made her turn her back on your cottage had certainly withered by the time I met her. Did you try and trace her?'

Sadly, he shook his head. 'I was angry. In those days, a man could pretty much wash his hands of a woman like Wendy. And that's what I did. I let my child be brought up a bastard.'

Diane objected, 'But even if Wendy had accepted your offer to keep her, if you wouldn't marry her then Gareth would still have been a bastard and still have to fight everybody at school who told him he was. Having a father who paid his mother's rent wouldn't legitimise him. He *minded* not having a father. It ate at him. Not knowing his father caused a gigantic chip on his shoulder, but I don't know whether having a father who tidied him out of sight would have been any better. And then his stepfather cleared off, leaving Wendy with two more kids to bring up alone. He couldn't even finish his apprenticeship because he had to bring in every penny he could for the family coffers.'

Harold's eyes shifted her way and she caught a glimpse of Gareth in the hardness of his stare. 'Quite.'

It was several moments before he spoke again. 'Eventually, I married Eleanor, Valerie's mother. I loved her in a quiet way and she was the right sort: nice family, decent education, properly brought up. But she never had half the strength of character of Wendy. And, I'm afraid, proved not to be an affectionate mother. Valerie always had to beg for her attention. I'm not sure I've done particularly well by either of my children.' He turned to gaze out at the garden. 'But I never forgot that I'd fathered another baby, although it might have looked as if I had. Then I began to suffer with angina and the doctor did a bit of straight talking about what might happen ... well, I realised that I didn't want to die without ever having met my son.'

Having let the rush hour grind by whilst she enjoyed a delicious meal and a cosy chat with Harold, the journey home was easy.

But, unlocking her kitchen door, Diane was struck by the difference between the silence of a *nobody's home just now but they'll be along later* empty house and a *you live here alone* empty house. It was like the difference between a daughter who was out hanging with her friends and a daughter who was half the world away.

She wondered when Gareth would return to their modest brick-built semi. Or if he would. Stripping off her laced shirt and zippy jeans in the bedroom she glanced at the double bed, as neat as a cushion of moss with its green quilt, and tried to imagine sharing it again with Gareth, lying beside the warm, snuffling, fidgeting body that never seemed to find tranquillity, even in sleep.

The next room was her sewing room, crammed and cramped. The overlocking sewing machine stood at one end; garments hung from the picture rail and wrapped about the tailor's dummy she'd bought eighth hand, its plush covering long ago worn shiny and the original maroon turned to rusty streaks. Shelves were buried by pots of beads and sequins, fabric, interfacing, thread, zips, and clothes that were destined to be unpicked for their fabric or other treasures – sometime. An octagonal Victorian sewing box that her grandmother had passed to her when Grandma's fingers had become too swollen to hold a needle, its mahogany as dark as treacle, stood on the floor beside a stack of glossy mags. Also passed on.

Automatically, Diane began to make her way through the comfortable clutter, but the ringing of the phone made her shift suddenly into reverse and run downstairs to answer with a breathless, 'Yes?'

'If Tamzin keeps her appointment, let her order what she

71

wants.' James's deep voice buzzed in Diane's ear. 'Tell her you've arranged it with me.'

'A big order will take time. I don't have a mini factory here – it's just me.'

'One item at a time will be fine. She's obviously taken a fancy to your work – and to you, I think – so I want to make the most of it. She pretty much disappears into a black cloud if I try and get her into a shop so I don't want her to be considering the money aspect.'

Diane tried to remember what it was like not to consider money. 'Perhaps now's a good time to talk about cost, then.' She pulled a face at her reflection in the window at the weediness of her voice. Negotiation wasn't her big thing, but she didn't want James to think that creating garments was something she did to occupy her hands whilst she watched *EastEnders*.

'How about your standard customer commission charge, plus twenty-five per cent?'

She paused, caught between curiosity and avarice. Curiosity won. 'Why plus twenty-five per cent?'

He laughed. She wasn't certain she'd heard him laugh properly before. It was a deep, dry chuckle that prickled its way along her hairline to settle right at the base of her skull. And spread lower. And lower. 'Because Tamzin might be a difficult client. And whatever you charge, I'll bet it's not enough. You're no toughie.' The laughter was still in his voice.

She was stung by this truth. 'Tough enough for you if I charge you double?'

He was unmoved. 'I'll pay if you do. Charge me garment by garment or weekly or something. I'll give you notice if I want to call a halt.'

'Thank you, that will help with cash flow,' she acknowledged smartly, in a way she imagined business people must speak. Maybe James's niceness wasn't a disguise for control freak tendencies, as she'd assumed. He actually wanted to be fair with her over money, and she was so damned used to people being *unfair* with her about it ... But she must start thinking realistically about cash. Gareth might be rolling in filthy lucre but his windfall wasn't in her hands, apart from what she'd lifted from his wallet. And she wasn't certain she wanted that. To take it had been a kick. Spend it and she'd have to be grateful.

'Cash flow must be a consideration, with Gareth in hospital.' James must have read her mind. 'I can let you have a deposit, if that helps. I don't ...' He hesitated. 'I don't want you to have to struggle.'

The words fell about her ears with a bang and crash like one of Bryony's drum rolls. 'Don't you?' she squeaked. Unexpectedly, her eyes filled up at the thought of a man not wanting her to struggle. 'Be careful or I might take advantage of you.'

His laughter rolled down the line again. 'Do try.'

It wasn't until the call was over that she realised why he found 'taking advantage' funny, and blushed. 'Grow up, Diane,' she scolded herself. 'You've got to think about earning money. Earn money, earn money,' she chanted. 'Toughen up, think about profit.'

Leafing through the spiral pad that served as her order book, she saw she had only to hem the prom dress for Maria Cuthbert's daughter's prom dress to complete the order; she could do that in the morning. Next on the list was an extravagantly beaded wedding suit for Trish Warboys, which required only buttons. Last time, Trish had said, airily, 'Leave your invoice and I'll get Jeremy to see to it.' Jeremy had taken six weeks.

'That's not tough enough.' Diane dialled the number on the top of Maria Cuthbert's order, beginning all in one breath, 'Hi, Maria the dress will be ready tomorrow. Shall I bring it round?'

'Oh, *brilliant –*'

And on the second breath, 'I've got your deposit so could you have a cheque for the balance ready for me please? Thank you.'

Maria squeaked like a startled chick. 'Oh, gosh! It might have to wait until my husband gets paid again.'

Diane slashed an angry question mark beside the order, though she forced herself to sound calm. 'That's OK.'

'Oh, *thank* y –'

'Just let me know when you can settle the account and that's when I'll deliver the dress.' Dialling again, she gave Trish Warboys the same treatment, clattering the phone back into its cradle with relish. There. Business could be fun!

Pity James hadn't been there to witness her being a toughie.

Chapter Seven

James halted just inside Valerie's room.

The setting sun was giving its last blast through her window. Valerie, her decency preserved by only one white sheet, looked hot, irritable and desperately uncomfortable. He went to the blinds and turned the slats.

A metal contraption skewered Valerie's right hip and one leg was in traction. The tide of bruising that rose from beneath the strapping on her ribs to her shoulder was streaking jammy red. The crescents beneath her eyes were purple and her poor broken nose looked as if it been put in the oven and risen unevenly.

Her expression was baleful when she answered his greeting but then, in hospital, there were no bottles of red wine to ignite her flashing smile.

The room, however well-equipped and pretty, smelled stale. He opened a small window.

Valerie already had a visitor. Diane was perched on a royal blue chair studying Valerie, a tiny frown curling her brow, hair a pale stream down her back. One elbow rested on her knee and he spent several seconds appreciating the way that her square neckline framed what lay beneath. Resolutely, he averted his eyes, determined not to be caught looking – again – like a teenager. But it was lucky that there were no Thought Police around.

He fixed his gaze on Diane's face so that he was smiling at the correct part of her when she turned to look at him. After a grave moment, as if perfectly able to read his thoughts, she let the corners of her lips curl up.

Valerie ran her fingers through her hair so that it stood up in crests. 'You already know Gareth's wife, I understand.'

James shucked off his jacket. 'How are you, Diane? Tamzin turned up for her fitting, I hear?'

'Why wouldn't she?' Valerie interrupted.

'Because she regularly fails to carry out planned activities?' suggested James.

Valerie made a face. 'You blow normal teenage behaviour out of all proportion. She's just a girl.'

James considered letting it go. But, on the other hand, the reluctance of both his wife and his daughter to face up to the realities of the condition of the other was constant grit in his eye. 'It's not teenage behaviour in Tamzin. She's clinically depressed.' He resisted the pleasurable pedantry of pointing out that Tamzin was twenty and not, therefore, a teenager.

Valerie dismissed him by turning to Diane. 'So Gareth is improving?'

Diane nodded. 'Still a mess, but less of a mess.'

'They won't let me see him.' Valerie plucked at the sheet.

James felt his eyebrows lift. 'Seems logistically difficult.'

'We can always rely on you to state the obvious, darling!'

Diane rose. 'I'll tell Gareth that you've been showing sisterly concern, shall I? He's been asking after you, too.'

Valerie blew out her breath in a frustrated sigh. Then she grinned and for a moment James caught a glimpse of the sexy, pretty woman he'd married, when every glimpse of her happy face had been a pleasure. 'You're nice. It was good of you to come and introduce yourself. I've often wondered about the mysterious sister-in-law. You're not at all as I imagined.'

Diane moved towards the door, her long black skirt flipping around her calves in a series of handkerchiefs. 'Well, as you see – quite ordinary.' With a last smile she melted from the room.

James didn't realise he was going to follow her until he

found himself outside the door. 'Can we talk?' he suggested. 'How about a drink – in an hour, say?'

She considered him, blue eyes curious. 'OK. I can hang around.'

Back inside the room he found Valerie had laid down her prickles, now that he was the only company left to her. 'My dear brother is playing silly buggers, James, isn't he? That woman's as normal as any of us.'

After a dutiful forty minutes with his wife, James found Diane waiting on a bench in the gardens, watching the dancing shadow of a rose bush, hair flipping in the breeze. Overblown roses had exploded in a lemon-and-pink confetti of petals around her feet, landing on the thin straps around her arching insteps. At least this time when she looked up, he was only staring at her feet. 'You're early.'

'Valerie's tired. I missed lunch and I'm starving. I hope you want to eat or don't mind watching me. I've had no time for anything since breakfast. Work was a nightmare of end-to-end meetings.'

'I could eat.'

He drove them to a large pub, one that was part of a national chain. He flipped off his seat belt in the car park but she remained motionless, her eyes running over the stitched leather car interior. 'This is a nice car.'

He patted the steering wheel. 'I love it. Expensive, but worth it.'

She turned to him with that long, assessing gaze. 'I can see it's pretty and shiny but I'm hopeless with cars. Is it a Mercedes?' She indicated the circular badge in the centre of the steering wheel.

'That's right. Mercedes E 55 AMG. Double spoke alloys, sports exhaust –'

'Is it fast?'

'Nought to sixty in 4.7 seconds.'

She made a face like a question.

He grinned. 'Fast, yes.'

Following a line of stitching along the dash with her fingertip, she glanced at his jacket. 'You like leather, don't you?'

Something funny happened to James's voice. 'Yes,' he croaked. And couldn't think of a single other thing to say.

Inside, the pub boasted pink-painted woodwork and exposed-brickwork walls. Framed sepia photos of bridges and barges and the River Nene hung between brass bugles, copper warming pans and corn dollies. Consulting the slightly sticky menu decorated with photographs of the food, James opted for the lamb steak and chips with onion rings and salad. Diane chose a beefsteak sandwich.

He ordered at the bar, returning with shandy for himself and pink grapefruit juice for her. 'So,' he began, taking the wheel-back chair opposite hers, 'what made you introduce yourself to Valerie?'

She shrugged. He had to fight to keep his gaze away from that square neckline. 'She's my sister-in-law, apparently, lying injured just along the corridor from Gareth. I'm sure it would be rude to ignore her. And I'd have to be made of concrete not to be curious, especially if what you say about the accident is true. She could've made me a widow.'

'And now you've met her?'

She sipped her drink. 'Yes. Now I've met her.'

He frowned. 'Now you've met her, what do you think?'

Another shrug.

He studied her narrowly. Nine out of ten women would exhibit huge curiosity about an instant sister-in-law. Valerie had certainly been agog about Diane and the screen of lies Gareth had erected between his wife and the family.

Her eyes flickered to his. 'She and Gareth seem very fond

of each other.' The pale brows shifted very slightly. 'To an ... unusual degree.'

James laughed. 'Whatever Valerie's foibles, I'm certain an unhealthy affection for her half-brother isn't among them.'

Her expression didn't change. 'But they enquire after each other like over-anxious lovers.'

The food arrived, plates in the hands and balanced casually on the forearms of a pretty, blonde girl who looked about nineteen.

James used his fingers to pop the first scalding chip into his mouth. 'In my view,' he said, when the swallowed chip lay like an ember in his gullet, 'it's about acceptance. I try and police her drinking, whereas Gareth actually enjoys her being her flawed self. Hence, he ended up aboard a helicopter she was piloting when she'd been on the pop.'

Diane was cutting her sandwich into tiny triangles. 'I've no idea what it's like to fly in a helicopter.'

'It's not much like being on a big airliner or even a small plane. The damned thing always feels as if it wants to crash, dancing about in thin air. Especially when it takes off, it's as if you're one of those plastic ducks at the funfair and some kid has just hooked you up in the air. It's flying for show-offs, so Valerie loved it. Her favourite, the newest chopper that the flying club owned – that's the one she crashed.'

'Do you think she'll go back to piloting helicopters, when she's fit?'

'If she can survive the Civil Aviation Authority enquiry into the crash and pass the medicals, I don't doubt it. But the CAA is deadly serious about air safety and regulation. They make the rules and pilots follow them – you can see where the conflict's going to lie between them and Valerie.'

'How will it affect her if she can't fly? Does she fly away on business, for instance?' A tiny frown pulled at her brow.

He laughed. 'Nothing so functional. Valerie flies for fun.

She does meet friends at the Fenland Airport for lunch or whizzes us off to Silverstone for the Grand Prix, occasionally. But, generally, she flies because she likes flying.'

Diane sipped her drink. 'I can see why Gareth's fascinated by such a flamboyant display of wealth. With her he could be Gareth-with-money, whereas he had to remain Gareth-without-money with me in order to avoid the sharing of it.'

Tucking into his lamb, James cocked his head. 'Why wouldn't Gareth want to share his money with you?'

She abandoned the sandwich, stretched – interestingly, he thought – and sighed. 'We've never had enough money. And my parents didn't want me to marry him, a boy from a council estate.' She laughed, but her eyes were angry as she balled her napkin and flipped it into the middle of the table. 'They said he'd never be able to give me what I was used to – they were right. But I didn't think it mattered.

'As well as giving me a clothes account my parents had bought me a brand new Mini Cooper, green, with white rally stripes. I loved it. After I got married we sold it and bought a cheap Ford Escort van and did some decorating with what was left over. I think Gareth hated the car as a symbol of what he couldn't provide.

'"Don't come running to us," my parents used to say. "You've made your bed. If we helped you out financially we'd be playing into his hands."' She sipped her drink.

'And they were right about us never having enough money, but it was almost as if Gareth manipulated things so that we wouldn't. He always "had" to help his family. First his mum, then his brothers, forever leaving us just that bit short. I don't know if he was punishing me for my parents' snobbery or if he thought that if we were perennially broke my parents would relent and help us.'

'He had to help his brothers? Even when they were grown men?'

'Still does. He's always sorted out everything for them with the result that they became adults who were bad with money, spending it the instant it landed in their hands. They award themselves a reasonable standard of living – Sky TV, cars, computers, things we don't feel we can afford – but they're always a payment or two short at the end of the month. That's when they come to Gareth.'

He couldn't suppress the question that was burning his lips. 'And did Gareth see you as a conduit to your parents' money?'

Her eyes were bleak. 'I've spent so many years denying it —' She sighed. 'But, yes, of course. I think that was why his love seemed angry – which was exciting for a long time but eventually crumbled under pressure. He was waiting for my parents to break. But they never did. Gareth blamed me for having all that financial potential and never realising it.'

James turned back to his meal, using the serrated knife to slice the steak into small pieces but not eating much of it. It wasn't very good. Veins of gristle ran end to end. Suddenly he wished he hadn't brought Diane here, where the dining was cheerfully cheap; where there were no tablecloths and the cutlery came wrapped in thin, blue-chequered paper napkins. It was all right, but all right was only all right. He would never have dreamt of bringing Valerie here, or Tamzin, Natalia or Alice.

As a director of Furness Durwent he received a big beaming salary, bonuses, dividends and profit sharing. Investments added to his income. Valerie had a private income from the chain of department stores that had eventually swallowed up *Myers*. All three of his daughters were beneficiaries of grandparental trusts.

His family were used to plenty: plenty of money, clothes, a lovely house, new cars; they were used to being pleasantly and materially spoilt.

He wished that he could return Diane to that kind of comfort.

Certainly, he could've taken her to a nicer restaurant – her clothes were slightly crazy but always good. She would've enjoyed a decent restaurant and he would have enjoyed her enjoyment. And they would have lingered longer over a meal that wasn't bashed out in the kitchen of a chain of pubs. It would have been good for both of them to lay down their respective burdens for a while.

'And did you blame Gareth?' he heard himself ask.

Thoughtfully, she shook her head. 'No, I never did. For being an ordinary man? It's hardly a crime, is it?'

'You must've loved him, to marry him?'

She smiled suddenly and he wished he could capture it, like a photo, capture the light in her eyes and the lazy way she turned up the corners of her fine mouth.

'Yes. I think I loved him. He was what Bryony would called "*so* cool" with his scooter and Parka. He stopped to help me when I had a flat tyre at the side of the road, me gazing at the jack, mystified. By the time he'd changed the wheel, I was in love. Gareth was quite –' She drew in a long breath. 'He was quite different then. Assured, capable, friendly, sexy, good-looking. He only had to smile and I'd melt. Of course, I quickly realised he had issues. He was all attitude and grievances, very *us and them*. It took me a while to realise that I would never be anything else but *them*.'

James's meal was only half-eaten but he was getting a bad taste in his mouth. He laid down his knife and fork. 'Surely that's not why he "forgot" to tell you about Harold and Valerie? And about the money?'

Her eyes managed a tiny twinkle. 'I'm afraid that was good old-fashioned tit for tat. My parents left everything to my brother, Freddy, when they died. I refused to allow him to make half over to me.'

James tried, but failed, to conceive of a grudge so black and bitter that it continued past the grave. Of parents who'd let their child and grandchild live in straightened circumstances while they rested on their fat bank account, a husband who'd condemn his wife to unnecessary adversity out of spite. It went against his nature. At various times his family had given him to understand that he was managing, controlling, overprotective and/or an obsessive provider, but if any one of them were to be listening to Diane, they might even begin to feel grateful. He was always there for his own, even though it was a long time since Valerie had deserved it. 'Has money ... been a big problem?'

She laughed, but he saw that her eyes shimmered. 'If you mean the lack of it, then desperately! And Bryony was ill so much that I was always rushing to the village shop for cough medicine and paracetamol stuff. The doctor used to put as much as he could on prescription for her but just getting to him – in Holbeach – was almost impossible, sometimes. Her asthma meant I couldn't hold down a full-time job. Hence the sewing.'

After coffee – as if to make up for the almost uneaten sandwich, she drank two cappuccinos, each with double sprinkles – they walked out to the car park. The air was soft with rain and the dusk smelled pleasantly fresh.

Inside the car, Diane patted the leather dash. 'So it's really fast?'

'Very fast,' he agreed, as he steered towards the exit of the pub car park.

'And it's an expensive car?'

'Pretty much.'

'I've never been driven really fast in an expensive car.' She turned and grinned, her eyes gleaming in the umbrellas of light cast by the enormous car park lampposts.

He tried to withstand the temptation. He was a responsible

adult. There were one-eyed monsters on every verge around Peterborough and he'd only just copped three points on his licence from one of the little bastards.

But he heard his voice say, 'Would you like to?' as the car purred up the service road and back onto the dual carriageway.

And before she could answer he thrust his foot down on the accelerator and the seat delivered a punch to his back as the car launched itself at the road ahead.

'Whoohoo!' She grabbed her seat.

James drove faster, surging along the dual carriageway from Paston Parkway to Perkins Parkway, weaving, overtaking taillights that were like red stars on either side until he hit a clear patch of road and he could really open up, enjoying Diane's yelps and whoops as she rocked in her seat and he let the car do what it was made to.

Her laughter bubbled around them. 'I hope you don't get stopped!'

'So do I.' One wary eye on his mirrors in case a flashing blue light materialised out of the dusk, he braked dangerously hard to pass a camera. But this was *fun*. And the woman beside him seemed to be having fun, too, clinging on and squeaking with delight at every swerve.

She gasped as he let the back end drift out. 'Wow, James!' He liked the way his name sounded on her tongue.

Eventually, he slowed.

The car slid sedately onto a slip road, past McDonalds and the cluster of car showrooms around the cinema, around a couple of roundabouts and into the Farcet Fen lane, safely reined in to thirty as they approached Farcet village. The main road through the village, busy during the day, was quiet now. Over speed bumps, they passed the school and friendly family homes in red brick and pebbledash. Just as the village became the countryside again he rolled the car to a stop in a lay-by beside the wall and railings of a small cemetery. The light had faded into the long deep twilight of a clear summer evening. No moon or stars yet, just infinite indigo sky.

Diane unfastened her belt and turned in her seat, breathlessly. 'That was great. Thanks for the ride.'

'My pleasure. We all need to kick back, sometimes. I do, anyway. That was irresponsible – but overdue.'

Her look was sympathetic. 'I suppose Valerie's drinking must be a strain. For the whole family.'

Usually, he blanked remarks like that, but Diane's husband had nearly lost his life as a direct result of Valerie mixing liquor with a helicopter. And he realised that he wanted to talk about it. It might be a relief to open up. Not to have to be the strong one. He sighed. 'Harold doesn't seem aware. The girls don't know the extent of it. Or, at least, I don't think so, although Natalia and Alice occasionally make remarks about boozing. Valerie drinks. It's part of her life. She *drinks*. Not just sometimes, not just socially – she drinks steadily. We have furious rows about her driving anyone else, especially the girls. She insists that she rarely drinks before six and rarely drives after. She's only rated to fly in daylight, too, so it's quite simple so far as she's concerned: only drink in the evening ... on good days. On good days, most evenings she drinks a bottle or two of wine. I rage about her still being over the limit in the morning but she dismisses it as "fussing".

'But sometimes she has bad days. On a bad day she manages a bottle of vodka, mixing it into orange juice or coffee, any time of day.

'I freak out and she treats me as a huge joke, won't discuss the problem because she hasn't *got* a problem, she says. Apparently, I'm a spoilsport. I take a few drinks much too seriously. I should lighten up.'

'But it certainly sounds like she's got a problem,' Diane observed. She hesitated. 'Does she have … you know – have help?'

He drew in a breath so deep that it dug a pain in his chest as her question chewed his conscience. 'Wouldn't hear of it. I suppose I ought to be going to one of these groups that support the family of a drinker. But then —' He blinked out of the window at the black shadows in the hedgerow. 'It would be an immense waste of time. She's headstrong and drinking has made that worse. I read that the decision to stop drinking has to come from the drinker and I let that excuse me from taking any initiative. The truth is that you can't help somebody who doesn't want to be helped, especially if they sneer at you for trying.

'And sometime I wonder if I'm the cause. Everything. Maybe it's me? Have I driven her to drink? But, if so, why didn't she leave?' *And why haven't I?*

In the confines of the car he could smell Diane's personal scent, warm and clean. He breathed it in. Soothing. Everything about her soothed him.

'So, to turn your earlier question back on yourself – you must've loved her, to marry her?'

He turned in his seat. 'I probably did love her but I was nowhere near wanting to marry. She was my girlfriend and I was happy with that. But suddenly she confessed that she was pregnant, with all the tears and fears and the interminable brave conversations about abortion that went with a surprise baby. I hated the idea of abortion. I knew that if we got married, she'd keep the baby. Natalia. It was the right thing to do.'

'I'm sorry,' she said, simply.

'What was done was done and soon and we were OK when the girls were babies. We were too focused on them to get on each other's nerves. But Natalia and Alice have grown up and moved out.' His shoulders tensed. 'And Tamzin and Valerie have a strange relationship. Close, but unhealthily tolerant. Blind to each other's problems, each effectively endorses the other's self-destructive behaviour.'

It felt quite natural to sit in the fast-growing dark confessing his problems to this unusual woman who seemed always to be so composed and pragmatic. He found himself wondering what his life would have been like if he'd shared it with a woman who didn't fall into banshee mode whenever … well, whenever she damned well felt like it. Imagine living in a home that was peaceful, with a woman who was restful instead of rocking the house with screams and bellows.

In the twilight, he could make out the curve of Diane's cheek and the straightness of her nose, the shift in the pattern on the fabric of her top as it folded around the contours of her breasts. And he was becoming aware of a need. The kind of need that a man might feel when tucked away with a woman he'd noticed from the instant he glanced across a waiting area and saw her staring at a policeman, a polite smile of astonished disbelief on her lips. If 'noticing' meant a clunk in his chest and eyes that refused to look away.

The need began to grow. He felt his breathing quicken.

'We've got more of a habit than a marriage,' he said, deliberately, trying to push her into a reaction. 'We share a bed but it's a big bed with a lot of space available. I've forgotten what meeting in the middle of all that space feels like. It's been a long time since we … met in the middle.' He waited, looking for signals.

But, no. No empathetic tuts or feminine clucks, no sympathetic hand on his arm. 'Difficult,' she agreed, neutrally, instead.

Irritation reared like a tormented bear inside him. He was spilling his guts about the situations he had to juggle every day and she called it 'difficult'! 'I'll tell you what's "difficult",' he snapped, goaded. 'Being alone with a woman like you and having to behave!' He froze as he realised that his thoughts had made it, uncensored, to his voice.

She shifted, minutely.

The silence magnified his words. They rang around inside his head. This, surely, would earn him a blast of indignation and fury. He braced himself for an icy, 'I think you'd better take me back to my car!'

But Diane seemed more curious than explosive. 'Why don't you want to behave?' She even sounded as if she might be smiling in the dark at his effrontery.

Having been honest to the point of lunacy, he felt obliged to crash on. 'Because my problems usually absorb all my energy but I've realised that I'm more interested in you than in my problems and I can't remember the last time I felt like that. I want to step off the world – my world – and into bed with you.'

She didn't react at all.

The silence drew out. She was utterly still, staring into the evening.

He sighed. He'd better apologise. Reassure her that he really was reasonably safe and that these uncharacteristic sentences would soon stop popping out. He'd got used to missing sex because he was the kind of man who expected to feel guilt about cheating on his wife. Fidelity was just another habit.

But instead of uttering an apology, his mouth seemed to want him to lean across and brush his lips gently across her temple. When she stiffened but didn't draw away, he let his mouth drift lower, feeling first the tingling brush of her eyebrow on his lips and then the soft flutteriness of her eyelashes. Her smooth cheekbone, her jaw. His mind churned with what the hell he was *doing* driving a woman off to dark lanes and propositioning her. It must be the stress. An urge for release.

Oh yeahhhhh ... He almost groaned aloud at the idea of finding release with her.

She was still.

And then he was kissing her mouth, his tongue stroking the supple softness of hers until, slowly, she responded, making his heart bump around with the pleasure of her proximity, her warmth. His hand wandered onto her upper arm, the back of his thumb brushing the side of her breast. And his palm moved in to investigate. He felt her jump. Tense. *I've passed her boundaries ...* he expected her to yank away with aghast demands to know what the hell he thought he was doing. He held his breath. But his hand continued to cup the delicious heaviness of her breast with a kind of helpless magnetism.

Then he felt her relax and her arms slide slowly about his neck, making him pull her against him as hard as he could, the stupid centre consol digging into his lower ribs and preventing him from feeling her body properly against his as he kissed and kissed her, shuddering, wanting her so much it sucked the air from his lungs.

'I don't want to go to bed,' she whispered. 'But I like your car.'

It took fully ten seconds for him to credit the evidence of his ears, wishing he could see the expression in her clear blue eyes. Ten seconds of listening to his blood pounding in his ears. 'Here?' It seemed a long, long time since he'd had sex in a car. It *was* a long time. He glanced at the steering wheel, the bulky consol, the automatic gear shift. His heart flailed about in the astounding knowledge that she seemed to want him, too. 'Let's go somewhere a lot more comfortable. With a bed.'

Instantly, she shook her head. 'A hotel, without baggage and a prior booking? Running the gauntlet of desk clerks trying to hide their titters? Between here and there I'll get cold feet.'

Personally, he felt the clerks could go to hell; hiding titters was in their job description. But he desperately didn't want her to get cold feet because, right now, she was so hot, plastered against him so that he could feel every beat of her heart. Even so, her words made him admit, reluctantly, 'If you're not sure perhaps we ought not –'

'It's been a long time since Gareth and I ... *met in the middle*, too. And I don't think I've ever had sex in a car,' she mused.

He groaned, willingly disconnecting with reality, tightening his arms so that her breasts pushed against him in a way that killed his last gentlemanly inclination. 'It'll be easier in the back – No, hang on, not here.' Limbs like rubber, he started up the car, pulled out into the road then backed up, swinging past the end of the cemetery wall and into a grassy track that ran beside it. Back, back and back, until they were fifty yards from the road.

In gallant mode, he raced around the car to open her door but, typically, by the time he got there she'd opened the door perfectly well for herself and was sliding into the back seat, leaving him to run a fruitless circuit of the vehicle, through the grass and nettles like an idiot, to reach the other door and fall in beside her.

The back seat was cold and the heat they'd begun to generate hadn't made the switch of venue.

With a nervous movement, she flicked back her hair.

Her hair was beautiful. He put out his hand to touch, stroke, slowly, from the crown of her head, feeling the silk slide beneath his palm until he reached the nape of her neck and could gather it into his fist and pull her gently, experimentally, to see if she'd come to his kiss. He watched her eyes close and her lips part as, slowly, tentatively, she did.

And then desire was a hot explosion and he heard her whimper as he kissed her too hard, threading his hands underneath her to drag her onto his lap, thrusting against her, running his hands over her bare legs and pulling her dainty sandals from her feet, touching each toe with his fingertips, breathing hard. The world outside the car spun away. He wished the seats in front weren't such an unaccommodating barrier, that the roof of the car wasn't bearing down, or the width of the car would allow him to lie her down and savour every inch of her body. And that it wasn't nearly dark. He wished he had all the space and light he wanted to undress her slowly and explore everything delicious that he had in his hands.

But it wasn't going to be like that. Not this time. He could wriggle off only some of her clothing because they were, after all, in a public place in their purple velvet evening and he couldn't discount the damage potential of someone walking up the track. But, on the other hand, he wanted her too much to call a halt.

He tried not to hurry. He desperately wanted to enjoy the moment, threading his fingers in her sinuous hair while he fed from the softness of her mouth and she clutched fistfuls of his shirt and got breathless. He examined the patterns of her spine and loved the softness of the nape of her neck. But his hands were programmed with their own course and in no time he was establishing that her pretty red buttons sprang open quite co-operatively, and that her breasts were cool and mobile and wonderful in his hands. He stroked her until her composure broke and she began to use her entire body to stroke him back.

Her sweet mouth inflamed him almost as much as hauling out her knickers from beneath her skirt. He went half-mad when she let her head fall back so that he could nibble at her throat, loved her erratic breathing, her clutching fingers.

'Don't stop,' she whispered.

'No longer possible,' he gasped.

He had forgotten how it felt to want somebody so desperately that he ached, arched, gasped, groaned, reached, lifted, slid ... *there*.

Sex had never satisfied him more.

Every limb heavy. Alive. Satiated. Replete. Complete. His heart slowing into a languorous, after-sex rhythm.

Her skirt was still gathered around her waist. His legs were uncomfortably confined both from her wonderful hot weight and from lack of space. If they'd gone to a hotel they would be stretched out together beneath the sheets, now, revelling in naked afterglow. He'd be able to feel the softness of her stomach and the firmness of her hips pressed against him, warmth against warmth, flesh against flesh. But he could put up with what he had.

At least, as hemmed in as they were, every inch of her was hot against every inch of him. 'Fucking hell,' he breathed. He meant to say: *that was fantastic, that was wonderful, you were incredible*. But all that made it out was, 'Fucking hell. Fucking *hell*.'

'Mm.' Her cheek squashed against his shoulder, her breath warm on the side of his neck.

He stroked her back, admiring the milky gleam of her skin in the glimmer of the moon, kissing the top of her head, tangling his fingers in her hair, hardly able to believe what had just happened.

She sighed. 'I suppose I ought to go back for my car.' She didn't move.

'Of course. I'll take you.' Neither did he.

'In a minute.'

'Yes. Soon.'

She yawned without lifting her face from the pillow of his

shoulder and her hair tickled his chin. Then she shivered. Feeling around in the darkness, he located his jacket and slid it around her shoulders.

She straightened, to snuggle into it, humming with pleasure. Her hair spilled around her shoulders and her breasts. 'You do like leather.'

Appreciation rumbled in his throat. 'I sure as hell like you in it. You look like my favourite fantasy.'

She wriggled and stretched. 'It feels lovely. The lining's probably pure silk.'

He stroked her hair over one shoulder. 'That's how you feel. Silk. Or satin. Your skin ...' He sucked in his breath as his hands found their way inside the jacket. Her hair spilled over the leather and over the whiteness of her flesh.

It was some time before he took her back for her car.

Chapter Eight

What have I done?

Riding back to the Ackerman, Diane felt as if she'd just become a complete stranger to herself.

She was super aware of the powerful Mercedes around her, the soft seats that had so recently been beneath her knees; their squishing swishing marking the rhythm of the sex she'd just enjoyed. Enjoyed a lot.

The tunnel vision of desire had shot past sense and integrity and she'd hurled away quarter of a century's monogamy. And enjoyed that, too.

In the close confines, James's thrusts had bumped her head on the roof. 'Sorry – too enthusiastic!' Even while he laughed, he was drawing her down to kiss her better, his laughter fading as he took up a slower, less boisterous rhythm.

What was I thinking?

I rode him as if frightened he'd stop. I didn't want to be brought back to my senses.

James had laughed again to find that all his change had chinked out of his pockets and into the dark recesses of the upholstery. Sex seemed a merry experience for James.

And she'd shared the joy.

Back in the car park at the Ackerman, she took a breath to say so as he rolled his car to a stop close to hers. But a shout whipped away her attention.

'Diane!'

She gazed in horror at two men barging out of the brightly lit hospital foyer, the heavy glass door closing slowly behind them.

James frowned through the windscreen. 'Who are these guys?'

'Shit.' She fumbled for the door handle, heart galloping, legs tangling, panic overhauling guilt by a short head. 'You'd better go.' She made – casually, she hoped – for her own vehicle parked under the sodium lights, hoping to hear James purr away equally casually behind her.

But what she heard was the engine being switched off and the creak and thud of a door opening and closing.

Trying desperately to ignore James, she watched the men stride towards her. A deep vertical line engraved the negligible area between the brows of the first man, his brown hair slicked straight back from his disgruntled expression. 'We've been looking everywhere for you.'

The second was a flabbier, taller, slightly younger version of the first, the vertical line less deep, the hair flicked to the side and over his face. The disgruntlement register was about the same. 'No one knew where you'd gone and why you hadn't taken your car. Our Gary didn't, nor the nurses.'

Diane unlocked her door. 'I needed something to eat, James gave me a lift.' It would be odd not to acknowledge him as he was leaning against the Mercedes with his hands in his pockets, dark brows low over watchful eyes.

Both men turned simultaneously to stare at James with identical *who are you and what do you want?* expressions.

James simply stared back.

Diane's pulse quickened. 'Have you met James North?' She managed to open her car door. 'He's Valerie's husband, Gareth's brother-in-law. James, this is Ivan and this is Melvyn, Gareth's half-brothers.' She inserted the 'half' deliberately. The Jenner brothers made such a deal of their blood being thicker than the proverbial water, none of them seemed to like being reminded that this especially thick blood was not drawn from identical gene pools.

James nodded.

Melvyn and Ivan merely stared.

Ivan was the first to look away. 'Can you come home with us for a while, Diane? We need a meeting about our Gary. You can come in my car.'

With a quick movement Diane threw her handbag onto her passenger seat and a twist of her body put her behind the wheel. 'I'll follow you.' Then, ultra casually, ''Bye James. Thanks for the lift.'

Slowly, James lifted a hand in farewell, exchanged one last stare with Ivan and Melvyn, and slid back into his car.

Diane let out her breath, giddy with relief.

Her hands, she noticed, were trembling. It took two goes to find the ignition with the key.

If she was a scarlet woman she was not much bloody use at it. How the hell did people carry on affairs? Her heart was bounding about as if already dodging accusations.

Half an hour later, ensconced on Ivan's huge sofa, she smiled, accepted a cup of tea from Megan, Ivan's wife, and began to relax and realise that her in-laws were behaving exactly as usual, so *I had sex in the back of a car tonight!* couldn't be emblazoned across her face as she felt it must be. Somebody would've mentioned it.

The sofa was constructed like three reclining chairs stuck together. Ivan and Megan liked gimmicky stuff and the room was overdone with elaborate curtains and nets and lampshades like crystal cakes.

Stella, Megan's sister, emerged from the kitchen with steaming mugs for Ivan and Melvyn. 'How's Gareth, Diane? Sounds like he had a close call.' Shadows beneath her eyes spoilt her usual prettiness.

'He's too cussed to die. Are you OK, Stella? You're very pale.'

'I'm fine!' Stella summoned a wide but not quite convincing smile. A small, brisk, blonde cutie, reminding

Diane of a beaming cherub, Stella was often around for Jenner gatherings, adding a welcome flavour of rebellion with her declared views that marriage was a prison designed to prevent women from achieving their desires. In contrast, Megan, and Hilly, Melvyn's docile spouse, were co-operative with their menfolk in a way that brought the word 'doormat' to Diane's mind and Stella's lips.

Stella had left her own husband during an affair with an improbably young teacher. Diane liked Stella and had been sorry the young teacher hadn't stuck around. Gareth, however, had been sanctimonious. Stella had got what she deserved, he declared, reaped what she'd sewn, eaten just desserts on the bed she'd made and must now lie upon.

Stella, presumably aware of his self-righteous condemnation, had been quiet in his presence.

And now, as Stella and Megan melted back into the kitchen, Diane nursed her steaming mug, waiting stoically as Ivan and Melvyn lit cigarettes and updated themselves on the European football results via Sky Sports. Rude of them, having invited her to the house.

Meanwhile, George, Ivan's eldest, clopped down the open-tread stairs into the sitting room.

Immediately, Diane forgot her brothers-in-law. 'George! How have you been?'

'Hey, Diane. Yeah. OK.' George grinned. So impossibly beautiful with bisque skin and gold-brown eyes to set off his tawny hair, so funny, bright and kind, Diane wondered how he could be Ivan's son. Or, for that matter, Megan's. George had been lucky with both looks and charisma.

No wonder Bryony called him Gorgeous George.

Diane suddenly missed Bryony with a physical pain behind her breastbone and a boiling in her eyes. 'How are things?'

He rolled his eyes. 'Uni's better than school. But reading and revising! *Waaaaaay* too much.'

'Stop fannying about and get a job, then,' Ivan demanded, without taking his eyes from the oversized TV screen.

Whether or not George went to university had been last year's family row. George had, with difficulty and because he was eligible for the full loan, won. Ivan didn't understand university and, as with most things he didn't understand, rubbished it.

Diane ignored him. 'Everyone hates revision, it's in the rules. How's the band?'

George flopped into the sofa and performed a yogic looking stretch to make his section recline. 'Amazin'. Been working on some new stuff, Marty wrote some wicked riffs. Got a gig Saturday – with the new drummer, Rob.' He'd hated having to replace Bryony and her pearl-white drum-kit. Bryony had told Diane that George sometimes sent her flyers announcing that Jenneration was to appear on Friday at The Bantam or Saturday at Dhobi Joe's. No letter, just the flyers, a silent but eloquent message that things at home were moving on without her.

'Hope it goes well.'

'Yeah, yeah. Anyway. Revision. Nice to see ya.' With a heart-stopping smile he loped from the room, chequered boxer shorts showing above the waistband of his jeans. If something that hung around his buttocks could be called a waistband.

''Bye,' responded Diane, sorry he wasn't staying longer.

She knew that George missed Bryony. When Bryony had lived at home he'd been huge in her life, so often a weekend guest that he was almost as familiar with Purtenon St. Paul as Bryony herself.

Diane thought of them making popcorn in her kitchen, a stereo playing Razorlight or The Arctic Monkeys; writing songs, arguing whether Bryony's new boots made her look like an American high-school kid. George was a happy, larky, lippy but likeable lad who'd filled that clichéd spot in Diane's heart of 'the son she'd never had'.

He'd taken Bryony's decision to work abroad personally, as if she was doing it to get away from him. Had tried frantically to talk her out of it.

Diane suspected that he felt more for Bryony than mere cousinly affection but Bryony pooh-poohed the notion, eyes big and curls bouncing. 'What are you on, Mum? George is my bezzy, not my boyfriend.'

'I know what he is. It's what he wants to be – that's the question.'

Interrupting these thoughts, Ivan pointed the remote at the flat-panel, large-screen TV and put an end to Sky Sports. Evidently, the conference was now in session.

Diane jumped in hard to put them off balance. 'So how long have you known about Gareth finding his father and sister?'

Ivan, having opened his mouth to speak, closed it, and glanced at Melvyn. Diane recognised the look of the Jenner boys getting their stories straight.

But Melvyn wasn't so easily steered off topic. 'Gareth's worried about you, Diane. Driving all that way every day.'

Diane began a snort of derision but, at the same time, she pushed back her hair and caught the unmistakable scent of sex on her hands and the snort emerged as more of an aghast sniff. After several horrified beats, she managed a squeaky, 'Why?'

Melvyn waved an airy hand. 'It's a long way.'

'There's petrol,' added Ivan.

'And the mileage clocking up. And wear and tear on all your vehicle consumables.'

Diane shifted her mug to a raffia coaster on the coffee table. It was difficult to concentrate on deciphering the subtext of this interview when her heart had just performed a gallop and buck like a naughty pony. The enormity of what she'd done tonight socked her in the head.

After 25 years of – admittedly hillocky – marriage to Gareth, she'd been unfaithful.

And here she was sitting with his brothers ... A cold nausea rolled over her like flu.

She stared at Ivan and Melvyn, who were staring back at her. Discovery seemed imminent, inevitable. Panic grabbed her heart in both hands and tried to stuff it up her throat.

She'd just had sex in the back seat of a car in a public place.

What if she'd been seen? What if someone told Gareth? Or Ivan? Or Melvyn? She'd be –!

She'd be –?

Bearing in mind everything she'd recently discovered, what was the worst that could happen?

She swallowed. *If you were discovered? If he divorced you? How would your life be worse? He can hardly prevent you having contact with Bryony – she's not a child.*

She picked up her mug to give her hands something to do. Separation and divorce.

Living without Gareth.

Being alone ... For an instant she knew a feeling of liberation so intense that it made her feel drunk.

In actual fact, discovery didn't seem too awful a prospect. For her.

Shit. She put her mug down again before she dropped it.

Two had tangoed. Gareth would be so furious he'd run to Valerie with his tales – OK, not literally, in view of his broken ribs, pelvis, tibia, fibular, etc, but figuratively. And James hadn't shown any desire to be divorced. There were significant issues with Tamzin's physical, mental and emotional health and Tamzin freaked out at the merest suggestion of acrimony between her parents. There might be money issues, too, for all she knew. Divorces tended to be expensive for those with money to lose.

He was probably standing under his shower at home right now, washing away the same secretions that she felt bathed in, thinking how much he enjoyed an occasional one-night stand. She doubted very much that he predicted major changes to his marital status.

She swallowed and tried to get a grip on the conversation. 'What are consumables?'

Melvyn assumed the role of patient adviser. 'Your tyres and brake pads, your exhaust, everything that wears out and needs replacing. The more miles you do, the sooner you have to replace them.'

'And that's what Gareth's worried about? Me wearing the car out and spending lots of money on petrol? The same car he drove on an almost identical journey every working day?'

'He's worried about you wearing yourself out, too,' Ivan added generously. 'That's why he suggested it.'

'Suggested what?'

Ivan gave her a puzzled frown. Maybe he'd explained all this once while she'd been suffering cold sweats about illicit sex. 'What?' she repeated.

'That you come and stop here. You'll be much closer to the hospital.'

'Hardly,' she disagreed, sharply. 'The Ackerman's the other side of Peterborough from this house. If you factor in extra traffic the petrol consumption's probably the same.'

'No, 'cos you can park your car here and come for visiting every night with us. I'll drive you.'

Diane laughed. 'What about our house? What about my work?'

'Well, that's what Gareth wants,' said Melvyn, decisively, in a *so that's that* tone.

Diane turned back to Ivan. 'How long have you known

that Gareth had found his father and sister?'

Although his eyes widened and his lips parted, Ivan didn't look any more ready with an answer this time than last.

She turned to Melvyn. 'How long?'

He shrugged.

'Since before the crash?' she guessed.

'It's not our business, Diane. It's between you and Gary.'

'Since before the crash.' She picked up her mug to take to Megan in the kitchen, then changed her mind and put it down. Megan had a nasty habit of throwing her arms around people and hugging them close. Diane felt as if she reeked of sex and Megan would know that Gareth was in no condition to provide it. She wiped a haze of sweat from her top lip.

'But when are you coming?' Melvyn frowned as Diane retrieved her bag from under the table.

She straightened. 'Where?'

'Here, while our Gary's in –'

'I'm not.' She fished out her keys.

Ivan's brows beetled in exactly the same way as Melvyn's. 'But Gary said –'

'I'm not coming.' Calmly. She raised her voice. 'Thanks for the tea, Megan!'

'You going, darlin'?'

Megan scurried out of the kitchen with her embrace ready but Diane was already on her way through the front door.

She whizzed home, mind racing. Why would Gareth want her to stay at Ivan's house? Ivan had only three bedrooms, all presently occupied; a guest would be an inconvenience. The petrol/wear-and-tear argument was an insult to her intelligence.

She pulled up outside the house.

So it must be ... She frowned out of the window at the

dark lane.

So it must be ... Come on, Diane.

So it must be ... it must be ...

The light in her brain came on slowly.

More stuff he didn't want her to find out.

Chapter Nine

Rich, dawn-pink fabric. Anything too pale would've been a mistake with Tamzin's bloodless complexion. Glass buttons, black embroidery silk, chrome rings in two tiny sizes, thread. The new-fabric smell enveloped her along with the steam as Diane ironed out the folds ready to mark out the garment on the laminate floor. She didn't have a table. Cutting on the floor saved space and money, both of which were at a premium in this house, although it did also mean fluff bunnies that collected in corners and rolled out to attach themselves to her fabric at the least draught.

A hard blue cushion was stuck with pins, red tailor's chalk lay beside the one-metre wooden rule and, pinned to a cork tile on the wall, the measurements that demarcated Tamzin's waif-like figure were written onto a female outline.

Diane looked at the materials around her. She felt scratchy eyed and light headed; not remotely like starting on Tamzin's mammoth order. But the garments wouldn't make themselves. Tamzin, although Diane hadn't seen her for over a week, had seemed to be looking forward to the new clothes and it was apparently a miracle for her to look forward to anything. Diane had an itch to help her if she could.

But she'd lain awake for too many anxious night hours recently asking herself what she'd done and feeling her stomach turning over at the answer. Twenty-five years she'd been faithful to Gareth, through thick and thin (or thin and thinner), good and, latterly, bad. After the row about Diane's inheritance – or lack of it – sex between them had faded until abstinence was habitual. Until then Gareth had never let anger interfere with his desire for her.

But there was something of which she was in no doubt: even if he no longer wanted her, he wouldn't want another man to want her.

She could just imagine his cold rage if he ever discovered her back-of-the-car sex.

How sordid it sounded! But it hadn't seemed it. James, both caring and urgent, had wanted her. And wanted her. She'd run with her instinct and satisfied a craving for human contact of the kind she hadn't even realised she'd been missing so badly. Waves of desire had washed her onto a dangerous beach.

But that had been then.

Before the cold light of several days had illuminated the fact that she knew almost nothing about James and only had his word for it that he and Valerie hadn't, um, met in the middle for years. And he hadn't said anything about meeting anybody else's middle. Casual sex could be his norm. It had seemed to come easily enough, complete with suggestions about hotels. She had come easily enough, too: one cheesy chat-up line and she'd hopped into his backseat like a curious teenager.

Carefully, she checked that her lengthways fold ran accurately along the warp of the fabric, then pinned and pressed it, a bad hang to a garment grating on her like a screeched note would on a musician.

She sat back on her heels and surveyed her sketch and the pattern she'd cut for a double-breasted shirt with collar and slightly gathered sleeves. Tamzin needed to avoid anything too fitted until she regained some weight. Either side of the centre panel Diane would embroider whorls of tiny stem stitch and French knots, working in and around the little chrome rings as she went. Subtle and unusual, Diane's offbeat ornamentation would suit Tamzin better than ribbon or ruffles.

She examined the cutting edge of her scissors. They'd soon need sharpening, and Gareth normally did them.

Downstairs, the phone rang.

Motionless, she listened. If she got to it before it stopped ringing, it wouldn't be James. He hadn't phoned on Tuesday. Or Wednesday or Thursday. The man didn't phone a woman after a one-night stand, she'd come to realise. That's what made it a one-night stand. Dur! So what did he do? Probably, he smiled with vague friendliness when he next happened to encounter her and maybe asked how she was. If he didn't mention the sex unless the woman was misguided enough to oblige him to, then it had been nothing special. He whistled in the shower as he swilled away Scent of A One Night Stand Woman and he forgot the whole thing.

The man certainly didn't swear and panic and attempt a belated douche job as an optimistic form of contraception, trying grimly to calculate when his period was due before hurrying off to Dr Cooke for advice.

The phone continued to ring.

Diane lunged inelegantly to her feet, a leg buckling because she spent too much time on her knees on that hard floor. She raced for the stairs, wishing she had telephone handsets all over the house so that she didn't have to drop what she was doing and fly to where the phone was fixed to the wall.

She jumped into the narrow hall. The phone still rang. She snatched up the receiver with a breathless, 'Hello?'

'Can we swap hospital visiting slots with you, today?' It was Ivan, blunt to the point of rudeness, typical of him that he didn't even bother with 'Hi, how are you?' Of course it wasn't James.

'OK.' She matched his economy with her own.

'You can go in the evening.'

'I can, can't I?'

'Only we want to go to the footie tonight and we've got half a day off.' Ivan and Melvyn worked at the same mammoth packaging plant.

'Have fun.'

'And you can stay over at ours.'

'I'll be fine.'

'But our Gary wants –'

'It's very thoughtful of you all to worry but I'll drive home.'

'It'll be dark.'

'I'll put the headlights on.'

Staring through the kitchen window after ending the call, she didn't immediately return to Tamzin's shirt. Clumsy and incompetent, Ivan was attempting to manipulate her. She would discover why – she'd had years of practice. It was just a question of being methodical. It would give her something to think about other than James.

OK, first – kitchen drawers.

No.

Sideboard. No. Gareth's wardrobe. Nothing remarkable in, on, underneath nor behind. Under one of the mattresses? No. Chest of drawers, bedside locker, behind the bath panel, under the bed, no, no, no, no. Every other nook and cranny, no. Purposefully, she clattered the stepladder up the stairs, heaved her way through the overhead hatch and into the loft.

Three hours later she was in the shower ridding herself of the dust from rifling every box and suitcase and cobwebby pocket of roofing felt that looked as if it might be a hiding place.

But, no.

Thoughtfully, she returned to the shirt, wielding the shears carefully along the pattern pieces, pinning the darts, tacking for the gathers at either end of the sleeves. She switched on the sewing machine and threaded it to wind the bobbin.

A car stopped outside in the lane.

She paused. Then stretched up like a meerkat to peep over the sill. A little white hatchback had pulled up and a young man stepped out and made for one of the neighbouring houses. She turned back to her work, wanting to spit like a camel. What had she imagined would be out there? A black Mercedes?

She paused. Her eyes returned to the view from the window.

In a moment, she'd stamped her feet into her canvas shoes and was jogging downstairs and outside, snatching up the car keys en route.

Why hadn't she thought of the damned car?

Glove compartment, door pockets, seat pockets, under the seats. Nothing. She threw open the boot, tipping out the contents of a plastic toolbox with a shrill scream of spanners. No. She halted, for the first time uncertain. No?

Then she saw a little loop, just below the boot catch. Pulling it up sharply, she found the floor of the boot came up and she was staring at the spare wheel.

And there, cradled by the hub, was a blue canvas pouch, neat and new.

She slid open the nylon zip. Inside laid a mobile phone, a set of keys and a blue building-society passbook.

Her fingertips went numb. She hadn't had much experience with mobile phones but knew enough from Bryony and George to switch it on and locate the phone book. The only entries read:

Dad
Ivan
Melvyn
STM
This phone
Valerie

The keys looked like a front door key and a back.
The opening balance in the passbook had been £200,000.
About £120,000 of it remained.

Diane sat in the car for several minutes outside Harold's lovely house, admiring the fish-eye dormers and the sweeping lawns. Gareth's father's house. It compared badly to Gareth's mother's house on the Brightside Estate – and that had been the best of a lifetime of bad lots. In the huddle of L-shaped terraces slotted like a jigsaw around car parks, greens and graffitied play areas, the Jenner house on the Brightside had been in a row with maroon front doors and a dustbin alcove alongside. The Brightside. The councillors must've been on something when they'd dreamed that one up.

When Gareth had first taken Diane home she'd been wiping sweaty palms on her jeans, she'd been so nervous.

'It can't be as bad as meeting your parents was for me,' he joked.

They found Wendy, a large, tired-looking woman, in her sitting room, setting small stitches in a ripped shirt pocket. At Gareth's laconic introduction, 'This is Diane,' she removed black-rimmed glasses to stare. Simultaneously, Melvyn and Ivan appeared, each as dark as Wendy, to have a peep at what Gareth had brought home.

The room was long and narrow with a dining table at one end. A brown suite surrounded a smoked-glass coffee table on a mottled brown carpet, and the walls were beige. With five people there, three of them strapping lads, the room seemed small.

'Pleased to meet you,' Diane offered, into the silence.

'You're easy pleased, then. Gareth says you've got your own car?'

Diane flushed at Wendy's offhandedness. 'A mini.'

'You must have a good job. Well, sit down.'

Diane, unused to having her life picked over so rudely, sat slowly. 'I work in a boutique. My parents bought me the car.'

Melvyn and Ivan exchanged grins.

Wendy stared harder. 'Must be nice to have things like that fall in your lap.' She set her mending aside. 'I suppose I'd better put the kettle on, you'll expect a cup of tea.'

Stiff with embarrassment at such ungraciousness, Diane refused. 'No, thank you.'

Gareth said, 'She takes one sugar, white.'

Wendy returned with a tin tray of mugs and continued her blunt interrogation. 'So what kind of a house do your parents live in? I suppose your friends are lawyers and bank managers and they all have cars, nice new cars. It's all right, isn't it, when you've got a bit of brass in the family?'

Gareth took a green mug bearing a picture of an improbably yellow, doleful sausage dog. 'We're getting married,' he said, quietly and without particular emphasis. He laced his fingers through Diane's.

Melvyn and Ivan gave vent to hoots of derision and old jokes about balls and chains but Wendy's hostile probing ceased.

Gareth took Diane home often in the few months before the wedding. Despite Wendy's resentment it was easier there than at Diane's house. They could go to his room and play records while Wendy sat downstairs in her armchair mending clothes and knitting jumpers in front of the TV.

It was on his own turf that Diane began to discover the complex person that was Gareth Jenner.

It seemed there hadn't been much money in the boys' childhoods. Equal pay for women had been still a few years away, which had meant punishing hours for Wendy. Now that all three Jenner boys were earning and Wendy semi-retired Gareth wanted the family to move, but Wendy wasn't interested. 'I'm too old to bother. And the boys need the money for their own lives. You'll always be OK, Gareth, you a miser all your life; you'll move on when you've hoarded enough. But Melvyn and Ivan have the arse out of their pants by Wednesday every week. They'd never cope with a higher rent.'

So they remained on the Brightside Estate.

Most of the petty criminals in the area had been housed in the ugly new beige-brick terraces and, although loosely law abiding themselves, the Jenners mixed comfortably with the dealers, thieves and hookers that lived beside them, treating the police like vampires – if you never invited them in you were fairly safe.

Diane won acceptance in the Jenner household, after a fashion. She might not be their sort but if she belonged to Gareth then she belonged to them and they made sure she never had a moment's trouble from the neighbourhood.

It was Diane's parents who fought bitterly and futilely to keep her from taking the name of Jenner.

So many rows. So many brutal words. So often that Gareth, pale with rage, had to stick out insulting disregard for his honesty and prospects.

Low life.

Wrong 'un.

Regret it all your life.

Underclass.

Don't come crying to us.

You've made your bed.

We expected better.

Diane shook her head clear of the echoes of her father's voice, and climbed from the car into spitting rain.

Harold answered the door looking as if he might just have awakened from an afternoon nap. But his bleariness soon vanished. 'Diane! Come in. You're a nice surprise.' Diane smiled at his pleasure, genuine she had no doubt, reflecting how little of this kindness she saw in his son.

How different would Gareth have been if he'd known Harold from the beginning?

Harold drew Diane through the house to a tiny sitting-room at the back with two cottage-style armchairs facing the French doors. This room was comfortably worn, the small table exhibiting a careless ring or two, the chairs bleached and shiny on the arms.

She surveyed the garden while he made tea, silently apologising to him for what she was about to do. 'Lapsang Souchong, Earl Grey or PG Pyramids?' he proffered through the kitchen hatch.

Her mouth watered suddenly at a smoky reminiscence. She hadn't had Lapsang Souchong for years. 'Lapsang, please. Any lemon?'

'Oh, yes. Lemon.'

She was glad to see he let the tea brew well in the small, elegant teapot. 'Have you visited Gareth recently?'

'Yesterday,' he confirmed, with a smile that displayed his fine dentures.

'He's worried, isn't he?' She sighed, shaking a regretful head.

Harold's smile switched off. 'Is he?'

'He's not used to being so isolated. He's normally in control. You know, finances, car services, household maintenance. He can't believe that I'm capable of writing a cheque for the gas bill. He's even worrying about me driving in and out to see him in hospital.'

Harold put down his china cup and stroked his large nose with one clean forefinger. 'Well. I hadn't realised. Do you worry about driving?'

Conveniently disregarding her initial wobbles, she gave a *pshaw!* of disdain. 'Of course not. But you know Gareth.

And I can tell he's worrying about the cottage, because nobody's been near it since the crash.'

Face clearing, Harold rediscovered his smile. 'But it's only twenty-five minutes from here. I can keep an eye on it.'

She tried not to let the triumph welling in her chest reflect on her face. She smiled gratefully, instead. 'Oh, you are lovely. I suggested it myself. But –' She paused, fidgeting, as if casting about for the right words. She let her voice drop confidentially. 'He won't hear of that, either. He feels so guilty that you had an angina attack because of him and Valerie.'

'But I'm quite over that.'

'I know.' She wrinkled her nose. 'But if I let you trouble yourself he'll go bananas. So I thought that you could give me directions and I could do it.'

'If you think that's best.' Despite his doubtful expression, Harold obligingly reached for a pad and pen. And Diane smiled.

Directions safely in her pocket, she finished her tea. 'Better get on, I have things to do before I visit Gareth.' She felt breathless with jubilation as he followed her down the hall, even if she'd had to fib – all right, lie – to Harold. For that she was sorry but would forgive herself.

He opened the oak front door. 'I hope he appreciates you; some people might feel he didn't quite deserve your support, all things considered.'

She stepped out over the high threshold and turned to kiss Harold's cheek. 'Actually, I can't wait to talk to him.'

Chapter Ten

James tried to feel sympathy for his wife.

But so many times he'd witnessed this same sad scene – Tamzin attempting to talk something over with her mother, Valerie waving it away – and it pissed him off. Valerie didn't dismiss Tamzin through being a bad person and it wasn't completely because Valerie drank more than was good for her or all those around her. It was because Valerie couldn't face up to Tamzin's problems. Better, much, to cram her life with fun and toys.

Valerie was reasonably good at pretending to listen, he acknowledged, observing her features fixed in an expression of interest. But poor Tamz, no matter how much she practised, never quite got the hang of being satisfied with pretence.

'Dad wants me to start my sessions with Lynsay, the therapist, again.'

Valerie smiled.

'But you don't think I need to, do you?' Tamzin waited. 'Mum?'

Valerie smiled more widely. 'Yes, darling.'

'Yes?' Tamzin's mouth turned down.

Valerie hedged. 'What does your father think?'

Tamzin responded patiently, her expression reflecting hope now a dialogue had creaked into being. 'That I should.'

'Well ...' Valerie paused and her eyes slid to the door to the room as if visualising herself slipping her body out of plaster and traction and sneaking out into her lovely fun world again. 'Tell you what, why don't you pop out to the coffee shop and I'll have a little talk with him?'

Tamzin nodded, not quite managing a smile.

When she'd shut the door, James propped his chin on his fist and waited. He knew Valerie wasn't going to talk about Tamzin.

'James.' Her voice was a murmur, her smile just for him.

He remained unmoved.

'Darling.' The smile widened. 'Darling, now I'm getting better, would you mind bringing me in something to liven up this bloody endless squash? Just a half bottle will do, some voddy or something. Or maybe a bottle and I won't have to ask you again for ages.'

'You know not to ask me, Val. Waste of breath.'

'Oh, James ...' She pushed her fingers through her hair. It was bushy and dull, probably she'd been pushing her fingers through it all day. The roots were quite grey, he noticed with a shock, a line marking her last visit to the colourist. She stepped up from wheedle to exasperation. 'Darling, don't be sanctimonious. I'm in pain and I'm terminally bored; a little drink will take the edge off.' Her eyes were still darkly bruised like a racoon's, the rest of her face turning sepia with brown accents. She sighed, shifting slightly, wincing.

'Sorry. No can do. Not unless you can get the doctor to prescribe it along with your painkillers.' There was no point getting angry with her, he reminded himself. It wasn't her – it was the drink.

But sometimes he was angry, unbelievably angry, with the woman that the drink had made her. Like over her mortifying performance at the Furness Durwent party last Christmas when she'd put her head down on the table, in front of everybody from Charlie, the CEO, to the lad in the post room, and gone to sleep. How could he forget the humiliation of hearing Charlie's wife say under her breath, 'Valerie's had too much to drink – again.'

He must remember that it *was* the drink. Not her, the

drink. He should make more effort to get her straightened out.

He tried to sound understanding. 'I'm sorry, Valerie, I can't bring you alcohol. Don't you think –' He decided to plunge in. 'Don't you think that it's time you got help to stop drinking? For your health? For Tamzin? Being in here is bloody awful, I know, but it's the perfect opportunity. You can't smoke and you can't drink. By the time you come home, you'll be off both.'

Valerie snatched up her jug of water, slopping it over a get-well card with a picture of a Spitfire. 'Oh, James, since when have I been an angel? Why expect me to start?'

Abandoning the idea that she might want to pull herself back from an abyss, he produced four envelopes from his inside pocket. 'Post for you.'

Valerie riffled through them, halting, as he'd known she would, at the one with the familiar dark blue and white logo. Hand trembling slightly, she ripped open the envelope and unfolded the letter. Then sagged, miserably. 'The CAA have suspended my licence pending investigation.'

He managed a neutral tone. 'I was afraid that that would be the outcome. They took a blood sample, didn't they?'

She nodded, just barely. All except her bruises had whitened, even her lips.

'You tested positive for alcohol?'

She shrugged, folding the letter over again and holding it tightly so that he couldn't read it.

'Was it a particularly bad day?'

She shrugged again, eyes lowered, a frown nipping a pinch of skin between her eyes.

Impatience reared up. 'God's sake, Valerie! You risked your life and Gareth's. What if you'd had one of our daughters with you? *My* daughters? You have to conquer this –'

Valerie snapped her head up, eyes glittering. 'Don't preach. I hate you when you preach, James.'

He took a deep breath, fighting hot red fury. It was a good time to leave the room. 'I'll collect Tamzin from the coffee shop.'

He stepped out into the carpeted corridor, shoulders rigid. It was not Valerie. It was the drink. He must remember that, when she snapped. It was not her; it was the drink. When she called him darling as if she still meant it – it was not her. It was the drink.

His attention fell on a hurrying figure ahead of him in a green summer dress threaded with white ribbons and his heart leapt. 'Diane!'

The hurrying figure froze.

'Diane?'

Slowly, she turned. 'James.' Diane flicked a smile on and off and turned towards Gareth's room.

A fresh wave of anger hit him. Diane wasn't Valerie and she had no business trying insincere smiles on him. Did she really think he'd be so easily dismissed? Three quick steps and he was able to grab her hand. 'We need to talk.'

At first it seemed she'd twist away but then she gave a tut and allowed herself to be towed past her husband's room and through the two cream doors that led to the comparative privacy of the stairwell.

She dragged her hand free as the doors swung shut behind them. Her eyes were slightly red-rimmed – had she been crying? – and she was pale and unsmiling. He made to pull her up against him but her coldness hit him like a truck.

'I'm sorry that I didn't ring you.' He prepared to explain what had happened, what had been happening, since the night in the back of his Merc. The night that had sustained him ever since.

Her eyebrows rose a fraction, as if she hadn't, until now,

noticed whether he'd rung or not. 'I expect you've been busy.' She sounded remote and polite and she let her hand lie flaccid in his.

He tried to connect with her eyes, to make her understand. 'Tamzin had a really bad week. She's hardly slept and neither have I. I didn't want to call you when I felt so —'

'No explanation necessary.' Diane removed her hand without letting him capture her gaze and turned back to the door, head high but hectic colour telling him that she might be pretending like hell to be cool but, inside, she was fighting mad.

Even as he shot out an arm to halt her, he cursed himself. All wrong, James. Wrong time (too late), wrong place (Gareth and Valerie in nearby rooms). Obviously she wouldn't want to talk about their recent sexual congress here at the top of the stairs with nurses passing the other side of the doors. But he tried to inject into his voice the familiarity there had been between them. 'About that night —'

She paused. Her voice was light. 'It's all right, I know the score.' She ducked his arm and shoved open the door.

'Diane! I should have —'

'We shouldn't have, more to the point. It was stupid and it was wrong.'

'It wasn't! It couldn't be more right.' Aghast, he watched her stalk off, her dress swinging against her bare legs.

He should have rung. Even if Tamzin had yanked him as taut as a violin string with her methods of expressing the deep melancholy that had sucked her into its scary embrace.

The ugly and frightening scores on her arm had been such a disappointment, after her recent good patch, that black moods had swum over him. He'd coped, he always did, but he hadn't wanted to taint his next conversation with Diane with the misery that permeated him so thoroughly.

Sometimes he could only deal with things by

compartmentalising. And so he'd tucked away the wonderful episode, to be brought out later and enjoyed.

With hindsight, one quick call to explain would've been a good plan ...

He shouldn't have presumed upon Diane's understanding, when he hadn't offered her anything to understand.

Chapter Eleven

It was a lovely place. Old red brick and bright white render with a tall chimney and a corner plot hedged in with glossy green privet. Highly desirable in today's market; so quirky and pretty it was an estate agent's dream. *Mature property on the edge of sought-after Whittlesey ... many original features, herringbone brickwork, latticed windows, decorative roof tiles ...*

The lawn was cut and edged, the shrubs trimmed. Diane wondered at the prideful rage that had caused Wendy to turn down such a sweetheart of a house and whether she'd often thought of it when she lived at Brightside or in even more grisly accommodation.

Principles. Harsh masters.

Inside, the cottage was a delight. The brand new leather suite in the sitting room could scarcely be compared with the balding green velour at home, which would've been laughed at by the sexy little stereo, wide-screen television and cream wool carpet that looked so elegant with the gold slubbed-silk curtains and red-tiled hearth gleaming with polish. Upstairs, she made the power shower in the bathroom whoosh into life and bounced on the king-sized bed, its mattress a foot deep, and looked out over a reedy brook to fields of sheep.

She opened every wardrobe and drawer and poked through the contents.

Thoughtfully, she wandered back down to admire the kitchen, fitted with 1920s' style painted cabinets and enamelled appliances. She helped herself to biscuits and tea and settled down at the oak table.

In silence, she drank an entire teapot, four cups – she had

to visit the luxurious black-and-white tiled bathroom – and ate half a packet of chunky Marks & Spencer cookies. The kitchen's colour scheme of cream and lemon with accents of forest green pleased her, all set off by the dried-blood red of the quarry tiles.

Even the china she was snacking from was tasteful, creamware with a pierced pattern edge.

As she ate, savouring the yummy chocolate chips in the cookies, she mulled over everything she'd observed in the delightful cottage. And so wasn't totally surprised to hear the front door open.

Shoulders aching with tension, she listened to somebody humming and rustling in the hall. Then the door swung open and a woman swirled in.

'Stella!' Stella: Ivan's sister-in-law, who Gareth had so often roundly stigmatised.

The small blonde squawked in shock, her hand flying to her throat. '*Diane*. You're not supposed to be here.'

Diane suppressed her desire to drum her fists on the table. 'No, I'm not, am I? I'm not to know about this place, or Gareth's money, or his father or his sister or his nieces. And, now, it seems, not about you. Sit down, Stella. I'll make you some tea.'

Stella hovered, glancing back at the door as if planning flight.

Then she flounced into a chair, folding her arms on the tabletop and regarding Diane warily.

Hospitably, Diane fetched another cup. 'So. Tell me all about your affair with my husband.'

Stella flushed. Her hair was carefully styled to frame her face, her nails were perfect ovals painted pale sugary pink with silver diagonal stripes. 'Gareth got in touch after I split up from my husband. It all went from there.'

'Rewind, Stella. There's more to the story than that.'

Stella met Diane's gaze with more defiance. 'All right. Me and Gareth had a thing, before that. I didn't want to hurt you, honestly, although I don't suppose you'll believe it. We were very, very careful. We even used to bicker at family gatherings, as a smoke screen.'

Diane flinched at just how long, and how easily, they'd fooled her.

'And then we had a big bust up. Gareth didn't speak to me for months.'

'He's good at that.'

'So I began the thing with that teacher to make Gareth jealous. It worked too well and he split on me to the old man.'

Wearily, Diane nodded. 'I hadn't thought about him being instrumental in the ending of your marriage, but it makes sense. Gareth isn't very good at sharing.'

Stella sniffed. 'Well, my marriage went for a burton and me and Gareth got back together. After a bit, Gareth got this place.' She encompassed it with a wave of her hand. 'I'm sorry, Diane.' She did look sorry – in a cross-to-be-caught-out kind of way.

Chin on hand, Diane gazed back. 'I used to like you. I called you my friend.' STM in Gareth's phone book, she thought, suddenly. Stella Teresa Musgrave.

'You don't live here, Stella, do you? You've got some shower gel in the bathroom cabinet and a couple of changes of clothes in the wardrobe but that's as far as he's let you encroach, isn't it?'

Stella looked found out. 'He doesn't live here, either.'

'So far as I can work out, he lives here two days a week plus an occasional evening,' corrected Diane. 'How often do you come? Once or twice a month?'

Stella jumped up, hunting around the kitchen as if looking for something to occupy her. Her voice wobbled. 'It's been horrible not knowing how he is. He borrowed someone's phone and sent me one text but I've been going out of my mind. I … I care for him.'

'I'll make sure he gets his phone.' Hearing her own voice, so cold and composed, a wave of nausea sluiced over Diane. How casual she could be about her husband having an affair. How unsurprised that it was Stella in his bed; Stella, who'd pretended to be Diane's friend. Nobody was reliable.

Not even herself.

And not James. Not James.

Chapter Twelve

Banging the door to Gareth's room open, Diane burst in like a gangster on a death mission.

Gareth jumped. 'Enter,' he drawled, pointing the remote at the television and pressing the off button.

Diane flung herself into the chair, breathless and flushed. 'Shall we stop pretending?'

'About?'

From her back pocket she extracted a navy blue passbook and threw it on the bed. Slowly, he picked it up, smoothing out the slight curve it had taken on from the shape of her behind. He didn't speak. Probably waiting to hear what she had to say.

Which was fine because she had plenty! The words tumbled over each other in their efforts to leave her mouth. 'I've been to see your cottage. Nice, isn't it? Nicer than our house, rather nicer furniture and decor, bigger garden – no vegetables in your garden, I see, but then you don't have to eke out the pennies as I do.

'Two hundred thousand pounds,' she hissed. 'And a house.'

He held on to the passbook, his eyes flickering. 'You wouldn't believe what those bastards took off me in tax –'

She leaned her elbows on the bed. 'Rich people do pay a lot of tax. They pay a lot of everything. Including alimony. And Harold paid the tax up-front and so you *netted* two hundred K, didn't you, Gareth? And as long as Harold doesn't die in the next seven years you won't have to pay tax on the cottage. Harold has just explained it all to me on the phone, very interesting, it was, about the financial specialist who negotiated with the taxman when Harold discovered his eldest child and wanted to make up to him for all the lost years.' Launching herself out of the chair, she prowled around the bed.

'Sit down. Calm down. Let's talk.'

She halted at the foot of his bed. 'OK, let's talk about Stella – who I met at the cottage, today, making herself at home in your absence.'

'She hasn't got a key,' he denied, instantly. And then, 'Oh, Christ!'

'Obviously, you've realised that she has. Your bit on the side.'

Gareth looked sour. 'Must've got a copy cut, somehow.' His injuries tied him to the bed literally and figuratively; the paraphernalia of the sick room, the bedpan and bottle in slots at the side of the bed; he looked exposed.

Abruptly, she returned to the chair and rearranged herself, calmly. Made her voice gentler, musing, though her heart still hammered with fury. 'It all came from me refusing my parents' money, I can see that, even your affair with Stella. But what I don't know is whether you only ever put up with me because you thought money would come your way eventually.'

'Of course I didn't only put up with you –'

'So it was all about revenge?'

He halted. He stroked his swollen jaw. 'See if you can get one of them nurses with some Tramadol, will you?'

'What hurts?'

He laughed, shortly. 'All of it, aching fierce. Head, ribs, hip, leg. And fingers. I need my pain pills and a nap, that'll put me right. They make you feel dead swimmy.' Then, when she didn't move, 'Diane ... love. I'm sorry I didn't tell you about my father, or Valerie or the money. I was just ...' He drew in a breath and winced, theatrically. 'You know

I've never had much. I kind of felt I deserved something.'

Slowly, she stood up. 'And I deserved you to punish me by keeping your sad little fortune to yourself? Revenge – not very attractive, but probably satisfying.' She glanced at the blue building-society passbook that still rested protectively in his good hand. 'What a lot of money you've got, Gareth. What a lot of lovely, lovely money.' She laid his mobile phone on the bedclothes. 'Happy texting.'

Diane rarely cried. But walking across the car park she felt as if her life was nothing but nasty surprises. There was no reason to stay with Gareth. She'd had a bellyful. And were her lies and betrayal OK because of his lies and betrayal? How sordid her marriage had become.

'Is there anything I can do?' A voice came softly.

She jumped, but knew before she turned that it was James. His presence was like a breath on the back of her neck.

He rose from a bench beside a fall of cream and pink honeysuckle. 'I don't like to see you crying.' His eyes were compassionate. The earlier frigid scene between them might never have happened.

'I'm teetering on the brink of thorough self-pity.' She wiped her cheeks, inelegantly, with the backs of her hands.

'There's a lot of it about.' He smiled, ruefully. 'Tamzin's a bit fragile.' He hesitated. 'In fact, I was hoping to see you. I was going to try to force you talk to me again by taking advantage of your kind nature – but I can see now's not the time to ask your advice.'

She sniffed. 'Ask. Might take my mind off poor little me.'

He sighed. 'It's Tamzin. She's been ill for so long. Your daughter had a sickly childhood – how did you cope?'

Diane looked at the frown lines between his worried eyes, and suddenly felt hugely sorry for him. 'She's lucky to have you.'

He grimaced. 'But it's so obviously her mother's approval that's key and Valerie has trouble facing up to Tamzin's situation.'

Somehow, Diane found that she was sitting beside him on the wrought-iron bench. 'Is that where the drink comes in? Valerie trying to avoid problems?'

'I don't know which is the grit and which is the pearl, frankly. Is Tamzin depressed because of Valerie's drinking? Does Valerie drink as a refuge from Tamzin's depression? The drinking seems to have been going on longer than the depression but how much has Tamz been hiding and for how long?'

Diane frowned. Behind the silver birches came the incredibly pure warble of a blackbird. The flowerbed blazed with marigolds, the sun lazed behind a sultry haze as a breeze scampered across the lawns. Pity that on such a perfect day two people should have nothing better to do than wrestle with problems. 'Bryony had good patches when she could race around like other children but there would always be a bad patch around the corner. We kept her away from animals but sometimes all it took was sitting with a girl who had a cat and she'd be in bed on the nebuliser – we bought a second-hand one because we're so far from hospitals in Purtenon St. Paul. And, bless her, she only had to get excited about a treat in the offing, a birthday party or Christmas, and she'd be wheezing. It made her a stoical little thing.'

'But she's OK now?'

'Much improved, thankfully. She began to grow out of it when she was about fifteen. I've never been so grateful for anything. She would never have been able to join this scheme in Brazil a few years ago. But now she can have fun like other people, if she's sensible.'

'That's all you want for them, isn't it? Just to be like other people.' He passed his hand over his hair, making it bristle. It changed colour like velvet, darker when brushed the wrong way. 'Tamzin had a good patch and I got over-optimistic. I think that's why this bad spell hit so hard. She really did have a shitty week, you know. I wasn't making excuses.'

Love for his daughter was in every line of his face. Diane identified with his corresponding lack of concern for himself – Parent's Disease, she called that, having had a hefty dose. 'She missed her fitting on Tuesday.'

His eyes darkened. 'But you can give her time, can't you? I'm sure contact with you is good for her. I don't know when she'll make another appointment, though.'

She let herself smile at the way his eyes were trying to compel her to agree – but not for himself, for Tamzin. She was still mighty pissed off at him, but this wasn't the moment to act it. This was about Tamzin. 'How about if I were to bring the fitting to her? She might co-operate if I just turn up.'

His eyes brightened. 'I ought to refuse; I live in Webber's Cross, so it wouldn't be a quick trip for you – but it would be brilliant. Thanks,' he added softly. His eyes smiled.

Despite the unresolved tension between them, she touched the warmth of his hand as she got up to leave. For an instant, his fingers tangled with hers.

Tamzin was in her favourite spot – rolled in her duvet like a giant larvae.

Gazing at the curtains, gold on pink and still drawn shut, she picked out the segment of pattern that looked like a wild-maned lion resting his chin on his paws. She saw things like that. In the grain of her bathroom floor there was a goblin, winking, and on the wallpaper in the hall a bishop, in profile.

Staring at the lion sometimes helped on a day, like today, when her organs felt too heavy for her body, except for her stomach, which felt hollow. A day when memories of the Coven made her inert with misery.

And though she had heard two knocks at her door, she kept her gaze fixed on the lion. It would be Dad. He'd knock once more and then look in. Check on her. She wished he wouldn't.

The third knock was louder and more impatient.

Then the door flew open. 'Hello, Tamzin!'

Startled, Tamzin watched as Diane, billowing with fabric, unloaded a basket onto the bedroom chair. 'I've come to do your fittings.' The curtains swished back and were snagged deftly behind their ties. From the basket, Diane plucked a tape measure to loop around her neck and a pincushion to clip onto her wrist. She looked at Tamzin expectantly.

Tamzin pushed back the duvet, slowly, and rolled to the edge of the bed. 'I don't really feel like it.'

'But I can't get on without a fitting. Are those pyjamas?'

Looking down at herself, Tamzin had to admit that they were. A white top with a piebald pony and non-matching yellow seersucker bottoms. Baggy.

'You'll be OK in jeans on the bottom half but can you put a decent bra on the top?' With an impatient movement, Diane consulted her watch then turned to the window. 'I'll admire your garden while you change.'

Tamzin gazed at the safety of her tumbled bed.

'Tell me when you're ready.'

Sighing, she clambered to her feet and opened her underwear drawer. Lying still for so long had left her feeling creaky, leaden.

She managed to find a bra and a pair of knickers respectable enough to be seen. From the wardrobe she selected a pair of black jeans that hung from her hips. She tried not to look at herself in the mirror, at her arms. Mingin. She curled up inside. 'I don't want to do this today.'

'But I'm here today.'

Sullenly, Tamzin climbed into her clothes. 'OK. Ready.'

Diane swung around.

Tamzin stared at the floor.

There was one still moment.

Then Diane swept up the pink fabric. 'This is the double-breasted shirt, do you remember? I've set the sleeves in but they're only tacked. I want to see how we are for length – left arm, please. Can you come to the mirror? Fasten the buttons, then I can see if I've brought the darts up far enough.'

Diane's busy fingers twitched and smoothed. 'The embroidery will be *here*, if you remember, with the little rings incorporated into it. I've done an experimental piece on this swatch, look, and I'm really pleased. Good, yes? I think the darts are OK, don't you? But the cuffs need lifting about half-an-inch.'

The fabric felt smooth against her skin. Tamzin risked a glance at her reflection; more sufferable now she was covered. The colour was well cool; in it, she didn't look like the neighbourhood ghost. 'It looks nice!' she observed, unwillingly captivated.

Diane laughed. 'No need to sound so surprised. Of course it looks nice, what with my sewing skills and your good looks.' She swooped suddenly on a wide-bristled hairbrush lying on the dusty dressing-table. 'Do you mind if I get your hair out of the way? Then I can see the shoulders properly.'

Tamzin looked away from the mat of old hair in the brush. Mingin. Meekly, she allowed her hair to be brushed, pulled back and swished up onto her head, not even complaining when the knots were tugged.

'What gorgeous hair you have – I wish mine had more colour.'

'But yours is so pearly blonde!'

'At least I've avoided going silver – so far. We'd be like the hymn about daisies and buttercups, then – me silver and you gold. Probably uncool, now, but it was my favourite when I was a child. Just let your arms hang while I pin.'

Scrutinising the collar and smoothing the shoulders, Diane began to sing, under her breath. 'Daisies are our si-ilver, buttercups our gold ...' Her voice was OK and she sang the hymn right through, all about diamond raindrops and emerald leaves, as she helped Tamzin carefully out of the pink shirt. Hymns reminded Tamzin of her primary school, a traditional private school where *All Things Bright and Beautiful* or *Morning Has Broken* contributed to the cosiness, along with blue gingham and grey serge. It had been a silken nest compared to university.

The other shirt was the delicate colour of clotted cream and the fabric as soft as tissue. Diane held it up. 'Don't be disappointed in the plainness, at this stage. The over-layer of gold gauze is going to bring out the lovely colour of your hair. Slide into it carefully ... there. That round neck suits you, Tamz. Your dad's invited me to stay for supper – are you in tonight?'

As if Tamzin was ever anything but 'in tonight', except for visits to the hospital. 'I should think so.'

'Great. Because I'd like to start on the decorated jeans, so we can throw ideas around. Your dad says he's grilling steaks. Can he cook?'

Tamzin watched Diane's efforts through the mirror, with growing interest. 'He can do anything he decides to. Ask him to make mustard sauce as well – it's wicked.'

Chapter Thirteen

Part of Diane's long hair was bunched up on the top of her head and the rest was a moon river down her back. Pleasurably, James turned over the memory of her hair tumbling around her nakedness in the back of his car. What had happened had happened only once and maybe he ought to be glad that his complicated life hadn't been sent spinning by it happening again. But he would really like to see her like that again. Daily.

Although it made him feel odd to see Diane here, in Valerie's home in the upmarket village of Webber's Cross, he couldn't stop watching her eating her steak and salad as if it was a treat – in stark contrast to Tamzin, who treated every mouthful as a trial. Finally, Diane sat back with a sigh. 'You were right about the mustard sauce, Tamzin, it was wicked. And the chocolate ice-cream with mini doughnuts, even wickeder.'

Tamzin just smiled. From her lack of participation in the conversation and her pallor, James could tell that she was shattered. Soon, she'd retreat to her room. But at least Diane's breezy presence had dragged her out of it for a few hours.

Sure enough, it was only five minutes later that Tamzin climbed slowly to her feet. 'I'm tired.'

Diane looked up. 'Going to bed? 'Night, sweetheart.'

'Night, Diane.' Tamzin wafted through the open French doors and marked her progress through the house with a trail of illuminated windows.

James, hoping that Diane wouldn't make Tamzin's departure a sign that she ought to be turning for home herself, poured her a fresh glass of fruit juice. 'She had a good evening. I haven't seen her so bright for a fortnight.'

'How do you feel about the quantity she ate?' Diane slapped at one of a squadron of bugs out on its evening sortie.

'For her, it was OK. Most of a small steak and salad, plus a small portion of dessert.'

Diane pulled a face. 'It's funny to think that Bryony and Tamzin are exactly the same age because they don't seem it. And Bryony would have eaten eight times what Tamzin ate. It seemed incredibly little.'

'I suppose it does, when you're not used to it.' The 'small' steak that Tamzin hadn't quite managed to finish had begun as the size of a modest burger; the salad consisted of a cherry tomato and two leaves of frilly lettuce.

'I could have polished it off in three mouthfuls,' said Diane, feelingly. 'I pigged out on a steak like a butcher's buttock, a mound of salad and coleslaw and what felt like half a French stick. Was it tactless to take a second dessert?'

He laughed at her guilty expression. 'Not at all. It's fine to eat normally in front of her. The only rule, really, is not to pressurise her to do the same.' The light from the house fell on one side of Diane's face. She looked relaxed, her legs stretched out, her elbows on the arms of the chair and her top clinging interestingly across her chest.

The house, once the vicarage, lichened grey stone with a slate roof and a gravel drive, stood in the centre of the village on a little square green. The village shop and the pub, The Old Dog, stood opposite, and provided them with a background noise of cars pulling up and their doors slamming. He crossed one leg lazily over the other and thought how comfortable he felt, lounging here on a balmy evening with Diane, listening to the rise and fall of her voice and her occasional flickers of laughter.

'It's been a pleasant evening,' she said, as if reading his thoughts. 'All I would have done at home alone is think what a shit Gareth has been.'

He could have made an anodyne response about enjoying her company. But he never let a sleeping dog lie if he thought he'd achieve more by giving it a good old shake. He let his voice drop. 'Is everything all right, after that night? Do we have any pregnancy worries?'

Diane was reaching for her glass and it wobbled alarmingly as she swung around to frown at him. 'I thought it was too good to be true that you were co-operating with me to forget that madness,' she whispered.

'How can I?' he murmured. Forget her hands, her mouth, the satin of her body, her pleasure in the act? In him?

She swallowed a mouthful of juice. 'Yes. All fine.'

'And you know ... how?' The light from the window hadn't fallen on him so she wouldn't be able to see his smile as he delved into the subject she so obviously wished left alone.

She sent him a darkling look. 'Dr Cooke is a sensible woman and pleasantly unshockable about prescribing the morning-after pill.'

'Good.' He paused long enough to let her think she might be off the hook. Then, 'You've never had to consult her about anything ... like *that*, before?'

'Scandalous, do you mean?' she returned, smartly. 'Or perhaps a 43-year-old woman who's had a one-night stand isn't scandalous, in your world? Maybe it's just what people do? And move on?'

'I feel terrible that I didn't phone you. It wasn't that I didn't want to, but Tamzin's been –' Having made the opportunity to talk about it, he hesitated, not knowing how to go on.

Then Diane sighed and the tension seemed to seep from

her. 'Yes. I can see how she's been. I'm glad you warned me before I went in – about her arms. I had no idea.' Her voice was sadder than tears.

He watched her shiver. The ladder of scabs and scars that ran up the soft inner of each of Tamzin's arms made him feel like that, too. Some fresh, some old, some no more than white or pink cords. Each scar an ugly statement he couldn't completely understand or a question he wasn't hearing. 'She tries to hide it. Self-harmers do that, they find it deeply personal.'

For a moment she touched his hand, her fingers cool in the evening air. 'I'm so sorry, James. Even though you'd warned me I'm afraid it took me by surprise. I don't think I quite carried on as if I hadn't noticed. I'd like to understand what makes her do that.'

He laughed, mirthlessly. 'So would I.' He fell silent. Tamzin was that rare thing – a problem he couldn't fix.

Diane reached for her bag and made an obvious attempt to change the subject. 'Look, I bought a mobile phone, yesterday. I've made one call on it to check that it works but I'm useless with it, really.' She held the flat black phone out for his inspection.

He took it. 'Sensible to have one.' His thumb moved over the touch screen. 'There. The first entry in your phone book.' He turned the screen so that she could see **James mobile** and his number. The thumb went into action again and he showed her: **James home.**

To view the screen properly, she had to draw close to him. And if he shifted his hand a little – even closer. 'So they're there forever, are they?'

'Yes, you press *menu*, then *phone book*, then the first letter of the name. See? Then press the green button.' After a pause a muffled buzzing soaked out into the evening air. He reached into his pocket and brought out his BlackBerry.

'Hello?'

She giggled, taking her own phone back and putting it to her ear. 'Hello!'

'Now I can put you in my phone book.' He showed her how to save the number and typed in **Diane mobile** beside it.

She played for several minutes inputting phone numbers. 'Home ... Freddy, my brother ... Rowan, the mean git who sells some of my garments at his shop ... the hospital.

'Right,' she said. 'Let's be adventurous. How do I send a text?'

'Not difficult.' He bent his head next to hers. 'Tap this icon, select me from your phone book, type the message, then press *send*.' In a few moments, his phone vibrated against his leg and a little envelope flashed on the screen, **Diane mobile** showing in his inbox.

They laughed at the message, '*I have a mobile!*'

Then, under the cloak of darkness, he took her hand.

She stopped laughing and examined the way his fingers enveloped hers. All the hairs on his arms stood up. Something in her faraway expression brought back the way she'd looked down at him when he'd been inside her, the wonder, the lust, that volcano of pleasure that erupted for him. The way she'd kissed him when she'd come down after the explosion, the sweetest, deepest, most perfect kiss. He remembered how to move, how to touch her to drive her crazy.

Gently, he squeezed her fingers. Even that chaste contact felt good. 'I wish I'd rung you when I should have. I wanted to see if we could make each other happy – but I was caught in the middle of Tamzin's black cloud and I felt as if I'd contaminate you with it. I had no right to ask, anyway. I'm stuck here and could never give you the relationship you deserve. And I'm being a presumptuous prick in disregarding Gareth. But I want you to know how I feel.

You don't have to say anything, I just want you to know.' His fingers tightened. 'I feel good just being with you. I think about you all the time. And want you. Our couple of hours at Farcet Fen was an oasis of pleasure during a shitty time. Your husband doesn't deserve you because he's an arse. I don't suppose I deserve you any more than he does – and I'm just as married as you are – but none of those things stop me wanting you.'

She sounded strained. 'I took it as a one-night stand.'

His heart began a long slow slide south. 'If that's what you want, it will be. Our secret.'

Abruptly, she closed her fingers around his, suddenly breathless. 'Let me think about it.'

A big meal, a long and emotional day, she was sleepy. She kept the car windows open and Lily Allen playing loudly on the stereo to keep her awake as she drove the hypnotically long, dark lanes.

Home. Her neighbours' houses were bright with windows where hers was dark.

Across the kitchen, through the dining room, up the stairs; a one-minute shower and she cleaned her teeth and fell into bed. She wasn't going to think about James and the words she'd been shocked to hear emerging from her mouth ... *Let me think about it*. She was going to sleep.

The phone rang. She groaned. *Stop ringing*! It stopped. Thankfully, she drifted towards sleep.

The phone rang.

Swearing, she rolled out of bed and staggered down the stairs. 'Hello?'

'Mum! Guess what? I'm coming home!'

Diane blinked, trying to engage her brain. 'Bryony, what's the matter? Are you ill?'

Bryony's laughter rocked around the earpiece, shrill and

excited. 'Dad rang me and we had a big heart to heart. He explained why he's been so odd. Isn't it cool about his father tracking him down? I've got a grandfather! Dad says he's sweet. It's so good that Dad finally told you. I saw him with a woman and I thought he was having an affair. It was so scary, even though he kept saying he wasn't. But she was his sister. He's *explained*. This is so good!'

'You saw him?' Diane repeated, blankly.

'And it was horrible thinking that he was having an affair – I mean, what was I supposed to do? Tell you and betray him? Or be quiet and betray you? I felt such a cow. But Dad wants me to come home and, like, see him, so we can all be together again, the three of us. I'm taking indefinite unpaid leave. Dad says he'll pay my fare. Isn't that cool? I'm so glad that you and Dad are OK. I've been feeling so bad, thinking that he had a girlfriend. I felt so bad about you.'

'Did you?' said Diane, shaken by the enormity of Bryony having known. Even if she hadn't known what she'd thought she'd known, she'd kept a huge secret. No wonder she'd been keen to get far, far away from home.

'I thought you guys were going to split up, I couldn't bear it. It was horrible.'

After a moment, Diane heard herself say, 'I can see how it was for you.' That was Parent's Disease again – sympathising with your child even when the same set of circumstances were so much worse for you. But she shoved the hurt to one side. Bryony was coming home. *Bryony was coming home*!

And she was thrilled that Diane and Gareth weren't going to split up.

Oh.

Chapter Fourteen

The wind thrashed her ponytail as she locked the car in the car park near Peterborough Cathedral. Diane wasn't going to see Gareth today. She'd sent him a text message, feeling, as she laboriously worked through the *txt talk* guide helpfully supplied with her phone, that she was finally in the twenty-first century.

Will nt b able 2 visit u 2day, have 2 c Rowan. C u l8r.

No kisses, no *Love Diane*. She felt neither kissy nor lovey. Every fresh revelation forced her old feelings for her husband through the mincer. And now he'd manoeuvred to bring Bryony home, which – obviously – was wonderful, because, ever since Bryony left for the steamy heat of Brazil, Diane had carried an ache around that was both hollow and heavy. But she was under no illusions that he'd done it to ease Diane's aches. Or even his own, although he missed Bryony, too.

No, he'd done it to make it more difficult for Diane to leave him.

And he wouldn't want Diane to leave him in case she took half of his stash with her.

Bryony, a forgiving little soul, had been moved by her dad's crocodile tears and intrigued by acquiring a grandfather and assorted other relatives. But it wasn't quite the same for Diane.

She set out for Rowan's shop in Rivergate Arcade, crossing at the lights into that segment of Bridge Street with a hundred other people.

Rowan Chater bought her garments for his idiosyncratic little shop, on what seemed a whimsical basis and with an air of doing her a kindness. She detested his condescension but income was income, so she'd put together a small collection of five pairs of decorated canvas trousers and ten colourful tops for the coming autumn season.

In the shop, Rowan, perched on a wooden stool behind the counter, was talking to an over made-up woman with a small child. 'Oh, hullo,' he drawled unenthusiastically, when he noticed Diane.

'Hi.' She gave what she hoped was a confident smile, hating having to hover with the heavy garments while he took his time nattering.

When woman and child finally left, Rowan gave a tiny sigh. Short stubble defined his jaw and head; he had seal-like eyes and a misleadingly sweet smile that he rarely bestowed upon Diane. His effete speech reminded her a little of Bryony, the way he emphasised at least one word in a sentence and used a final upward intonation as if statements were questions. 'Shall I have a look?' he suggested with the air of doing his good deed for the day.

Silently, slowly, he turned over each item. Diane ran her eyes over the racks, the torso mannequins, the garments hanging sideways with broomsticks through the sleeves.

None of her work, boasting the little label in the neck with *DRJ* embroidered in turquoise on a bright yellow ground, was currently displayed in the shop. She tried a bit of casual self-promotion. 'The last batch all sold, did it?'

He turned another garment. 'In the end.'

She subsided. She didn't want to ferret for details only to find that he'd had to slash the price to get her stuff off his hands.

'Mm,' he conceded. 'Good colour choices, anyway.' He always seemed to have to cast about for some detail to praise. He folded back the final garment – a bronze linen tunic embroidered with a goldfish, bubbles rising in the form of clear washers. Sighed. Raised his eyebrows. Tapped his fingertips on the counter.

Diane held her breath.

'Yes, OK,' he agreed, eventually. 'I can usually put a "Hand made" label on them and make them go. Send me an invoice.' He wrote a figure on the back of a brown paper bag. He always did that, as if it might invoke bad luck to speak money aloud. It was exactly the same price per garment as the last lot. And several prior to that.

Diane bit down on her disappointment and the urge to point out the 70% mark up he put on the garments. The important thing was that Rowan was already writing a cheque.

'Overheads are escalating,' he mentioned, conversationally.

'Mine, too.' Perhaps she could find an outlet where the proprietor didn't make her feel as if she ought to be so damned bloody grateful all the time. Cambridge, maybe? There was money, there.

To cheer herself up she found a coffee shop and ordered a cappuccino. It came in a glass cup with not enough sprinkles but she settled at a table near the window to savour it as she watched the people milling along Bridge Street.

An imperious series of beeps from her pocket almost made her drop the cup. She plucked out her phone. **James mobile**. After a bit of fumbling, she opened the text. Tamzin @ Nat's. Need dinner companion 2nite. How u fixed?

Thoughtfully, she laid the phone on the table and returned to her coffee, staring out at mothers with buggies, lads in jeans that swung like satchels from skinny backsides. The planters that decorated the street were filled with the kind of geraniums you're supposed to call pelargoniums, as jolly and scarlet as Bryony's favourite nail varnish.

The phone beeped again. Diane wondered if she'd ever be the nonchalant phone user that everyone else above the age of six seemed to be. I promise 2 behave. Strictly no pouncing. Will pick u up@8. She grinned and ordered another cappuccino. She always considered herself a strong woman but she discovered herself quite powerless to resist the idea of dinner with James, with his dark grey eyes and lightning smiles.

When Tamzin's phone rang, the next morning, **Dad** showed on the screen. Tamzin rolled herself a little more tightly in the covers of Nat's spare bed before she answered.

James sounded as if he'd been up for hours. Which he probably had. 'I can drive you to Diane's today, as it's Saturday.'

Unfairly, she snapped, 'Oh, *Dad*, I can drive myself. It's a good day. You can't be in control all the time.' And she pressed 'end call' on her phone.

Then she felt mean. She wasn't fair to him. She knew that. On bad days she wanted him to be the man with the answers even while she resented him for having them. But, on good days, she'd shoo him away.

Still, half-an-hour later, she was parking beside the hedge outside Diane's redbrick house. She knew, now, to knock on the side door. It seemed better manners to go to the front door but it was swollen shut and if you rattled the pitted brass knocker Diane had to come out of the side door and find you, or shout directions through the letterbox.

'Great to see you, Tamzin.' Diane beamed as she opened the door. She glanced over Tamzin's shoulder.

Tamzin giggled and gestured to the empty space behind her. 'Look! No Dad.'

Diane's eyes returned to Tamzin and she smiled. 'So I see. It's great you could make it. Let's take some tea up to the workroom with us and we can start decorating your jeans.'

Tamzin whisked a bag from behind her back and

flourished a pair of soft grey Levis. 'I'm all ready.'

'Wonderful – and don't you look good, today? Your hair looks great with that pretty dress.'

Diane's approval puffed Tamzin up. The blue cotton dress was one Alice had bought in an optimistic moment. The ruching that had given her an elephantine bum suited Tamzin's snakey hips.

'Oh. My. God.' Tamzin paused on the threshold to Diane's workroom. It was more of an Aladdin's Cave than even on her last visit. 'Diane, I want bling-bling buttons like those.' She pointed at six bright, glass-encrusted buttons knotted together with wool and hooked over a nail in the wooden shelves that could have been the store of a giant magpie. Folded fabric, funny felty white stuff, braid in twenty colours, sequins, buttons, beads, buckles … It was a treasure trove.

'You have those, if you want. Don't think they're right for either of the tops I've fitted you for, though. Maybe something darker?' Diane looked at Tamzin with her head on one side. 'Dusky red? That would suit you. Do you like zips? Or, I know!' Diane seized a pad and scrabbled for a pencil. 'How about, instead of a normal seam we have a run of clear circlets up the outside of the sleeve? They'll go well with the buttons.' She sketched rapidly, then turned the pad to Tamzin.

'Oh, yay, that'll look so cool!' Tamzin paused. She checked her sleeves were rolled down. 'You'll see my arms between the circlets –'

'Only on the outside, here, from your shoulder. That'll be all right. And we could make this a bib neck, three buttons either side running vertically.' She sketched again.

'Brilliant. You're so kind.' Tamzin gazed at the drawing. Her throat was suddenly tight with tears.

Diane took the cream shirt from its hanger. 'Kind! This is

my business, Tamz. I send bills to Daddy. Now, you rootle through those shelves. There are catalogues on the bottom shelf, look through them, too.'

Willing the tears to subside, Tamzin examined tubes labelled *bugle beads* and *seed beads*, silver, gold, scarlet, black and some blue that shone purple depending which way you looked at them. Depression was shitty. Sometimes she was so sad that she couldn't cry, descending instead into a bleak and frozen landscape where tears might've been a relief. But make her happy and she cried? Er, right ...

She picked up a big black buckle that fastened with three circular plates like her old school belt, stroking the satin matt finish.

Behind her, the sewing machine began to chatter. She glanced around. Diane was absorbed, pale head bent over the cream shirt as it passed smoothly under the machine's foot.

Hooks and eyes, poppers, Velcro dots, rings the colours of brass, pewter, silver, gold. Thin cord. Tamzin popped open an old circular biscuit tin and found a feast of embroidery silks, a hundred colours from the subtlest silvery blue to flaming scarlet and lime green. Broad black ribbon gleamed dully at her, and she put it aside with the buckle.

'Got some stuff that appeals to you?' Diane snapped off the threads and examined the stitching on the cuff.

'These?' Tamzin showed her the black buckle and the ribbon.

'OK.' Diane put the two things together on her work table. 'Can you pass me that red tin? It's filled with buckles.' She flipped the top off and shook the contents. 'What else do you like?'

Tamzin peered in, her reflection slithering around in the battered silver interior. 'This ... and this.' A silver S buckle, a black one without a prong but with serrations at the sides, a buckle that looked like a flower with six petals and one with two prongs.

Diane picked up the original black buckle. 'The obvious thing to do with this is to make a belt. Let me look for some webbing of some kind. The rest of the buckles can be threaded with ribbon and then fixed all over the jeans. The S should go in the small of your back, I think, and then down the side – Oh – here's George.'

Tamzin followed her gaze out of the window to where a tall lad with a baseball cap was locking up a deep blue car outside. The cap hid his face. He turned, took two strides, hurdled the hedge and loped up the path.

Diane grinned. 'You must meet George.' She paused, wrinkling her forehead. 'He's your cousin. Or your half-cousin or half-second-cousin or something. Gareth is half-brother to both your mother and George's father so you must be related, somehow.' She beamed. 'George is one of my favourite people.'

'Oh.' Tamzin felt suddenly flat. If Diane got chattering to this George about people Tamzin didn't know, Tamzin would no longer have Diane's attention. She glanced at her watch. 'I'll say hello before I leave.'

'You'll like George,' said Diane, as if plucking Tamzin's misgivings from the air. 'Bryony adores him. They used to be in a band together, Jenneration. Do you like Indie Pop?'

'Can't bear it.'

She skulked downstairs behind Diane and hovered silently while Diane stood on her tiptoes to hug George. 'You jumped my hedge.'

'Gates are for boring dudes.' George flipped off his baseball cap and threw it on the seat of a chair.

Tamzin felt her jaw drop.

George's hair was the colour of a lion's mane and clung around his head in quills, framing his eyes and pointing up his impressive cheekbones. Soft, youthful stubble defined the slant of his jaw. His eyes were brown-gold. They settled on Tamzin and she felt the tiny hairs on the back of her neck stand up.

Then his lips curved slowly. 'All right?'

She felt herself flush but she managed the accepted response. 'Not bad. You?'

'Yeah. Good.' His gaze remained on her.

She was glad all over again for Alice's dress. And that she'd washed her hair.

Diane began to explain. 'This is Tamzin, who –'

'Yeah, I get who she is. I'm still trying to get my head round Uncle Gareth having, like, this whole other family, though. Amazin'.'

'I'm still getting my head around it myself. Sit down, you two.'

Tamzin forgot all about leaving after saying hello and chose a kitchen chair. Presently, lunch was set before her and she didn't even realise what she'd eaten until the soup bowl was empty and all that was left of her roll was crumbs. But, apparently, this had happened while George attempted to explain the Jenner family tree on the inside cover of Diane's address book, and Tamzin put in the missing family on the other half of the page, beginning with Pops and ending with herself, Natalia and Alice.

'So my grandmother was naughty with your grandfather,' observed George.

Facing one another over the kitchen table they talked non-stop whilst Diane cleared up and reflected on how it would reduce James's stress levels if Tamzin had more days like this.

Much of his conversation over dinner, last night, had revolved around Tamzin. Parent's Disease. Diane understood. She'd spent so many anxious years on tenterhooks over

Bryony's health.

The restaurant James had chosen backed onto Stamford's water meadows and from the rear terrace they'd watched the ducks flying circuits and coming in to land as the sky turned purple and dark pink. 'When one of your children is ill it's like a spiky burden you carry around with you,' he'd said. 'I think about Tamzin all the time. I expect I talk about her all the time.' His dark grey eyes crinkled. 'But you've seen her on a bad day.'

'It's such a shame for her – for you all. Hasn't she worked or studied since she left uni two years ago?'

'Some days she won't get out of bed.'

'But she has nothing to get out of bed for. I thought that one of the symptoms of depression is feeling purposeless – isn't that aggravated by her genuinely not having a purpose?'

'The therapist said occupation can help some people. But it's a vicious circle. She couldn't hold down a job or attend a college because she's too ill.'

They'd talked for hours: how excited Diane was about Bryony coming home – perhaps as early as next week – and how proud James was of Natalia and Alice. 'Especially of how good they are with their little sister ... And now I've brought the conversation back around to Tamzin.'

He'd driven her home at a reasonable hour, the journey in the soft black night seeming woefully short. Diane felt the back seat like a spectre and she almost expected it to rear up behind her booming: 'You can't ignore what happened here!'

But she had tried her best to, even when James kissed her goodnight. It had begun as such a quick kiss – his lips brushing briefly over hers. But then he'd gathered her up against him and let the kiss deepen, slowwww downnnn, sending goosebumps straight down her back. He was so warm. Her fingers had tangled themselves in his hair and she hadn't wanted the kiss to stop.

And all day she'd nursed the memory of the evening like a happy secret.

'How about we go down to one of the village pubs? Fancy a swift half at The Dragon, Diane? *Diane*?'

She jumped out of her daydream. 'Not me today, George. Too much to do. I said I'd visit Gareth and I've just seen the time. Take Tamzin.'

'Yeah, good one. OK?' he said to Tamzin.

'OK,' she said, as if it didn't matter one way or another.

'So, are you into Indie pop?'

'Oh, like, yeah,' Tamzin breathed.

'My band's playing a gig on Friday. How about you come? We're Jenneration.'

'Could do. I'll visit my mum in the afternoon then I'll be free in the evening.'

George banged open the kitchen door. 'So we could meet up for pizza, if you don't mind hanging around while we sound check? See you, Diane.'

'Bye, Diane. Yes, that would be OK. I'll give you my mobile number and you can text me …' The door shut behind them.

'Bye, then.' Diane plunged the plates into white, glistening suds, letting the tangy smell of Fairy Liquid rise around her in a cloud of steam. Maybe a little attention from a looker like George would do more for Tamzin than doctor's pills.

It was brilliant to see Tamzin looking so much like a normal twenty-year old.

Even if it meant that Tamzin hadn't needed James to accompany her to Diane's house when, actually, Diane had been looking forward to seeing him. Even though she knew it was quite the wrong thing to do.

Chapter Fifteen

Chadda-chadda-chadda. The now familiar sensations of lift, the seat kicking against his legs and back as the helicopter pauses in hover and the rotor chops the air.

Then they're being snatched up and hurled towards the trees as if by a giant trebuchet. He bellows, 'Put us down! Put us down! You idiot, why are you flying like this?'

Valerie, chewing gum, turns. Gareth's image is reflected in her aviator glasses but she ignores his howls.

'Watch out, Alpha Zulu, you're close to the Eastern perimeter trees,' *warns the unseen air-traffic controller.*

Higher, closer come the trees, thrashing, tossing in the wash from the rotor. 'Climb. Climb. Climb! Climb now! Valerie, climb!' *Gareth clutches his seat and thinks of Diane, what she'd say if she could see him perched in this mechanical dragonfly.*

'Shut up. There's only one pilot on this aircraft.'

'Alpha Zulu! You are too CLOSE –'

Abruptly, Valerie yanks the cyclic lever back until there is only sky. With horrible inevitability she shoves it forward again and grenades and rifles fill his head as the helicopter hits the trees, plunging and lurching like a furious horse. It pauses … then pitches earthwards as if spat from a cyclone.

Valerie screams and screams …

Gareth's head snaps helplessly forward, back, and his legs and arms flail into Valerie's as Valerie's limbs windmill uncontrollably into his.

The engine shrieks and the machine thrashes itself to death against the unforgiving earth.

Sirens. Shouting, closer. Running feet. Panted words.

'There's fuel every-bloody-where. Valerie North has managed to miss the sky.'

Gareth can hear himself groaning.

A flash of high-viz clothing appears in a gap in what was left of the acrylic bubble. 'All right, mate. You're all right. The paramedics will have you out. Can you hear me? We're the fire crew, and we'll see you're OK. You stay with me, all right? The paramedics will get you to a hospital.'

The groans get louder. Hospital! Sensation floods in – the cage of his chest is on fire, his fingers have been slammed in a car door, his arms wrenched from their sockets, a giant has stamped on his legs before giving his head a proper kicking.

Diane's going to find out — !

Gareth smashed into sweaty consciousness with his lips stretched into a silent squeal of fear, not the rotor but his heartbeat's *whump-whump-whump* filling his ears.

He couldn't move – his fingers or his arm or his legs; he was fast in a giant spider's web. He was paralysed, he was stuck, he was helpless … No. No, he was hurt.

Gradually, he focused on the pins protruding from the ends of the fingers bound into plastic troughs and at the prison of white plaster immobilising his legs. The hospital bed. And then Stella, sitting on the edge of a visitor's chair, her eyes huge, frightened, fixed upon him. 'You were dreaming, Gareth.' Her voice was an uneasy whisper. Moisture glistened in the minute lines that were beginning to hatch the soft flesh below her eyes.

He licked his lips, trying to calm the galloping in his chest. 'Yes. Yes, I must've been.' His ribs ached; he'd probably been trying to flail around. Come to that, most things ached. Where was that bloody Tramadol?

Stella neatened her blonde waves with nervous fingers. 'I was scared you might hurt yourself. I nearly called the nurse.'

'Glad you didn't,' he said, shortly. 'I don't want a load of nurses standing round while I squeak like a guinea pig, do I?'

Stella pulled her chair closer. Her lips trembled. 'Gareth – oh, poor you!' She stroked his face with the back of her hand and then with her fingertips. Stella had sexy little hands and took care of them with hand cream and rubber gloves. He had a thing about Stella's hands. They were white and soft where Diane's were red and scratchy with housework and pins and needles. Whenever Stella touched him his skin would shiver in response.

He closed his eyes and thought of her undressing him, stroking each part of his nakedness as it was revealed so that by the time she was ready to slide his boxers off he was primed to explode and would be quite unable to undress her slowly in return. Instead he'd haul her from her clothes, making her squeal and giggle. Marvellous skin she had, soft as rose petals and as fragrant, because she was a pampering sort of woman who moisturised her entire body every day. White and velvety as marshmallow, delicious little thing.

Her soothing fingers stroked his cheekbones and what had been the hollows of his cheeks, his swollen chin and jaw line, his temples.

'Poor you,' she repeated. She stroked every millimetre of skin: face, neck, hands – so gently over the damaged one. The hip and thigh between gown and plaster, and Gareth felt himself sink into the bed as if it were angel hair. With him, all trace of Stella's usual bolshiness evaporated to leave only softness and compliance. She was his indulgence.

'You know that Diane knows?' Her voice was still a whisper, her tip-toeing fingers still working their magic.

'Yes.' His lips barely moved.

'She was lying in wait for me, all scary and sarcastic, you know how she gets. I couldn't think of a credible lie. But …

perhaps better that she knows? She seemed to take it quite calmly.'

He thought back to Diane hurling threats and accusations at him like flaming arrows, lighting the room with her rage, searing him with disgust, her single plait rearing from high on her head and swinging like a grumpy cobra as she strode around the room. An in-built stressometer.

Despite himself, he smiled. 'She wasn't very calm when I saw her.'

The stroking fingertips returned to his forehead. 'That must have been horrible for you. But the worst's over.'

'Where did you get the key?'

The cool fingers halted momentarily, then returned to his cheeks, careful, soft. 'The key?'

'To my house, in Whittlesey.'

The caresses moved to his ears. He had sensitive ears. If she wanted to get round him she always began there with her fingertips and perhaps her warm, quivering tongue. He let himself be temporarily distracted, even wondering whether the doctor had been right about the huge number of blood vessels around the pelvic area and a broken pelvis being likely to affect the ability to get an erection.

He couldn't make love to her. But perhaps her mouth –

No, probably not.

'It was the key you gave me, Gareth.'

'Once. Once to let the carpet fitters in. You were supposed to put it back in the kitchen drawer.' He kept his eyes shut.

'I must've forgotten.' She sounded defensive. 'Then when I heard through Megan and Ivan about your accident I thought you'd want me to go and check that everything was all right –'

He opened his eyes. 'Even though you might bump into my dad or my wife?'

She looked anxious. 'Not your wife, Gary. Diane didn't

know about the cottage –'

'So how come she was sitting there waiting for you? Didn't you think that because I was in the accident with Valerie that secrets would come out? But she needn't have found out about you. Until you strolled in and advertised the situation.' Of all the things he hadn't wanted to happen, it was for Diane to find out – about his family, his money or his lover. Especially the Diane who fairly crackled with fury.

That Diane, the angry, intransigent one, rarely appeared. Rage, for her, was like a comet: it came only every few years to sear across the cosmic landscape. But then it threatened everything in its path.

That Diane could alter orbits.

And while he hated her for defying him, at the same time he had a grudging admiration for what his mother would have called her piss and vinegar.

Stella's eyes pinkened. 'But at least she knows now and we can be together. We can be together!'

Oh ... *dangerous.*

With his good hand he covered one of hers. Her soft little hand with cute dimples over the knuckles. He sighed and made his voice as kind as he could because Stella had been his mistress for a long time. 'It's not Diane that I have to part from, Stell.'

After Stella had stumbled out he stared out at a colourless, hazy sky. He was going to miss her. He'd enjoyed the affair from its slap-and-tickle beginnings to its surprising metamorphosis into an actual relationship. He'd even sort of enjoyed the break in the middle, the aggro, her stubborn refusal to realise that her role was to come back to him. She'd gone too far by going off with that younger guy but he'd ended both that and her marriage with one whisper in the ear of her husband.

Stella hadn't been right for the husband; she was too wilful, too much fun. A lot of fun, was Stella. But the unpalatable truth was that he couldn't – for the present – have both his wife and his girlfriend.

He picked up his mobile phone, selected **Valerie**. She picked up curtly. 'Yes?'

She was missing the pop; it was bound to make her grumpy, going cold turkey on both cigarettes and alcohol. Economically, he told her about Stella.

'Sorry to hear,' she returned.

'I'll miss her.'

'I'm sure.'

'We had a lot of fun.'

'That's the idea.'

He hesitated. 'What's up?'

She sniffed. 'I have the arse with you, dear brother. You've been lying to me about your wife. She's not a reclusive agoraphobic or a sobbing mess scarcely able to look after herself. Why did you lie? To me?'

Concern creased his brow. Valerie actually sounded angry. In the last two years he'd intrigued, interested and amused her and she'd confided in him. She had not been annoyed with him.

He gave vent to a gusty sigh. 'Why does anybody lie about a thing like that? Because they wish things were different. I'm trapped in my marriage and I tried to pretend that I wasn't. I'm sorry.'

'Trapped? But I respect her. She's a valiant sort of woman. Scraping along financially while you laze around in your cottage with your bit on the side or shoot about in the chopper with me. I like her, too.'

Alarm blossomed in his chest. Gareth admired Valerie to the point of hero worship and never felt impatient with her as he did with Melvyn and Ivan who were, let's face it, low-achieving but high-spending. He loved them, but it was a job – his job – to keep them out of the Small Claims Court and out of the hands of the cops. Ivan was bloody silly and would buy anything from some junkie down the pub, even when it was quite obviously so hot that it glowed. And Melvyn had to have every new gadget that hit the High Street, all of it on the never-never. BlackBerry, TV, camera, DVD, MP3.

He loved his brothers but they were exasperating, the way they needed pulling out of the shit all the time.

Yet he was proud to share blood with Valerie, who he'd never had to help with a damned thing. Her mind was fast, her opinions decided, her finances awesome.

'It's not like you to be snotty about something so trivial as my maritals,' he said, abruptly. 'What's really the matter?'

'Nothing.'

'Come on.'

'Nothing unexpected.'

He waited.

Her voice filled with tears. 'The CAA have taken my licence away. James brought the letter in today.'

Cautiously, 'You must've expected that. They'd already suspended your medical certificate.'

'But that was because I've suffered multiple fractures. Not because I was unfit to fly.'

He let his voice become censorious. 'In what way were you unfit to fly?'

A pause. 'Alcohol above the permitted limit.'

He sighed. Balls. Here he was again – listening to the troubles of a sibling. 'I could've told them that. Having been the poor sod in the helicopter. You've told me the "eight hours from bottle to throttle" rule, and you do tuck it away, Sis. You should've stuck to your rule about not drinking before a flight.'

'Like you should've stuck to your non-basket-case wife?'

Chapter Sixteen

George, as he'd promised but Tamzin had hardly dared hope, rang her mobile, making her feel all skippy inside. 'On Friday, we've got sound check at six but we're not on till half-ten. Jenneration's headlining. So we'll eat in between, yeah?'

'Yes, OK,' she answered breathlessly, hoping it didn't sound as if it had been so long since a boy rang her that she'd forgotten how to talk to one.

'Good day?'

'All right. Visited my mother in hospital. That metalwork that goes into her hip is really gruesome though. How about you?'

His voice came back rich with the fun of living. 'I've had an amazin' day at uni. I got my exam essay in on time. And my car number plate was read out over the PA because I parked it on the end of a row. I was waiting to go into an exam and had to run off, with everyone laughing, and move it. The Director of Learning was standing by the car when I got there. I asked him if he was the car-park attendant.'

Tamzin giggled.

She went to bed feeling cautiously happy.

But woke in the morning with the familiar feeling of anxiety squeezing her head between its hands.

She curled up in bed, stomach churning. What should she wear to a live music gig? What were all the people like that George knew? She'd have to drive into the city and park. And drive home in the dark.

The desire to get out of bed drained away. Also the desire to eat, although her father knocked on her door and offered her a slice of toast and jam.

She closed her eyes on the snakes of fear in her belly and drifted back to sleep listening to the comforting and familiar sound of James working from home for the morning in his study, videoconferencing through his laptop, his dark voice rising and falling.

Her mobile woke her again – and it was George. Again! She tried not to sound as if she had just roused because he had been revising all morning and sounded full of life. 'Shall I pick you up instead of meeting you in the centre?'

It wasn't fair when her own car stood outside doing nothing, but, pathetically, she gasped, 'Oh yes, please!' And then, 'Oh no, because I need to go shopping.'

But, after complicated negotiations and shouted conversation to her father downstairs, she managed to arrange for James to take her into the city en route to the office, and George to bring her home later. All parking and driving in the dark problems solved, she showered, ate a tomato sandwich that James made her, his smiles giving away how much he liked to see her happy, and hopped into the leathery seat of the Merc.

James dropped her right up by the cathedral, although it would mean him fighting his way out of the city again to his office. Tamzin clutched her bag to her chest and prepared to get out. 'Explain to Mum, tonight, won't you? And I'll see her tomorrow.'

'She'll understand.' James winked. It was nice that he was pleased she was going out, but she wished he wouldn't make his eagerness for the old Tamzin so obvious. The old Tamzin had been shed and left behind, like a spider's exoskeleton that looked real but wasn't.

It was tiring battling the Friday afternoon shoppers at the clothes racks. She found black jeans with silver stars embroidered on the hips but the tops all seemed either unbelievably plain or low-cut where she was not so ample as before and – worse – short-sleeved. After trudging the equivalent of a marathon, she found a lace-covered white top with wizard's sleeves and a belt below the bust. She could've bought the top in black but that would've meant a new bra, too, and she was fast losing the will to shop.

She trudged to the Ladies in John Lewis's to change, pulling and biting the price tags off. She glared into the mirrors above the basins. Not bad. But now she was stuck with a carrier bag of clothes she'd changed out of. She shoved it into the bin. She wasn't going to turn up for a date with George carting a carrier bag of raggy old crap.

To make reparation for using John Lewis's loos when she hadn't bought the clothes there she went into their coffee shop for a latte, bought breath freshener from Boots afterwards, used it so thoroughly that she felt as if she'd been gargling neat disinfectant, then wandered along to Cathedral Square where she had arranged to meet George, window-shopping so that she wouldn't be early.

But he was late.

She gazed across the square at the acres of paving and the neat row of shops. He was late. Ten minutes. He wasn't coming, then, obviously. Something had come up – something better. Someone. The aroma from the nearby takeaway kiosk began to make her feel sick.

Standing alone near the Guildhall, its arches making it look like a building on stilts, while the late shoppers threaded past her on both sides, her heart slithered, by degrees, to her feet. He was late.

Fifteen.

He wasn't coming. He'd found someone else to take, or decided to go with his mates. She looked at her watch. Twenty.

Exhaustion began to buckle her limbs. She'd been taut all

day but now she was coming unstrung and she wanted to droop, collapse, close her eyes and …

'Hiya! Sorry I'm late.'

Her eyes flew open.

'Some arse has let his car break down right in the entrance to the car park. Amazin' chaos. You look well cool!' He took her hand. 'Better run or I'll miss our sound check.'

His hand was warm as he pulled her along. 'Marty plays lead guitar, he's got a Les Paul, and I play rhythm on my SG, and sing lead. Erica is bass and backing vocals, and then we've got Rob on drums. Course, my cousin, Bryony, she used to play drums before she went to Brazil.' He paused. Laughed. 'Your cousin too, right?'

Tamzin strained to keep up both with the conversation and with his enormous strides. 'Half a cousin, because of Uncle Gareth.'

'I guess the other half of her is my cousin. Crazy. Marty's got my gear in his van. We're on with other bands but we have to sound check first because we're on last, have you been to Danny Boyes before?' He glanced at his watch and speeded up.

She had to run a few steps. 'Don't think so.' Her breath was beginning to burn her throat.

'Nearly there. Sorry. But if I miss our sound check everyone'll hate me.' In fact it was several minutes of George's seven-league strides before they reached their destination and by then Tamzin's legs felt like boiled spaghetti. George showed no sign of distress but loped along like a particularly good-looking giraffe.

Danny Boyes was a scruffy-looking pub painted in midnight blue with a mixture of matt and gloss. The bar was open but held only three girls in the corner drinking WKD and five older men in cardigans with a grey whippet lying beside them. 'You get all sorts in here because the beer's cheap,' George explained, hopping over the whippet.

As they ran into an echoing back room a crash of drums made Tamzin cry out in shock. An ironic cheer went up at the sight of George.

'Sorry, sorry! Crappy traffic.' He released Tamzin's hand and ran up the room to where two lads and a girl hovered disconsolately on the small stage, shouting back to two men behind a console at the back of the room, 'Sorry, sound engineers.' The unsmiling sound engineers were clones of each other – middle-aged bald men with ponytails.

A boy who looked about twelve, but was probably Tamzin's age, smiled at her. 'Hi, I'm Simon, the promoter.'

'Oh. Hi.' Tamzin didn't really know what a promoter did. She hauled her shaking legs up onto a bar stool while George took a flying leap onto the front of the stage, grabbed a guitar off a stand and threw the strap around his neck. He panted into his microphone, 'Tuning,' and played a few notes, twisting the machine heads, strumming, picking, frowning as he poked at pedals with his feet. Several minutes of absorbed twiddling later he'd got his breath back. 'Ready to go.'

'OK, let's go, drums,' sighed the sound engineer.

The sound men fiddled with levels as a thunder of drums made Tamzin wince. Feeling as out of place as a nun at a rock festival, she gazed around a room once painted orange but now showing hundreds of white slashes where posters and cables had been stuck up and pulled down. Small round tables and squat stools edged the wooden floor with no polish other than from years of feet, fag ends and beer.

'OK. Erica on bass.'

The bass didn't assault the ears like the drums but merely shuddered through Tamzin's seat and up her spine, to clamour uncomfortably in her head. Would it be really rude to jam her fingers in her ears?

Erica, with her black pelmet skirt up around her chunky thighs, stick-straight hair and the eyeliner of an ancient Egyptian, looked like a sulky child until her smile transformed her into a cherry-lipped, chubby-cheeked doll. Her blue-black bass guitar was slung as low as her fingers could walk the strings.

Members of supporting bands began to wander in, propping their instruments against the wall, lifting their hands in greeting. Erica, playing on, smiled her dolly dimple smile.

'OK. Rhythm.'

George's electric guitar ripped across the tail of Erica's bass line.

Forgetting noise oppression and spare-part anxieties, Tamzin watched his fingers flying over the frets as his feet and his head kept time. George was good. She felt a little wash of pride and reflected glory.

But when the mixer said, 'OK. Marty, lead guitar,' and the other guitar rang out like joy and pain, Tamzin realised what good was. No one from the other bands spoke or even moved, all faces were turned towards the stage.

A sound engineer broke the spell. 'OK. George, voice.'

George folded his arms loosely on top of his guitar. 'One two one two one two, three three three, four... four... four...' His voice ran effortlessly up the scale.

Tamzin felt the hairs on the back of her neck stir. It was a voice like suede: smooth but with texture.

'Words, please.'

George abandoned the scale and took up a tune.

'Tamzin, you're coming for a pizza,
I was late when I went to meet ya,
Now you think that I'm all scummy
And you've got a poorly mummy...'

Everyone – except the expressionless sound engineers –

laughed and Tamzin felt her face burn with embarrassment. But also with pleasure. George was singing to her – only a silly ditty, but for her.

'OK. That's the headline band, Jenneration. Can we have Average Spoonful, please?'

A new band hopped up onto the stage as the members of Jenneration stowed their instruments in the band room and, with Tamzin, were soon stepping outside into a rapidly cooling evening.

Tamzin trailed the others past big houses made into flats and small houses made into shops to the steamy warmth of a pizza parlour beside a launderette, wondering how she'd keep her end up in conversation that was all about music and performance.

She knew all about being excluded.

Memories of uni crowded in. The elite kids who had been known as the Coven, with their sly grins and sarcasm, their pointed silences. Their remorseless ability to make her feel stupid and rejected. Her breathing began to hurry.

But at a booth of slippery red seats and a scratched plastic table Tamzin found herself dragged from the back of the group and wedged between the wall and George. He grinned at her. 'Gotcha!'

The Coven faded from her mind. She realised that she was grinning goofily back when Erica had to flap a laminated menu to get her attention. 'Tamzin, are you up for sharing a pizza?'

Tamzin was relieved and disappointed to break the eye contact with George. 'Um, yes; I can't eat a whole one.'

Erica sighed. 'I can. And it goes straight to my bum.'

Marty laughed. He'd put on silver-framed glasses as soon as he got off stage and they glinted in the strong overhead light. 'Don't let her eat a whole one, Tamzin, or there's not going to be room on the stage for the rest of us.'

Erica snorted. 'Oh, right, Mr Strange Hair! If you use any more hairspray –'

'It's not *hairspray*, it's *straightener*, don't tell Tamzin I wear hairspray. And what about your skirt, then, Erica? Man, it's a parachute –'

Tamzin giggled, hardly daring to believe that the members of George's band might be ... friendly.

'Hey.'

'Yes?' She glanced up at George. Immediately, he kissed her. His lips were like velvet. Gentle. When, tentatively, she kissed him back, he kissed her harder, giddily. Her heart began to patter.

'Tamzin, do you like Hawaiian?' Erica interrupted, as though nothing extraordinary was happening, as if the world was just the same as before George pressed his hot lips to hers.

Tamzin, who felt as if she'd just woken up after a hundred years, couldn't even remember what a Hawaiian pizza was. 'Whatever,' she agreed, breathlessly.

The others took their pizzas much more seriously and embarked upon a summit meeting over the extra toppings and garlic bread possibilities.

George put his lips to Tamzin's ear, so that his voice buzzed through her hair. 'Sorry. I got a bit juvenile, there, in front of everyone. I got an urge.'

'It's OK.' She tried to sound casual, as if men were always losing control of themselves over her. A place behind her breastbone was filled with enough fairy dust to set her entire torso tingling.

'Really OK?'

'Really OK.' Tamzin had once had a Tiger's Eye ring and the stone had held just the golds and browns of George's eyes.

He grinned. 'So I could do it again?'

Trying to control her inanely grinning lips, she nodded.

And while the others argued about whether Pepsi Max was better than Cherry Coke, George did it again.

And Tamzin fell in love.

Back at Danny Boyes the place was filling up with teenagers, the bar was busy and two girls with kohl-rimmed eyes, studded noses and sequinned cheeks had taken up station behind a cash box at the door. Tamzin realised instantly that she should've bought a dress or skirt. All the girls wore hiked-up skirts or clinging dresses. She was, like, nearly the *only* one in jeans. Like, *noo-oo*...

But, before she could be totally swamped with anxiety, she was enchanted to find that not only did she not have to pay £5 to earn an entry stamp of wiggly lines on her hand but that when George said, 'Tamzin's with me,' she received a stamp that declared in thick green ink, BAND. Instantly, she felt sorry for all those who not only had to pay but also received the stamp that marked them out as audience and not as BAND. She was BAND. How cool was that?

One of the other bands was on stage. A portion of the audience stood directly in front, watching, heads nodding. Conversation was impossible, the bar staff must've been reading lips as George managed to procure a Breezer for her. She felt pleasantly part of everything with Jenneration around her like minders around a rock star.

Between sets it was possible to talk. That was when the band members slapped palms and linked thumbs with favoured acquaintances – unless the acquaintance was female, in which case they hugged – and discussed the previous band.

The first sign that Jenneration was preparing to go on stage was when Erica unbuckled her belt. 'Can you hold this for me, Tamz? It scratches my bass.'

Marty dug his money and his phone out of his pocket. 'Yeah, do you mind? All this crap gets on my tits.'

'And my phone,' said Rob.

'And mine.'

'Sure.' Tamzin threaded her arm through the belt, tucked the money in her pocket and held the phones, still warm from pockets.

The promoter materialised. 'You guys ready?'

'Yeah, yeah.'

And suddenly they were streaming away from her through a door beside the bar, reappearing a minute later on stage with instruments around their necks or drumsticks in their hands, green strobes playing over the audience while the stage flashed silver. It was very *Alice in Wonderland* – they'd stepped through a looking-glass and become a band.

A cheer, whistles, whoops and much of the audience surged raggedly towards the stage, glasses hastily abandoned on tables. Immediately, Tamzin saw that the number abandoning their stools and pressing the stage was four times what the other bands had attracted.

Guitars plugged into amps with a *thunk*. George and Erica said, 'One-two,' into the microphones. The guitars and bass tuned up briefly, the drums rolled experimentally. Rob moved the snare drum closer to him, flipped a drumstick in the air and caught it. Waited.

Tamzin began to catch something of the expectancy of the crowd edging around on their toes and gazing at the band.

The promoter jumped onto the stage, having to tiptoe to shout into George's mike. 'And about time, too! This. Is. JENNERATION!'

The drums banged *one, two, three*, the guitars raged in on *four*. George closed his eyes and opened his mouth and the dancefloor exploded as it was hit with a wall of sound.

Tamzin stared at the heaving bodies. And at the band.

Whoa! They were good enough to be in *the charts*! Excitement burst inside her.

With fumbling fingers she fastened Erica's belt – pulled in a lot – around her waist, forced all the dosh and phones into her pockets and pushed her way into the crowd. It was hot and difficult to keep her feet as the dancers bounced wildly into her from all directions.

It was delicious.

She let loose her hair, threw her arms in the air and whooped as the crowd tossed her around like a cork on a stormy sea. It was wicked.

Chapter Seventeen

Diane stood on James's doorstep, feeling like an idiot. 'Tamzin's out? I'd forgotten it was tonight that she was going out with George.'

James leaned on the doorframe and raised lazy eyebrows. 'Tonight it is.'

She groaned. 'I should've rung first. I just thought I'd surprise her with her final fitting, with time dragging while I wait for Bryony to come home. And I was so pleased with the tops when they were finished.' She waved the hangers, sighed and turned away. 'I'll ring tomorrow.'

It wasn't until she was unlocking her car and hooking the garments above the back door that she realised James was right with her, pulling on a wolf-grey fleece. 'How about a drink at The Old Dog?'

She glanced across the green. In the softening summer evening the windows of the pub glowed yellow. Homely wooden tables stood between tubs of marigolds and children dodged among them while their parents tried to relax.

'Let me buy you dinner,' he added, persuasively.

'I've eaten,' she admitted, sadly, thinking of the sensible but not very interesting chicken with jacket potato and a book propped open for company.

'You can watch me eat, then. Come on! There's something I'd like to talk to you about.' He was very close and warm.

She fiddled with the car door. It wouldn't do any harm, would it? Bryony's room had already been given the welcome-home treatment and the freezer filled with her favourites. Alone, Diane would probably spend the evening unable to concentrate on a film or a book or even her sewing while she waited for the clock to tick around to the day after tomorrow, the day that Bryony's plane landed.

And she hadn't eaten dessert …

They chose to sit outside with the midges and the kiddies. Both were a nuisance but it was a still evening and Diane liked the idea of letting the dewy twilight close peacefully around them, rather than be seated inside in the cheery but artificial light, washed by roars of approval or groans of dismay according to the fortunes of the darts players.

The creaking pub sign sported a beagle with an erect tail. 'I call him Frank,' said James, following the direction of her gaze. 'He's a randy old dog with an eye for pretty ladies.'

'And an up-for-it expression.'

'Always. He's currently sniffing around Charlotte the King Charles Spaniel, who has a coquettish eye patch and a cute little nose. He can't wait to get his paw over.' His eyes crinkled. He hadn't shaved and the stubble accentuated the hollows of his cheeks.

Diane snorted inelegantly. 'How sad – you have a prurient interest in the imaginary sex life of a painted beagle.'

James settled more comfortably on the bench and sank the first half of his pint efficiently. 'OK, let's talk about your nephew, George – as he's taken my fragile daughter out tonight.'

Diane lowered her glass. 'They were getting on brilliantly the other day. I was pleased to see her cheerful and doing something as normal as taking an interest in a boy. Aren't you happy?'

He waited as his lamb tikka was placed before him, ripping into an oval of naan bread before replying. 'Of course I am, because, as you say, it's normal for a twenty-year-old and Tamzin hardly ever behaves like a normal twenty-year-old. But I have this urge to charge round to George's house, pin him against the wall and tell him the boundaries.' His jaw hardened. 'I hate it that he does drugs. It just needs her to fall for this clown – if he treats her like rubbish, she could be right back at square one. Depression, starving, self-injuring –'

'Whoa!' Diane's voice emerged loudly in the still evening air and two little girls with bunches paused in their game with a toy horse to gaze, wide-eyed. She lowered her voice to a fierce growl, her words rushing over one another in irritated little leaps. 'George is all right. He sings and plays guitar in a band, he goes to Anglia Ruskin uni, he's pleasant and polite. He's been very close to Bryony and has never acted like "a clown" with her. And. He. Does. Not. Do. Drugs.'

James brought his face close to hers. 'I'm afraid he does,' he whispered. 'I heard Tamzin on her phone ask him what was so special about an E and why he had to have one.'

Slowly, Diane relaxed. 'Don't be such an arse.'

James hesitated. 'What?'

She felt the corners of her mouth begin to curl. 'The only E he uses is his *harmonica* in the key of E. The key of E is his favourite vocal range. But you might have heard her talk about C or G, too.'

'Oh ...' Slowly, James's smile crept across his fine lips. 'That is such a relief. I didn't even know that harmonicas were in specific keys.' His grin widened. 'All right, I'm sorry. You can stop your scary voice.'

Laughing unwillingly, Diane pulled a face. 'Sorry. But George has a special spot in my heart.'

He began to eat. 'So I see. Quite reassuring, the way you jump to his defence.'

Diane struggled with her conscience. Presently she said, 'Of course, he's not a saint. He's a nineteen-year-old boy and I can't pretend that he won't ...' She hesitated. 'I mean, they're young adults – '

'I get the picture,' he said, shortly. 'Testosterone will kick in.'

Diane reached out and pinched a piece of his naan and a plump cube of lamb to go with it. 'Like you?'

His eyebrows almost flew off his face. 'What?'

She picked up his fork and stole some more lamb, with rice this time. 'I said, "Like you?"' She pointed his fork at him. 'People in glass houses shouldn't throw stones. Judge not lest ye be judged. If you're the pot, don't call the kettle Burned Arse.'

'Oh.' He picked up his beer and stared sightlessly at the tubs of flowers losing their colour in the twilight.

She took up the dessert menu. Chocolate fudge cake. Very pub grub. Probably sticky toffee pudding, too. Yes, there it was near the bottom. Ooh, cherry crumble … Mmm, summer pudding … Lemon meringue, ice cream sundae. 'What's dime cake, do you think?'

'No idea.' James balled his napkin and tossed it onto the table where it unfurled and hung in his tikka. Diane flinched automatically at such a waste but her mind had turned to dessert. 'Would you like –?'

'No, thanks.'

She wiggled her fingers to catch the attention of a waitress who was clearing nearby tables, ordered, then sat back and awaited the arrival of her dime cake, while James scowled into his beer.

The dime cake arrived – chocolate biscuit base, chocolate mousse, marshmallow, meringue and chocolate sauce. Slowly, she dug her spoon through the squidgy mousse and broke into the base. And groaned. The first mouthful was orgasmic. She shut her eyes the better to concentrate on the mousse's contrast with the biscuit and meringue and the rich chocolate that pervaded them all.

She opened her eyes ready for the next bite to discover

James's gaze fixed on her. She offered him a spoonful.

For a moment he did that thing where his eyes smiled but his lips didn't bother. Then he leaned forward to close his mouth gently around the spoon. His eyes widened. 'Mm.' He signalled a thumbs up. 'Mm-*mmm*.'

She agreed with a, 'M*mmm*,' of her own. His hand closed over hers to guide another load between his lips.

When the last skerrick of mousse and crumb of biscuit had been scraped from the thick white plate by the surprisingly intimate act of taking turns with the same spoon, James sighed. 'So. Now you've had some time to think about it, what's the state of our relationship?'

Heart thumping suddenly, she blinked, licking crumbs of chocolaty meringue from around her lips. 'You're my husband's brother-in-law?'

'I made love to you.'

Her blush was so hot that she could've doubled as a patio heater and she glanced around to check that they couldn't be overheard. 'I hadn't forgotten. But not every sexual encounter ... I mean, it doesn't follow that you've necessarily got a relationship ... there are one-night stands.'

He folded his arms on the edge of the table. 'I don't want it to be a one-night stand.'

'But,' she pointed out, 'it was just the one night.'

'That's just how it worked out. To me it was ... an experience. I began the evening hardly knowing you, thinking that you were quiet – if quietly stroppy, sometimes – and probably a bit doormatty where Gareth's concerned. After all, he'd somehow pulled that crappy trick on you without you even noticing – or you simply hadn't wanted to see what was under your nose.'

'So, naturally, you wanted sex with me,' she observed. 'Everyone gets uncontrollable passions for quietly stroppy, dim doormats.'

His eyes smiled again, as if he didn't want anyone else to know that he had something to smile about. 'I had already noticed you, physically,' he murmured. 'Not being blind. Then as we talked over dinner I realised what a great person you are, how switched on, how courageous, how principled. I took the Merc for a burn up purely to show off to you. And when we were alone in the dark, I experienced all the lust of a teenager on viagra. Afterwards – I drove home absolutely dazed. Then I messed everything up by not ringing you the next day, which was bloody crass. But while I was listening for hours outside Tamzin's door, wondering if she was OK, wondering whether this would be the time when she would slice a vein, all the time I tried to keep that night with me, thinking that when Tamzin's crisis was over I'd have this thing with you to explore.' He drew in a deep breath. The smile in his eyes had vanished. 'Only to find, of course, that the last thing I had was a thing with you.'

The gnats were being a nuisance, spinning around the lamps until they were dizzy and then splashing down in glasses of beer. Weary children were being gathered up by patient parents, the local teenagers had congregated in the middle of the green, their shouts of laughter drifting through the evening.

He slapped suddenly at his arm. 'Bloody bugs! Come on, I'll walk you back to your car.' He settled the bill with a young waitress called Sarah, asking how her sister was doing at uni. They turned through the gap in the flower tubs and headed for James's house, leaving their footprints in the dewy grass. The part of the drive where Diane had parked the car was screened by rounded green hedges, throwing the area into deep shadow. As she turned to say goodnight she found herself sandwiched between the car at her back and James at her front, a breath away, the heat of his body radiating over the space between them.

'I want to make love to you again.' His voice was quiet and almost conversational. 'Lots of times. Now. In the future. All the time. I want privacy and light and comfort so I can relax and enjoy you. Your body.'

His fingertips brushed against her left hip.

She sucked in her breath. She hadn't realised she had quite so many jangly nerve endings there. 'You mean an affair?'

'Yes.'

'We're both married.'

'We were last time, too.' He lifted his hand to her face, stroking her cheekbone and down to her neck, pushing back her hair. His skin was hot, yet Diane shivered. 'Diane, it seems to me that your marriage is in injury time and you might be thinking about leaving Gareth. And I shouldn't have feelings like this about another woman but I view my wife as a responsibility and she views me as an annoyance. Still, I can't leave home at the moment, regardless of Valerie being stuck in hospital or whether she even cares about me. Tamzin couldn't handle it.

'But none of that stops me wanting you. I want to be with you, to hear your opinions and laugh at your jokes. When we're alone I want to be able to kiss you and hold you and touch you. I can't offer you much – certainly not anything that's fair or equitable. I'm just telling you what I want. However messy.'

Straining her eyes to see his expression in the darkness, her heart thudded so hard that it was almost unpleasant. 'I haven't thought about leaving Gareth. Much,' she amended. 'Bryony's coming home in two days and she's full of happy family stuff. She's made up a misunderstanding with Gareth – I think he orchestrated that. I –' She paused. 'I don't know what I want.'

'But it's not me?' His voice was gentle but gravelly with disappointment. His hand dropped from her hair.

She caught it and held it between both of hers, her voice husky. 'That's not true … I don't know if there's any point in beginning an affair. And I don't know if I can do it. Sneaking around, lying to everyone. Making do in the backs of cars or in fields. Or checking into hotels for a few hours here or there and the staff being terribly polite but *knowing*. And I'd still be living with Gareth – wouldn't you mind?'

He laughed shortly and his fingers tightened over hers. 'I already mind. I mind that you're his wife, I mind that he's a shit, I mind that he's slept with you for years. And, obviously, I'd mind about all the sneaking around, that that's all I can offer you and all you can offer me. But millions of people do it. They meet when they can and take what happiness there is.' Each of his fingers slid slowly between hers, lacing their hands together. 'I think that that's all there is for us, for now. I'm prepared to take it. Are you?'

She let her head droop until her forehead was lodged against his collarbone, hard and warm and real. 'I don't want a lovely thing to be squalid.' Two hot tears escaped from her closed eyes.

His voice was deep and low. 'I'll make it as unsqualid as I can. You won't have to face staff in hotels. I'll arrange something.' Lifting her face to his he kissed her damp eyelids and leaned against her.

'I don't know if I can,' she repeated, weakly. 'It's so deceitful. I don't know if I'll cope. The guilt.'

He sighed. 'You could always ask Gareth how it's done.'

'Ouch!'

He kissed her, quickly, his mouth firm and hot. 'Sorry. It can't have been nice for you to find out about that. But you *did* find out. You know that he has someone else. Doesn't that clear your conscience?'

'Or make me as bad as him?' The summer night had thickened around them, the air full of the scent of damp grass and the sound of a thousand insects. Diane allowed herself to relax into his arms, feeling the thud of his heartbeat. It felt safe.

They stood, bodies pressed together, for so long that night-time creatures began rustling the hedges around them.

James said, quietly, 'We could make each other happy.'

Chapter Eighteen

Diane squashed in, forcing herself as close as she could get to the barrier.

Other bodies jostled, other heads craned. She'd almost made it to the front of the mob by the time the one she awaited emerged beneath the brightly lit Arrivals sign, squinting with tiredness, short brown curls on end as she fought an airport trolley stacked with scratched suitcases and a brightly coloured backpack.

'Bryony!' The name burst from the depths of Diane's lungs and a woman in front of her winced in irritation. Diane only shouted louder. 'Bryony, here, darling!' And she squirmed out of the press, thrusting aside elbows and shoulders, to sprint around the length of the barriers. In seconds she could crush her daughter to her for the first time for almost a year.

'Mum!' Bryony's embrace was just as fierce. 'I'm so glad to see you. Thanks for driving all the way down to the airport. We had turbulence – I was sick. And when they could finally serve icky dried-up meals I didn't feel like eating, so now I'm empty.' She rubbed her tummy under a yellow-and-green shirt that looked at least two sizes too big.

Diane turned towards the nearest coffee shop. 'Let's get you something. I could murder a cappuccino. Let me push the trolley, darling – you've enough luggage. Oops, sorry,' as she cornered awkwardly and clipped somebody's suitcase.

Eventually she was able to park the recalcitrant trolley and Bryony on the edge of a seating area while she queued along the shiny stainless steel counter for cappuccino and a scone for her and water and what looked like a yard of cheese-and-pickle baguette for Bryony.

Bryony was home! As she queued she darted looks at her daughter, almost excited enough to bubble and steam like the cappuccino machine.

'Now,' she said, back at the table, passing Bryony her baguette, plus a chocolate brownie that she'd picked up knowing how Bryony adored them. 'Tell me about Brasilia and the orphanage where you worked and everything.'

'God, Mum. It'll take hours.' But Bryony began, between bites of baguette, and the subject lasted her through her meal, into the car park, around the M25 and up the M11. The people, the wealth and the poverty, the institution at Lago Norte, the towers of Congress on the skyline, the vast expanse of City Park, the yellow-flowered trees and how it was rainy in summer but dry in winter. 'It's tropical downpours there, Mum. You want to see the rain. You could shower in it. Honestly, you could rinse your hair.'

For the first time, it occurred to Diane that, with all that money in Gareth's account, they *could've* seen it – and Bryony. The hollow, pulsing ache of longing for her only child could've been assuaged if Gareth hadn't hoarded all his riches to himself like Scrooge McDuck.

As they approached Peterborough, Bryony began to yawn, giant, eye-watering yawns.

'You need to be in bed. Not long now.' To be truthful, Diane wouldn't have minded a nap herself. She'd hardly slept for the last two nights for thinking of Bryony. *And James*, a little voice added.

Bryony stretched. 'After seeing Dad.'

Diane shifted her eyes briefly from the thundering lorries ahead. 'You want to go now?'

'Of course. He texted me the minute I landed. He says he's counting the hours. What sort of shape is he in?'

Diane checked her mirror and moved over into the inside lane. 'He's improving all the time.' And, honestly, 'But pretty horrible.'

A nursing sister intercepted Diane as she crossed the foyer. It was Kirsty, the lovely Irish nurse who was one of Gareth's favourites because she could make him laugh. 'He's not quite so well today, Mrs Jenner. He's got a water infection so we've turned some fans on him and the antibiotics will start to work very soon. But he's hot and uncomfortable until they do.' She turned her smile on Bryony. 'If you're Gareth's daughter then I think there's a welcome waiting for you. He can't wait for you to turn up. In fact, he's having such lurid dreams with the infection that twice he's been convinced that you've been already.'

Bryony beamed. 'Poor Dad. I can't wait to see him, either.'

But when they reached Gareth's door they discovered that they were not the only visitors. Harold looked to have arrived just before them and Gareth was glaring at him balefully across the white and ordered room, challenging, 'So, where were you?'

Diane halted, recognising the sound of Gareth getting something off his chest. 'This might not be a good time,' she muttered, sliding her arm around Bryony.

Harold was wearing an astonished frown. 'Am I late?'

Gareth reached for his iced water, eyes moving feverishly. 'A few bloody decades. Where were you when Mum took up with Denny and had Melvin and Ivan, then Denny left us and we were shoved away in a damp, rat-infested dump because he turned out to be just another bastard who sent no fucking money for his own kids?' His voice rose. 'The benefit system wasn't quite so generous, those days, you know. Where were you when I had to leave school, when Mum and me had two jobs each and there was no one much to look after the little 'uns and they ran around like hooligans? When I had to give up my apprenticeship because it didn't bring in enough?

Where were you?' Fresh sweat ran down his forehead.

His gaze dropped to the small basket of fruit that his father clutched, done up with cellophane and a curly gold ribbon. 'You can fuck off with that! I'm ill, I can't eat. I just want to know where you were.'

Harold looked bewildered. 'Gareth you know how sorry I am but I can't change history –'

'I'll tell you where you were, shall I? You were sitting on your posh arse in the back of your Rolls Royce, with your posh wife and your spoilt little daughter. And I'll tell you what you weren't doing, too, shall I? You weren't finding out what happened to the girl you got pregnant or your child that she'd given birth to. You waited until I was forty-bloody-three and that girl was dead as a door knob before you got off your posh arse and did that.' He wiped his face roughly with his good hand.

'*You* are criticising *me* for depriving my family of money?' barked Harold, evidently spurred into giving as good as he got.

Gareth fell silent. The two men glared at each other like pitbulls.

Then Bryony pushed past Diane, bursting onto the scene, brown eyes round under aghast eyebrows, and broke into noisy sobs. 'Oh, my God! Oh, my God! Oh, *Dad*. Your face!'

Gareth turned away from Harold as Bryony dashed forward and bent awkwardly to hug what she could of him. 'Dad, the reality didn't sink in. Oh, Dad, you nearly died.'

Automatically, he put his left arm around her, exchanging an uncomfortable look with Diane, hovering in the background. 'I didn't realise it was time for you to be here. I keep having these dreams.' His face softened, even as he grumbled, 'You're making me hot, sobbing down my neck.' But he closed his eyes and patted her back.

'Perhaps I'd better give you some time alone.' White and shaken, Harold climbed to his feet.

Gareth lifted his eyes to his father. 'You bloody stay where you are and meet your granddaughter. Bryony, this is Harold Myers, my father.' Diane heard the pride in his voice.

Theatrically, Bryony sprang up, wiping her eyes. 'Oh. My. God!' And she flung herself around the bed and into Harold's arms as if she'd known him all her life.

After a startled moment, Harold beamed. 'Hello, young lady,' he said, quietly.

Gareth looked up at Diane and she saw the pride of parenthood in his gaze. They still shared Bryony.

Chapter Nineteen

Tamzin rang Diane. 'Can I come over, today? Or do you want to be left alone with Bryony? I understand, if you do. But if I do come, can I bring George? He's got no exams this morning so he said he'd pick me up and bring me over.'

She heard the smile in Diane's voice. 'Yes, come. Bryony won't wake until afternoon, I'll bet. She's shattered.'

The journey to Purtenon St. Paul took twenty-five minutes. Thirty-five if you counted the initial ten minutes spent kissing in the car, slewed around and scrunched over to avoid the hand brake. It was George who broke it up, golden-brown eyes regretful. 'I could do this all day but I suppose we'd better hit the road or I won't get back for uni.'

After they'd cleared Crowland and turned right off the main road he picked up her hand from where it lay on the seat and placed it just above his knee. Whenever his left hand wasn't occupied on the gear stick or the steering wheel, he dropped it casually on hers. His flesh was warm and firm through the fabric of his jeans and she went suddenly breathless and shy.

George treated her like a proper girlfriend and his friends had made themselves her friends, too, slicing through the distrust for groups and gangs that the Coven had given her.

'The others want to see a film tomorrow night at The Showcase. I said I'd see if you were up for it.'

'Yes!' she squeaked, before she could think about being cool or laid back. 'What are we seeing?'

George glanced in his mirror, indicated and turned left. 'Erica and Marty are still bickering about it. What's your sort of thing?'

'Not horror, not cowboys.'

'You're such a girl.'

Tamzin giggled. 'It seems a while since anyone noticed.'

She thought about being alongside George in the darkness of the cinema. Probably holding hands. About the way their relationship was going. How long it would be before he went for it, sex-wise. Her heart bumped, uncertainly. Sex hadn't happened for her until uni. Was that what had marked her out to the Coven as different?

Certain that all she had to do to be accepted was bin her virginity like a dress in last year's colour she'd thrown herself into bed with Lucas – until Lucas began referring to her as his 'fuck buddy'. Pathetically, hoping he thought she didn't care, she moved on from unprotected sex with Lucas to unprotected sex with others. She'd been so lucky not to get herpes or chlamydia.

At least she'd guarded against pregnancy with the pill. Some days, it had been her only solid food.

Since then, she'd discovered that counsellors link casual sex with depression, risky behaviour and low self-esteem. A counsellor wouldn't demand, 'What were you *thinking*? That letting boys you hardly knew inside your body would solve something?' But, instead, would explore good-for-me and bad-for-me relationships, carefully avoiding passing judgement.

But Lucas had been bad for her. So had all the others. She didn't need anyone to tell her that.

Tamzin hadn't had sex since she'd left university. Sexual opportunity didn't leap out at you when you lay alone in bed or on the floor or hung out with your mum and dad.

But it could be pretty important to the girlfriend of a funky young god who was something of a local hero.

'Diane, this is amazing!'

Diane beamed as Tamzin stroked the ivory fabric of the first top. The slightly boxy style made her appear slender rather than thin. And maybe she was putting on just a pound or two? She looked miles better, with a flush on her cheeks and her hair brushed into a corn-coloured sheet.

While Bryony slept the sleep of the jet-lagged upstairs they'd indulged in a cosy half hour around the kitchen table with coffee and a biscuit tin and Tamzin had eaten two biscuits that George selected for her. She was certainly going through what James termed a good patch. Diane let her mind linger on James: his smiling eyes, his brushy hair. She'd received a text from him this morning: Thinking of u. Want 2 b with u.

She had still been considering her reply when her text alert beeped again. Can u come here alone? Would like 2 talk.

But it was from Gareth.

She'd flushed with guilt, as if Gareth's text could somehow look into her inbox and scurry back to him to report. She'd returned, OK, will have 2 b 2morro. Fittings 2day. Perhaps, by then, she would have decided on a path to dance through the marital minefield. She really didn't see that she was going to be able to bring herself to have a relationship with James without distancing herself from Gareth, but Bryony wanting to play Happy Families made that difficult.

Unnerved, she sent to James: Me 2. And turned to applying her talents to dressing his daughter in something more flattering than shapeless T-shirts and old oversized jeans.

Rewardingly, Tamzin looked like a model in the creamy top with the brassy gauze. Diane saw her looking at George for approval and ached. She wanted to warn, 'Don't, Tamzin! Don't expose your fragile heart. George is a good boy but he's ... a *boy*. He doesn't think in the long-term or that you might fall to bits when it ends.' But, of course, she just smiled auntishly. And she crossed her mental fingers really hard.

Tamzin's eyes were shining. 'It doesn't need any alteration, does it, Diane? It doesn't. It's so cool, I want to take it home.'

'Cool,' George agreed.

Diane walked around her, critically. 'What do you think about the length?'

'Great.'

'And the sleeves?'

'Excellent.' Tamzin put her arms out at her side like a scarecrow.

George blew her a kiss. 'You look amazin'.'

Immediately, Tamzin declared the top to be perfect and rushed off to the bathroom to change to the pink one. When she reappeared, she was beaming at how the beautiful, delicate colour lent its blush to her skin. George ran his fingers over the clear washers and black embroidery. 'You design cool stuff, Diane. When the band's famous I'm going to get you to do all my stage stuff. Tamz just looks really wicked.' He gave Tamzin a hug.

… Just as Bryony bounced through the door in pink shortie pyjamas. 'George, I heard you – Oh. Who are you?'

Diane's heart sank as, looking about ten, curls on end and a thunderous scowl on her sleepy face, Bryony glared at Tamzin.

The warming tone of the blouse couldn't disguise Tamzin's sudden pallor.

George looked at Bryony as if trying to remember who she was. 'Wow,' he said, at last. 'Hey, Bryony. Great to see you.' He let go of Tamzin long enough to stoop to kiss his cousin's cheek. 'Wow, can't believe you're home. Diane said, like, you'd be asleep until this afternoon.'

'I heard your voice.' Bryony's dark gaze flipped from George to Tamzin.

'Oh, right, sorry. Diane kept telling us to be quiet but I forgot.' George laughed. 'This is Tamzin, by the way. She's your half-cousin, same as I'm your half-cousin.'

With a frozen smile, Bryony said, 'Hello, Tamzin.'

With an uncertain pucker between her eyes, Tamzin returned, 'Hello, Bryony.'

They stared at each other until Bryony said, abruptly, 'I met Granddad, yesterday.'

Tamzin nodded, slowly. 'The rest of us call him Pops.'

'Shall we get on?' Diane pulled her tape measure from around her neck. 'George has to get off to uni after Tamzin's fitting. There's plenty in the fridge if you're hungry, Bryony.'

Bryony shrugged. 'I think I'll go back to bed now I've said hi to George. You're all obviously ... busy.' She turned on her heel and stalked from the room.

'Right, Tamzin,' said Diane, ignoring both Tamzin's uneasy expression and Bryony's less-than-perfect manners. 'I've decorated the first two pairs of jeans. Hop into a pair and we'll see how you look.'

Diane waited until she'd seen Tamzin and George off and then made two cups of tea and a couple of slices of toast to carry upstairs to the room at the front of the house where her daughter had slept since she was a few weeks old. Knocking, she walked in. The curtains were closed and the room thick with the mustiness of sleep. Bryony was a shape beneath the quilt. 'I've brought your breakfast.' She didn't insult Bryony's intelligence by pretending she thought Bryony might be asleep.

Slowly Bryony stirred. 'You shouldn't have.' Her voice was dull.

'It's been ages since you ate.' She waited while Bryony hauled herself up, propping her pillows between herself and the pink-buttoned headboard, then deposited a mug on the bedside and passed over the plate of buttery toast before opening the curtains and a small window.

Bryony regarded her toast with a noticeable lack of enthusiasm. A blue inhaler lay on the bedside table and she took two puffs from that instead. Bryony would always have an inhaler and use it several times a day.

Diane was just grateful that modern drugs let her lead a normal life with so little intervention and pushed away the memory of the years of Bryony's childhood, when that certainly hadn't been the case.

She parked herself on the foot of the bed and blew across the surface of her tea to cool it. 'Is it very odd?'

'What?'

'Coming home after a year. Is it like Narnia? You feel as if you've been away for ages but now you're home nothing's changed?'

Bryony nibbled one corner of the toast. 'The opposite. It's as if I've been away no time but everyone else thinks I've been away forever.'

'Dad's narrow squeak must have rocked you.'

Bryony nodded and swallowed with an obvious effort. Before bursting out, 'And then there's the secret family thing – Mum, what's been going on?' Her eyes were as dark and shiny as Galaxy Minstrels. 'When Dad phoned me to tell me I was, like, so pleased that there was some kind of explanation that meant he wasn't having a scuzzy affair. And he'd had this mega accident in a helicopter and I got all emotional because he could've been killed. But in the next few days I couldn't stop thinking, and it seemed really strange. It is strange, isn't it? He's got this family and he kept us secret from them. I mean, you call them his secret family but I think we were the secret. Is he ashamed of us?' She discarded the plate on the bedside and it wobbled around in a noisy circle before settling.

Moving up the bed, Diane reached out to stroke Bryony's pillow-matted curls. 'I don't think you need draw that conclusion, darling.' She searched for a way to soothe her. 'You have to remember what an underprivileged upbringing Dad had. In those days being poor meant more hardship than it does now. Benefits weren't plentiful, especially not for single mothers. Granny and Dad did everything humanly possible to keep the family all under one roof. Wendy worked hard but women earned less than men.' She knew the story by heart; Gareth had chewed over and over his childhood until his words ceased to have an impact.

But, for the first time for years, she felt touched by those old troubles. She remembered the worn but clean home, furnished with second-hand bargains. And that was the Jenner world well after Wendy and Gareth between them had hauled the family away from the breadline.

'But we've always been poor, Mum, we know about it.'

'Sweetie, we've never been poor! We've had to be careful; we've not been well off. But we've never gone hungry, never been without shelter. How can you say we're poor when you've spent all that time working in Brasilia and seen what real poverty is?

'I think that when Dad eventually met his father and sister, he didn't know how to react. When Harold wanted to make things up to Dad financially ... well, it was such a huge amount of money to Dad that he literally didn't know what to do with it. For a while he just kept the knowledge to himself. And,' she hesitated, 'he has always thought that I betrayed him by not challenging my father's will. That I'd cheated him – and you – out of a more comfortable life. He feels that what he did was no worse than what I did.'

Bryony snuggled her head into the crook of Diane's neck like a child, arm around her waist. 'That's a crock of shit. You refused money your parents didn't want you, or him, or me, to have. I don't think I would've wanted it, either. But he's lived a double life and kept us hidden so that he could keep all his money to himself.'

Diane couldn't think of a reply.

'So that girl is Dad's half-sister's daughter?'

'That's right. Tamzin. I'm making her a load of clothes.'

'And her folk are rich, I suppose.' She wriggled herself into a more comfortable possession of Diane's shoulder.

'By our standards.'

'What's her problem? Is she anorexic, or something?'

'Something. Unhealthily thin. She's suffered from depression for the past couple of years. She's going through a good patch, at the moment.'

'Is she … is she George's girlfriend?'

Diane's arms tightened around Bryony's body. Not a frail, bony body, like Tamzin's, but a warm, fleshy, curvy young woman's shape, on the verge of plumpness. Diane had always been too busy and too short of money to gain weight but Gareth's mother had been a size in the last couple of decades of her life. She hoped Bryony wouldn't go the same way. It would be so bad for her asthma.

'It looks like it. Although they've only just started seeing each other.' She hesitated. 'I expect it took you by surprise, her being here.'

'I felt so stupid. I crashed in expecting a big hug but George had his arms full of her,' Bryony complained.

Diane continued absently to stroke her daughter's warm back as she had done a thousand times when shocks, fears and spills had brought Bryony into the sanctuary of her mother's arms. A lost toy. A scraped knee. Not getting the part of Angel Gabriel. A fickle friend. A fickle boyfriend.

And soon she felt the telltale hot wetness against her neck and the tiny shudders of the body pressed against hers. 'Darling,' she murmured. 'Everything will be fine when you've settled back at home and decided what you want to do next. If you don't want to go back to Brazil, you could probably go to university now.' Some good might as well come out of Gareth's money.

Bryony's sobs only increased.

'Or travel somewhere else? Or get a job here?'

The rounded shoulders heaved. 'No I can't. Oh, Mum – I'm *pregnant*! The father's name is Inacio, he doesn't know about the baby and I don't know where he is. And one of the other girls says he's *married*!'

Chapter Twenty

'I have to tell you something.' Diane sank into the visitor's chair. She had rung Ivan and Melvyn and told them she wanted the evening visitor's slot, and sorry if it cut across their plans. They hadn't minded. There was an athletics meeting on Sky Sports.

Gareth's still-bloated head turned her way, brown and purple in the pouches and furrows as if he'd been washed carelessly. The bladder infection had disappeared almost as suddenly as it had come and the electric fan was gone. 'I think I'd better go first. It's quite important.'

What Diane had to say was pretty important, too. But then she remembered Gareth's text. No doubt he assumed that she'd travelled in specifically to discover what he had on his mind. Not long ago she might have done that very thing.

But now she was different. Deceived, betrayed, hidden; she was the kind of person who made choices unhampered by unearned loyalty. She'd made James her lover and, today, under the guise of taking a walk in the sunshine, she'd called him for the comfort of hearing his voice as she tramped the matted verges, whilst Bryony recovered from her storm of weeping in a hot bath.

James's voice had been deep and warm and full of pleasure. 'When can we be together?'

'Bryony's home.' But she couldn't resist adding, 'Though I'm planning to go to Cambridge on Wednesday.'

'I'll clear my diary. I'll drive you. I want you.' His voice was dark and rough, making the hair on the nape of her neck stand up.

I want you sent her giddy; images of them in the back of his car flashing across her mind. The heat, the laughter, the stroking of his hands. 'I'll meet you there because I'll have my car packed with sample garments. I'm seeing a woman who owns a boutique.'

'Pity. I love having you in my car,' he said, deadpan.

Her laughter rose up into the sunshine, above the country lane. It was almost an hour before she'd ended the call, hot with joy at the prospect of a few hours with him. She'd hugged the thought to her ever since, dreaming off into space whenever she had five minutes.

'The most important thing,' Gareth was saying, reclaiming Diane's attention, 'is that I've ended things with Stella.' His pause was heavy with significance.

Diane raised her eyebrows. 'It's wonderful how many people do end their affair the instant it becomes untenable to continue.'

He managed to look injured. 'You don't think I'm ending it just because I've been found out?'

'Yes.'

'It's not like that. You're not looking at it from the right angle. I never realised how much I might hurt you until I saw how it made you feel to discover –'

'It made me bloody angry,' Diane interrupted, dispassionately, deciding that now would not be a good time to leap onto her high horse about fidelity. 'What *hurt* was that you hid me from your new, wealthy, desirable family and luxuriated alone in your lovely cottage.' She jumped up and prowled to the window to gaze out of the window at the lawns, conscious of having to inhale the sweetish disinfectant smell of hospitals instead of fresh cut grass. 'But none of it's particularly important at the moment.'

'Of course it's important.' Gareth sounded peevish. He shifted on the bed, pinned by the paraphernalia of his injuries. 'I realise that I acted badly. Like a child that's had too many presents on Christmas Day and doesn't want to share. I realise, I *realise*.

'But now it's all out in the open I feel relieved. You were right – I was paying you back for what happened over your dad's will.' His voice dropped. 'We can start again, move to a nicer place. You can give up your dressmaking.'

Slowly, Diane returned to her seat. Gareth held out his good hand to her but she pretended not to notice. 'Gareth, you're insulting my intelligence with this sudden munificence. All that's important about the money is what it's made you become. You're only beating your chest in case I make you share your horrible filthy bank balance.

'But I can't worry about what's left of our marriage right now. I came here to tell you what Bryony told me this morning – because, believe it or not there are things more important than money. Even your money.'

She paused to give him a moment to refocus, to switch his mind to his daughter. 'Gareth, Bryony's pregnant. She doesn't think she'll be seeing the father again, and she needs both of us on her side for a while. So let's worry about that, rather than balancing the scales of retribution.

'That's what I came to tell you,' she continued unemotionally, though she saw the colour had drained from his face. 'The father's name is Inacio, he's a Brazilian that Bryony saw for a few weeks. He's about 27 and, apparently, is "well fit, with black eyes that send you funny". She fell hard for him. She thought it was the start of something. But he stopped phoning and when she called his mobile he was offhand.

'It took her a few weeks to realise that she was pregnant. Then somebody told her that Inacio's married.'

Gareth drank from his spouted cup before he spoke again. 'Bastard!' he hissed, a clammy sweat of fury on his forehead. 'Wait till I get my hands on him, that shit –' He halted, glancing down at himself, pinned together like a mannequin, plastered into immobility, muscles wasting with disuse. 'What's she going to do?'

Diane sat back with a sigh. 'She won't contemplate abortion and I think she's possibly too far on, anyway.'

'Will she keep it?'

'I think so. I've made her an appointment with Dr Cooke tomorrow. She'll need to have a check up and be put into whatever the programme is now for pregnant women. Tests and scans.' *Pregnant women.* It was only a minute since she'd been her little girl, with merry dark eyes and a giggle that rang out like a xylophone.

'Is she all right, do you think? She wasn't herself yesterday but I put it down to tiredness.' His voice was gruff.

Diane nodded. 'Anxious, of course, and shocked. But she seems healthy.'

'I must see her, talk to her. I feel so helpless lying here.'

'I'll bring her tomorrow afternoon. She'll be living with us for the foreseeable future, I think. There's the money for you to give her a car now, isn't there? It's murder living in Purtenon St. Paul without one.'

His face flooded with colour. 'I'll arrange to have some transferred to you –'

'Arrange it with her,' she said, flatly.

He hesitated. 'Are you all right for money, Diane? Are you managing?'

A smile crooked her mouth and she gazed at him with curiosity. 'You've lain here with all that money at your fingertips and that's the first time you've bothered asking. Your boss phoned to check I was getting your sick pay, your union rep asked if I'd like to draw from the welfare fund, Harold offered help and Freddy wanted to send me a cheque. Thanks, Gareth, thank you for finally bothering about me but I'm OK. For now, your sick pay's covering the mortgage and I'm meeting everything else myself. I've even got in all the money Trish Warboys and Maria Cuthbert owed.'

Silence. Then, 'I still love you.'

She made a rude noise. 'Words are cheap.'

Fresh sweat broke out on his face. 'We can get through this. I'll have counselling. Some people don't cope well when they have a big windfall. They go on the spree. I just did the opposite, that's all –'

'How did it happen?' she interrupted.

'What?' The afternoon sun slanted low into his window, making him squint.

'When Harold got in touch with you. Did he write? Phone? Just turn up one day when I wasn't there?'

She watched the expressions chase across his face – indecision, guilt, guile. He cleared his throat. 'A bloke waited outside for me one day. I sent him on his way.'

'Why?'

He grinned. 'I thought that Melvyn or Ivan had got in bother with a loan and maybe got a bit creative with my signature and put me down as guarantor. You know how those lads expect my help.'

'Yes, I do.' She didn't smile.

'Then a letter arrived at our house. It was directly from my father. I was … flabbergasted. Blown away. You can't imagine – '

'Was I there when you read it?'

His eyes flicked left and she knew he was searching for the politically expedient reply. Probably he knew that the wrong answer would ignite her simmering fury. 'It was a Saturday, you were upstairs in your workroom when the post came. I don't think I meant not to tell you. But it was unreal. That's it, honestly – unreal. I didn't know what to do. He said that the agency believed that I was born to Wendy Jenner and he was likely to be my father. And he would very much like to meet me.

'I couldn't get my head round it. Didn't want to be made a fool of by it turning out to be some crackpot joke.

'I had to answer a load of questions about Mum's age, height and colouring and the names of her parents and siblings. I had a meeting with somebody from the agency, then I had a meeting with my father.' His voice shook. 'It was at the Great Northern Hotel. You know how swanky that is.'

'Yes. I haven't been there since before we were married, of course.'

The eyes dropped again, uncomfortably. She so rarely alluded to the fact that marrying him had sent her finances hurtling downhill as fast as a bob sleigh. 'We met for dinner. He was there, waiting for me. I was nervous, didn't know what to expect. I'd bought a new white shirt so that I didn't feel like a tramp in that swish dining room. I dropped my spoon in my soup and was so concerned with checking my new shirt that I didn't realise I'd showered his suit. I felt such a berk! The waiter looked at me as if I'd come in on his shoe. But Harold just laughed and told me not to worry.'

'Did you have blood tests?' Diane felt a creeping sensation of unreality that Gareth, her husband, could have been living in the same house as her yet keep hidden all these momentous developments in his life. Was she blind? Complacent? Stupid?

'Yes. Neither of us wanted to find later that we'd believed in something that wasn't true. Diane, he's a really good bloke and we get on well.'

'Yes, he's a gentleman.'

'Then he took me to meet Valerie, and we hit it off, too. She took me out in her sports car and up in her helicopter. I mean – a *helicopter*. My relationship with her is all novelty.

195

Not just the flying, not just that she's a sister instead of a brother – but because she doesn't expect me to make her decisions for her.'

'And it was all just too nice to share?'

He sagged wearily on his pillows, hunted and grumpy. He was being honest(ish) and she was still responding with her sour little comments, not cutting him any slack at all. In a minute he'd lose his temper and ability to apologise and this cautious, uncomfortable conversation would be wasted. Implacable, angry Diane was wearing to deal with. The normal Diane, the one who liked a quiet life, was easier to manipulate. He studied his wife. She looked half her age today in cropped jeans with a red and gold cuff at the bottom. He thought, irrelevantly, that he'd forgotten how blue her eyes were. Blue steel.

But maybe it was time for a controlled offensive. 'You know how I feel about what you did to me about your parents' money. And you know what lies are like. Suddenly, I was creating a whole new life for myself. For *me*. Not for you, not for my brothers or mum.'

'Nor for your daughter,' she added, helpfully.

He hesitated. Thought about Bryony and the baby. 'I'm going to make it up to her.'

'Put her in your will, do you mean? So she'll have to wait about 30 years, but if there's anything left, she'll get it?' Diane laughed.

Abruptly, the hold on his temper snapped. 'Oh, fuck off!'

'Good idea. I'll drop Bryony off to see you tomorrow afternoon.' And she sauntered out of the door, humming.

He seethed out at the sky and the treetops for a long time. It wasn't fair of her to stroll out on him when he couldn't chase her!

And … it was worrying that she didn't seem to give a

bugger for his opinion any more. He had never actually wanted his marriage to end or he would've ended it. It was just that his feelings for Diane had been coloured for such a long time by resentment.

He sighed, wondering how long it was since he'd had sex with his wife.

See, that was a bit of carelessness, to get out of that habit. Just because he was being nicely looked after by Stella he'd sort of let things slide with Diane during the cold war and, once intimacy had lapsed, it could be bloody awkward to make it routine and natural again.

Sex was a great destroyer of barriers. Which was probably why he hadn't wanted sex with her, because he wanted the barriers up, to punish her. But he'd expected her still to be waiting at the barrier when he chose to haul it aside.

The crash had mucked everything up. He'd had everything under control until then but now he had the feeling that nothing was under control. Particularly Diane.

He picked up his mobile and pressed the speed dialler. 'Guess what?' he said. 'I'm going to be a grandfather.'

His sister's precise tones were amused. 'Good God! I didn't know your daughter was in a relationship.'

He laughed shortly. 'It was over before she realised she was pregnant, unfortunately.'

'What does Diane think about it? Is she pleased?'

He realised, belatedly, that he hadn't enquired. 'I think she's concerned for Bryony, and that Bryony makes the decision that's right for her.' He was on pretty solid ground with that, Diane would be putting Bryony first; she had for all of Bryony's life.

They performed the routine comparison of recovery rates, then Gareth said, 'Can I ask you something, between you, me and the bedpost? Haven't you got a close buddy who's a lawyer? Would she come over and see me for an hour one morning? I need some information on something.'

A pause. Then, instead of agreeing instantly, Valerie said, 'I don't like being brought into your nefarious schemes.'

'Who said it's a nefarious scheme?'

She laughed. 'Why don't you ask your wife to arrange it, then?' A longer pause. 'No, I don't think I'm going to do it, Gareth. You've been perfectly bloody to your wife and I don't want to be any part of it. You'll have to pull this one off on your own.'

Dumbfounded, he hung up. She'd said no! His *sister*. Hadn't she read the unwritten rule that siblings said yes? She'd been brought up as an only child, and it showed. Melvyn or Ivan wouldn't have said no. Ever.

Chapter Twenty-One

'This is *so* weird.'

'You don't have to do it today if you don't want to. You've had an emotional few days; be kind to yourself.'

'I want to do it. It's just weird. I can't believe that I've had all these relatives all my life, and I'm twenty, and you have to introduce me to them.'

A dozen paces out of the lift stood a leather chair pushed up against the wall of the corridor. Bryony sank down in it. 'My legs are wobbly.'

Diane fetched a waxed paper cone of cold water from the dispenser for her. 'Why not leave it for today, sweetie? It's been a trying day, seeing Dr Cooke and then the midwife.'

Immediately, Bryony climbed back to her feet. 'No, I want to do it; I'm dead curious. We can see Dad later.'

There was no 'we' about it. Diane intended Bryony to see her father alone today. Bryony and Gareth needed time together – and Diane and Gareth needed time apart.

At Valerie's door, Diane knocked and stuck her head into the room. Tamzin and James were seated at the far side of Valerie's bed. Tamzin beamed delightedly to see her; James smiled with his eyes. Diane smiled back, but addressed Valerie. 'Is it a good time to bring Bryony in?'

Valerie brightened. 'Oh yes, let me meet my niece!'

Bryony was already squeezing past but paused as her eyes fell on her aunt. 'Oh. My. *God*. You and Dad are a real pair – you look as if you've been run over by a truck. Oh, hello.'

'Hello,' replied Tamzin, briefly, as she scooted around the bed to hug Diane.

Diane gave her a big hug back. 'You're looking good.'

Even though Tamzin wore a white top – it looked new – she had some colour in her face. Her hair had been brushed, too, the top pulled back into a red scrunchie and the rest rippling down her back.

'I feel amazing.'

Valerie, too, was looking better than when Diane last saw her. Her hair was glossy and she had less of a preoccupied and anxious air.

Diane broke away from Tamzin. 'Valerie, this is Bryony.'

Valerie smiled. 'You're like your father, Bryony. But prettier.'

When Bryony beamed, Diane suddenly saw a flash of resemblance to Valerie, too. There was something about the mouth and the way Bryony held herself. It was unsettling.

'And this is James, Bryony.' Diane had known that James would be there from a text conversation conducted late last night as she snuggled under her duvet. All day she'd looked forward to the meeting with tingling warmth, catching herself smiling at the thought of being near him. And she'd thought herself prepared to see him with his wife and daughter – but found herself trying to remember how to act normally around him. Disconcerted, she flashed a panicky glance at Valerie and found those hazel eyes regarding her almost with affection.

Guilt lurched through her like the first downwards drop on a roller coaster.

In cold blood, she was planning to have an affair with this woman's husband.

Valerie – her husband's half-sister and Tamzin's mother. If she were to go through with it, it would always be this way. There would be one relationship with James in public and another when they were alone. Echoes of Gareth and Stella. Had they felt like this? Guilty and remorseful? Or had they hugged their secrets and giggled over them when they were alone?

To hide the sudden trembling of her hands, she pushed the chair set out for her back from the bed, and from James, so that Bryony could sit close to Valerie.

Tamzin, luckily, was uncharacteristically streaming with chatter about her sisters' envy of her new clothes and all Diane had to do was listen and nod and smile, screamingly conscious of James's hands, resting loosely, still and calm, on his jeans-clad thighs. The same hands that tomorrow would be holding hers in the streets of Cambridge. Perhaps sliding beneath her clothes in the privacy of a car in a secluded spot … Pleasure and self-reproach butted heads and she felt sick.

As Valerie talked a wide-eyed Bryony through the helicopter crash and the complexity of lift offs – without actually mentioning the role of alcohol in what went wrong – Diane felt the truth of what she was contemplating like spicules of ice in her stomach.

There were so many people who could be affected. Valerie, Tamzin, Natalia and Alice. And, most of all, her own Bryony, sitting beside Valerie's white hospital bed and getting to know her family. Family that first Gareth had kept from her and now Diane was going to risk alienating.

People with whom Bryony and the tiny life she cradled inside shared blood.

Clammy horror climbed up on her shoulders.

She'd been thinking that she was only betraying Gareth. But that wasn't true at all. She rose jerkily. The conversation halted. 'Excuse me,' she mumbled.

Outdoors, she blinked in the sunlight, as confused as if she'd just arrived by Tardis. She felt like hell. Like such an evil bitch that she didn't want to be with herself. She crossed the car park and climbed a bank, skirted a big bed of red roses and dropped to the grass between it and a Leylandii windbreak. Rolling onto her back she slung her arm over her eyes, pressing with her forearm until her eyeballs ached, trying not to see a mental image of Bryony and a baby, both dark-eyed and cherubic and in need of a happy home.

Then Tamzin's face floated in front of her. A face that had suddenly remembered how to look cheerful, lit from inside by first love. And Valerie, plastered and pinned, and with plenty to cope with. Not really in any condition to fight for her husband.

The thought made her feel sick.

The thought of being without James made her feel worse.

It had taken a long time but it was as if she'd been drunk on joy ... and here came the hangover.

Her phone rang but she didn't even take it out of her pocket. She just lay with her face turned towards the sky, utterly miserable to realise how taking what you wanted could mash the hearts of other people.

Finally, she trailed back in through the automatic doors. The carpet, the hospital smell, the smiles of the nurses, the low key buzz of the place – all drearily familiar. She trudged up the stairs to the first floor and knocked gently on Valerie's door.

Valerie lay alone, staring out of the window, a magazine face down beside her.

Diane halted. Somehow she'd expected Bryony and Tamzin and James.

Valerie turned, forehead puckered with concern. 'Are you OK? You've been gone almost an hour, the others wanted to send out a search party. Bryony's gone to visit her father and Tamzin and James have left. I think James wanted to hang on and be Sir Lancelot but Tamzin's made arrangements to meet this new young man, so she hauled him out.'

'George,' Diane supplied, automatically.

'He's a relative of Gareth's, isn't he? If you're not in a dreadful hurry, why don't you sit down and tell me about him? According to Tamzin he's a god.' She reached over and pressed a button on her panel. 'You look as if you could do with a coffee. Are you all right? Shall we get a nurse to fetch Bryony?'

'I'm fine. I did feel strange but it's passing.' Awkwardly, Diane sank down onto the chair while somebody brought in coffee and a few biscuits on a little blue plate. She waited silently while the nurse put Valerie at a more comfortable angle to drink and joked gently about whether the coffee was strong enough to melt tar, the way Valerie liked it.

'Only because they won't put any scotch in it,' Valerie added under her breath as the nurse rustled out. 'So, is this George character the wonder that Tamzin insists?'

Diane forced a smile. 'George isn't perfect but he's no more likely to play Tamzin up than any lad of nineteen – and a lot less likely than some.'

'I suppose James has already given the poor lad the third degree. She'll never grow up if he has his way. She needs to get out and about; she shouldn't really have been allowed to flunk out of university.'

'But her depression …?' began Diane, doubtfully.

'Oh no, has James been filling you up with that?' Valerie closed her eyes and groaned theatrically, so, hopefully, missing Diane's horrified blush at the mention of James filling her up. 'Young girls get the blues, it's nature. Periods, boys, hormones – all part of the agonising process of being a teenager. Isn't Bryony the same?'

'Not really.'

'Lucky you. Pain in the derrière.' She switched subjects before Diane could protest that clinical depression was a million miles away from teenage moodiness. 'My dear brother tells me you're going to be a grandma. Congratulations!

What a scream to be a granny in your forties. Gareth was a bit shell-shocked but I think he was pleased. Are you? Takes a bit of getting used to, I expect, but new babies are so delicious. Tamzin was a perfect poppet.' And then, with hardly a pause for breath she added, 'I've enjoyed chatting, I hope you'll come again. And could you bring me in a little bottle of voddy next time? Do you think you could? I get terribly peed off without even a glass of red to liven up meal times.' She laughed, lightly, as if to show how unimportant the subject was.

Carefully, Diane replaced her coffee cup in its saucer and pushed it onto the little side table. 'Sorry,' she said, awkwardly.

Valerie looked knowing. 'Because James will make a fuss?'

'Um … because I'm not happy doing it.'

Valerie turned to pull open the little door to her locker. 'I'll give you the money, of course, I'm not asking for an early Christmas prezzie.' Deftly, she extracted a £20 note from a dark-red leather purse and tried to push it into Diane's hand. 'That's lovely, thanks such a lot.'

Shaking, Diane put the note back down beside Valerie's cup. 'Sorry,' she repeated, weakly.

Valerie's colour rose and her eyes glittered but her tone remained friendly and polite. 'Don't worry. Doesn't matter.'

Diane found Bryony waiting at the car. Her sweet little face was white and shuttered and she sat in silence as Diane drove.

'Dad offered me money for a car,' she burst out, finally, as Diane steered through the lanes towards the safety of Purtenon St. Paul. 'He said that I'd need it if I wanted to live at home for a while with the baby.'

Diane pulled her thoughts away from James. The heat

in his eyes, tonight. 'You will feel isolated without a car. I should know; I've done it for long enough.'

Bryony turned to stare out of the window at the garden-like fields. When she spoke again her voice was small. 'I must be more like you than I realised, Mum. I told him to stuff his money. He hid it from us until it was forced out in the open, didn't he?'

Diane concentrated on slowing the car enough to get through a speed camera – just around the slight bend after a long, inviting straight – without sullying her virgin licence.

'Didn't he?' repeated Bryony.

Diane sighed. 'Yes. But he says that he had his reasons.'

Bryony snorted. 'I can afford a banger with what I've got in the bank. I'd rather have that. If I let him buy me a car, every time I get into it I'll remember he doesn't really want me to have it.'

Diane sighed inside for her daughter and her hurt, pinched, little face. It was a strange thing for her to have to cope with, fatherly deceit on a grand scale. 'You know, don't you, that what he did was aimed at me and not at you?'

'Does it make any difference?'

'I'm not sure,' Diane answered, slowly, 'but I think so. Your father loves you very much, whatever his faults are. His love for you is beyond question.'

'Right,' said Bryony ironically. 'It's a neat theory that his crappy behaviour was all about you and old grudges but your motivation was good. He kept his shitty money to himself for selfish bastard reasons. And Granddad did almost exactly the same thing: he didn't leave you any money so that automatically cut me out, too!'

Diane let out a gurgle that could've been either laughter or a sob. 'I'm sorry, Bryony. My bad relations with other people have rather deprived you, haven't they?'

'None of it was your fault.'

'Neither Granddad nor Dad would agree with you there.' Diane drove on in silence, powerless to do anything but let Bryony glower out of the window in peace.

Presently, Bryony shifted in her seat. 'I'm getting too fat for these trousers. Mum, if I buy some maternity jeans, will you make them really cool for me?'

'Of course I will.' On impulse, she slowed the car. Here was something she could do to make her daughter feel better. 'We can go shopping now, if you want?'

Bryony brightened, though protesting half-heartedly. 'But we're nearly home.'

Diane began an eleven-point turn in a widish bit of lane. 'Doesn't matter. We'll buy you some jeans and then we'll have pizza in town. What do you say?'

'Sounds like a plan. That's cool, Mum, thank you.' After a few minutes she added politely, 'Of course, you've got all those clothes to make for Tamzin.'

'But I can squeeze you in, sweetie.'

They were almost into Peterborough again when Bryony sighed. 'Do you think Tamzin and George are serious?'

Diane followed the signs to the city centre. 'I think they're very new and exciting to one another at the moment.' She indicated to change lane. 'Have you told him that you're pregnant?'

'I haven't had the opportunity.' The hurt note was back in her voice.

Diane drove into the car park and found a space and ferreted out her change purse for the Pay and Display machine. 'It hasn't been an easy homecoming for you, has it? Perhaps you ought to ring round your old friends tomorrow – Stephanie and Katie and everyone. Pick up the threads of your life.'

Bryony nodded unenthusiastically. 'What about George? Do you think it'll be all right to ring him – you know, with

Tamzin?'

'He's still your cousin, Bryony. He's been your best friend since he was old enough to crawl about after you, so I don't see why that should change.' And then, because she knew her daughter's faults as well as her wonderful strengths, 'It's not as if you're immature enough to play any of those silly power games with Tamzin, is it? Vying for George's attention and making her feel the interloper. Tamzin is your cousin, too. She's very fragile and I think she'd be hugely relieved if you were friendly towards her.'

Bryony sighed again.

Chapter Twenty-Two

James was to meet Diane at Jesus Green, between Jesus College and the River Cam. He was supposed to be working from home but he'd diverted his calls to Lawrence and was playing hooky.

He was early enough to have a mooch around the pathways, enjoying the pleasantly shaggy Jesus Green, his heart doing flick flacks each time he thought about Diane.

She hadn't coped well with being in the same room as him and Valerie; her sudden exit from Valerie's hospital room could only have been guilt-driven. However tough a cookie she wanted him to believe she was, she had her marshmallow moments. He'd wanted to go after her, wanted to wait until she returned. Neither had been possible. He wasn't precisely certain of affair etiquette but the number one rule had to be not to exhibit undue public concern for the other party.

Now he'd probably have to persuade her that even though an affair might engender emotional situations she hadn't anticipated, it was *possible* and it was *worth it*.

He'd planned the day with care. A walk, here, on Jesus Green, where nobody was likely to know them and they could talk and laugh without being overheard. Then a meal in a quiet little place. He would be warm but not hot. She'd been spooked and needed reassurance that a relationship with him wasn't going to be scary and full of stress.

They would plan meetings. He was good at meetings.

They would be super careful.

They would manage. She would relax and he could tell her about the arrangements he'd already made.

'Hello,' she said, from behind him.

He swung round, heart leaping to see her standing there with the sun streaming all over her. 'You're early! I thought we were meeting at the entrance at noon?'

She smiled, her blue eyes and palomino hair shining in the sunlight. She was as beautiful as summer in a dress made of a collection of blue fabrics. She wore denim sandals and he felt unexpectedly turned on at the sight of her toes and slender, arched feet, reminding him of that evening in the back of his car when he'd been fascinated by her toes. He'd never been a foot man, till then.

'The drive didn't take as long as I'd thought, so I was killing time. I saw you by chance.'

He stepped closer, pulling her to him. 'More time together.'

Ignoring passers by, eyes fixed to his, she ran her hands slowly up the outside of his arms to his shoulders, then pulled herself up on tiptoe and touched her open lips to his mouth. With a shock of desire he put a hand in the small of her back, pressing her to him. She kissed him hard, urgently, her tongue hot and sweet and he pressed the hardness of his arousal against her warmth as he concentrated on the wonderful feeling of wanting to be inside this woman. Again.

The kiss seemed endless. She was feeding from him and he forgot they were in the middle of a public park with children giggling and traffic grumbling nearby and focused only on her and this heart-thumping, scalp-prickling kiss.

Until she dropped back down onto her heels, pushed herself out of his embrace and stepped back. Her eyes burned with pain. 'I can't do it,' she whispered.

His heart was still going like a train. 'What?'

'I can't have an affair with you. I can't do it to Valerie and Tamzin. In their different ways, they need you. You belong to them. And now that Bryony is home and pregnant I think she needs me and Gareth to be together for a while, too.' She took another step back. 'I could probably cope with the subterfuge and the guilt, but I can't cope with hurting other people. Now's not the time for us.'

He took a step after her, disorientated by the sudden, brutal reversal in his fortunes. 'Let's discuss it –'

She shook her head and tears slid from each eye. 'If we talk I might not be able to stick to it. And I've got to.' Then she whirled on the dusty path and ran away, her hair streaming out behind her like a scarf.

As winded as if she'd kicked him in the balls, he dropped down on the unshorn grass and watched her go.

Grit stuck between her toes and beneath the soles of her feet but she ran on. She ran until her lungs burned and her knees hurt. Tears curved around the apples of her cheeks and prickled down her neck. People with dogs and children tutted as they hauled their charges aside to let her skitter past, running from the hurt on James's face.

Finally, she stumbled to a halt, breath dragging at her throat, legs like string, miserable with the knowledge that she'd made a complete pig's breakfast of things.

She trudged towards the nearby Grafton Centre in search of a ladies' room, glancing from habit at the corner house in Fair Street with the flood gauge on its wall that had held a ghoulish fascination for a younger Bryony. Through the sliding glass doors in the giant conservatory-like edifice that was the entrance to the Centre she made her way to Debenhams' toilets where she washed her hands and face and brushed her hair, trying not to look her reflection in the eye, furious with herself. She'd hurt James. Oh, how she'd hurt James! The expression in his eyes had switched in a heartbeat from joy to pain. And she'd done that. She'd put that pain in his face.

He probably wanted to throttle her – how could she have kissed him like that and then given him the push? Angel and devil in one instant.

He must think she got off on hurting people.

The room was empty so she filled a white oval basin with warm water and was hopping on one foot dunking her dusty toes, her dress hiked up to her thighs, when three silver-permed ladies entered, handbags swinging from their elbows.

Ignoring their pause for disapproval, she soaped and rinsed the other foot and dried both feet with paper towels. After plaiting her hair from the nape of her neck she made herself look properly in the mirror. She looked OK. A bit pale, but she wouldn't scare the horses.

Christ's Pieces, in contrast to Jesus Green, was a manicured, colourful array of marigolds and canna lilies. Diane paced sedately beneath the central avenue of trees, no longer the woman who galloped gritty paths like a bolting horse. She'd bravely driven right into Cambridge's manic city centre this morning and, after innumerable slow tours, secured a space in nearby Lion Yard car park. Now she returned and dragged out her load of garments, working automatically through her plan, glad it wasn't too much of a trek through the market place to Rose Crescent.

Still, her arms were cracking by the time she reached the shop at the end of the crescent farthest from the market on the brick-built side, not the stone-built side. Nothing hung outside, not like Rowan's shop; here at Unity's the stock was safely contained behind windows. Shops in Rose Crescent catered to a discerning clientèle – even McDonalds looked slightly self-conscious with a Sunday-best timber frontage.

She would normally have been nervous, but she just felt too bloody miserable to stress over a mere business meeting. She paused by a topiary box tree to remind herself that what she was doing was important, she couldn't give in to the overwhelming urge to ring James and cry out that she hadn't meant it. That they could make things work, somehow ... No. She couldn't. Shouldn't. Wouldn't.

She clanged in through the brass-framed glass door with a lump in her throat and an image of James's stricken face hanging before her eyes.

The shop was painted a colour that wasn't lavender and wasn't grey, but possibly both. The highly lacquered woodwork was blond and halogen spotlights angled towards chrome rails.

Few items in the shop had a price ticket under three figures and the most important part of a garment on these rails was the label.

What. Was. She. Doing. Here?

Competing with Ghost and D&G? This was going to be the dreariest waste of time. Maybe she should just turn around and shuffle back to the safety of Peterborough. Rowan was a condescending little turd but it didn't stop him taking her stuff.

But then, her voice as steady as if she did this every day, she heard herself say, 'Hi,' to the woman looking up from some task behind the counter. 'I'm Diane Jenner and I've an appointment to show my work to Unity.'

The woman uncoiled slowly. The layers in her dark red hair flipped back from her face like the petals of a flower that topped her long, slender stem of a body. She looked old enough to have experience and young enough for confidence. 'Oh yes, my mother said you'd be calling. I do like to sell some original garments.' Encouraging, until she added, 'But she should've told you that I'm fully stocked. I take it you've brought autumn? My autumn stock's already on order. Soon I'll be reducing summer.'

'Autumn/winter,' Diane responded, stretching a point. She hesitated. With such a heavy heart to drag around she wasn't sure she had the strength to get her garments out just to pack them away again.

But then Unity smiled. 'It won't hurt to look. I'll tell Jasmine to come into the shop.' She led the way into a back room, white and bright with fluorescent lights. Several chairs were scattered around a freestanding clothes rail near a compact kitchen area and, around an L, a sewing machine on a long table. 'Alterations,' she explained. 'I have a lady come in.' Unity detached Jasmine, a young, dreamy girl dressed entirely in pink, from her task of unpacking bead belts, to look after the shop.

'Hang your stuff here.' With one slender manicured hand, Unity swept a few clothes and empty hangers to one end of the rail. Then she turned to answer the telephone, giving Diane time to slide off polythene slips and shake out creases. Choosing a blouse, a skirt and a dress, she turned the hangers so that the garments faced the room.

Unity was evidently getting impatient with her telephone caller. 'So what's happened to the jackets? Look, I must have jackets, they bring customers into the shop in autumn. Yes, the size eights are all very well for the window but I need other sizes. You know, for real people.'

Diane sorted through for a jacket, dark red needle cord and denim, and pulled that out, too.

Unity clicked the phone down, a pucker of irritation on her forehead. 'OK, let's see what you've got.'

She looked without speaking for a minute then picked up the blouse, one made from panels and patches of white voile and cotton, frayed and unfinished as fashion demanded, fastening with white frogs down the front. She examined the back. The stitching. Then moved on to the skirt, dark grey glazed cotton with inset godets overlaid with dark green lace, a wraparound that fastened with three ties, one at the waist and two at the hip. 'You'd have to tie that realistically to stop it riding up,' she commented.

'Yes. Flattering for the snake-hipped rather than those built for comfort.'

Unity put her head on one side. 'It's lovely for the sizes, say, up to 14, but I suppose you could do a waist-tie only version for the larger? Wraparounds are popular with the bigger women but you have to go for flowing rather than fitted.'

'Of course.' Despite her wretchedness, Diane's heart suddenly began a tango.

The dress was cinnamon-coloured slubbed linen with a fringed hem above the knee and a crossover bodice, pin-tucked above the breasts and beaded with gold. Unity glanced inside. 'This says it's a ten. Do you mind if I try it? Then I can see how your sizes come up.'

Even as Diane said, 'Please do,' Unity pulled her top over her head and wriggled neatly out of velvet jeans, unselfconscious in bra and pants as she slid the dress from the hanger, undid the side zip and pulled the fabric over her head. Diane zipped it up for her as Unity fluffed out her hair, then slipped into her heeled mules and went to the wall mirror.

Diane crossed her fingers. And then her ankles. She ought to be doing something more constructive, telling Unity that it could've been made for her, it flattered her, that her svelte figure and endless legs did wonders for the dress and she ought to have been a model. But Unity didn't need Diane to say any of those things. The mirror had already said it.

'Wow, it even gives me a bust,' exclaimed Unity. 'I love it.'

By the time Unity had looked at every garment, trying on a blouse and a skirt along the way, Diane was beginning to dare to get a good feeling.

'I think we've earned a break.' At last, Unity moved towards the kitchen area. 'Would you like a cup of tea?'

'Yes, I would,' said Diane, frankly. 'Strong with no sugar, please.'

Obligingly, Unity gave her the cup with the tea bag still floating in it, and they sat down at the table. Unity was drinking a pale brew, camomile or lemon or something equally healthy.

'This is all autumn stuff and I'll have no room on my racks for it,' she said, waving her hand at the clothes spaced along the length of the rail.

Diane's heart began a long, slow swallow-dive to the pit of her guts.

For an instant, hot tears pricked under her eyelids. She'd become sure that Unity would take *something*, even if were only the dress for her own wardrobe. She'd even planned to make a gift of it as a sweetener. Misery rushed in to swamp her and she dipped her face to her tea mug so that Unity wouldn't see.

'But it's so good, and so well-made, so original, that I want to have it anyway, if we can come to terms.'

Miraculously, Diane's eyes cleared and her head shot up. 'What? All of it? Um, I mean, yes, let's talk.'

'Ideally I want at least one of everything in sizes 8 to 18 but I'll settle for 10 to 16 if it's too short notice. And if you can give me two of 10, 12 and 14 in the jacket, I'll snatch your arm off. And can you get some new sew-in labels made? *DRJ* is nothingy; how do you feel about *Diane Jenner Original*? I want to sell them top end so we need to push the individuality angle.' She grabbed a pad and pen and began a series of calculations. Then she turned the pad to face Diane. 'Look, this is what I'm in the market for paying. I think these figures are reasonable and I'm going to devote a bit of shop space to you. I'll need delivery, latest, absolute latest, by mid-September. Are you selling your stuff through any other local shops?'

Diane's lips had gone stiff with shock, but she managed, 'Rowan's in Peterborough.'

'Can you stop?'

'Yes. The relationship isn't satisfactory, that's why I'm approaching you.'

Unity frowned. 'I don't want anyone else local selling you, ideally. They might undercut me. I'll give you another ten pounds on each garment if you don't sell to anyone else in a 50-mile radius of this shop.'

Slowly Diane nodded. She sipped some of her tea, the teabags bobbing against her lips. 'What about customer commissions?'

Unity shrugged. 'Yes, OK, small, direct-to-customer commissions are the exception. I take a full-page ad in the local paper at the beginning of each season, so we'll launch Diane Jenner Originals in the autumn one. Will it be OK to have a pic of you and like a news flash about how well you're doing and how lucky we are to be able to buy your original garments locally?'

'I … I expect so.' This was beginning to seem like a dream.

'Are you going to be able to handle the order?'

Diane gathered herself. 'Yes. These are only garments, there's no hand embroidery and not much beading – that's what takes the time when I'm doing customer commissions. And I'll use help for the basic stuff, you know – cutting out, tacking in interfacing, sewing on buttons. My daughter's just come home from Brazil, she might want to help.'

Unity's eyes were gleaming. 'Embroidery? In a few weeks we'll have to start talking about Christmas, and embroidery, beading and lace will be snapped up. Do you produce drawings?'

Diane thought of her children's sketch book full of line drawings, a bit wonky sometimes. 'Not what you'd call *drawings*. Not like on a commercial pattern.'

'Can we have an ideas meeting, in that case? Say at the end of August?'

'I'm sure I can fit that in.' Diane could scarcely believe it was her speaking.

'I think this is going to work,' Unity mused. 'Lots of my ladies will go for a fresh, exclusive but local designer.'

Diane let out a strangled laugh. 'Let's hope so.'

Unity helped her gather up and re-cover the garments before seeing her to the door of the shop. 'Where did you do your training, by the way?'

Diane grinned. 'Which? The A-level needlework or the evening class in pattern-cutting?'

It was peculiar to be in a haze of happiness and a nightmare of misery at the same time.

Diane tracked back to the car in the afternoon breeze on wobbly legs, not knowing whether to sing or weep. Nobody would know, if she cried, that she was crying for James and the big emptiness that the joy of Unity's contract had not filled up.

At the car park she was only half-surprised to find him leaning on her car boot. Glowering.

'I've spent hours looking for your Peugeot,' he said, sourly. He took her key and opened the boot then took the clothes, lying them as flat as possible without having to be told. His forehead was a frown and his slate eyes didn't smile at all.

'I'm sorry,' she said, unhappily. 'I told you really badly, didn't I?'

'Brutally. I still need to talk to you, even if it's to work out how we're not going to have an affair, rather than how we are.'

She sighed and followed him to a pub. She couldn't remember the last time she'd been in a pub in the afternoon. But she ordered a glass of wine when he asked for a bottle of beer and they sat at a small round table on an inadequately padded bench as far from the few other patrons as possible.

'What if I were to leave Valerie?' he demanded.

She gazed at the grim resolve in his eyes and wanted to slide comforting arms around his firm body. Instead, she said, gently, 'But you don't think that's the right thing to do, do you? Tamzin's doing better but she's so terribly brittle. She wouldn't cope. James, think how we'd feel if she crashed back into depression and began on her arms. Or worse. You might not feel guilty about Valerie but you would about Tamzin.'

'I don't feel guilty about Valerie.' But he didn't disagree about Tamzin. His glance flickered over her face. 'So you're going to stay with your lying, deceitful husband and I've got to stay with a wife who doesn't much like me? And do without each other?'

Under the table she took his hand and felt his electricity cross to her body. His flesh was warm and smooth and strong. 'I think that that is exactly what we have to do. At least for now. Until Bryony and Tamzin can stand on their own feet.'

'But we could make each other happy.'

'And all the people we love unhappy,' she whispered.

There didn't seem to be much more to say. She blew her nose a couple of times and told him glumly all the marvellous, wonderful news about the Unity's contract and he turned his stormy eyes to her and told her, grimly, how pleased he was.

'You'll need some capital,' he pointed out.

She sighed. She'd shoved that aside to think of later. 'I will, especially if I'm going to pay somebody to help me with the basics, and that's before I start thinking about materials or what I'm going to live on. Maybe I'll go to the bank.'

'You don't want to use Gareth's money?'

She was shaking her head before the sentence had ended.

'I can lend you what you need. Say £5,000, so that you don't have to worry until you get your first big cheque.'

She burst into tears. 'I couldn't do that but you're so kind,' she sobbed.

'I don't feel kind,' he snapped. 'I feel like shaking you.'

He watched her until he couldn't stand to see her shoulders trembling any more. 'I suppose that if you're going to a bank you'll need a business plan,' he said, eventually, to distract her.

'Yes,' she sniffed, emerging from her tissues, 'but I don't know what one is.' Her eyes were pink.

'They're quite easy. Especially for such a small venture. You can find templates on the Internet.'

'If you have a computer,' she agreed, dolefully. 'Maybe the bank has a form.'

'I could give you a few headings and you could just fill it in.'

Her eyes swivelled to him hopefully, and she blew her nose. 'Really?'

'Really,' he sighed. He wished he could stop being the guy who wore the white hat but when she looked at him as if he'd just solved all her problems ... He searched through his pockets and came out with a folded envelope. Diane found a pen with a broken end, in her bag.

'Introduction.' He underlined the word. 'Just give them an overview of what you're going to do. Business opportunity.' He underlined that, too.

'What's that mean?'

He considered. 'It's what you plan to sell, and how.'

She groaned. 'Same thing, different words, yes. What else?'

'Your marketing and sales strategy.'

'I've marketed it. I've sold it.'

'Personnel?'

'Me. Maybe Bryony. Even Tamzin, if she fancies it.'

He began to feel like laughing. 'I don't think you're going to chase Jaeger out of the market, do you?'

She shook her head. There was a glimmer of a smile.

'Premises?'

'Home.'

'Equipment?'

'Only when I take on another machinist. But maybe I need a new table. Materials and money to live on are my priorities.'

'Financial forecasts?'

She looked horrified. 'Are you absolutely certain a bank will want a business plan?'

He kissed the tip of her nose and tucked the folded envelope into her hand. 'Or you could just smile at the bank manager and he'll lend you the money.'

She gazed at him reproachfully. 'She's a woman.'

'Better write the business plan, then.'

They kissed for the last time before he walked her back in silence to her car. There was none of the heat and passion of the back-seat episode. He cradled her against him and explored her mouth as if committing it to memory. He kissed her throat and the palms of her hands. Then waited, impassive, while, her lap full of tissues, she reversed out of the parking space and drove home to Purtenon St. Paul.

Chapter Twenty-Three

Tamzin had been going out with George for three weeks. Three blissful weeks of holding hands. Kissing. Laughing, talking. Eating fast food.

George had such a huge appetite and punctuated his days with, 'I need a McDonald's,' or, 'How long till I get a pizza?' Tamzin was actually beginning to gain weight because she sat beside him and opened her mouth like an obedient little bird as he fed her titbits of pizza dough festooned with cheese or strips of spicy chicken, while he ate.

Besides Erica, Rob and Marty, George had loads of friends; it made her head spin how many. He fell over them at every pub, club and gig.

In the busier of these, Tamzin withdrew – and tonight was happy-cheapy night at Danny Boyes, so mega busy. As the place heaved and voices rose she grew sweaty and tense. To her surprise, George seemed to realise and, when holding her hand didn't make her feel any better, just whispered, 'Let's go,' in her ear and led her out into the night, out of the rafter-shaking racket.

'Are you a panicker?' He pulled her close to kiss her.

She snuggled into his arms, the evening air chilly after the cheerful fug inside. 'Kind of. I'm sorry if I spoilt your night.'

'So what is it? Crowds?'

She felt her hands become fists. 'Not always. It's certain kinds ... Certain people. It sounds so stupid when I say it aloud.'

'It can't be stupid if it makes you feel so crazy bad.' The street was quiet. He pulled her down beside him on a wall. 'Tell me about it.'

'You'll think I'm babyish.' She shivered.

He squeezed her tightly. 'I'm on your side, Tamz.'

She leaned her forehead against his collarbone, squeezing shut her eyes as if it would be easier if she couldn't see him, and took a deep breath. 'You know that I dropped out of uni in my first year? I had problems with some people.' She swallowed down her thudding heart. 'They were known as the Coven, this group. They appointed themselves arbiters of popularity; decided who was in and who was out. They had this well cruel sense of humour. You were OK if they thought you were cool, and OK if they ignored you, but if they *picked* on you – they just made life hideous.' Her voice was muffled.

He kissed her hair. 'Girls can be bitches.'

Moisture leaked from her eyes and onto his T-shirt, anxiety rising in her throat. 'The Coven weren't girls. They were all clever and good-looking blokes – and hateful! Patrick and Lucas were the leaders. They'd select somebody and ridicule them constantly, for entertainment. The somebody was me.'

She hid her eyes against him. 'It sounds so childish. But they condemned every aspect of my life, my clothes, music, car, accent, hair, skin, body. I began to smoke dope. I'd never smoked it before but some of the girls thought it would help me chill. It didn't. I had a thing with Lucas and the Coven used it to spread lies about my supposed perversions. I smoked and smoked but I couldn't chill. I couldn't not care.'

She choked on a sob. 'I got terrible downers. And as the coming down got worse and worse, I smoked more and more.'

'Cannabis would only fuck you up more, you poor little sod.' He rocked her in his arms. 'Those shitty bastards. I'd like to rip their fucking heads off.'

The ice of his anger somehow began to make her feel better. 'Dad came and got me. He wanted to bring in the police, lawyers, make them pay, shave their heads, put them in the stocks. But I just wanted to go home and curl up and forget it.'

George's arms tightened around her. 'You can forget it now.'

Being in love with George made Tamzin something she'd pretty much forgotten how to be. Happy.

George was wicked, George was amazing, and every time Tamzin thought about him the space between her shoulder blades prickled and the pit of her stomach felt hot.

So it was a small blow a couple of days later to find him full of what, to him, was good news. 'Bryony's going to meet us at the pub, tonight. Be amazin', we've hardly seen her since she came back.'

Tamzin smiled as her heart sank.

It had never really struck her that a lot of George's friends would have been Bryony's friends, too, even though first Diane and then George had told her that they'd been buddies all their lives. If she'd thought of Bryony at all it had been as safely out of the way in Purtenon, with Diane, or perhaps visiting Uncle Gareth in hospital.

She hadn't envisioned her borrowing her parents' Peugeot and bursting right into the middle of Tamzin's good time. But there she was, hurling herself at Erica and Marty for joyous, wet-eyed hugs. 'Oh, oh, it's so good to *see* you! This is so *cool*.' And then George, an especially long, meaningful hug. 'I've missed you, Gorgeous.'

George laughed. 'Yeah, so much you'd forget to email me for weeks 'n weeks.'

Bryony pouted. 'I didn't have my own computer, I had to wait to get to a cyber café and there were none near to where I worked. Hello.' She sat down with a brief smile and nod to Tamzin. George reclaimed his seat and even gave

Tamzin back his hand to hold but his eyes and ears were Bryony's for the next hour as she poured out her life since she'd left Peterborough. 'The school, the school needed so much doing to it and the children, the children were so beautiful but so poor. We talk about underprivilege here but it's nothing, *nothing* like there.'

Rob, across the table from Tamzin, was the only one to look unimpressed. He even yawned a couple of times. Tamzin, who found yawns contagious, had to struggle to suppress her own, causing Rob to wink conspiratorially at her.

Tamzin liked Rob. There was no bullshit about him, he was just a nice guy who usually had too many zits to shave and the face fuzz didn't show because his bedhead hair hung all over his face anyway.

Rob began to tell Tamzin about his college course and the part-time job he'd just started at a care home and how, on his first day, he'd somehow managed to kick an elderly man's stick out of his hand. 'Luckily I caught him before he hit the deck.'

She grinned. 'I bet the old ladies love you.'

'Yeah, as it happens. I put new batteries in their hearing aids for them.' He nodded towards Bryony and dropped his voice. 'Bet she wants to come back to the band.'

Tamzin's lip dropped in dismay. 'Can she? You're the drummer, now.'

Rob shrugged, drawing a sad face on the table in spilt beer. 'Suppose. But bands are democratic. If the others say they want her instead of me, then I'll, like, have to go. She and Georgie started the band. She's one of the Jenners of Jenneration.'

'But she left.'

'Like that's going to change anything.'

'Oh. Right.' They turned to look at Bryony burbling at

the end of the table, looking like a busty imp with her dark eyes and curly hair and curious low-waist jeans with braces that Diane had apparently already been let loose on, judging by the tawny embroidery and silver oval beads.

But it wasn't long before the burbling had died down to a sputter, and Bryony's eyes were filling up. Tamzin felt a spear of jealousy to see her put her forehead against George's shoulder, much as Tamzin had done the day before. 'I'm pregnant,' she confessed.

'No!' everybody breathed.

And among the gasps of surprise and murmurs sympathy, Tamzin couldn't help but meet Rob's eye. He grinned and mimed a drum roll on the tabletop.

At the end of the evening, Tamzin and George saw Bryony to her car. It was dark because some of the streetlights were out; even the moon seemed to be having a bad cloud day. George held Tamzin's hand, although both Bryony and George were so quiet that Tamzin began to wonder whether they wished she wasn't there. But Bryony drove straight off and George watched the tail lights disappear. Tamzin had brought her own car, feeling really cool and brave to have brought it all the way into the city. Climbing into the passenger seat, George flung himself back with a sigh.

'What do you think of that, then?'

'Bryony's news?' she asked, cautiously.

'Yeah.' He shook his head. 'She's pregnant by some guy she has almost no chance of getting any cash or help out of. *Pregnant.* I can't believe it. What the fuck was she thinking? Doesn't she carry condoms? And the way she announced it, as if she expected us all to rally round.'

'People get pregnant all the time. Contraception fails – '

''Specially if you don't use it.'

Ignobly, Tamzin felt a burst of happiness. All evening

she'd dreaded discovering that George's affection for Bryony was more than cousinly, but it seemed that George was more irritated than enthralled.

'You have to be careful,' he insisted. 'You just have to be careful. I'm always careful. Aren't you?'

Tamzin nodded. 'I used to be on the pill but I haven't … there hasn't been anyone. Since uni.'

Slowly, George turned towards her. 'You haven't since uni?'

In the darkness, the air felt as if somebody had charged it with static electricity. 'I told you about having a bad time,' she whispered.

George didn't move but still somehow seemed to get closer. 'Has your doctor or therapist told you not to?'

A nervous giggle. 'Of course not.'

He laughed, too; low, husky. 'That's a good start, then.' He slid his arms around her. Very softly, gently, he kissed her. 'Did you hate sex?' he whispered, his mouth touching hers.

'No.' Her heart broke into a canter.

'Did you like it?' His hand stroked her back, and she shivered.

'Sometimes,' she croaked.

He laughed again. 'I'd like it with you. Do you think you might like it with me?'

She shivered. 'I might.'

He nuzzled her neck and let his hand glide down her back to her hip. 'I think you would. I think it would be amazin'. You don't have to. But I really want to, Tamz.'

She felt giddy and panicky all at once. 'I haven't got anything.'

'I have. I'm always careful. It's all right if you don't want to – but I totally want you to want to.'

She giggled again as he kissed her ear, her heart soaring at the heady experience of being the object of desire. 'I think I want to.'

They drove out to a place near one of the lakes, a place George knew – there was no way it was going to work out in Tamzin's little hatchback with somebody George's height. By the time they were lying on the bumpy grass together, she was shivering.

George crushed her in his arms as if he was doing his damnedest to become part of her. 'You can change your mind, Tamz, if you don't want to do it.'

'I think I want to but … you know. What happened before.'

'Pretend it's the first time,' he whispered. 'It's something amazin' and new, just for us.'

He was gentle and slow, his fingertips fluttering over her like butterflies, sealing her and him into a world of dewy grass and twilight where her skin tingled and her body melted. 'It's the first time. Just the first time.'

'The first time,' she agreed. Fears slithered away, taking all those hurtful old images with them. This was the first time. And it was amazing.

Chapter Twenty-Four

It nearly killed Diane to admit it to herself as she stood on Freddy's doorstep on a storm-darkened Sunday afternoon. But her father had been right about Gareth.

For years she'd genuinely thought that he'd put up with her parents' awfulness for her. It wasn't until she refused the money from her father's estate that it became plain that all those years of exemplary behaviour had been no more than an investment. Gareth had possessed a fine perception of which side his bread was likely to be buttered. All he had to do was wait it out and half of Diane's parents' money would surely come.

She remembered his face, black with fury, when she'd refused Freddy's offer to share the inheritance. 'You're entitled! It's your right.' Whereas, it was clear to her now, he'd meant *he* was entitled and it was *his* right.

To force the memories from her mind, Diane admired the green sweeps of Freddy's lawn, the elegant might of the monkey puzzle tree and the banks of lilies on the shady side of the garden. And she thought of James.

She seemed to be thinking of James every waking moment.

His smiling eyes, the hot sex in the back of his Merc, the way he'd accepted her decision to end things before they began with huge regret but no word of recrimination. It was astonishing how empty she felt without him. Which just went to show – you *could* miss something you'd never had. Or only had once in the back of –

She twitched her thoughts away at the sound of the front door opening. Her brother blinked at her through his glasses. 'Diane!'

'Hello, Freds.'

Freddy grasped her hands and kissed each of her cheeks. 'It's been too long since I saw you.'

Diane found she actually had to swallow a lump in her throat at the pleasure in her brother's eyes, always magnified by his glasses. She wished suddenly that she hadn't allowed Gareth's animosity to make it difficult for her to visit her brother.

He showed her to the conservatory that wrapped around the back of the house. One of the doors to the garden was open. 'This is my favourite spot. I can sit here in all weathers and never get wet.' He halted suddenly. 'Anyway, what's it to be? Cup of tea?'

'Bring the pot.' She chose a thickly padded cane chair and kicked off her shoes to settle back and watch the purple sky become lower and darker until smudgy clouds dropped the first raindrops as big as pennies on the yellow York stone of the patio. Faster. Harder. Noisier. Until the rain was pelting the windows. Freddy reappeared. 'I hoped we'd have a storm – that's why I was in here.' He wound up the roof blinds so they could watch the water washing summer leaves from the glass as shrubs thrashed in the blustery wind. From outside came the rotting smell that came with rain after a long dry spell.

Admiring thunder crash and lightning flash, Diane propped her feet on the coffee table. 'Do you think you should shut the door?'

Freddie poured the tea. 'I'll mop up before Sîan comes home.'

Lightning hung among the clouds as the next roll of thunder shook the sky. The rain redoubled, began to hiss. Diane tipped her head to watch it sluicing down the roof.

A puddle began to spread across the terracotta tiling towards them. Gleefully, Freddy lifted his feet to join Diane's on the coffee table. He had to raise his voice to be heard as the rain lashed. 'This is exhilarating.'

Diane laughed. 'I suppose it is. It's a while since we had an adventure together.'

'The last one was when you pushed me out of the tree house – '

'You fell!'

'Only because I jumped at you and you moved. I broke my arm and my fingers came up exactly like sausages.'

'And what about being nearly cut off by the tide at Wells? Do you remember how Dad bellowed?'

'Missing our lift home after a party in a barn.'

'Getting drunk on whisky.'

'Getting drunk on all kinds of things.'

'You thinking you'd got Miranda Thingy pregnant.'

Freddy choked on his tea, spattering dark drops down his polo shirt, eyes watering behind his glasses. 'I didn't know you knew about that. I still come out in a cold sweat when I remember. I used to pray that either she'd get her period or I'd get knocked over by a bus before Dad found out. Luckily it was the former. She finished with me in relief.'

'I would've tried to talk to him for you.'

'You were always a good sister.' He pushed back the dark, slightly old-fashioned wing of hair that fell over his eyes. 'I wish you'd taken your half of the money.'

She sipped her tea. Not bad, but could've been stronger. The thunder's bark moved further away and the rain dropped a note. The puddle on the floor had crept under the coffee table. 'When I married Gareth I knew I was letting myself in for a lifetime without frills. But I also knew that there were more important things than money.' She sighed. 'But I am here kind of on the trail of filthy lucre. Have you still got that jewellery for Bryony? She's twenty-one in September and I'd like her to have it.'

Freddy turned his head slightly, eyebrows lifting. 'Of course I still have it. It's in the safe. I'm glad you're taking it.'

'There's something else.' She hesitated, feeling foolish. 'I wouldn't ask this, except it's for Bryony. Do you remember Mum and Dad buying her £100 worth of premium bonds for her first Christmas, but not actually handing them over?'

'Do I! The Christmas Day from hell. Yes, I've been meaning to speak to you about that. There was an account with about £1,000 in it, and I think that must be the prizes it's won over the years. And I cashed in the £100, too, so that can be added to it.'

Diane gazed at her brother with affection. He was such a soppy old sod in his sheepskin slippers and golf shirt. 'Oh, Freddy. You're a bloody bad liar. There *were* no premium bonds in Dad's things, were there?'

Freddy pulled a shamed face. 'No.'

'And therefore no account with £1,000 in?'

'No.'

'He never bought those bonds, did he?'

A big grimace. 'I didn't find any evidence of them.' He hesitated. 'I never talked to you about it because Gareth asked me for them after Dad died and I told him the bonds weren't there. He asked for £100 out of the estate and I said only once I'd talked to you about it. He didn't seem to want to take it any further.'

Diane looked out at the dripping garden and heaved a great sigh. Puddles stood on the lawn, the earth baked too hard for absorbency. 'I didn't know that. Of course, he might've meant to pass the money on to Bryony.'

'Or keep it safe for her.' Freddy's glance was sympathetic. 'Let me give her the £100 – it was promised to her.'

Diane debated. Her first instinct was to refuse. But then she remembered that it wasn't actually her £100. 'I'll talk to her about it. She's going to need money.' And she told

Freddy about Bryony's pregnancy.

At home in Purtenon St. Paul, Diane found Bryony sitting at the kitchen table and sighing, the ever-present inhaler beside her. She was wearing panelled maternity jeans that Diane had embroidered and the kind of frown that changed her appearance from elf to imp.

Diane was familiar with that pucker on her daughter's forehead. She dropped her bag on the kitchen chair. 'What's up?'

Bryony shrugged and turned a page of her magazine. 'We haven't got a computer and there's no cyber café in the village. I want to email my friends in Brasilia.'

'You can come into Peterborough with me when I visit Dad tomorrow, do it then.'

'Yeah. Guess.' Another page flipped over. Then, casually, 'None of my friends here seem free to go out much.'

'You went out with them last night.'

The magazine shut with a slap. 'Yeah. Some. But that's evening. I want to meet my old mates and go shopping and have a laugh. Claudia and Bella, for instance.'

'Where are Claudia and Bella?'

Bryony's fingers drummed on the front of the magazine, right on the sensational cover-model's blinding white teeth. 'Claudia's on a gap working in a taverna on a Greek island and getting browner and beautifuller. And Bella's doing work experience for the BBC in Manchester, meeting loads of cool people.'

Diane washed her hands ready to prepare the evening meal. 'What? They've had the temerity to get a life while you've been overseas? Shame on them.'

A reluctant smile curved Bryony's mouth. 'Get over yourself, Mother, being a smartmouth doesn't suit you. I had one phone call, though.' She hesitated. 'From Pops.'

Diane smiled. 'I like him, your new grandfather.'

'He's invited me out to dinner, tomorrow evening. He wants for us to get to know each other.'

'Sounds wonderful. I'll make sure you can have the car.'

Bryony hesitated. 'Well ... he says he's sending a car for me. You know – like with a driver.'

Water dripped on the floor as Diane turned to stare. 'Wow! Get you.'

Bryony blushed. 'It's really cool, isn't it?'

'Really.' Turning back to the chicken breasts that she was washing, Diane debated whether to go to the fag of peeling potatoes or whether to microwave the chicken then chop it up and chuck it in with some vegetables and a jar of curry sauce. Microwave, she decided. 'So, did you meet George last night?'

Bryony's smile faded. 'Yeah.'

'Have a good time?'

'Yeah. OK.'

'Was he with Tamzin?' Diane washed her hands again after handling the raw chicken and poked around in the bottom of the fridge for onion, feathery-ended celery and a mini tree of broccoli.

'Yeah.'

Diane put the oil on to heat and turned the cold water on the vegetables, releasing the smells of onion and celery into the room. 'They seem to have quite a thing,' she said, cautiously.

'Yeah.'

The vegetables didn't take long to soften and the chicken to par-cook. In ten minutes Diane was able to push the curry into the oven and sit down at the table. 'I have something to show you.'

'Yeah?' Bryony looked up.

From the cupboard under the stairs, Diane took out

the dusty black leather box that she'd brought back from Freddy's and, tipping it, let the jumble of gold slide heavily onto the cheap, scarred old table and all over Bryony's magazine.

Bryony froze. Aghast eyebrows slid slowly into her hair. 'Oh, my God. What have you done? Oh, *Mum*.'

'What on earth do you think I've done?' Gently, Diane wiggled free a thick gold rope threaded through with fine black ribbon and then a large oval Victorian locket. She frowned as she noticed that the clasp was broken on the locket. She'd have to take it to a good jeweller and get it fixed. Probably cost megabucks. That was the trouble with gold.

Bryony still didn't touch any of the booty. In fact, she pushed herself slightly from the table. 'You realise you're putting your fingerprints on it?'

Bubbles of laughter rose up inside Diane. 'Don't be ridiculous, Bryony! I haven't stolen it.'

'Is it yours?'

There was a round gold brooch that Diane could remember being shown as a child, enamelled heavily with turquoise and red. It had been her grandmother's. Picking with her fingernail she managed the awkward little clasp. Inside was a tiny brown lock of hair. A baby curl of her mother's. 'Well, no, it's not mine.' Piece by piece she laid the entire collection in rows so that Bryony could see it. Necklaces, bracelets and bangles, brooches, rings and earrings.

She put her hand over her daughter's, taking the pleasure of the smooth whiteness of Bryony's skin next to the rough redness of her own. 'It's yours.'

Bryony's wide-eyed gaze flew to hers. 'All this? How can it be?'

'Uncle Freddy's been keeping it for you in his safe and I think that now you're nearly twenty-one and going to be a mother it's time it came to you. It's your inheritance. These things were your great-grandmother's – my mother's mother, that is. And these, my mother's. Some things will need attention before you wear them. The ribbon on this choker is useless, of course, but the cameo is very fine, apparently. My grandfather bought it for my grandmother when he came back from the Great War.' The ribbon was frayed and faded to a purply grey from the black she remembered curving around her grandmother's stocky neck.

Cautiously, as if still not quite believing that what they were doing was permissible, Bryony opened another locket. 'Who's in here?'

Diane inspected the faded sepia inside. 'That's my mother and her two brothers. And these, here, are Granny's wedding and engagement rings. And these are Great-Granny's.'

Bryony picked up her great-grandmother's engagement ring and twirled it in the light from the window. 'That stone's like a small egg. What do you think it is?'

'It's a diamond.'

Bryony put the ring down as if it was hot. 'You're kidding.'

'Not at all. She always used to say, "It's too big to be pretty but that's what your grandfather wanted me to have." She used to turn it underneath her finger when she wore gloves so that it wouldn't snag. Granny's ring is diamond, too.' She moved it around with her fingertip on the table, remembering how she'd loved to clean it with a little toothbrush when she was a child.

With an expression of awe, Bryony picked up the diamond cluster and slid it onto her finger. 'This is mega, too. Your father must've loved her.'

That was one thing Diane understood about her father. 'Oh yes. They were a good team – he was the general and she was his lieutenant.'

They continued sorting through the heavy jewellery,

Diane telling her the stories attached to the pieces, dull with dusty neglect.

It didn't take long for Bryony to ask the obvious question. 'And why didn't you inherit all this? Why has it hung around in Uncle Freddy's safe?'

Diane got up and took the curry out to stir it, hiding her face in the cloud of steam. 'More of the same old boring feuding, darling. Granddad didn't want me to have it; Uncle Freddy was desperately embarrassed when Granddad tried to give it to him. We each refused it, and came up with the idea of it coming directly to you. I'm rather glad, now.' She closed the oven door. 'It's only just coming home to me that by refusing my share of Mum and Dad's estate, how much I cheated you. That's what your dad said at the time but I wouldn't listen.' She explained about the £100 of premium bonds, too.

Bryony's young eyes were shrewd. 'But if Granddad had wanted me to have it, and your share of his money, he would have left it in a thingy for me. A trust.'

Diane's head was beginning to ache and she thought how nice it would be to go and lie in a deep bath and shut out the world. And think of James. No! Not think of James. It might make her cry. Cry for the moon.

She took Bryony's hand. 'You can go around in circles about the rights and wrongs of it until you're demented. But I am glad that I accepted this stuff on your behalf. So you've got something worth having.'

'And can I sell it?' Bryony frowned again.

'You can do anything you please with it.'

'Does Dad know I've got it? That it was left to me?'

Diane hesitated. 'No. It was between me and Freddy.'

Bryony nodded slowly. 'So you didn't trust him, either?'

Diane flushed. 'Apparently not.'

'You kept this a secret from him like he kept his money a

secret from you?'

Something shifted unpleasantly inside. 'I suppose I did,' she said, slowly. 'I'm not as blameless as I like to think, am I?'

'I don't know.' Bryony frowned as she wound the rope of gold into a spiral like a snail's shell. 'It all depends on motive. You acted to protect what was mine. I'm so angry at Dad.' Bryony turned to the enamelled locket and touched the curl of hair. 'But there's something inside me that makes me want to forgive him.' She shut the locket and sniffed.

'He loves you very much. But he's a very complex character and trusts nobody else's judgement.'

'Control freak.'

'A bit.'

Bryony stood a silver-and-jet bangle up and rolled it from side to side. 'Can I ask you something else, even if it might hurt you?'

Through the glass aperture in the oven door the curry bubbled and the spicy smell began to fill the room. It was past time to put the rice on but Diane didn't want to break the spell by leaving the conversation now. 'Yes, ask,' she said, softly.

'Do you think he's got a woman?' Bryony blinked.

Diane felt sadness settle over them both like a sootfall. 'He did have. He says it's all over.'

Bryony flashed a look of horror at her mother and then concentrated fiercely on rolling the bangle. 'Don't you *mind*?'

'Not now.'

Bryony propped her head on her hand and sighed. 'Are you just being, like, really forgiving? Or don't you care?'

The kitchen seemed to be getting hotter and hotter. Diane wiped her forehead with the back of her hand. She felt as she used to when her father found her out in some childish misdemeanour and she had to face his questions. 'What happens between me and your father doesn't affect how we feel about you –'

'I know you both love me. I'm asking you whether your feelings for Dad are so crappy that you don't care if he's cheating on you?' A tear rolled off the end of Bryony's nose and onto the table. 'I'm sorry, but it's really, *really* important to me. It's not as if I'm a kid any more, but –'

Aching for her daughter, Diane struggled to be diplomatic. 'At the moment, it's difficult to feel about him as I once did.' *Please don't ask me if I've cheated on* him. 'We've each done things that the other sees as hurtful and selfish. It's all to do with money. And family. And principles. And who thinks which is most important. But that's not to say that we won't get over this.'

'You're not planning to leave him?'

Oh James. 'No immediate plans.'

Bryony stood another bangle up. It was of dark yellow gold and in the shape of bamboo. Diane remembered her grandmother wearing it. It had come from Malaya. Tears dropped off Bryony's chin. Her voice broke. 'I still love him.'

'Of course you do.' Diane slid her arms around the warm, quivering body of her daughter. 'I know this is all hard for you.'

Sobs began to escape. 'When I decided to come home, I was, like, coming home to be safe. I could bear it that Inacio had turned out to be a married bastard who'd seen me as a stupid little girl he could amuse himself with. I could cope with being pregnant, because I was coming home. I knew Dad was in hospital, but I thought he'd soon be out – '

'And nothing too bad could happen while you're with me and Dad? That's all still true, darling. Still true. You're safe here. I love you. And Dad does, too. We've always kept you safe.'

'And what about the baby?'

Diane's arms tightened around her daughter. 'We'll keep the baby safe, too.'

Chapter Twenty-Five

Sleepless at midnight.

Diane's mobile rang. **James**. She rubbed her thumb gently over his name on the illuminated screen. Should she answer? No, she shouldn't. They should learn to deal with not being together.

If the phone rang unanswered seven times the call would be diverted to voicemail and she'd have to get her instruction book out and learn how to retrieve the message. Because she wouldn't be able to leave it unheard.

She pressed the green button and put the phone to her ear without lifting her head from the pillow. 'Hello.'

'Hello.' His voice was low.

Pause.

'Am I disturbing you?'

'I was awake.' She ached to be holding him, drawing strength from his warm body. She swallowed. 'How are you?'

'Apart from having my guts drawn by a fine woman? I'm great.' He sounded weary.

Tears began to leak from Diane's eyes and slide down the sides of her head. She scrabbled in the drawer beside the bed for a tissue.

His sigh whistled in her ear. 'Sorry. I wanted to know that you were OK. Even if you don't think we can be together I can't stop thinking about you and wondering if you're coping and whether Gareth's sprung any more nasty surprises.'

'Nothing new,' she managed. She tried to blow her nose quietly.

'But you're OK?'

How can I be? I'm in pieces. I can't remember feeling like this before. I want to run to you, to feel safe. I hadn't realised properly how I felt until hope was removed. 'As well as can be expected,' she said, like an old-fashioned nurse.

'I rang to tell you something.'

She swallowed tears with a little gasp. 'What?'

'That I love you. I want you to know. Just in case it makes you reconsider.'

She began to cry. 'No. No, it doesn't. But I love you, too.'

Chapter Twenty-Six

It was a solid month before James rang her mobile again.

They'd seen each other, of course they had, chance meetings in the hospital corridors or the car park, when Diane's heart would do a hop, skip and jump. Occasionally, Valerie rang and begged Diane to call in to prevent her going stir crazy and once James had been there, making the visit bitter-sweet. Tamzin came to the house for fittings of the dresses, tops, skirts and cropped trousers that Diane made for her. She was swimming to the surface of her depression and Diane had even got her helping with some of the cutting-out for the Unity's order. And she could pump her gently for precious news of James.

James had played fair. There had been no more midnight phone calls and only one text: *I miss you.* And so it was a surprise to see, when the phone rang, **James**. Her breathing quickened.

'It's me,' he said.

'Yes.'

'I need to see you.'

She hesitated. *It would be so easy.*

'It's not ... it's to do with you rather than us.'

Her eyebrows rose. 'Me? What?'

He hesitated. 'I really can't do it over the phone because there's something I have to show you. Come and have lunch with me at The Old Dog. I'll behave. No unwelcome declarations, no heartfelt persuasions.'

The beginning of the school holidays had brought a cold spell. Diane let James install her in a cosy corner of the bar while he collected drinks and menus. She stared out of the window at clouds marching across the sky and the pub sign swinging in the wind.

James brought over lager for him, pink grapefruit juice for her and cappuccino for them both.

He didn't try to touch her or kiss her cheek but his haunted eyes scrunched her heart.

'How are things?'

He dropped onto the banquette beside her. 'Tamzin's transformed and spends one half of her life with George and the other half talking about him. Valerie is fruitlessly dreaming up ways to get the CAA to reinstate her licence. Neither of them seems to need me. Remind me exactly why we're giving up what we're giving up?'

She picked up her teaspoon and made a pattern in her cappuccino froth. This didn't sound like *no unwelcome declarations, no heartfelt persuasions.* 'Tamzin's only going through a good patch. She's in love and she's ecstatic. But ecstasy is tenuous. And what if the relationship ends? I've already had her at my house in floods of tears because she'd had a silly spat with George – you must know that he isn't a miracle cure. There's a risk that her moods will confuse him, she'll be too needy. He's a nineteen-year-old boy, not a saviour and he won't always want a girlfriend he has to wear around his neck like a baby chimp.'

She stirred the chocolate flakes and cream into the coffee with angry little chops. 'She'll need you more than ever when it ends.'

James blinked. 'Don't sugar the pill, will you?'

Without missing a beat, she continued, 'And in a few weeks Valerie will be home from hospital and need care. I know —' She put up her hand. 'You'll hire a nurse. So she'll want company. She's bored out of her skull in hospital and the boredom won't lift until she gets her mobility back. It'll be a while before she can drive her sports car and what's she going to do to replace flying? And you'll find yourself watching her booze intake because she'll soon be on crutches and able to get about the house and find it, if not at home then in this pub which is, conveniently, just across the green. You'll rage at her about it and you'll fight her every inch of the way but you won't leave her to drink herself into a hole in the ground because that's not how you're made.

'And I've made an undertaking to Bryony that I'll stay with her father, at least for now. She's going to be a single parent. A grandchild will be living with us, a grandchild who deserves the nearest to a happy home that we can give it. And, anyway – I thought the thing you had to talk about wasn't us?'

James picked up his cappuccino and drank, sipping slowly, flinty gaze fixed on something outside.

She'd infuriated him. She knew that she'd been blunt, but he'd *promised*. And then made her go over all the hellish reasons that they couldn't be together. *Again*. He shouldn't be saying things to make her eyes smart and her heart stretch out to him in longing. His eyes shouldn't be spreading heat through her. He shouldn't be tying her in knots.

When his cup was empty he replaced it carefully on the table. 'Natalia spent the weekend in London.'

'Lovely,' she said, automatically.

'She visited Covent Garden Market, she always does. She loves the street performers and the quirky shops. She's a mug for even the most expensive. She brought home a dress she fell in love with.' He dragged out a carrier bag from under the table and turned it upside down, letting fabric slither out.

After a pause, Diane picked it up.

It was bronze grosgrain with fat, chocolaty lacings up the front and the back. The label sewn into the neck said, *DRJ*, embroidered in turquoise on a bright yellow ground.

Bewildered, she stared at him. 'Was it a shop that sold second-hand clothes?'

'No. I checked.'

'But this is something I made for Rowan.'

'Thought so.'

She was aware of a slight nausea, disorientation, like the onset of travel sickness. 'So it couldn't be for sale in Covent Garden.'

James reached into his pocket again and came out with a receipt. For £209.

She gasped. 'Oh ...'

'I'd say he's ripping you off. He's buying stuff off you for a song, then selling it on to this shop for a significant mark up.'

Anger made the backs of Diane's eyes burn and her vision of the dress wavered. She clenched her fists. '*Bastard.*'

James smiled the first real smile of the evening. 'If you want to leave him to me I'll be happy to put the fear of God into him –'

Diane almost knocked the table over as she leapt to her feet. Her breath came choppily, making her feel dizzy. 'When did I ask you to take it over?'

He gazed up, looking injured. 'I'm trying to help.'

'Well, forget it. It's my business and I'll sort it.' She saw that she'd caught the attention of quite a few of the other customers and sank back onto her seat, fighting to regain her composure. It took several deep breaths. 'I'm very grateful both to you and Natalia for bringing it to my attention, but I'll take it from here. OK?'

Chapter Twenty-Seven

Diane had spent the last hour in the coffee shop sewing a pattern of silvery buttons onto a black top for Tamzin so that Bryony and Gareth could have some time to talk. Their relationship was under repair. Diane wanted Gareth and Bryony to have a relationship because it would be good for Bryony and, presently, Bryony's child. Bryony was unarguably warming to her father again and if Gareth chose not to look any further than superficially good relations then Diane wasn't about to interfere.

Then Bryony, not yet having found a decent car to suit her bank balance, had taken the Peugeot into Peterborough City Centre for a late lunch with her grandfather – she was seeing him most weeks – and Diane was stuck at the hospital until she brought it back. Now, sitting beside Gareth's bed, still sewing, the whiteness of the room made her head ache and her sleep-deprived eyes scratch against her lids. For hours, last night, she'd lain awake, seething, rehearsing what she'd say to Rowan, the bastard.

Oh, to go home and put the sewing away for a bit, open a bottle of wine and nibble her way through a pack of Devon cream toffees over a library book. Instead, she was stuck here, listening to Gareth congratulate himself on how well he was getting on with his daughter.

She examined his self-satisfied smile.

It might make her feel better if she could wipe it from his face.

She searched her mind for a suitably sore subject. 'Have you had any contact with Stella?' Gareth's granite forehead immediately closed down over his eyes. *Good choice.*

'Why should I?'

'I notice that you don't actually answer yes or no. Why should you have contact with her? Because you've been having an affair with her for years and she might want to talk about why it's ended? Or you might want to start things up again? Or the whole finale was just a charade for my benefit?' She bit off her thread and unwound more from the spool with swift, assured movements. She'd been working like a maniac on the order for Unity's. This special piece for Tamzin was something she'd slotted in as a favour. Jenneration had secured a spot at The Cavern in Liverpool – so long as they could take at least a coach load of paying guests with them – and Tamzin wanted something really special for the gig to go with black jeans with junk jewellery dangling from the waistband.

'Don't be stupid,' he replied.

Diane threaded the needle and knotted the ends. There could be few requests more likely to enrage her than that she refrain from being stupid.

Although, sometimes, she thought she had been very stupid indeed.

In the weeks since she'd quashed the possibility of an affair with James she'd seen the world in greyscale. The meeting at The Old Dog yesterday had come perilously close to a row because she hated seeing James without being able to touch him, kiss him, or know the pleasure of his body. What if Gareth felt the same about Stella? With a man less controlling and possessive she might even have suggested a little reciprocal blind-eye turning, but not with Gareth. It had been bred into him never to let another take what he considered his. No matter what he'd done himself there would be no hope of maintaining the semblance of a relationship even for Bryony's sake, under those circumstances.

She set the first stitch and prepared to ascend new heights

of stupidity. 'You've got your metalwork off your hip and you're out of traction. You'll be home in a few days. I just wondered how the land lay. If you'll be expecting me to drive you out to your cottage for meetings.'

He set his jaw. The swelling had almost all gone now and also the bruising, returning his face to its habitual hardness. 'Are you deliberately trying to start a row?'

She selected a button, a really tiny one, and held it to the fabric with her thumbnail while she thrust the needle through. 'I don't have to try.' She dropped her work on the bed and slipped her hand beneath his pillow.

'Don't you dare!' he snapped in outrage, but even though his arm was out of plaster and into some stretchy supporting affair, he was no match for her agility. He turned puce as, safely out of his range, she scrolled down first his Dialled Calls and then his Received Calls.

'You're a fibber,' she announced, in mock reproof. 'Stella is ringing you and you're ringing her. You rang her yesterday.' She tossed the phone down beside him, and retrieved Tamzin's black T-shirt from the floor where it had fallen. 'I thought I'd make it plain that I'm finally awake to your games. I expect openness from you. However shitty the truth.'

His mouth was a straight line.

'I don't care about Stella for myself but Bryony cares a lot. She's going to have a tough time bringing up a baby without a father and we've agreed to be there for her. But you're not keeping up your end of the bargain, are you? For the sake of your wallet you seem to want me to stay, so, for the sake of your daughter you're going to have to give up your lover.' *Like I had to.*

She gave him a few minutes to chew that over before introducing the next irritating subject. 'I've bought a new bed; it was delivered yesterday.'

'What was wrong with the old one?' He rapped it out in the old Gareth way, expecting her to run every decision past him for approval. Well, he could bloody well stop all that nonsense.

'Actually, it's so ancient I'm surprised you can lower yourself to use it after the luxury of the king size at your cottage. But I didn't buy the new bed to replace our old one. It's as well. I'm making the dining room into my work room, as we generally eat in the kitchen, and my old work room into my bedroom. I no longer want to sleep with you.'

She selected another button, glancing up. 'You surely don't think that after all the nasty tricks you've played that I want intimacy? If it weren't for Bryony's situation I would be looking for a divorce, frankly. But she needs the comfort of a friendly family unit, right now. The only way I can remain friendly with you is to have my own room. I'll be your nurse until you're fully fit again, then I'll be your house-mate – but I won't be your lover.'

Gareth took a sip from his squash before answering. He was drinking from a normal glass now. His voice was thin, surprised. 'But what will Bryony think?'

Diane put her work down on her lap and gave him the benefit of her direct blue-eyed stare. 'She thinks that our relationship has undergone a radical change and that the situation is irretrievable, because that's what I've told her. The truth. I've explained that, us all being grown ups and probably reasonably fond of each other under it all, this is the best way forward.'

Gareth's eyes were hazel pools of shock and, as he seemed temporarily lost for words, Diane picked her work up again. She was sick to her stomach of sewing; she was sewing her fingers off. She wished she could take a week off, like normal people did. Perhaps she'd jump on an aeroplane after she got the balance of her money from Unity. The

249

school term would've begun and Spain or Italy would be lovely and quiet. She could read, eat ice cream, drink coffee, swim in the turquoise sea. If Gareth wasn't able to take care of himself by then he could hire a nurse for a week. It wasn't like he didn't have the funds.

She picked up a big saucer-like button, mock mother-of-pearl. The hospital seemed incredibly noisy today. There had been a loud beeping coming from somewhere and what sounded like a rugby team racing around the corridor. 'While we're laying out ground rules for the new order of our marriage, let's talk about money.'

That got his attention. 'What about it?'

'I've opened a couple of accounts in my own name. I propose that we split all household bills down the middle, ditto the groceries, and apart from that keep our money separate.'

His eyebrows flipped up. 'Should I be asking if there's a catch?'

'Not so much a catch as a few provisos. The mortgage stands at just under £20,000. I want you to pay it off. And I don't want you ever to query what I do with my money and neither will I with yours. In other words, you get to keep nearly all your cash in your own grubby paws. Right?'

'Right,' he agreed, cautiously, as if looking for a catch no matter what she said about provisos.

'And I have a new money-making scheme for you – sue Valerie. I think it's an interesting point whether you will do this to a sibling. But I was reading in the paper about claims for damages and you've certainly been damaged, so I thought I'd mention it to you.'

He replied, stiffly. 'In fact, that's common practice. Valerie wouldn't pay, her insurance company would. But I haven't seen a solicitor.' His eyes lit up suddenly. 'In the next couple of days the nurses are going to get me used to a wheelchair and take me in to Valerie's room. I'll talk it over with her.'

Diane put down her sewing to give him her best school marm look. 'Gareth, you *have* seen a solicitor because one of the nurses let it out accidentally. No doubt you were establishing what you can do to protect your fortune if I go for a divorce … hell's bells, what's that?' She lunged to her feet.

The scream had been unearthly.

Gareth tried to pull himself up, glancing towards the door. 'Is it human?'

'It's a woman.' Diane frowned and cocked her head. Then she caught a familiar voice.

Quickly, she threw down her work and crossed to the door. Hesitated, hand on the chrome door plate, frowning. She opened the door a few inches; the heartbreaking wails becoming louder – and the familiar voice also.

She pushed the portal wider and darted through.

Chapter Twenty-Eight

James felt as if his insides had been turned to stone.

He held Tamzin in his arms. Not the happier Tamzin that he was daring to get used to but a gasping, keening, grey-faced Tamzin whose arms and legs jerked out of control.

Her wails of anguish, '*No! No! No!*' were choking her. Crowing for breath, she ripped sobs out from the pit of her stomach.

James tried to hold her tightly, to keep her tipping into hysteria. 'I'm here, Tamz.' But her frantically pedalling legs trampled his toes and drew lines of fire down his shins.

Two nurses encouraged her back down the corridor, voices soothing. 'Let's get you to the relative's room, dear. You'll be better, there.'

It was ineffective.

Tamzin was in some private agony zone and seemed quite unable to control her pumping legs.

And then, like an answer to a prayer, Diane was racing up the corridor towards them, compassion all over her face. 'James?'

Tamzin yanked herself free and threw herself at Diane. 'Diane! Oh, Diane. Mummy *died*. Right there in front of us. She began to gasp and panic and Dad pressed the red button and people raced in and they were trying to help but she just *gasped* and gasped. And then she stopped. ' Her voice spiralled. 'She *stopped breathing*!'

Diane cradled the shuddering body, her horrified eyes seeking James's. Dumbly, he nodded. Stroking Tamzin's back, Diane murmured, 'Oh, darling.'

With her other hand she reached out to James.

Helplessly, he let her arm slide around him. But the bad stuff didn't go away. It was like the sweating, terrifying kind of nightmare when a family member is torn away by the slavering fangs of a monster. This time the monster was death and there would be no grateful awakening.

Diane helped him haul Tamzin along to the relative's room and a doctor came and gave her something to calm her. James held her, repeating endlessly, 'I'm here. I'm here, Tamzin.' Eventually, she slumped, her head on his shoulder, quieting in the protective circle of his arms.

James began to shake as awful reality sank in, the images of the last few minutes hanging ghastly before his eyes. Valerie's strange colour. The life draining from her face. She had always been so alive, so animated, her eyes alight with laughter or gleaming in scorn. But never as they were now – with no expression.

He thrust away the image of what he'd just witnessed, letting his tendency for logic and control carry him into action. 'I must tell Natalia and Alice, and Harold. Be with them.'

Diane was seated on his other side. He could feel her hand, firm on his arm. 'Do you want to leave Tamzin with me? You could break the news, gather everyone at your house, then I'll bring her along. Just give me a few minutes to tell the nurses so that when Bryony comes –' She halted, suddenly. 'Oh, no. Gareth.'

They stared at each another bleakly. Diane grimaced. 'I'll have to tell him. Stay with him.'

She helped James down to the car with Tamzin sleepwalking between them, James half-carrying her. She weighed no more than a child. Diane took his keys and opened the car door and they loaded her into the front seat and fastened the seat belt.

The car door shut, Diane put her hand on James's forearm.

253

'I'm so sorry.'

'Yes.' His voice was a croak. Nausea waited in his throat.

'If you want to talk, ring me.'

For an instant, normality stirred. 'Could I?'

'Of course. Of *course*. Don't be the strong one all alone. Everyone will need you. It's OK for you to need somebody.' Her eyes shone with sympathy.

He managed, 'Thank you.'

Diane made her way slowly back upstairs to tell her husband that his sister was dead.

Gareth went a brilliant, startling white, a contrast to the rainbow face he'd sported until recently. 'But I was going to visit her tomorrow. Tomorrow. They were going to put me in a chair and let me see her. She was nearly better. Wasn't she nearly better? She was going home, like me.'

Shoving all the hurts and frictions aside, Diane took his hand. 'I know. It was a complete shock. James and Tamzin were with her and called the crash team but it was so quick.'

'How could she die? She was never in danger from her injuries.'

'James assumed it was her heart but the team are talking about pulmonary embolism – a blood clot that went to her lungs.'

'But she was nearly better.'

'I know.'

Presently, Bryony crept in to give her father a huge hug. 'Dad, the nurse told me. Poor Valerie! Dad, poor you. And Pops and Tamzin and everyone.' She put her head down on her father's chest and began to cry.

Diane didn't feel she could leave Gareth until well on in the evening but did have to take Bryony home in the end, promising Gareth that she'd be back in the morning and that they'd talk to the doctor then about getting Gareth to the funeral. 'I must get to the funeral,' he kept saying. 'I've got to be there.' Fixating on it, where it would be and when it would be and how he'd manage.

Diane drove home in a dream, Bryony beside her, dazed into silence, apart from the occasional, 'I so can't believe it. Poor Dad! Poor Tamzin. Poor, poor Pops, he was so happy this afternoon.'

And Diane's automatic, practical, 'We'll have to help everybody as much as we can.'

She didn't think she'd sleep but she climbed into her new bed in her new bedroom to watch mindless TV for a while. Bryony padded in, her big spotted T-shirt making her look about twelve – if not for the bump of the baby. She perched cross-legged on Diane's bed. 'I've got something to tell you. It's been such a weird day.' Her eyes looked very big in her pale face.

Diane reached up to tug a curl. 'We're going through a weird time, aren't we? Poor Valerie, Dad in hospital, you going to be a mum, me to be a grandmother – I haven't got my head round that, by the way.'

'There's something else for you to get your head round.' Bryony looked sheepish, almost embarrassed. She hesitated. 'Pops told me today that all his grandchildren come into some money when they're twenty-one. He set up a trust, or something.'

Diane felt a smile spread across her face. 'Does that mean that you'll get a bit of money on your birthday? He's such a sweetheart.'

Bryony looked awed. 'I get forty thousand pounds.'

Chapter Twenty-Nine

Tamzin had spent the night in her bed, curled on her right side.

She wasn't aware that she had slept. Whatever the doctor had given her had locked her up like a fly in amber so that she felt immobile and remote.

And it hadn't altered the horrible truth.

Now, as the light stole around the curtains, she tried to make herself believe that her mother was dead.

Mum's dead. Mummy. My mother is dead.

She can't be. She was right there, propped up in bed and talking about coming home in a few days and how odd her legs felt and that the physio was a sadistic bastard and then she began to frown and get short of breath. My God, James, open the damned window, I think I'm having an asthma attack. Gasping, panicking, grabbing her chest, coughing for breath, suddenly white and waxy and Dad shouted her name and slammed his hand against a red button on the wall.

People had run in like a scene from Casualty. Heart monitor. Oxygen mask. A tube in Valerie's arm. Then Valerie passed out. And even though they tried, even though they'd worked and worked, ignoring Tamzin and her dad backed fearfully into a corner, Tamzin had known that Valerie was dead before they stopped trying.

But still she'd wanted them to carry on, had even shouted, 'Don't stop!'

Horror.

My mother is dead.

She can't be. She was right there in the room with me. She was coming home.

Tamzin thought about the house without Valerie in it, not just as it had been the past few months, waiting for her to return. But forever. The same house she'd grown up in. But different.

Growing up with Valerie had been like being a living doll. Natalia and Alice were tomboys who were always building tree houses that were too high for Tamzin or jumping brooks too wide for her to clear.

So Tamzin had hung out with Valerie. She could still hear her mother's proud laugh. 'You should hear my baby fuss about her hair. Everything has to be just so for my pretty princess.'

But that had been then, not now. In the last couple of years, when the pretty princess had been wandering the grey caves of depression, Valerie had done exactly what Tamzin wanted everyone to do. Leave her to find her own way out.

Her gaze fell on the shelf above her computer. Empty. At some time since coming home from the hospital her CDs had been whisked away. James, probably, or one of her sisters, had – as they thought – removed temptation from her path.

Slowly, she straightened her legs, waiting out a storm of pins and needles. Sliding to the edge of the bed she rose, feeling the familiar whiz in her head that told her she hadn't eaten recently. Opening the wardrobe doors she found her old brown suede coat and felt in the big square pocket at the front. The pocket was just the right size for the CD case. And if it wasn't there she knew where there were others. Taped beneath the wardrobe, slotted behind the chest of drawers. They waited, like best friends, to be needed.

Back on the bed she drew the quilt around herself and carefully prised the CD case apart with her fingertips, discarding the dark grey inner and the paper inserts with the retouched photos of a moody-looking band. Her counsellor had known that most people like her had a favourite instrument – scissors, knives, shards of plastic. Tamzin had denied she had one, because she liked to keep bits of herself private. What was that phrase? *Knowledge is power*.

Delicately separating the clear plastic parts she chose the front and began to flex it between her hands, forcing it into a curve with her two thumbs.

It snapped almost immediately with a satisfying crack. It always made her jump, that bit. But she liked it.

She selected the biggest piece. It had broken on the angle to leave a long, knife-sharp diagonal edge. She pulled up her left sleeve and set the broken edge of the plastic against the soft white underside of her arm just below the elbow. Drew the clear plastic slowly across the skin. She winced. The first stroke always sent a strange sensation up the back of her neck. She waited for the beads of blood to appear. Grow.

And then came the burning that made her gasp and curl her toes. The throbbing would come later, so tender that she'd feel shadows glide over the wound. But at least she would feel something. Know that she was still here.

James had dealt with the formalities surrounding the deaths of each of his parents but that hadn't prepared him for doing the same for Valerie.

An untimely death, he discovered, meant a lot of new stuff to deal with. There would be a post mortem and Valerie had been moved to the mortuary at the district hospital.

Two of his daughters were distraught and one had, quite obviously, retreated into her grey caves. His father-in-law had aged ten years overnight to become a silent old man.

Harold's doctor had attended him at James's house and pronounced himself concerned. Harold didn't have much medication with him and the doctor left a prescription but there was nowhere in Webber's Cross to fill it. James had to wait for a phone call from the mortician. Arrangements could only be pencilled in until James had a death certificate and the funeral director had a body.

Valerie's body. The words made him feel sick. Once Valerie's body had been something that filled him with desire. Now it was the name used to describe the husk left chilling in a drawer.

'I don't mind driving to the pharmacy in Wisbech,' Natalia offered. 'But I haven't got my car because I came here in yours last night.' She swallowed. 'I suppose I could take Mum's ...'

Valerie's car waited in the clean expanse of the garage and it was almost an obscenity that such a piece of machinery should stand unused. He'd given it a run periodically while she lay injured but it took too much driving for his taste. And it was so much Val's car ...

'Mum's car isn't insured for you and neither is mine. There's Tamzin's –'

'For God's sake, Dad!' Natalia exploded. 'Now is not the time to obsess about details. Who gives a crap about insurance, today?'

James kept his voice neutral. 'I don't see that you getting prosecuted for driving without insurance will make any of us feel better.'

'I've been driving nine years and never been asked for my insurance details. How many years have you been driving? And have you ever been asked for yours?'

'It doesn't matter,' offered Harold, trying to sound firm. 'I'm absolutely fine.'

'It does matter,' declared Natalia and James, simultaneously.

'Couldn't she drive Tamzin's car on her own car insurance?' suggested Alice.

'Oh, I expect that only covers me third party or some

other bloody fusspot thing,' declared Natalia, before James could say that it was insured for any driver, because he'd seen to it.

He hung on to his temper but he felt it swelling behind his eyes. Why was Natalia giving him such crap for making sure things were done? Did she see it as her role now that Valerie was gone? He had a sudden vision of Valerie lighting a cigarette and leaping up to grab a bottle of wine from the fridge, crying, 'For God's sake, James. Lighten up!'

But it had always been his job to keep everything together, to know that everything was insured, maintained, arranged, booked, working, even though he was completely sick of the role, because Valerie would let everything go to hell while she cantered about –

It hit him like a blow. *He would no longer have to worry about Valerie. Not driving or flying, smoking or drinking.* It had all finally ceased to matter. A hole opened in his chest and grief flew in to squeeze his heart.

Then the mortician rang for James and the doorbell chimed and the argument had to be postponed.

When James returned from the phone he halted, shock bolting up his spine. Diane.

She wore a straight denim skirt and her plait gleamed like an ornament over the shoulder of a plain navy shirt. Her eyes looked very blue and she gave him a tiny smile. He thought he had never seen anything more reassuring in his life. 'I came to see if you needed anything.'

Your tranquility, he told her silently. 'We seem a bit disorganised,' he said. *And they're not playing nice. I need help with them.*

'I can be useful.' Diane began by making everybody tea and toast, two slices each, seeming to understand that nobody had eaten that morning – possibly explaining the shortness of tempers – as if to have done so would somehow besmirch Valerie's memory. At first Harold refused brusquely, but Diane crouched before his chair and took his hands and explained how worried she was about him and he came to the table like a lamb and ate half a slice of toast and drank two cups of tea.

The final slices of toast she put down at an empty place, left the room and returned five minutes later holding Tamzin's hand as if she were a little girl. Dressed in last night's clothes Tamzin was silent but at least she was there and some food passed her lips. Everybody ate something, even if not much more than four mouthfuls, and Diane cleared away.

She seemed to have appointed herself general factotum. 'OK,' she said, returning to the table. 'What needs to be done?'

James explained about his appointment with the mortician at four, Harold's prescription, Natalia's car. *It's too difficult*, he added, with his eyes.

'I could drop Natalia off to pick up her car while you keep your appointment, so she can fill out the prescription.' Diane turned to Tamzin. 'Will you come with me to Pops's house and pick up some things for him? Your dad thinks he shouldn't go home alone yet and I expect that we all agree. Alice, will you stay here with Pops while she's gone?'

And everybody nodded, preparing to perform their allotted tasks without a grumble.

James, when he went out to his car, found Diane right behind him.

'How are you?' Her voice was low and sympathetic, and he was ashamed that he wanted her to hold him. Just for a moment.

Instead, he leaned against his car, letting her presence comfort him. 'It's a nightmare. I see her everywhere. I feel as if I let her down. I let her die.'

Her eyes brimmed with sympathy. 'But it's not true,

James. You couldn't stop her dying – that's not the same thing as letting her die. Nobody could stop her. Fully trained medical staff with all the gadgets and gear tried and failed.'

'But I keep wondering if the kids think I let her die.'

'I'm sure they don't.'

He touched her hand and she didn't pull away. 'The guilt's incredible.'

'It always is.'

'I don't mean about being alive when she's dead and the usual survivor's remorse. I mean because I was thinking about you when she began to struggle for breath.'

She nodded, once, jerkily, and blinked. 'Bryony's with Gareth. I feel guilty that I've left him to come to see if you needed help. But I had to.'

James was finding everything painfully unreal by the time he got home after keeping his appointment with a kindly mortician and a doctor from the Ackerman in a sterile-looking room that smelled funny and then having to fight rush-hour traffic that seemed intent on siphoning him into lanes he didn't want to be in. He'd grown so used to the thorn of Valerie piercing his side. But now the thorn had been removed, without anaesthetic, and with no dressing to keep his guts from spilling out.

Emotions were racketing around inside him like bagatelle balls. But he wasn't certain what the emotions were.

In his kitchen he found Diane sliding a chicken casserole into the oven.

The sight of her in the house he'd shared with his wife for twenty-seven years screwed with his heart. He'd wanted to leave Valerie for this woman. He'd made love to her while his wife lay in traction. He'd planned an affair; even taking a six month lease on a flat where they could meet on the outskirts of Peterborough, a flat that he was now arranging to be sublet because Diane had pulled back.

When Valerie had begun to arch and gasp on her hospital bed had he leapt fast enough for the red button on the wall? In the seconds that seemed hours before the staff burst into the room could he have done something to save her?

Guilt rose in his throat like black bile.

Diane met his eyes and seemed to read his mind.

She whisked off the tea towel that had served as an apron around her waist and picked up her car keys. 'Harold's watching the news and Natalia and Alice are keeping him company.' She hesitated. 'I hope it's OK, but I rang George. He's up in Tamzin's room with her. I had a word with him, told him to let her grieve, just to keep her company – he's never had to deal with anything like this. I'll leave you with your family now.'

He nodded, too scoured out with guilt and grief to speak. As he made his way to the sitting room he heard her car start and the crunch of tyres across the gravel.

When he entered the room, Harold pointed the remote control at the television and cut off the *Look East* presenter mid-sentence. James sat down heavily, suddenly sick with fatigue. All eyes were fixed on him, the family focused on every detail of the process of losing Valerie.

He reported his meeting bluntly. 'They asked me formally to allow a post mortem – although I'm not sure I really had a choice. It'll take place tomorrow, and after they've given me the result I can get a death certificate and arrange for her to be moved to the funeral home.'

After several moments, Harold murmured, 'Does she really have to be ... disturbed?'

'They have to know how it happened. We all need to.'

The evening stretched ahead. Abruptly, fiercely, James wanted Diane back, making them cups of tea and knowing what to say.

A curious aimlessness descended. No plans could be made without the death certificate. It felt indecent to sort through Valerie's things so soon. He hadn't told their solicitor of her death. Or the bank. Or, indeed, her friends or any family but the most immediate. He could begin on the family this evening –

But he remained in his chair, eviscerated by death and tragedy. He shut his eyes. So tired. Soooo tired ... He'd do it in the morning. She'd been only in her forties. It no longer mattered how she abused her body. Never again would she endanger herself or anyone else. She had made him angry and made him sad and he'd wanted rid of her.

But not dead.

He managed a few hours sleep, which helped. Awake since dawn, he sat down at the kitchen table with a spiral-topped pad from the kitchen drawer and began to list necessary phone calls. *Solicitor, bank, insurance companies –*

He'd been sitting there for a couple of hours, trying to force his brain to work, when an unfamiliar cough mad him turn. He found himself staring at George Jenner.

George hovered awkwardly, hands jammed inelegantly in the back pockets of ripped jeans so that his elbows stuck out like cup handles. 'Um, I gotta go, 'cos I'm on a work placement. Tamz said it's OK. I'm already having time off for the gig in Liverpool on Friday.'

'No, of course. Right.'

George shuffled and cleared his throat. His eyes flicked to James and away. 'Um ... did you know ... Tamzin's done stuff.' He fidgeted. Itched his calf with the opposite foot. 'To her arms.' He took his hands out of his pockets to make a tentative cutting motion with the side of his hand to the inside of his elbow.

James felt his stomach plummet. 'Oh hell, has she?

Very bad?'

George cleared his throat again. 'Like, about three ...'
He made the cutting motion again. 'That's to do with this
depression she had, right?'

'Self-injury. It seems to be a reaction to when something
bad happens that she has no control over.' James pushed his
fingertips through his hair.

George shook his head. 'Amazin'. And you can't get her
to stop?'

James decided to ignore the faint note of accusation.
George had no experience of dealing with self-injury. As
Diane had pointed out, he was a nineteen-year-old boy.
He was talking so awkwardly not because he was rude or
inarticulate but because he was excruciatingly embarrassed.
He and James scarcely knew each other. 'Not so far. Unless
you've got any bright ideas?'

Slowly, George slipped his feet into a pair of oversized
trainers that seemed to have spent the night with the family
collection of footwear in the corner. 'I dunno. It's weird.' He
hesitated. 'Would it help to, like, make her do stuff?'

James fought down irritation. 'Do what kind of *stuff*?'

'When my granny died Dad and Uncle Melvyn and Uncle
Gareth had a load of stuff to organise, the funeral and that.
There's always a load of stuff, isn't there, when somebody
dies? I'd make her do that. *Ask* her to do that, for her mum.
She'll do it for her mum. Then maybe she'd have less time to
rip herself up. But you'd probably have to, like, let her think
you really needed the help, not that you were just trying to
get her out of her room.'

'So you think it's wrong, do you, for her to be left alone in
her room?' James was curious. This lad had become hugely
important to Tamzin in a few weeks – maybe he might be
the one with the insight?

George rubbed his chin. 'I think she needs to be out of

there but you've got to do it without letting on that that's what you want. Make it something real or she'll just get the meanies. She's like it with food. If I act like I don't care whether she eats or not, she shares my meal. If I make a thing about it or buy her a meal of her own, she hardly touches it.'

When George had gone James stared at his list, at his angular handwriting. George made him feel old and cranky, to think in uncharacteristic phrases such as, *young man, I believe I know my daughter* and, probably, *better than you.*

He'd been desperate to end Tamzin's nightmare.

He'd thought Valerie unfeeling when she said he was making too much of Tamzin's problems. Depression was a medical diagnosis, not some babble he'd picked out of a trendy magazine; his instinct had been to make things easy for his daughter. Unlike some households, her lack of occupation hadn't mattered, financially. She could be safe at home for however long it took for her to find her way out of the grey caves.

But ... in taking all possible pressure off, had he removed 'motivation to progress' as Cherry in HR would say? Both George and Diane plainly thought that Tamzin should be steered towards occupation.

He wrote, *Ask Tamzin for help* across the top of the list.

Stared at his words on the page. They seemed so foreign. So against the natural order of things. She didn't give him help – he gave it to her. But, with a mental shrug, he threw down the pen and went to knock on Tamzin's door. On the third knock, she answered through the door, drearily, blearily, from the depths of her despair.

'I'm stuck,' he called. He didn't have to contrive the flatness in his voice.

A long pause, before her voice came again, puzzled. 'On what?'

'On what to do next. There's so much to do. My head hurts and I've hardly slept and I can't think straight. Any chance that you could help me?'

A long pause. He could imagine her, rolled in her bedclothes, a frown curling her pale eyebrows. 'OK,' she answered, cautiously. 'I'll get dressed.'

Whilst he waited for her to appear, he made them each a slice of toast and a cup of tea. Following Diane's example of the morning before, he simply put food down in Tamzin's place and began to eat his own. She arrived with her hair pulled up into a navy blue scrunchie, blinking. She looked at the toast as if it were left there by aliens but picked up the cup of tea as she sat down.

'So, what have we got to do?'

He shrugged, palms up. 'I'm trying to make a list of people we have to tell about Mum. Things we have to do. I can't think straight.'

'Oh.' She picked up a pen and wiggled it. Skewed her head to see what he'd written.

Inform:–
Solicitor
Bank
Insurance companies

'Rellies?' she asked. It sounded like the kind of word George would use. 'Let's begin with her cousins.'

Wordlessly, he passed her the pad and, after a moment's surprised hesitation, she began to write down the names of Valerie's cousins, going from the oldest to the youngest, in order, to ensure nobody was left out. Then they began on Valerie's aunts and uncles, then friends. 'She had so many,' observed Tamzin, rubbing her eyes. 'Let's work through them by place – you know, flying club, village, school ...'

'Great.' He got up and made a second cup of tea. Tamzin worked at her list methodically, James tossing in names if he thought she'd missed any, carefully making no remark when she dipped a corner of toast into her tea and ate it. Valerie had hated her dunking, said it made her look like a navvy.

He didn't care in what form food got into her stomach. Just that it did.

She heaved a massive sigh. 'We've got to sort out a funeral, haven't we?'

Without knowing whether he was comforting her or himself, he took her hand as he dropped heavily back into his chair. 'Yes. I think we need a family conference about that. What do you think?'

A tear tipped over her lashes. 'Yes, better talk to the others. Do we have to put a box in the newspaper, too? Dad, this is really horrible.' The tears began to slide slowly down her cheeks.

He slid his arm around her weightless shoulders. 'We'll have to be strong for each other.'

'OK,' she whispered.

Chapter Thirty

'You're not going to be able to manage me.' Gareth's fingers moved restlessly over the spokes of the wheelchair.

Diane didn't pause in her task of transferring things from her usual old handbag into a small black one, new, that she'd bought to go with her dress. 'I can get you into the car – you're mobile enough on your crutches in short bursts. Melvyn and Ivan will help at the church.'

'I feel funny about Melvyn and Ivan being at Valerie's funeral. They've hardly met her but it hasn't seemed to occur to them not to go.' His brows were hard over his eyes.

Diane found her keys. 'She's the half-sister of their half-brother. They have a pronounced idea of family.'

'Did you get directions?'

'Yes.' Her stark black dress showed not a flash of white or even a gold-coloured button. She glanced in the mirror. It was amazing how well black suited her and her pale hair. She hadn't bought anything of such quality since before she met Gareth and was entranced by the way the fabric hung and moved.

He was watching. 'So where's that dress from, then?'

She looked up. 'I bought it at cost from Unity's because I've had no time to make anything suitable.'

'You seem thick as thieves with this Unity. I heard you, on the phone, turning away work from Trish Warboys.'

She looked down into her bag. It had a bright paisley lining but she was sure nobody would mind that, or notice. 'I've too much to do for Unity's and she wants more for next season. It's more remunerative than doing occasional commissions for Trish Warboys. Good job I've moved into the bigger workroom. I'm working flat out, even with Bryony helping.' She didn't tell him that she'd successfully negotiated working capital both via a deposit from Unity and a small bank loan. Let him wonder.

'It's a regular little rag factory in there.'

She didn't answer. It was one of her new strategies. Whenever Gareth sneered, she fell silent.

'I don't want to be late,' he snapped.

'We won't be.' She looked again in the mirror and brushed the shoulders of the dress.

'Where's Bryony?'

'In the bathroom.'

'Again?'

'She's pregnant and she's nervous because she's never been to a funeral before. She'll be OK.' She reached for her jacket.

He looked around the modest, old-fashioned kitchen. 'I'm thirsty. Any chance of a cold drink before we go?'

'Yes, you get it. Up on your feet little and often, that's what they said, wasn't it? You can shout if you get stuck.' She left the room and went upstairs. At the moment, he was easy enough to avoid. During the day, he had the choice of the sitting room or the kitchen, to avoid the undignified palaver of scooting upstairs on his behind. Good job they had a downstairs loo.

He hobbled around, his progress slow on crutches because of his wrist.

By the time she had to help him into the car, he'd taken refuge in grumpiness. He wasn't taking well the cool way that Diane was ignoring his wishes and also his temper. Her absence from the marital bed. The segregation of their finances.

She was a remote Diane.

She smiled to herself as he glowered out of the car window at a field of stubble. No way could he look after himself as yet, so having support at home had been fundamental to his discharge from hospital. But if he'd thought that Diane not leaving him when his secrets popped out like naughty children meant they'd return to their old relationship, then he couldn't have been more wrong. With cool courtesy Diane helped him wash and dress; she also prepared his meals and did his laundry.

But she didn't discuss her movements nor seek his opinions. She offered him no company other than at meal times and her conversation consisted of finances, hospital appointments and the information that she had booked a local gardener to transform their garden into an easy-care oasis.

Even Bryony, silent in the back seat, wasn't demonstrating her love in the unconditional, effusive way that she used to.

For Gareth, his life had changed when his father found him. And now, if it was changing again ... well, that was unfortunate. Diane could no longer live her life to suit him, she reminded herself, picking up speed on the straight lane.

But then he disarmed her by muttering, 'It's unfair that somebody who loved life so much shouldn't have it.' And she realised that his surliness wasn't necessarily about her. He was missing Valerie, who'd represented fun in his life in the last two years. No more helicopter jaunts. No more sitting in her large, beautifully equipped kitchen and listening to her describing the childhood he never had. Discovering how comfortable wealth made things.

'I know you miss her,' she said, gently. And how much did he miss Stella? Not as much, she was sure, as she missed James.

As St. Agnes-in-the-Field Church was only around the corner from Valerie's house there was no motor cortège to join. Diane took Gareth directly to the pointy Norman greyness of St. Agnes's and Ivan and Melvyn were waiting to lift his wheelchair from the boot, steadying it on the lane's bumpy surface while Gareth hauled himself across from the car.

The hearse carried Valerie's oak casket from her home with the family walking behind.

James. Harold. Natalia. Alice. Tamzin.

In the pause while the casket slid smoothly from the hearse and on to a gurney, Diane wheeled Gareth to join the family group.

'Dad.' Gareth put his hand out to his father. Harold was pale and his nose looked larger and more heavily veined than ever.

'Gareth,' said Harold, hoarsely. 'At least you're still here –' His lips set tightly. Tamzin, a liquorice stick in a straight black dress, took her grandfather's hand. Diane pushed Gareth slowly, behind the casket, up the sloping path to the dim interior of the small village church. But she watched James, in front, James who set his shoulders and looked only straight ahead.

Gareth let Melvyn hoist him onto his crutches to shuffle between the scarred old pews, flinching each time he put weight on his leg. Diane left him and Bryony in the family pew and she melted back into the body of the church to stand with Melvyn and Ivan.

She wanted to put space between herself and James. If she could have avoided the funeral she would have. It felt wrong for her to be there.

The church was cold and smelled of hymn books. She watched Gareth casting his eye over the simple village church, without stained glass, silver ornaments or gilded crosses and only worn old flagstones to floor the nave and the aisles. Then frown at James, as if wondering why the funeral hadn't been held somewhere grand.

But there was a nice enough choir and a breathy organ

and the red-faced vicar, raising his voice to the rafters, managed to avoid giving that speech about the deceased having merely stepped into the next room, which, far from comforting the loved ones, usually left them enraged.

And one of Valerie's friends read a eulogy about keeping Valerie alive in their minds – especially whenever they heard a sports car gunning past.

Gareth listened, motionless. Harold's complexion was so grey that he could have been carved from the same stone as the church. James stood between his softly weeping daughters, holding their hands.

Chapter Thirty-One

Had she ever been so busy?

These days, Diane's 'to do' list was as long as her arm. Top of the list was Unity's order, which she had scheduled by the simple expedient of calculating how many garments there were left to make and dividing that figure by the number of weeks before delivery was due, which left her still three garments to make each week; frightening, bearing in mind that she had to take Gareth to his outpatient appointments and physio, which always took hours.

And Diane found herself calling at the supermarket on the way home from these appointments because the fridge and the cupboards emptied themselves quickly and thoroughly now that Gareth and Bryony were both living at home.

Bryony contracted a stubborn chest infection and a cough like an old coalminer, making her hot and listless. Because of her pregnancy, she didn't want to use a steroid inhaler. Diane, dropping automatically into worried mum mode, found herself driving Bryony to her antenatal appointments even though Bryony had bought a little Ford KA now. Lots of the mums-to-be seemed to have their mums or friends with them, either for moral support or to look after existing children during check-ups and Diane loved the feeling of being involved, but then had to work long into the evening to keep up with her punishing schedule. Somehow she'd squeezed in the meeting about Christmas stock with Unity, resulting in an order that she was trying not to think about, yet.

When Bryony began to get better she embarked on a shopping spree for the baby, an activity that Diane just couldn't entirely resist.

And when she was at home visitors were a constant interruption. Melvyn and Ivan persuaded Gareth into spending some of his money on an immense new television and satellite TV box – whereupon they called much more often.

Bryony visited Harold to keep him company in his desperate mourning for his daughter and reported that, filleted by his grief, he didn't seem to care whether he ate or not. Very worrying. Diane began inviting him for meals.

George brought Tamzin to visit Diane 'to cheer her up', although Diane did keep explaining to him that Tamzin wasn't suddenly going to get over her bereavement, as if it were a bad cold.

In between, Diane kept her head down, battling grimly to deliver Unity's order on time.

Then there was James. Before she crashed into all-too brief sleep, sometimes she'd send him carefully friendly texts. *How r u? How r u coping? How r the girls? Do you need help?* He'd reply, *Lots of crap to get though. Taxman a pain. Tamzin worrying but Nat and Ally spending lots of time with her.* Occasionally, he drove Tamzin to the house and Diane's heart bled at the shock in James's dark grey eyes as he somehow steered his family through the uncharted land of grief.

One task on her 'to do' list kept sliding down the order: Diane still needed to investigate why a shop in Covent Garden Market was selling her garments at a huge mark-up. But then the day finally came when she could deliver her entire order to Unity – feeling quite important at drawing the Peugeot up to the delivery entrance.

'I never thought you'd manage the whole lot,' confessed Unity, slender in a gold tunic that brought out the lights in her hair. 'You must have worked your poor fingers to the bone.'

'I did.' Diane hung the last garment on the hanging rail with a, 'Phew!' ready for Unity to inventory and price.

'You deserve a rest. But I will need the first of the Christmas order ASAP ...' She pulled an apologetic face.

'Some of the fabrics have arrived and I'll get onto it in a few days,' Diane had promised. But she knew that before she plunged up to her eyes in beads and bows, she had to face the evil hour.

The train to London took only an hour from Peterborough, yet Diane hadn't been to London for years. At least ten. She tried not to look too country-mousey as she stepped down from the train and shuffled along the platform at King's Cross, the voices of fellow passengers battling the thrumming of the trains in the echoing station.

Country Mouse had wanted to wear her 'best dress', the beautifully cut black number from Unity's. But Idiosyncratic Fashionista had dressed in a skirt in dingy pink and drab blue – wonderful colours – overlapping and pockety, and every edge unfinished, dark-pink corduroy dancing slippers belonging to Bryony and a white top spattered with appliquéd metallic blue shark fins.

Almost falling into the stairwell, she descended into the tiled corridors leading to the underground station. Although she'd pored over the map in the back of her diary and knew very well that Covent Garden Station was only three stops down the Piccadilly Line, the diagonal, dark blue one, she still checked again with a large map on the wall before committing her travel card to the slot in the barriers.

Clutching her safely returned ticket, her stomach rose to meet her heart as she descended into the warm air of the subterranean network. Where were all these people going? Why was she the only one who had to pause to scan each colour-coded sign before selecting her route?

She wished she could have come down to London when she had first learned what was going on and was still good and angry. Then she wouldn't have felt so trepidatious about storming into some swanky shop in Covent Garden.

The tube was almost exactly as she remembered it; first a crowded platform and then a crowded train, the passengers divided into sitters and standers – the sitters having to watch their feet weren't stood upon by the standers – breathing overused air as the hissing monster trains clattered and whooshed through the tunnels. Diane clung to a metal pole near the doors and tried not to think about a breakdown in a tunnel. She alighted at Covent Garden and became one of a block of passengers herding into the big sheep-pen lifts. There, she tried not to think about a breakdown en route to the surface.

Relieved to reach fresh air, outside the station she was transfixed by a shop mannequin, wearing a red suit and a stupid hat, unaccountably left on a picnic chair in the middle of the pedestrian street with a guitar across his lap. Three giggling teenaged girls were waving their fingers in his face. Diane seemed to be the only one astonished when the 'mannequin' came to life and played a few bars on his guitar. He must be one of the famous living statues she'd read about.

'What a bloody tedious way to make a living,' she muttered, disgusted. Further down the busy paved street she found another of these curious creatures, painted entirely in silver and striking a pose he was only motivated to change at the chink of money in his basket. Mr and Mrs Tourist and all the little tourists were out in force and seemingly willing to break off their chatter in order to donate coins to this end. Good luck to them.

Diane turned her attention to the right and a columned

building, *Covent Garden Market* arching over the doorway in gilded lettering.

The shop was in there, somewhere. The Monkee Box.

A highly unlikely name for a clothes shop, it prompted an unpleasant uncoiling sensation in the pit of Diane's stomach each time it floated through her head. On the journey down, surrounded by passengers on mobile phones or listening to MP3 players, she'd tried, and failed, to visualise marching in and challenging the origins of the shop's stock.

Too scary! She needed more time to gather herself and 11.30am didn't strike her as the best time to confront the manager of a busy shop. She would wait until the other side of the lunch-hour and, meantime, explore this famous area of the capital city.

Soon she was absorbed in testing hand creams in Crabtree & Evelyn and drinking tiny samples of tea in Whittards, entering from The Piazza and accidentally leaving by the other door.

And there, on the other side of The Apple Market, hung the newly familiar words. The Monkee Box.

No! She wasn't ready! Heart fluttering, she swung back towards The Piazza.

A street entertainer was preparing to walk a tight rope slung between two of the four enormous columns of St. Paul's Church. Diane joined the crowd craning to see him try. But when, after quarter of an hour, all he'd done was *talk about* walking the tight rope, she detached herself from his audience in favour of a tour around the covered market hall, pausing to admire stalls full of glass and silver jewellery.

At the end of The Apple Market – no apples on sale, but prints of watercolours of London scenes and elegant jewellery that she eventually realised with astonishment was made from forks – she was drawn by the aroma of coffee. Her stomach gurgled. She checked her watch.

After queuing for ages, she then found it difficult to choose between creamy pasta dishes and exotically filled baguettes. Finally deciding on a parmesan chicken baguette, she got flustered trying to order cappuccino where she was meant to order food and then waiting for the food when she was supposed to move to where the food would be waiting for her. She somehow managed to order the cappuccino twice, but that, looking at the length of the queue behind her, was fortuitous, and she settled down at a table to enjoy her meal and watch over people's heads as a man on a unicycle juggled bright blue clubs, coaching his audience to cheer, clap or boo on his cue.

After the meal – very nice – Diane followed her ears into the next hall and downstairs into the lower courtyard where a string quintet was simultaneously creating wonderful rousing music and causing gusts of laughter. Intrigued, Diane bought a glass of red wine and took one of the little green tables – well back, because it was evident that the musicians considered those in the front row to be targets, especially two polished women who giggled and tossed their expensive haircuts as the musicians stole sips of their champagne.

Diane resolved that one day she would buy champagne at Covent Garden – with money that she had earned *herself* – and sip away the afternoon, laughing and clapping and tossing her hair.

At three, she could shelve the purpose of her visit no longer.

She ate a mint, used the public toilets and forced her anxious legs to carry her to The Monkee Box.

Although she had the garment Natalia had purchased with The Monkee Box and the astonishing sum printed on the receipt, it still seemed too incredible to Diane that something she'd made could sell here for £209. She half-expected that somehow there would prove to be some plausible explanation that would make her feel foolish, but relieved, and counting the cost of a wasted day.

Forcing her chin up, she made her way to where The Monkee Box was painted in yellow above a royal blue frontage. Inside the door, a young member of staff beamed at her. 'Hi!'

'Hi,' responded Diane, politely.

'If you need any help at all, please ask any member of staff.' She had a slight, pretty accent, perhaps Scandinavian.

'Thank you.' Diane moved over to the first rail wondering if that poor little girl had to spend her working life parroting the same redundant phrase to everyone who wandered in. She must be nearly fainting from the monotony.

The shop was laid out on two floors, ground and basement. The clothes hung on simple chrome rails and Diane was soon engrossed in the ground-floor garments. The prices! £209 wasn't unusual for a dress in The Monkee Box – which maybe should be renamed The Monee Box – and there were loads priced higher. And, astonishingly, although silk and linen were immensely popular, sometimes those prices were charged just for polyester. She couldn't believe it.

The current fashion for unfinished seams and hems had apparently been readily embraced by The Monkee Box clientele, although a requirement for lavish detail did kind of balance that out so far as the work involved was concerned. Diane could see how her own brand of boho would fit right in here, the diaphanous layers, threaded cord, D rings, straps, sequins, lace, rick-rack, ribbon, dull buckles and gleaming eyelets. She drifted among the rails and down to the basement, almost forgetting her original purpose as she stored in her memory bank diagonal waists and big floppy bows.

As she studied a devoré skirt on a rail at the foot of the stairs something caught the corner of her eye. And there it was – a grey linen dress with pink ribbon executing a single twist each time it tacked from side to side of the garment. Snatching it up, she checked for the label and saw the familiar turquoise and yellow. And the price … £229.

Angrily, she flicked through the rails but found only one other garment, a red skirt with a black lacing and flick-up hem. She carried them upstairs and pre-empted an offer from a smiling member of staff to show her to the fitting room by announcing loudly, 'I need to speak to the manager about the origins of these garments. Immediately.'

Like magic, an elliptical woman with skin of amber and a frizzy bun on the back of her head materialised. 'Can I help?'

Diane held up the two garments that almost blurred before her eyes, she was shaking so much. 'You can explain to me how my work makes its way onto your racks – as I don't sell it to you.'

In seconds she was ushered to another door revealing another staircase, upwards this time, and the woman was settling her into a green leather chair and pouring coffee from a jug kept on a hotplate near the window, saying, 'I'm Amelia Fountain, the manager. I'm astonished by what you've just said. Can you add detail?'

Amelia was short and dumpy and draped in a khaki angora shawl over a long linen dress in shades of mud and a silk scarf belt coloured like a sunset. Her hair looked as though it could be knitted from angora, too, and she had a sweet voice that seemed at odds with her forthright manner.

Still trembling, Diane laid the two garments over the pine table that served as a desk. 'These are mine – at least, I designed and made them. I sold them to Rowan Chater at Rowan's in Peterborough for sale in his shop.'

Amelia nodded, her elbows out and her hands laid one on top of the other on the table in front of her. 'There can be no mistake? Similar garments? Copies?'

'None. My garments. My labels. My stitching.'

Amelia nodded again, thoughtfully, reaching to finger the pink ribbon as if it might tell her its secrets. Her gaze was direct. 'Are you accusing this company of shady dealings?'

'I don't know. Are they shady?'

'I'm not the buyer,' said Amelia, 'but I do sometimes make recommendations and I recommended these garments be bought in. Rowan Chater came to the shop with an introduction from somebody I used to work with. He made a lot of being in the trade, wishing he could move his operation here, all that kind of thing. He said he had a local designer who was wasted in a small provincial city.' Amelia replaced her hands tidily in front of her. 'I agreed to look at it. I liked it. He said that he'd arranged to agent the designs and was taking 15%.'

Diane choked back a laugh that might have become a sob. 'Agent! He pretended that he sold them in his shop and had a job to get rid of them. He paid me peanuts. And all the time the slimy bastard was bringing my garments to you and making a big profit.' She swallowed, hard.

Amelia's eyes were sympathetic. 'It's been going on for some time.' She rubbed one of her hands on another as Diane fought her tears. 'I'm sorry,' she added. 'But I don't think anyone's done anything illegal and I had no reason to believe that he was pulling a fast one. Unless you had a contract that he would sell what you sold him from a specific outlet, I think he's free to sell stock on.'

Diane nodded, throat stretched with tears.

Then the urge to cry vanished as an interesting thought blossomed. 'Did they sell? My designs?'

'Oh, yes. No problems there. I like your stuff.'

Sitting up straighter, Diane fixed on what she hoped was a businesslike expression. Miraculously, her trembling ceased.

'So would you buy garments directly from me?'

Amelia reached again for the coffee jug, with a glimmer of a smile. 'It does seem the best arrangement. Let's talk Monkee.'

Back in Peterborough, James was waiting as the train groaned into the station. Carried by a wave of joy, Diane had bounced over to hug him before she remembered that she wasn't supposed to.

'How did you know where I was?' Somehow, her hand touched his.

His eyes smiled, despite the sadness in their depths. 'Tamzin and George tried to ring you and Bryony told them that you'd just texted home with the time of your train. I came to see if you'd fill me in with what happened at Covent Garden.' He grinned. 'I promise not to press my unwanted and unwarranted advice on you.'

Across a table in the steamy coffee shop she told him about her confrontation of Amelia Fountain in the Monkee Box. 'It's Rowan, exactly as I suspected. Nasty little worm. *And,*' she paused, impressively, 'I offered to sell my garments direct to the Monkee Box and Amelia said yes!'

His face lit up. 'You're officially a successful business-woman. Congratulations.'

She laughed. Then she stopped. 'Was I rude when you offered to help with Rowan?'

'Bloody rude, but I didn't offer to help, I tried to take over. A fault of mine. Sorry.' His eyes smiled.

She put her head on one side. 'Humility doesn't suit you.'

'Nothing suits me.' His eyes stopped smiling. 'I'm in a nightmare. My wife's dead, my daughters are distraught, my father-in-law is the personification of grief and I think it's only his anger at his loss that's preventing his heart from sending him after his daughter. Tamzin has announced that she's done seeing doctors, counsellors and therapists.

'Valerie's affairs are orderly but complex and I'm her chief executor. I would never have believed that she could cause me more stress and paperwork now than she did when she was alive. And the girls are intelligent enough to realise that although it was her injuries that made her vulnerable to the embolism, being a heavy smoker and drinker almost invited it. So their emotions are all over the place.

'And through it all, the weeks of hassle and heartache and the regret and even despite the awful, ever-present *guilt*, a tiny piece of me wants you to be sewing something quietly in the same room while I deal with the paperwork tsunami. Whenever the girls dissolve into tears I want you to appear with understanding words and hot, buttered toast.'

He smiled, painfully. 'You didn't know how right you were going to be proved about it being the wrong time for us.'

She sighed in unhappy acknowledgement. 'Apart from Valerie, Bryony needs family stability and so do your girls.'

He examined her hand, caressing the rough patch on her left forefinger with one square fingertip. 'Do you think you'll ever leave him?'

'I don't know. I'm trying to keep my marriage going in some form for Bryony and her unborn baby. I can't see far past that, right now.'

'I suppose you're right to do that.'

'I suppose I am.' Despair tugged at her chest.

He sighed. 'So I'd better go home and cope with stuff.'

'Me, too.'

In the car park, they kissed cheeks by her car in an unexceptional manner.

Chapter Thirty-Two

Diane picked up her bag and car keys then tapped at Bryony's door. 'Come on then, if you want a lift into Peterborough.'

Bryony's voice was muffled. 'Two minutes.'

Downstairs, Gareth was already settled in his armchair, the newspaper and TV remote balanced on the arms, his crutches beside him and his legs on a stool. He frowned over his reading glasses as she passed through the sitting room. 'Going out?'

'Peterborough. Bryony's coming, too.'

'What are you going there for?' His heavy brow shut down over his eyes.

Had she always reported her movements to him automatically?

He'd never seemed to feel a need to reciprocate, and somehow she hadn't really expected it.

An appointment at the bank was scheduled and she had no intention of sharing that information with him, nor the update to the business plan that James had shown her how to draw up, to her an unnecessarily formal method of saying, 'I need more money because I now have two fabulous outlets to supply and will have to buy another machine and somebody to use it.' To cope with Unity's Christmas orders, plus supplying The Monkee Box, she was going to need someone who could cut patterns and machine- and hand-sew as soon as possible and Gareth was bound to explode when he discovered there would be a strange person in the workroom – which he insisted on still referring to as the dining room – every day. Until that hurdle had to be leapt she intended to keep her business as just that – her business.

'I've got a few things to do. I'll be back this afternoon,' she answered. 'There's plenty of soup in the cupboard for your lunch, or you could make a sandwich.'

'I suppose I can manage,' he said shortly, and pointed the TV remote at the set.

'I'm sure you can.'

Bryony padded down the stairs. Her pregnancy showed itself as a soft segment of big naked tummy looming between her maternity jeans and a top the colour of blackberries. Diane wasn't keen on the look. When she'd been pregnant the idea had been to cover up the bump and distract the eye with flamboyant collars, not display it for everyone to admire. But such observations only drew Bryony's most exasperated, 'Oh, Mum!'

'See you this afternoon, Dad.' Bryony dropped a kiss on her father's cheek.

His forbidding expression melted into a smile for her. 'Mind how you go, darling.'

'Want anything from Peterborough?' Bryony perched on the edge of a chair and slid her feet into gold-coloured trainers with dark turquoise laces, bending awkwardly.

Gareth's smile broadened at her concern. 'I could do with a new box of tissues –'

'Kitchen cupboard,' offered Diane.

'– and a pen that works –'

'Kitchen drawer.'

'– and a sudoku book.'

'I've never seen you do sudoku,' commented Bryony, standing up.

'Got to keep the little grey cells going.'

Diane looked at her watch and moved towards the door, heroically suppressing an unworthy remark that yes, he would need to find some activity to replace the deceit and duplicity with which he'd exercised his mind for so long.

In the car, as soon as Gareth was safely out of hearing, Bryony burst out, 'Well? Was it really your stuff on sale in Covent Garden?'

Diane cast a glance behind her as she pulled away from the house, as if Gareth might be tuned into their conversation, somehow. 'It was. But it's all working out, because now I'm going to supply The Monkee Box myself!'

Bryony's dark eyes sparkled. 'That's so *cool*. A Covent Garden shop wants to sell your stuff. How cool is that? That's *so* cool.'

Turning into Purtenon St. Paul's main street, making sure that she got out ahead of an oncoming tractor to avoid following it at 15mph for miles, Diane laughed. 'I admit I hadn't seen it in quite that light. I've been focusing on how some shit's been buying stuff off me cheap and selling it on heavily marked up.'

Bryony's brows shot up. 'Oh, yeah. So, are you going to speak to Rowan?'

Diane accelerated away from the village. 'He's going to be my first call this morning.'

The brown eyes shone again. 'Can I come? I haven't seen you in a strop for ages.'

'If you think me in a strop is particularly entertaining.'

Bryony giggled. 'I love to watch you giving someone shit.'

'Problem is that it doesn't seem as if he's done anything illegal. I didn't sell him the stuff with any provisos.'

'You could give him shit, anyway. He's totally out of order.'

They found Rowan's shop busy, Yummy Mummies flexing their credit cards now that the children had returned to school for the autumn term and shopping, once again, had become an indulgence rather than a hideous endurance test.

Rowan's glance lit on Diane over the head of a customer

in a floor-length, pale-grey, knitted cardigan that matched the colour of today's sky. His hair was cut so close, it was like suede. 'I'm busy, can you come back in an hour?' His dismissive tone would have been perfect for the hired help.

'No.' Diane began to flip through the rails for her own stuff.

Rowan made his way over. 'I don't have time to look at your things right now.'

'I haven't brought you anything to look at.' She carried on scraping the hangers methodically along the top rail.

He threw her a baffled look and turned back to the lady in the long cardigan, now at the till with aubergine capri pants in one hand and credit card in the other.

Diane worked through the wall rails and then the floor-standing ones while Bryony settled herself in the chair for customers.

When the shop was still full but Rowan was no longer actively serving, Diane opened her green corduroy shoulder bag and pulled out the dress that Natalia had bought in The Monkee Box. 'Look,' she said to Rowan.

Rowan's eyes flicked to hers. He shrugged. 'What?'

'A garment that I sold to you.' She made sure that her voice was audible all over the little shop. She waved the cuff under his nose, the one with a price ticket from The Monkee Box for £209. 'Look!' she repeated. 'It was on sale in Covent Garden Market.'

He hesitated, eyes narrowing. Then he smiled and tried to take her elbow. 'Come through for a chat.'

'No, thanks.' She folded the dress and returned it to her bag. 'How have garments I've sold to you ended up being sold elsewhere at an enormous mark-up?' Every prospective shopper had paused to listen by now. 'You've paid me peanuts for years. You pretended that you had difficulty selling my stuff and I ought to be jolly grateful for what I got. Yet you've been selling it on to The Monkee Box and pocketing a big profit.'

A couple of shoppers drew in breath. One tutted.

Diane held up her hand. 'And don't pretend that you haven't, because I've had a frank chat with Amelia from The Monkee Box, and she's been kind enough to share the figures with me.'

Rowan's face turned a dull puce. 'I don't have to be spoken to like this in my own shop.'

'I don't know how you're going to avoid it.' Slowly, Diane smiled. 'I'm telling the truth and you can't lay hands upon me because all these nice people are witnesses. You could ring the police, I suppose.' She folded her arms. 'Why don't you? You ring the police and I'll ring a reporter, and we'll see how it looks in the paper.' Her smile grew into a grin. 'Or you could ring Amelia – but I think you'll find that you're blacklisted as a supplier so far as she's concerned. From now on, when Diane Jenner Originals appear in her shop, Diane Jenner will be making the profit out of it. Not some talentless third party tosser.' With a defiant flick of her plait, she spun on her heel.

'Like your husband?'

Diane halted in mid-stride. Turned slowly back. 'What?'

'Like your husband.' Rowan's lips twisted.

Diane's lips went numb. 'What's he got to do with it?'

His face shone with spite. 'He walked past one day and recognised the stuff I was loading into the van. It took just thirty quid for him to keep his mouth shut. Thirty measly quid for every batch.'

The blood in her cheeks boiled. Her ears sang. Diane heard a couple of customers murmuring. Sympathy! She despised it. She clawed her tattering dignity around her. 'I don't know why you expect me to be surprised. He's as big a shit as you are.'

Outside she put her arms around Bryony, who was white, even her lips, and guided her out of the arcade over to a black-painted bench where the fresh air might revive her. 'Oh, darling, I'm sorry you heard that.'

Tipping her head to rest it on her mother's shoulder, Bryony sighed. 'I'm a big girl, Mum, I can handle it – like you. I just feel a bit ... wobbly.'

Diane debated her next move. She didn't want to leave Bryony here, the bench was cold metal and the breeze had enough edge to chill a body through. She needed somewhere warmer if she were to even consider leaving her alone for an hour while she put her business plan before Ms Rhianne Andrews, at the bank.

It's never far to a café when you're in a city centre and in five minutes Diane had Bryony drinking hot tea.

Bryony was still shivering. 'It can't be right, can it, what Rowan said? Dad wouldn't?'

Diane hesitated. 'I don't know. I hope not.'

A chalky Bryony fell silent. Even after two cups of tea, she was shaky.

Diane rang the bank and rescheduled her appointment with Ms Rhianne Andrews for the end of the week. She tried not to sigh, remembering that she'd meant to use the excuse of reporting on how the business plan had been received to ring James that night. To hear his voice. To check that he was coping.

'Shall I take you home?' she asked gently.

Bryony blinked. 'I don't know. Dad will be there –'

'But Dad will be downstairs until I help him to bed, later. I think you could do with a few hours chill time, snug in your own room. Buy a magazine on the way back to the car and you can put your feet up.'

Compared to the cheery, chatty journey into the city earlier, the journey home was a wet weekend. The parkways were busy and Diane knew from experience that it was easy to want to leave one and inexplicably find herself still on it. She concentrated on the traffic and left Bryony to stare silently at the scenery.

Until they reached the quiet of the Fen lanes, the land stretching flat on either side of the road. Then Bryony burst out, 'Are you staying with Dad for me?'

In her surprise, Diane almost let the car run into a ditch. For safety's sake she pulled over, half on a humped grass verge. 'That came a bit out of the blue!'

'Sorry.' Bryony paused to feel around for her inhaler and use it on a big in-breath. She paused before letting the breath out again and gave a little cough. 'It's dawning on me exactly how crappy Dad's been to you. And I bet I don't know the half of it. Because people's relationships are private and mostly others don't see the real picture? Sometimes people inside the relationship don't. Like I thought my relationship with Inacio was so cool and that he always came to my area because he didn't want me crossing the city at night. But it wasn't cool, it was crappy, because he was actually going home to his wife.'

She coughed again and paused over another puff of her inhaler. 'And I don't want anything to do with Inacio, because he lied and lied and lied. And I just thought … well, Dad's lied and lied to you and you're still with him. So I wondered if there was a reason. And then I wondered if the reason was me. But I suppose I shouldn't have asked because it's your relationship, yours and Dad's.' Bryony rubbed her eyes, like a child. 'I still love Dad.'

'I know.'

Diane stroked Bryony's cheek, unsure of what she could say to make this less hard on her daughter. Because she was staying with Gareth for Bryony's sake – but she didn't think it was necessarily the best thing for Bryony to hear.

Chapter Thirty-Three

Troubled that she'd somehow let her daughter end up in the middle of things despite all intentions to the contrary, Diane didn't immediately notice anything missing when they trailed silently into the house.

It was Bryony, dragging her bag as if even that little weight was too much, who said, 'Where's Dad?'

His chair in the sitting room was empty, his crutches gone. They looked in the workroom and checked the downstairs loo. Both empty. Slowly, they moved towards the stairs. Diane took the lead. For a reason she didn't examine too closely, she trod as quietly as she could.

The doors to the bathroom and the other rooms were wide open, showing empty rooms. But the door to Bryony's room stood only a little ajar, and through the gap Diane could see Gareth sitting on Bryony's bed, his back to the door, hunched over something in his lap. She hesitated.

With a mew of distress Bryony thrust past her, hurling the door back on its hinges. 'Dad, how could you go through my things?'

Gareth's head flew up, his face pulled wide with horror. One of his crutches lay across the duvet, the other was propped against the wall. The large drawer beneath Bryony's bed was open next to his feet. A black leather box was open inside the drawer.

And Gareth's lap glistened with the jewellery that had belonged to Diane's mother and grandmother.

Beside him sat a blue canvas money belt, the one he took on holiday to keep their spending money safe. Several pieces of jewellery could be seen through its gaping mouth.

Bryony swayed on her feet. Diane guided her hurriedly into the pink basketwork chair. 'Sit down, sweetie.' All they needed was Bryony fainting.

Gareth's hunted gaze flicked from daughter to wife. He cleared his throat and looked down at the brooches and chains laid out neatly across his legs like bizarre decorations. 'I –' He cleared his throat again.

In slow motion, Bryony stooped awkwardly for the box and held it out. Like a naughty child, Gareth put everything back. First the pieces from his lap: gold, silver, diamonds, emeralds, jet, amber; then from the pocket of the belt. Bryony checked inside. 'Is that everything? Or do I have to frisk you?' Her voice trembled.

Gareth nodded. 'Everything.' He picked up his crutches and threaded them onto his arms. Then he sat, silent, staring at the carpet, caught red-handed and stuck for an explanation.

Gradually, colour began to return to Bryony's face. Her eyes glittered and Diane recognised anger. She was glad. Anger would serve Bryony better than shock and horror.

'Mum, do you think Uncle Freddy will put these things back in his safe for me?'

'I'm sure he will.'

'Good. I'll go over there now.'

'I'll come with you. Probably better if you're not alone.'

Gareth turned quickly. 'Bryony, darling, I'm sorry, I shouldn't have been looking without asking but ...' He scrabbled for words. 'I was only looking. The stuff in my belt – you don't think I was going to take it, do you? No.' He halted, licked his lips. 'I was just going to get it valued.'

Bryony shook her head, her eyes as big as pansies. 'Don't expect me to believe your crap. Who needs a father like you? Not me – in case you were wondering.' She turned her agonised eyes to Diane. 'I mean that, by the way.' Bryony made it from the room before she began to sob.

Diane hovered, not knowing who was the more devastated, Bryony or Gareth.

For herself, she was shocked. The implications of Gareth's latest perfidy were almost too huge for her to dare to believe and she felt as if, for once, the light at the end of the tunnel could be daylight, rather than an oncoming train.

'Why do you have to be so greedy?' she whispered. 'Why couldn't you be satisfied with everything you already have? We'll talk more, later, but I want you to move out of here in the next few days. You can live in your cottage. I don't want your money and if you go without a fuss I won't ask for any.'

'How can I? I can't live alone,' he answered, gruffly. He flicked a glance her way. His eyes were ... what? Not hurt. Worried? Probably, a bit. But angry, too; annoyed with himself for being careless.

'Well,' she said, preparing to follow her daughter. 'Whether or not you can live alone, I think it's time we lived apart. Maybe you could go live with your dad for a while, he could use the company. Or you could hire a nurse. Spend some of the dosh on yourself – you seem to be able to do that OK.'

Chapter Thirty-Four

Diane's footsteps pattered down the stairs and her receding voice called after their daughter, 'Bryony, I'm so sorry ...'

Painfully, heart thumping, Gareth laboured to his feet. Found his balance with his crutches. Punting himself out of the room and across the landing he could still hear Diane's voice, then Bryony's, high and tearful. His heart gave a massive squeeze.

'Bryony?' He sagged against the doorjamb of what used to be his and Diane's room but was now his, leg and hip throbbing.

He blinked fiercely. Bryony had looked at him with such pain and repugnance in her eyes. 'Bryony!' he shouted hoarsely over the banisters. 'Bryony!'

But there was no pause to show that Bryony was listening. Her voice ran on in her sweet, over-emphatic way. High and rapid with emotion. Then Diane's again, lower, soothing.

He heard the back door open. And shut, snipping the voices off mid-sentence.

With a heave, he lurched and limped to the window to watch Bryony and Diane heading for Bryony's baby blue KA, a real girly car, as cute as his daughter. Bryony throwing her hands around, talking, talking. Diane, skirt swinging as she walked, resting a calming hand on Bryony's shoulder. Bryony pointing her key unit at the car, a flash from the indicator lights as it unlocked. Both women climbing in.

The car was small enough to turn in the lane. The engine note climbed. Then they were gone.

After a minute, he backed away from the window. Dropping his crutches to the carpeted floor he lowered himself onto the bed, swung his legs around in stages and then inched up the mattress until he could lie with his head on the pillow. He wouldn't go downstairs yet. The stairs were murder without help. It had been painful to get up here on his own without Diane to hold his crutches and steady him as he went up one step at a time on his backside. Going down on his backside was a proper bastard, his healing limbs shrieked whenever he tried to use them to haul himself forward.

Tears pricked suddenly. He hadn't cried since his mother had died. And then it had been only one hot, fat tear as the coffin was lowered into the ground. What would Wendy have had to say about all this caper?

Closing his eyes, he tried to hear her voice. *Look after ...* Look after your brothers. Look after yourself. *Look after your family ...* Shame melted him into the bed, spreading itself over his limbs and weighing him down. He shifted, uncomfortably. He would've been on the wrong end of one of Wendy's tongue lashings for this because he hadn't looked after his daughter.

Not like Wendy, who had looked after him until it had become time for him to look after her.

She wouldn't have minded that he hadn't looked after Diane. Wendy had never been fortunate enough to find a man who put her first, so why would she want it for Diane? Women had to be strong and look out for themselves. That way they'd never be disappointed.

He'd often seen Diane disappointed.

But Diane was strong, in her quiet way. Damned woman, you could push her and push her and she'd bend to your will, but you could only ever bend her so far. She'd never break – just suddenly rebound and slap you in the mush. And it stung.

He knew better than to expect her to calm down and

retract her decision. Yes, she was angry but anger wasn't driving her. She would be as composed and positive about leaving him as she had been about marrying him. If Diane in a temper was a comet, she was just about as likely to change course. He might as well resign himself to moving out or, he was quite convinced, she'd make it her business to take as much of his money as she possibly could, even if she didn't want it. Bloody woman. *Bloody* woman.

Bryony would be different. He could work on her, in a while; get her to see that he'd been stupid, not dishonest. Bryony would forgive him in the end.

His painkillers were downstairs. Shit. He settled his bad arm gingerly on his chest and the good one over his eyes to block the light. The sun had muscled through the clouds to glare into his window, making him sweaty and uncomfortable. He didn't feel like putting himself through the pain of getting up to close the curtains. His hip throbbed. Daggers shot through his leg.

That fucking helicopter. It had taken everything from him. Valerie, Diane and, at present, Bryony; he'd lost them all as a result of the crash. *Chadda-chadda-chadda*, how that noise used to excite him! Sitting in the left-hand seat with Valerie in the right doing the hocus pocus of the pre-flight check before flinging that whirly bird up into the sky. It had been brilliant. Racing their shadow over trees and fields, houses and roads, chatting through the headsets. He didn't suppose he'd ever get into a helicopter again and feel the vibration shaking through him as they sat on the ground waiting for clearance.

There was so much still to heal. Bones that had thickened, joints that would never move as they had.

And Valerie had gone.

The helicopter that she loved so much had snuffed her out.

He missed her. He'd known her for such a short time, but she was in the compartment in his heart marked *Family*, just like Ivan and Melvyn.

He felt in his pocket for his mobile. In his phone book he hesitated over **Ivan**, then scrolled past. **Melvyn**. He hesitated longer. He thought of his brothers, each living in a nice little semi full of family. He tried to envisage himself moving in for a while, just until he was well. Being looked after by a sister-in-law.

Being stuck in the house all day with a sister-in-law.

His sisters-in-law were OK, as brothers' wives go. But not bright, not snappy, not interesting company.

He scrolled down once more. **STM**. His thumb hovered over the green button. He missed Stella. He let himself think for several moments about Stella's soft little hands stroking his clunky, painful limbs. He really missed her.

He pressed the button. 'Oh God, Stella! I miss you.'

And her voice, breathy and sexy, surprised, incredulous. '*Gareth.*'

Two hours later he was swinging himself down his garden path with Stella wobbling beside him in shoes that sank into the grass. 'Can you cope with getting into the car? I can't believe this. I can't believe you're really leaving home. I had to pretend to my boss I felt ill, to get away.'

The car journey – in another titchy girly vehicle – was a bit teeth-gritting, even worse than getting back downstairs had been. But he'd taken his Tramadol and they were making the pain fuzzy at the edges.

Stella was taking him to her flat for now. He'd arrange the move into the cottage from there. Stella's apartment block had a lift, there were no stairs at all. Bliss.

He couldn't perform in bed, of course. Not perform as such.

But it was a treat to let Stella take him out of his clothes and swing his legs into the bed. She shucked off her own kit so that he could admire her generous little body for the first time in months, then lay down beside him, running deliciously smooth hands over his hurts. 'Poor you!' she exclaimed. 'Poor, poor, Gareth. You're still bruised. And I don't think your face is entirely right yet, is it? Oh my *God*, is that where that thing went into your hip? Eeouw! You've had so much pain, darling.'

They spent the rest of the day in bed. Dear Stella, she realised he wasn't up to sexual acrobatics, not yet. But she did one or two very nice things for him. Including making him egg, bacon and chips.

Finally, he was ready for her to switch off the bedroom television and the light and give him a bit of space so that he could sleep.

'When I'm a bit better,' he said, drowsily, deciding that the settling-down-together glow was a good time to broach a fresh start. 'I'll move back into the cottage. Will you come, too, darling? Live with me full time?'

Stella stopped stroking his bad leg. 'Live with you at the cottage?'

'We could be happy there. It would be fantastic if every day was like this one.'

Stella removed her hand. She inched away. 'Fantastic for you, maybe. I don't need a job. And certainly not as a housekeeper.'

He laughed, without opening his eyes. Stella had a great sense of humour. 'I'm not offering you a job as my housekeeper. I think a little more of you than that.'

Still, she kept her distance. 'So we're going to get married.' Her voice was flat.

In the darkness, his eyes flew open. He tried to answer as though she hadn't just frightened him to death. 'Not unless you've completely changed your tune about all that "marriage is a prison for women" stuff. We'll live together in the cottage. It's what everyone does these days. Marriage – who needs it?'

Stella rolled further over to her side of the bed. It was a big bed, king size, plenty of space. 'But prisoners always know where they are and what's what, don't they? I have changed my tune because I need that kind of security. I'm suddenly in the mood for commitment. I'm not going to live with you, Gareth, so that I can look after you for free and you can chuck me next time it's expedient.'

'That's not what I mean,' he began, alarmed.

'No? Not bloody much. I'm up to your caper, Gareth Jenner. *This* is my home and this is where I'm going to live, no-one to look after me and no-one to look after. And I've got to go to work tomorrow so you'll have to watch the telly.'

Watching the telly while Stella went out into the world as usual? Gareth had envisaged something altogether cosier. That she'd help him wash and they'd laugh over the warm sudsy water. Stella had always liked doing things for him; she'd help him with his physio and fire up her laptop to begin all his change of address letters. She was sweet about things like that.

Across the dark divide of the bed, he reached out to run his fingers coaxingly down her ribs to her hip. 'But if you come live with me you won't have to work, I've left Diane for you –'

'You've left Diane but I doubt that it was for me.' She sighed gustily, but her voice was hard. 'You can stay here for a few days, but tomorrow we'll discuss how we're going to organise things. I suppose I'd better get up early to catch the supermarket while it's quiet before work, because you eat like a horse. We can split the bill when I get home. And then you can either marry me and treat me properly or fuck off to your own place.'

In the following icy silence, Gareth stared up into the darkness in astonishment. *Stella* was giving *him* the flick! Astonishment gave way to dismay. He pictured his new life in his nice cottage – but alone. A pretty chilly prospect. One by one the women in his life had deserted him. Valerie had gone for all time and Diane was almost as unreachable, bloody woman. Bryony, his Bryony, was hurt and wary. Well, buggered if he was going to let Stella push him away, too.

Him and Stella could be good together. Stella would bring warmth and affection to his life, a life that, suddenly, was in danger of becoming a bit bloody bleak.

Awkwardly, painfully, he dragged himself over to where she clung frigidly to the mattress edge and eased her reluctant body against his. 'Marrying you is going to be a lot of fun, Stella. A woman who tells me to fuck off when I'm out of order has got to be good for me.'

By degrees, he felt her body soften and curve around his. 'All right, I'll marry you but remember I've taken all the shit I'm taking from you. And I've been one of your little secrets for too long, too. If you want us to be an item you have to tell your brothers and your daughter that we are.' She thought for a moment. 'And your wife.'

'Yeah?' He paused, turning her words over in his mind. 'Yeah, I could. I will, Stell. We'll start out with everything in the open. Married life without subterfuge and secrets.'

He didn't know, as Stella snuggled up contentedly at his side, whether he could ever get used to such a marriage. But, there was no harm done by going along with Stell for now.

Divorces took a year or two, didn't they?

Diane lay awake.

There was no moonlight and, because the house stood on a country lane, no street lights.

She stared up into the complete darkness and hugged herself with joy.

It had been a shock to come back from Freddy's and find Gareth already gone. He'd left a note in Bryony's room that Bryony had read but not shared with Diane.

And, ever since, relief kept breaking over her like a benign and gentle wave.

She. Was. Free.

Chapter Thirty-Five

Tamzin's palms sweated and her legs felt as if they'd been filled with sand.

Seated on the edge of her bed, she stared at George as if he'd just turned into a monster.

George, in fact, was alight with joy, beaming, fizzing with energy as he strode around. 'It's just amazin', Tamz. A-fuckin'-*mazin'*. Hamburg! Gigs in clubs in Hamburg. The scout who's offered us it has watched us three times and we didn't know. It's such an opportunity. I can't believe it. My dad says I can't go, but I'm going, obviously.'

She unfroze her lips. 'What about the others. Are they all going?'

''Course! Erica, Marty and Rob are taking a year out of uni, like me. We've got to totally take this opportunity, Tamz.' He threw himself down at her feet and hooked his warm hands around her legs. 'If we didn't take it we'd, like, kick ourselves for the rest of our lives.'

Her throat had turned to sandpaper. 'How will you survive, financially?'

'No idea. We get paid, of course, but it's bound to be difficult. Most of the bands out there have part-time jobs in bars and stuff while they're getting established. The agent helps you find digs.' He leapt up and began to pace again, fizzing with joy, too hyped to contain himself.

'So you speak German?'

He paused. 'Um … no. I'm going to get one of those language discs and learn, though. I expect we'll all learn. We'll have to, won't we?' And he pulled her up off the bed and into his arms and whirled her around the bedroom.

Her legs moved stiffly like a peg doll's, her heart as still as glue. She wanted to fling herself onto the bed and have a two-year-old's tantrum, letting the awfulness of one grief upon another press her down into the quilt. He would have to stop whizzing her round or she was going to be sick. Sick from grief and disappointment. The disappointment was the worst. Because she'd really thought … She'd honestly believed – that he loved her. Even losing her mum was less hideous than it could be, with George around.

George yanked her against his chest, laughing, staggering dizzily. He stroked her hair and kissed her forehead. 'Will you come with me, Tamz?'

Six words – and her heart unglued itself with a joyous thud. 'With you? With the band?' Her voice squeaked.

'Yeah. I know it's selfish but I don't want to leave you behind. I don't know when I'll get back to visit, I don't think I'm going to have much time or money and we've got to rehearse and write new stuff and everything. I might not come back for months. For years. You could try it for a month, couldn't you? See if you like it.' He was coaxing, now. 'You could always come back, we'd find the money somehow.'

'I've got money,' she pointed out, dazed. 'I can speak German. I learned to speak German at school. It's a lovely, easy language. I can be useful.'

'*Ja! Gut!*' George roared. And began again to whiz her around.

And, this time, Tamzin's heart whizzed, too.

Chapter Thirty-Six

Diane had left a message on his phone, last night. 'I've got something to tell you!'

But James hadn't returned her call because he wanted the excuse to turn up at her house.

The lack of Valerie had taken some getting used to. It was like having an abscessed tooth out – the unanaesthetised surgery had cured the fiery pain but he'd had to get used to the gap it left. And he knew that there was a 'decent period' meant to pass before bereaved spouses moved their lives on. But he was so desperate to see Diane. Just to see her. He'd make do with that.

He'd enquire after Gareth's health and ask her advice about Harold's worrying colour. That would be perfectly OK.

Even with Val gone, Harold and Gareth were family.

Diane swung the door open at his knock and beamed with reassuring joy. 'James!' Her hair, unbound, flowed over one shoulder like winter sunshine and her T-shirt's neckline was low enough to grab his attention. His heart stirred into a rapid boop-de-boop.

Far from being annoyed that he'd swanned up without notice, she grabbed his hands and fairly dragged him across the threshold. 'I've got so much to tell you.'

He took in her flush of excitement. 'The new business plan went down OK with the bank?' he guessed.

'The what? Oh yes, and the bank's up for it. I read so much in the papers about the big bad banks not lending businesses any money these days, that I was quaking by the time I got there. But they're increasing the loan on the business account for *Diane Jenner Originals* and giving me an overdraft in case I need it. Which I shouldn't. They're happy because I have firm orders and my margins stack up, my cash flow's realistic and ... oh, I can't remember all the business-speak. Just that they said yes.'

She looked so bright-eyed and beautiful that he risked a soft *hello* kiss on her cheek. 'Fantastic.'

'That's not even the biggest news, amazing things have been happening.' She thrust him down into one of the old kitchen chairs as she danced through the ritual of making coffee in a brass-topped cafetière and hardly drew breath in her description of the meeting with the bank and how she was rearranging the workroom and had bought a new machine that would be delivered on Monday along with a work table. And she was going to *interview* someone. 'I've never interviewed anybody in my life.'

When she was finally sitting opposite him, the steam from their coffee rising between them, he managed a foothold in the conversation. 'Are Bryony and Gareth here?'

She grinned. 'No, neither of them. Bryony's out with George and Tamzin, apparently. She's picking up her old life, which I think is a good thing. She was a tiny bit jealous to come home and find George so besotted with Tamzin and the band happy with their new drummer, but she's getting her head around it, now the baby is well on the way. And *Gareth* ... I've got to tell you about Gareth, James –'

His mind seized on the incredible fact that she seemed to be alone in the house. 'But he's not here? Nobody's here?'

'Just me, but, listen – '

All the pent-up tension and guilt, the pain over his daughters and his father-in-law in their grief, gurgled away at the news that Diane was alone. For just a little while he could have her to himself. His hands slid across to take hers and he drew her over the tabletop so that he could kiss her gentle mouth. 'Diane,' he murmured, against her lips.

She answered with a kiss of her own, parting her soft lips and sucking his tongue into her mouth in a way that scorched straight down to his groin. He found himself straining over the damned table, the edge digging into his lower ribs. He half-stood, hunching over to maintain the contact as he inched around the table and she turned in mid-air as he lifted her up until somehow he was taking her chair and pulling her astride himself. It felt so fantastic to have her body against his that he let common sense flee the scene without compunction. Her arms and legs wound around him and he buried his head against the softness of her neck, aroused in a heartbeat, breathing her in, his lips on her warm skin, feeling her hands caressing his shoulders. His hands fitted themselves naturally to the curves of her buttocks and his thumbs stroked the fine skin between her waistband and her top. 'You feel fantastic.'

He shifted his mouth to the soft skin in the V of her T-shirt, tracing her cleavage with his tongue tip. He groaned, and let his hands slide up her ribs, feeling the shapes beneath her skin, bunching the fabric, bulldozing it with his hands until he had a nice expanse of bare Diane. 'You taste good, too. And smell good. I want you like crazy.'

'James –!' Her voice was husky but not horrified. It was enough encouragement. He ran his hands all over her naked flesh as if frightened she'd suddenly come to her senses and push him away.

'James, I have to tell you –'

Her bra was blue and made of some silky stuff and he was successful with the clasp first time. He flicked the fabric aside, she spilled out into his face and he sucked her into his mouth. '*Oh* – !' She stopped talking. She groaned.

And the door burst open.

'Mum, I've brought – Oh!' Bryony stopped dead.

'Shit!' Diane yanked down her top and James whipped away his hands and mouth as if her breasts had grown teeth.

'– Tamzin and George home,' Bryony finished, lamely.

Diane bounded to her feet, eyes huge with horror and, helplessly, James rose to stand at her side.

'Oh. My. God.' said Tamzin, faintly, from the doorway. Her eyes, fixed on James, were horrified. Bewildered. Accusing. Hurt.

James felt pinned to the spot by her repugnance. 'Tamz,' he croaked.

George, behind Tamzin, murmured, 'Amazin'.'

Tamzin's freckles stood out like tiny wounds against her pale skin. 'Dad, what about Mum? Oh, poor Mum! She's hardly been – Did she *know*?'

His lips felt as if they didn't belong to him. 'She didn't know. Nobody knew. We were trying hard not to let it happen.' He took a step towards Tamzin, wanting to hug away the pain he'd just caused her. But he halted when Tamzin took a step back. If only she hadn't come in exactly then – or, for that matter, any time in the next hour – he wouldn't have hurt her. However much he'd wanted Diane he wouldn't have allowed his lust for her to hurt Tamzin.

In slow motion, Tamzin turned her gaze to Diane. 'You, Diane. You!'

'Mum!' said Bryony, on a long, scandalised breath.

First Bryony and then Tamzin bumped down into kitchen chairs.

James felt like hell. He wished he hadn't given in to the yearning to see Diane. All their lives he'd filtered situations to protect his three daughters, but this time he was the cause of Tamzin's pain. Apologies dried in his throat like breadcrumbs. He had no idea how to begin to explain that people stayed with bad marriages because they had to, even when they wanted someone else all the time. And occasionally gave in to the wanting.

It was Diane who tried, blue eyes burning with distress. 'I'm sorry. We tried. We both meant to hang in there with our less-than-ideal marriages, we took that decision. But, today ...'

She stumbled to a halt.

Tamzin buried her head in her hands. 'Daddy. How could you?'

Tentatively, James slid an arm around her thin shoulders, hating himself. Was aware, with another part of his mind, of Bryony and Diane speaking in low voices. Of Diane justifying, explaining.

Bryony staring at her mother as if she'd never seen her before.

With a cursory wipe of her eyes, Tamzin jerked away from James. 'Right. Well. We have some news of our own. I don't suppose there's any point breaking it to you gently, now.'

Her reddened eyes were suddenly filled with purpose, and even defiance, as she looked from her father to Diane. 'Jenneration has been offered the opportunity to play the venues in Hamburg. You know, like The Beatles did. George is taking a gap year so he can go.

'And I'm going with him.'

'You can't.' The automatic objection was out before James could stop it.

'I *can*.' Tamzin pulled away from him.

Chapter Thirty-Seven

Diane was aware of Tamzin hurling her bombshell at James and of James turning to stone.

But most of her attention was on poor, bewildered Bryony. 'Sweetie, I'm sorry you had to find out like this. Well, to be honest, I wasn't even certain that there was anything to find out. We've tried to stay apart and mostly we've succeeded. But – !'

'It just happened?'

Miserably, Diane nodded.

Bryony didn't cry. Her pinched, wounded expression was worse than tears. She dropped her forehead in her hand and rubbed her back. Her tummy swelled a little every day but she wasn't sailing through the final trimester in the golden glow that the books suggested she might. She felt in her pocket for her inhaler.

'I'm sorry,' Diane repeated, helplessly.

Bryony didn't look at her as she took the two puffs that would give her a bit of space in her lungs. 'I know. I think I know, Mum, honestly. Dad hasn't always been the easiest and you've had to struggle with money the way you have and then find out that he's been rolling in it for ages must be totally crappy. You were, like, totally loyal and he didn't treat you right.'

'But he's still your dad?' Diane suggested, gently.

Bryony's lip trembled. 'That's right. And even though I had to put that jewellery in Uncle Freddy's safe, in a way I still love him.'

'Of course you do.'

'And I still love you.'

Diane laughed shakily. 'That's a relief! Will you still come shopping with me, on your birthday? And have lunch?'

'Yeah. 'Course.'

'You know that I'll be here for you, you and your baby, and Dad's going to want to see you often.'

Bryony smiled, just, without disturbing the mesh of frown lines that corrugated her brow. 'Don't take this as a punishment or anything, Mum. But I think I'm going to go and live with Pops. For a bit, anyway. He's so sad. He needs someone to look after him. When Dad left and he'd behaved so badly, I thought I'd better stay here, with you. But now I don't want to feel as if I'm taking sides. He might even want me to stay after the baby because then he won't be so lonely. Will you tell Dad? About James.'

'I haven't even thought about it. It might be better not to.'

Bryony brought her hand down onto the tabletop with a slap, eyes sparking with fury. 'But if you don't, you leave me in the same situation that he did – of choosing either to tell him or to keep it a secret from him! *It's not my secret.*'

Diane blinked at her cross little elf and hastily reversed her decision. 'OK, I'll tell him.' She tried to smile. 'It'll be something to look forward to.'

They spent another stilted hour together, the five of them. Diane moved around the kitchen with automatic hospitality, making drinks and putting biscuits on plates, for nobody to eat. Trying not to think how she'd been judged and found wanting by her daughter.

And James's daughter. Tamzin's eyes, wells of injury, avoided Diane's.

Even George looked at her with a kind of wondering dismay.

When Tamzin and George left – with not even a peck on the cheek for Diane or James but they both hugged Bryony –

Bryony took herself immediately to her grandfather's house to propose to him that she become his housemate.

Diane and James ended up where they'd begun, staring at each other over the kitchen table.

'Well, that was horrible.' Her voice trembled as images of all those young accusing eyes rose in her mind.

James smoothed his hair. 'I feel a worm. And I can't believe what Tamzin's going to do. To go to Hamburg with the band! There's no job lined up, she's just going to see what happens. She thinks she's going to help manage the band because she's got A-level German. Fucking hell, she can't manage getting dressed, some days. She's been depressed for two years, she doesn't eat, she hurts herself –'

Diane cut in. 'I think she's coped with Valerie's death brilliantly. She only seemed to lose it occasionally. The rest of the time she held herself together. You should give her credit.'

He recoiled, eyes blank with disappointment. 'So you think I'm exaggerating the way she's been, do you? Like Valerie?'

She took his hand with both of hers, wrapping her fingers around his solid warmth, feeling the goodness in him through the pores of his skin. 'I never thought you exaggerated the way she's been. But it's just possible that you aren't quite grasping how she *is*. She's improved, James. She's improved out of all recognition just in the few months I've known her. And she might not sustain it, she might not hold it together in Hamburg without you, one day soon you might get a phone call crying, "Daddy, come and get me!" But you can't expect her to live her life in case she can't cope.'

Frustratedly, he shook his head. 'I sometimes think that nobody but me sees her as she is.'

'Maybe we don't,' she said, touching his cheek with one fingertip, smoothing the lines of sorrow. 'Or maybe we do.'

He kissed her wrist. 'When I met you I felt I was trudging around carrying huge burdens. One was Valerie and her drinking; the other was Tamzin's depression. I was constantly under the pressure of thinking for them. Neither could be trusted to fill in a form or anything else essential but mundane. They had to be protected from themselves and their own actions and others had to be protected from them. And I dragged them along, minding but trying not to mind, knowing that it was my role to be the reliable one. It was my job to take the shit.

'And now Valerie's gone and Tamzin has pushed me away. I've got what I wanted.'

'Have you?' She stroked his knuckles with her thumb.

'I'm beginning to think I haven't! I feel bloody.'

'Your girls will always need you. Maybe not so much and maybe not all the time, but they need you.'

He freed a hand and stroked her hair, gathering it like a skein in his hand and smoothing it back over her shoulder. Then his hand stilled. 'What was Bryony saying about her dad leaving?'

Her heart gave a great wriggle. 'It seems like a lifetime since he left, not just a day.' Even in the present awful circumstances Diane couldn't help beaming. 'That's what I was trying to tell you! But you ... Um, we –' She blushed.

'I meant to plod on but he did a couple of things that opened Bryony's eyes and she asked me not to stay with him for her sake. And, James, I'm so liberated. I feel as if I could float up around the ceiling if I took a breath big enough. I've got this house and he's got the cottage and that's pretty much the end of the settlement, although it'll have to be written up legally.'

His eyes, dark with shock, were fixed to hers. But then his slow smile began to break. 'So we can be together? Perhaps not yet, not living together. But in a year, say, or two, so that it doesn't hurt the girls too much. We can sell both houses and buy one that's "ours".' He kissed her, tasting her. 'I love you.'

Diane kissed him back. 'I love you, too.' Her hand tightened on the warmth of his and she made her voice persuasive. 'But try to understand, James. I'm going to trade from here until I can afford other premises and I'm going to live off my own earnings, not yours. I'm going to make my own life. I don't want to live in anyone's shadow any more.'

He snatched his hand away as if she'd bitten him. Fumbling his way to his feet, he glowered down at her, his voice tight. 'We're not going to be together? When we're finally free to? For fuck's sake, you just said that you love me!'

She rose, stretching on tiptoes to kiss his lips, his cheeks, his jaw line, desperate to make him understand. 'James, I want "us" so much I ache. I want us to love each other and make love to each other. But I'm never going to be dependent on a man again.'

He stared, understanding warring with disappointment in his face. Understanding won. His voice began to relax. 'So you do see us going somewhere from here?'

She grinned. 'Absolutely, I see us being together. As long as you want the real Diane, the one who has a business to run and might not always be able to put you first. The Diane who is looking forward to living alone for a while … and having a lover.'

He frowned. Slowly, the idea seemed to grow on him. 'I certainly want the real you.'

Her voice dropped. 'I could also see us taking up from where we left off.'

The tautness began to fade from his face and a smile tug at the corners of his mouth. 'And where was that?'

Slowly, she eased her T-shirt up to where her bra, still undone, straggled above her breasts. 'I think you'd got to just about here ...'

His eyes fastened on her and his hands followed; hot, hungry. He murmured, 'Even though we've just caused the most godawful scene and pissed off everybody we love best, all I can think about is that at least we don't have to hide what we want.'

Diane sucked in her breath at his touch. 'Mmm. And as we're so thoroughly in disgrace I think we might as well act disgracefully.'

'Fantastic,' he breathed, sucking, nipping, licking, kissing. 'But pack a bag because I don't do backseats of cars in daylight. We're finding a hotel.'

Slowly, she let her head fall back. 'Yeah, well. We both have plenty of baggage.'

About the Author

Sue Moorcroft is an accomplished writer of novels, serials, short stories and articles, as well as a creative writing tutor and a competition judge.

Her previous novels include *All That Mullarkey, Starting Over, Uphill All the Way* and *A Place to Call Home*.

She is also the commissioning editor and a contributor to *Loves Me, Loves Me Not*, an anthology of short stories celebrating the Romantic Novelists' Association's 50th anniversary and the author of *Love Writing – How to Make Money Writing Romantic or Erotic Fiction*.

www.suemoorcroft.com
www.suemoorcroft.wordpress.com
www.twitter.com/suemoorcroft

More Choc Lit

From Sue Moorcroft

New home, new friends, new love.
Can starting over be that simple?

Tess Riddell reckons her beloved Freelander is more
reliable than any man – especially her ex-fiancé, Olly Gray.
She's moving on from her old life and into the perfect
cottage in the country.

Miles Rattenbury's passions? Old cars and new women!
Romance? He's into fun rather than commitment. When
Tess crashes the Freelander into his breakdown truck, they
find that they're nearly neighbours – yet worlds apart.
Despite her overprotective parents and a suddenly attentive
Olly, she discovers the joys of village life and even forms
an unlikely friendship with Miles. Then, just as their
relationship develops into something deeper, an old flame
comes looking for him...

Is their love strong enough to overcome the past? Or will
it take more than either of them is prepared to give?

ISBN: 978-1-906931-22-3

Revenge and love: it's a thin line …

The writing's on the wall for **Cleo** and **Gav**. The bedroom wall, to be precise. And it says 'This marriage is over.'

Wounded and furious, Cleo embarks on a night out with the girls, which turns into a glorious one night stand with …

Justin, centrefold material and irrepressibly irresponsible. He loves a little wildness in a woman – and he's in the right place at the right time to enjoy Cleo's.

But it's Cleo who has to pick up the pieces – of a marriage based on a lie and the lasting repercussions of that night. Torn between laid-back Justin and control freak Gav, she's a free spirit that life is trying to tie down. But the rewards are worth it!

ISBN: 978-1-906931-24-7

Why not try something else from the Choc Lit selection?

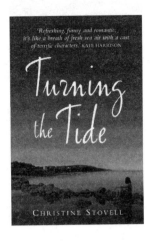

All's fair in love and war?
Depends on who's making the rules.

Harry Watling has spent the past five years keeping
her father's boat yard afloat, despite its dying clientele.
Now all she wants to do is enjoy the peace and quiet of
her sleepy backwater.

So when property developer Matthew Corrigan wants
to turn the boat yard into an upmarket housing complex for
his exotic new restaurant, it's like declaring war.

And the odds seem to be stacked in Matthew's favour.
He's got the colourful locals on board, his hard-to-please
girlfriend is warming to the idea and he has the means to
force Harry's hand. Meanwhile, Harry has to fight not just
his plans but also her feelings for the man himself.

Then a family secret from the past creates heartbreak
for Harry, and neither of them is prepared for
what happens next ...

ISBN: 978-1-906931-25-4

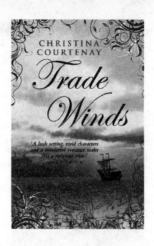

Marriage of convenience – or a love for life?

It's 1732 in Gothenburg, Sweden, and strong-willed
Jess van Sandt knows only too well that it's a man's world.
She believes she's being swindled out of her inheritance by
her stepfather – and she's determined to stop it.

When help appears in the unlikely form of handsome
Scotsman Killian Kinross, himself disinherited by his
grandfather, Jess finds herself both intrigued and infuriated
by him. In an attempt to recover her fortune, she proposes
a marriage of convenience. Then Killian is offered the
chance of a lifetime with the Swedish East India Company's
Expedition and he's determined that nothing will stand in
his way, not even his new bride.

He sets sail on a daring voyage to the Far East, believing
he's put his feelings and past behind him. But the journey
doesn't quite work out as he expects....

ISBN: 978-1-906931-23-0

A modern retelling of Jane Austen's *Emma*.

Mark Knightley – handsome, clever, rich – is used to women
falling at his feet. Except Emma Woodhouse, who's like part
of the family – and the furniture. When their relationship
changes dramatically, is it an ending or a new beginning?

Emma's grown into a stunningly attractive young woman,
full of ideas for modernising her family business.
Then Mark gets involved and the sparks begin to fly. It's just
like the old days, except that now he's seeing her through
totally new eyes.

While Mark struggles to keep his feelings in check, Emma
remains immune to the Knightley charm. She's never
forgotten that embarrassing moment when he discovered
her teenage crush on him. He's still pouring scorn on all her
projects, especially her beautifully orchestrated campaign
to find Mr Right for her ditzy PA. And finally, when the
mysterious Flynn Churchill – the man of her dreams – turns
up, how could she have eyes for anyone else?

The Importance of Being Emma was shortlisted for the
2009 Melissa Nathan Award for Comedy Romance.

ISBN: 978-1-906931-20-9

If life is cheap, how much is love worth?

It's 1914 and young Rose Courtenay has a decision to make. Please her wealthy parents by marrying the man of their choice – or play her part in the war effort?

The chance to escape proves irresistible and Rose becomes a nurse. Working in France, she meets Lieutenant Alex Denham, a dark figure from her past. He's the last man in the world she'd get involved with – especially now he's married.

But in wartime nothing is as it seems. Alex's marriage is a sham and Rose is the only woman he's ever wanted. As he recovers from his wounds, he sets out to win her trust. His gift of a silver locket is a far cry from the luxuries she's left behind.

What value will she put on his love?

ISBN: 978-1-906931-28-5

February 2011:

How much can you hide?

Jemima Hutton is determined to build a successful new life and keep her past a dark secret. Trouble is, her jewellery business looks set to fail – until enigmatic Ben Davies offers to stock her handmade belt buckles in his guitar shop and things start looking up, on all fronts.

But Ben has secrets too. When Jemima finds out he used to be the front man of hugely successful Indie rock band Willow Down, she wants to know more. Why did he desert the band on their US tour? Why is he now a semi-recluse?

And the curiosity is mutual – which means that her own secret is no longer safe ...

ISBN: 978-1-906931-27-8

Introducing the Choc Lit Club

Join us at the Choc Lit Club where we're
creating a delicious selection of fiction
for today's independent woman.
Where heroes are like chocolate – irresistible!

Join our authors in Author's Corner, read author interviews
and see our featured books.

We'd also love to hear how you enjoyed *Want to Know
a Secret?*. Just visit www.choc-lit.co.uk and give your
feedback. Describe James in terms of chocolate and
you could be our Flavour of the Month Winner!